SICK HEART

NEW YORK TIMES BESTSELLING AUTHOR

JA HUSS

SICK HEART

NEW YORK TIMES BESTSELLING AUTHOR

JA HUSS

Copyright © 2021 by JA Huss
ISBN: 978-1-950232-61-1
Edited by RJ Locksley
Cover Photo: Sara Eirew
Cover Design: JA Huss

This is a work of fiction. Names, characters, businesses, places, events and incidents are either the products of the authors' imaginations or used in a fictitious manner. Any resemblance to actual persons, living or dead, or actual events is purely coincidental.

About the BOOK

Cort van Breda is the undefeated Ring of Fire world champion. An MMA circuit so deep underground there are no rules and only the winners get out alive.

They call him the Sick Heart.

They say anyone who sees him fight has to live with the nightmares after.

They say he's a shameless monster, they say he's a ruthless killer, they say he's as twisted as the man who owns him.

They say a lot of things about Cort van Breda.

But in my experience, it's what people don't say that counts.

In our world violence is money, and money is winning, and winning is life, and life is the only thing that matters.

But he wasn't meant to win that last fight.

And I wasn't meant to be his prize.

But he did win.

And I am his prize.

Sometimes love isn't a choice, it's just a set of circumstances. It's situational, it's transactional, and sometimes it's even survival.

This is *not* how I fell in love with the Sick Heart.

Even though our story starts out in all those ways.

This book is for us.
The survivors.
Never let them shame you into silence.
And never, *ever*, apologize for winning.

CHAPTER ONE

Cort van Breda's body conjures up images of sculpted marble, the pages of a master's sketchbook, or the god Adonis come to life.

Eyes are drawn to him and once your gaze lands, it's caught. Like a prisoner. He is a cage with steel bars and bulky locks with large keyholes.

His dark hair is cropped short, but he runs his hand over his skull like maybe just yesterday there was something there. Something to feel that has since been removed. He pauses for a moment, taking in the ship and the people around him. This gives the reporters an opportunity to swoop in, but one of his entourage pushes the people back with force. And even though I can't hear what he's saying, I read his lips.

"Get back! Get the fuck back!" He's pushing them. Hard. Making a scene.

But it works, because Cort is ushered into a cleared area by some mercenary types and I get an even better look at him as he's led down the stairs closest to me. No shirt, so I can see the dozens of tattoos on his upper body with perfect clarity as he walks towards the command center.

He looks over his shoulder, down the main deck of the ship. His father's ship, so he's probably been here many times. His expression is flat and unreadable and if I were pressed to pin an emotion on him, I would call him indifferent. Maybe even apathetic.

I'm six stories up in the reception room above the command center. Which is not that close, so maybe I'm wrong.

But I doubt it.

I'm very skilled at reading men.

I've read up on Cort van Breda. He's the reigning superstar of the underground fighting ring my father and his ilk are obsessed with. Cort was on the cover of *Ring of Fire* three months ago when this match was announced, and after my father was done with the magazine, and I was sure he wouldn't notice that it went missing, I took it and read every word about the man they call Sick Heart.

He's ruthless, they say. Undefeated for the past twenty-two years, which is almost unheard of in this world we live in. He has won every fight they've put him in since he was placed in his first fight-to-the-death match at age five.

There are no real records of those fights. No vids or even an article. Five-year-old fighters aren't newsworthy. They almost never turn into a Sick Heart. But I wish there were. I would like to see those fights. My mind begins to picture this man as a boy, all those years ago, and all the things he's had to do to stay alive since then.

I quickly rein those thoughts in. There is no point.

He is six foot two, a hundred and seventy-five pounds, and covered in tattoos. The *Ring of Fire* article was obsessed with his body art and so am I.

Skulls. He is partial to skulls. And each one—if the rumors are true—represents someone he's killed. He didn't admit that in the article, of course, so it's just a rumor. But there are rumors and then there are reputations. Cort van Breda, the Sick Heart, is more of a reputation guy at this point in time, so even if you've never seen him fight it's not hard to imagine that the rumor might be true.

His eyes in the photographs I studied were a deep, soulful, silver-gray and when his gaze wanders up the side of the command center it feels like they land right on me.

I take a quick step back from the window. I don't want his attention. No one in their right mind wants his attention. Men like him—men who fight in these fights—they don't make it to twenty-seven years old still psychologically intact.

It's not even remotely possible that Cort van Breda is sane.

The article didn't mention much about his personal life. Didn't say anything about his wives or where he lives. Didn't give anything up about his hobbies or interests. In fact, it talked more about the entourage of friends following him down on the deck right now than it did him.

Two are not fighters themselves, but trainers in Cort's camp. All the Ring of Fire fighters run training centers. It's the only way to keep these fights going because there is a dead body at the end of every match.

These men, they only exist to kill one another.

This is Cort's last fight. I overheard my father saying so a few weeks back and Cort is not the favorite tonight. He's been around too long and at twenty-seven, he's two years older than his opponent, Pavo.

That's two additional years of abuse.

Two additional years of hardcore training. The type of training that breaks a body down quicker and quicker with each passing year.

Two years is a big deal in the ring. Cort has had at least a dozen more fights than his opponent tonight and in this world, too much experience is a liability.

The article was mostly the rules tonight, the opponent, the prize, and, of course, the ring.

There are no rules. It's fight to the death by any means possible.

The opponent is Pavo Vervonal. A ruthless man I've known my whole life because my father owns him and the training center he runs.

The prize is complicated. As is the ring. Because it's not a ring at all, it's a ship. These fights never take place in a gym or an event center. That's far too dull and banal for the people who run my world. They need drama. They thrive on it.

The ship, called the *Bull of Light*, is definitely dramatic. It is a massive, floating oil-rig installation vessel currently carrying a fully-assembled five-story oil rig that will be carefully placed on a platform in the Gulf of Mexico sometime next week, but for now is being used as a hotel for over a hundred and fifty invited guests.

We're in the South Atlantic, somewhere between Vila dos Remédios and French Guiana. My family arrived yesterday. Pavo, the Sick Heart's opponent, is… family, for lack of a better word. He needed time to acclimate to the sea because he trains in Thailand so we came early.

I guess Cort van Breda didn't feel the need for the same consideration because the fight is tonight and he, obviously, just got here.

The ship is not just the ring, but also the prize. Part of it, at least.

Cort's father—for lack of a better word—is Udulf van Hauten. He currently owns an eighty-one-percent controlling interest in this massive two-point-eight-billion-dollar ship. But if Pavo wins tonight, my father will knock him down to forty-nine percent and the majority of the ship's profits will change hands.

The prize is as complicated as the ring. Because if Pavo loses, I will change hands as well.

I wonder what the Sick Heart thinks about that?

I take a quick step towards the window again so I can watch him as he approaches the command center. And just before he disappears inside, he looks up and pauses. Watching me watch him.

Then his friend pushes him inside and he disappears.

I walk over to one of the overstuffed leather couches and take a seat. It's nice and cool up here in the reception room. Almost chilly, since I'm the only one here. But I enjoy it while it lasts. It's sticky hot outside and later tonight, after the fight is over, all the important people will be up here for the celebration and I will have forgotten all about what it feels like to sit in cool comfort, alone and unbothered.

And just as those thoughts manifest in my head, right on cue, the door flies open with a bang and Bexxie, my nine-year-old sister—for lack of a better word—comes racing in squealing with delight.

"Oh, my God. Oh, my God. OMG. OMG. OMGeeeeeeeee! Did you *see* him?" She places a hand over her heart and sighs. "Ahhhhhhh. I'm dead. *Dead*, Anya. Were you looking?"

I nod at her.

"Of course you were looking." She giggles. "You should've seen the lady crew from the laundry. They were all dy-*ing*. Dying, Anya! Falling over dead. He's so gorgeous. Don't you think?"

I, of course, do not answer her. But someone else does.

"No."

Bexxie and I both turn towards the door to find Pavo walking in to the reception room. He's looking very put-together. Short-sleeved collared shirt, dark, pressed jeans, mahogany hair slicked back. He even smells good.

He walks over to me, extends his hand, and pulls me to my feet. He spins me around, leans his mouth in to my neck, and whispers, "Do you find him pretty, Anya? Are your panties wet for him?"

I roll my eyes.

Bexxie makes a face. "You're gross, Pavo. You should not talk to us like that."

Pavo laughs. "Get the fuck out of here, you little baby brat. I need some time alone with your sister."

"She doesn't like you." Bexxie sneers at him. "In fact, she *hates* you."

"Doesn't matter, does it?" Pavo *licks* my ear. Bexxie and I both make a face. But I don't move and neither does she. "It doesn't matter if you like me, does it, Anya? Because after I win this fight tonight, you're mine. Forever."

Bexxie frowns. "She's not yours. And you're not going to win. Cort is."

Pavo pushes me off him and crosses the distance to Bexxie in an instant. Her face is red from the slap before I can even move to stop him. "Shut up, you little whore. Go find your stupid daddy. Anya is mine."

Bexxie—not the kind of girl who can be deterred by a single slap—plants her hands on her hips and tips her chin up. "No. *You* go find my stupid daddy. And make sure you tell him you called him stupid. Because I will if you don't." She points to her cheek. "I hope it's nice and red. So when he asks, 'My dearest Bexxie, why is your cheek red?' I will say, 'Fucking Pavo did it because I told him he was going to lose and Anya would never have to let him lick her ear again!'" She screams this. Then makes a face and shivers. "Girls don't like ear-licking, Pavo. Even a child knows that."

I love her. I really do. She is the very best thing about my life. But Pavo is just like any other fighter in the Ring of Fire circuit.

Ruthless.

Violent.

Intolerant.

Insane.

He grabs her by the hair and drags her through the open door. My mind follows the sound of their feet stomping on the metal stairs as they descend. Then Bexxie is screaming and wailing and I know she is putting up a fight.

I let out a long sigh and sit back down on the couch.

Less than a minute later Pavo is back. He slams the door closed as he enters and the banging echoes off the high ceiling of the large room. "She is a stupid little whore. Stupid. Fucking. Whore."

I don't say anything. There's nothing to say anyway. Pavo will rant no matter what I do. And even though I'm ninety-nine percent sure that Father won't beat Bexxie over this, it still makes me mad that Pavo caused a scene.

I don't like scenes. I like calm.

"You are mine, Anya. You know that, right? When I win tonight, you will be mine. That's my prize. Your father can have control over this stupid ship. I don't want it. I will take you back to Thailand and you will never see that stupid bitch of a sister again. Do you hear me?"

Of course I hear him. He's yelling in a reception hall that echoes.

The door bangs open again and both Pavo and I startle and turn.

"Oh, hey," the man says with a broad smile. He's one of Cort's friends. The inner circle entourage people. Maart, if I remember his name correctly from the Ring of Fire article.

But then he's pushed out of the way by...

I stop breathing.

Cort van Breda's steel-gray eyes find mine, but he looks away, searching the room. Then, without comment, he turns towards the bar at the far end and starts walking that way.

Pavo and I are silent as Cort reaches for a bottle of electric-blue liquid on the top shelf. But then Pavo snaps out of it. "What the fuck do you think you're doing? You can't take that. It is Bokori."

He's referring to the bottle of Lectra in Cort's hand. And Pavo is right. Cort is insane if he thinks he can just walk in here and steal a hundred thousand dollars' worth of Lectra. Since Cort's father is the host

8

tonight, the rest of the families have to bring gifts. This bottle is the Bokori family party favor. It goes to the winner. And clearly, there is no winner yet so...

"Did you hear what I just said?" Pavo is crossing the room. "You can't fucking take that!"

"Listen," Maart says calmly from his position by the door. "You can argue with him all you want, but he's taking the fuckin' bottle. If you want to have your fight, right here, right now, well, I'm pretty sure that's not gonna go over well with the hundred and fifty VIP's currently placing bets in the topside mess hall. So you should maybe shut the fuck up and back off before he and I kill you and put an end to this night before it starts."

My mouth makes a little o shape. And then I laugh. I can't help it. This is the first truly funny thing I've witnessed in a very long time.

Pavo is speechless. First, my bratty nine-year-old sister yanks his chain. Now, his current mortal enemy is stealing something precious—something he very much thinks is his—and there's nothing he can do about it.

Cort turns and heads back towards his friend at the door. But his eyes narrow down into slits as he passes me. I meet his gaze and realize... he is everything they say about him.

Ruthless.

Violent.

Intolerant.

Insane.

Just like every other fighter in the Ring of Fire.

But I drop my eyes quickly and then get a good, long look at those skulls on his body.

This is the moment when I believe the rumors.

This is the moment when his reputation sinks in.

This is the moment I know in my heart he is *sick*.

He has won thirty-five Ring of Fire death matches.

This does not include all the people he fought on his way up as a child.

Because there are a lot more than thirty-five skulls on his body.

A lot more.

When I look up again his steel-gray eyes find mine.

And I feel like his next victim.

CHAPTER TWO

Hot.

Everything about this day is just fuckin' hot. So before I even get out of the helicopter, I take my shirt off and throw it aside.

We exit, Maart first, so he can speak for me. His loose button-down shirt flaps in the vortex of wind created by the propellers. His slicked-back hair barely moves, and even though this day will turn into something shitty and dark no matter how it ends, I take a moment to internally grin as I admire Maart's commitment to his fucking hair.

Evard and I jump out next. He's nervous, I can tell. But he's still very young and those nerves are for me, so I don't complain or poke him when he presses too close.

Rainer brings up the rear. His bulky body outgrew the fights long before they got too serious. He was lucky in a way. All that muscle made him far too slow for anyone to take much notice of his strengths. But he's a damn good fighter. God help you if you find yourself this man's target. He's pushing people out of our way like the Hulk, shoving this way and that.

11

People stumble backwards and then decide they don't want to push him and stay where they land.

We walk forward towards the *Bull of Light* command center and I look up, expecting to see my father pointing me out to his friends on the bridge.

He's there. And he does point.

But my attention goes up one floor higher where a blonde girl stands in the window.

She takes a step back when she realizes I've noticed her, but reappears a few seconds later just before Evard and I pass through the door out of sight.

The stairs leading up are crammed with workers, but they press themselves against the open railings so we can pass. None of them look me in the eye.

Who was that girl?

Evard reaches for my hand, but I shake him off and shoot him a stern look.

"Sorry." His voice is low, just a mumble. "But I don't like this."

"Shut up." Maart's words are harsh and curt. He's not in the mood for whining. This is a fight day. First one in over a year.

First one Evard has ever been to, as well. Which explains his fear.

"Don't be a dick, Maart." Rainer grabs Evard and holds him in place as I keep moving. They stay several steps behind me after that. I can hear Rainer whispering something to the kid, but he's being discreet, so I don't catch the pep talk. I can imagine it though.

He's gonna win, don't worry. He always wins.

Which is true.

If you're still alive at the end, you win.

And I'm still here.

SICK HEART - JA HUSS

Pavo Vervonal is no slacker, but I *am* going to win. He *will* lose. We trained together when we were small and he was good. But we went our separate ways a long, long time ago for a reason.

Only boys like me end up where I am.

He is no me.

Suddenly Maart stops and when I look up, I realize there's a crowd of people on the landing just below the command deck.

"We just want an interview." It's an older woman making this demand. She's still pretty. Was probably someone important twenty years ago. But she wears too much makeup and her clingy, revealing red dress is far too much for this sticky day.

Her cameraman stands behind her, his equipment perched on his shoulder, his eyes only on me. There is a flashing red light indicating that he's already recording.

"You know press time isn't for another three hours." She's not going to get anywhere with Maart. He has one job—keep all the no-brain fucks away from me. And he's pissed about the ambush. You don't have to know him to hear the anger in his voice.

"Just a word." The reporter pushes her hands in the air, one clenched into a fist and holding a mic. "Just one question. It's for *Ring of Fire*. One question!" Then her gaze lands on me. "Cort, do you think the prize is fair?"

She only wants me to answer one question and that's the one she asks?

Like I give any fucks at all about the prize.

Nothing about this fight is about me.

Not one moment of it is about *me*.

13

Maart is beyond pissed now. "He doesn't do interviews." He shoves her out of the way, then stands in front of her so I can pass. Rainer and Evard come up behind me, but Maart hangs back to insult the washed-up reporter.

The mercs take over at the bridge and the door opens as I approach. When I walk through I'm hit with a rush of cold, conditioned air.

That feels good. I suck in a breath and smile internally when I hear Evard do the same behind me.

Then my father is walking towards us with Pavo's sponsor. A little girl—blonde, striking blue-green eyes, pigtails, striped, sailor-suit dress—grabs the sponsor's hand and giggles excitedly as they stop in front of me.

My father grabs my upper arm and squeezes. Then he pulls me in and kisses me on both cheeks before letting me go to turn towards his guest. "You remember Cort, right, Lazar?"

Lazar is pushing the little girl away, telling her in Hungarian to go upstairs and find someone called Anya. I take a moment to pause and wonder if Anya was the blonde girl I saw in the window.

The little girl pouts, but doesn't argue.

Lazar has a Mediterranean look about him, like he spends a lot of time in Greece. Very tall, very tan—almost ludicrously tan. And his white linen shirt highlights this. His hair is blondish. Dyed. Or maybe it's truly sun-bleached, but somehow, I doubt it.

Lazar offers me his hand.

I stare at it for a moment. Normally, Maart would run interference for me in this type of situation, but he's still back near the door with Rainer and Evard.

I look back up, meet his gaze and narrow my eyes.

Lazar laughs. "Sick. Heart." He says the words in two separate sentences, the way they are supposed to be said when spoken out loud, but something about it rubs me the wrong way. So when he takes a step forward and claps me on the shoulder—

Well, that's it.

The next thing I know my knuckles are stinging, his nose is bloody, and several of the soulless mercenaries are pulling me off him and holding me by the arms.

Lazar wipes his hand across his upper lip as the mercs push me away. But then his tongue darts out to taste the blood and he chuckles. "Boy," he says, meaning me—I am 'the boy'—"you turned out well." His accent isn't thick, but it's there.

My father does not apologize. But he does shoot me a look. "Go clean up, Cort. Grab a drink, for fuck's sake. Calm down a little. The fight won't start for seven more hours."

"I have brought tribute." Lazar's teeth are stained with blood when he smiles at me. "It's upstairs in the bar. You may have it early, boy. If you are man enough to take it."

I shoot a dangerous, sideways glance at Lazar and find him smirking at me.

I suddenly want to kill this man. Not sure why. Not sure I need a reason why. I just want to kill this man.

My father spins me around, points his finger in my face. "Do not drink it, Cort. Do you hear me? Do not." His eyes shoot to Maart. "Give him a whiskey."

"Why not?" Lazar is laughing. I really hate that laugh. "Pavo will be on the Lectra when he fights. It's only fair for your boy here."

"You will not." My father is deadly fucking serious as he looks me in the eyes. "Do you understand me, Cort?"

I sneer at him and he smiles. Then he squeezes my shoulder again and leans in. "Don't look at me that way. It's my job to keep you in line tonight. It's an important night for you as well as me. Tonight, we are a team and we don't want anything to go wrong."

Tonight, we are a team. Interesting way to put it.

"Yes," Lazar says. Fuck. Why can't that man just shut up? Every time I hear his voice, I get the urge to throttle him. "The stakes are high tonight."

"Not now, Lazar," my father cautions him.

"Why not now? Surely your *son* would like to know what he's fighting for?"

I know what I'm fighting for. It was explained to me in the contract. Keeping our family's controlling interest in this ship.

It doesn't sound like much, but this is no ordinary ship. A heavy-lift construction vessel, it's a floating city—and presently the only one of its size. When it's in international waters—and it almost always is—it's practically a nation state. Impervious to the laws of others. Not even the Americans can stop the business we do on this ship.

And my father owns most of it. Not all of it—the network would never allow one man to hold *that* much power. But most of it is practically the same thing.

It generates an obscene amount of legitimate money each year installing topsides onto oil rig substructures. Tens of billions of dollars. But the illegitimate money is just as precious.

These fights, for instance. This night is just one of dozens each year. But they host more than fights on this ship.

"We will talk about this later."

I nod at my father. I don't care about the prize. The winning lost its shine more than a decade ago now. I fight because they make me.

I turn and walk towards the door. The mercenaries open it and I slip through first, then Maart, then Rainer and Evard in the rear.

"We're going this way," Maart says, heading down.

But I go up.

"Guess we're not." Rainer laughs.

"Wait here," Maart orders them. Then he races up the steps ahead of me. "Cort." He pauses in front of the door. "You do not want that bottle. Do you understand me?"

I push him out of the way, but he's not afraid of me and pushes me right back.

I *will* hit him. Any fucking time I want. But I'm not going to kill him and Maart is no pussy. He will retaliate and he and I are well enough matched that I will probably come out ahead, but just barely.

He knows I'm not going to hit him today. Not on a fight day. I will have enough bruises when I step off the platform tonight. I don't need any extras going in.

"You do not want that bottle. Do you hear me?"

I want that bottle. And he knows it. That's why he feels the need to repeat himself.

"Fuck." He sighs, then opens the door with a bang. "Oh, hey!"

I am not in the mood for one of his charismatic long-winded speeches to explain my actions, so I just push him out of the way and enter the reception hall.

My eyes take in the massive room and… well, well, well. There she is. The girl from the window.

Anya, Lazar called her.

She is young. Much younger than me. *Maybe* eighteen. But probably not.

I know how these people work. I know their sick hearts better than I know my own.

But she *is* very pretty. Slender and willowly, like a ballerina. But on the small side. Fragile and strong in the same breath. Her hair is light blonde, very straight at the moment, and long. Her fair skin and soft features tell me she is not actually related to Lazar. There is no resemblance whatsoever. He calls her 'daughter' in the most derogatory way possible. Same way my father calls me 'son.'

The other little girl is missing. They look enough alike that they might be real sisters, but again, I doubt it.

Anya. I say her name in my head. Memorizing the way it feels. Enjoying the hate it conjures up.

Not for her. I do not give a single fuck about her.

Lazar. He's familiar in an unfamiliar way. And everything about that is ugly.

My gaze wanders over to the bar and I stride towards it with purpose. Everyone is silent as I reach for an electric-blue bottle on the top shelf.

"What the fuck do you think you're doing?"

I look at Pavo, then down at the bottle of Lectra in my hand, taking a moment to appreciate the almost-glowing light-blue color of the drug inside. It doesn't look like water. You don't need to be smart to know this is not colored water. It's too thick. Viscous. Like an oil. But it's not oily going down. It's cold. Ice cold. It burns your throat, then your stomach, then—just a few minutes later—you *float*.

You float through worlds. You feel like Superman. You want to kill people and save the world in the same instant.

It's indescribably seductive.

And addictive.

I look up and study Pavo for a moment, looking for the tell-tale signs of Lectra addiction, but he's too far away to see the blue ring around the iris.

I'll be close enough tonight to solve that little mystery.

"You can't take that." Pavo is still moaning. "It's Bokori."

It's fucking tribute, is what it is. And we both know I will win this fight tonight, so even if Lazar didn't say I could have it early, I could take it anyway.

"Did you hear what I just fucking said?" Pavo is crossing the room. "You can't fucking take that!"

"Listen." Maart says this word calmly, still standing by the door. "You can argue with him all you want, but he's taking the fuckin' bottle. If you want to have your fight, right here, right now, well, I'm pretty sure that's not gonna go over well with the hundred and fifty VIP's currently placing bets in the topside mess hall. So you should maybe shut the fuck up and back off before he and I kill you and put an end to this night before it starts."

Anya's laugh almost startles me. It's so... I dunno. So out of place here. So musical and happy that I almost ask her to do it again.

What?

I have to shake my head at that last thought.

Her veins might not have Lazar's blood running through them, but she is the enemy's daughter.

I lock eyes with her as I cross the room. She lets out a breath like she's about to piss herself with fear. Good. *You should fear me, little girl.* Everyone should fear me.

Because inside my chest beats the sickest heart on this whole ship.

And if I win, none of the guests will rest tonight.

I don't care how many fights they've been to—I don't care how many ways they've seen it end—I will give them a show they will *never* forget.

I will haunt their sleep like a monster.

I will fill their hearts with terror.

I will ruin them… with the memory of *me*.

One floor down Rainer and Evard are waiting for us. Evard's eyes go wide when he sees the bottle of bright blue liquid in my hand. I shove it into his chest and he wordlessly clutches it. I catch the mercs standing guard at the command room door eyeing the kid, probably imagining ten or twelve different ways they might steal that bottle from him.

But then one of them—the leader, I think—locks eyes with me. He looks away real quick.

Forget the fact that my "father" is Udulf van Hauten, the man who controls this ship. I might not have an arsenal strapped to my body the way this merc does, but I'm not a guy you fuck with on a whim. It would be a very stupid move to steal that bottle of Lectra from my boy, and that merc gets it.

I go down the stairs and my team follows. This ship is only four years old, but there are others. Older ones, smaller ones that I spent far more time on. Hell, I practically grew up on the *Deep Sea Galaxy*. But I know my way around the *Bull of Light*. My last four fights have been hosted here.

My team and I have dedicated quarters on the deck below the command center. I push through a door, take us out onto a catwalk, and then enter the port side structure where my family compartments are.

This is Evard's first time here, so when I step into the main room and wave everyone forward, it's his face I concentrate on.

I really like to make the stupid kid happy for some reason. Maybe because I remember all too well what it was like for me when I was his age.

He doesn't disappoint. His smile is broad and real as he crosses the room and stands in front of the window, looking out at the work happening down below us.

We have a perfect view of the massive crane on the port side. It's not busy right now, but it's still something impressive. There are dozens of men down on the deck. It's actually quite a nice place to people-watch, if you're into that sort of thing.

"Wow." Evard is properly impressed.

Rainer walks over and takes the bottle from him, holds it up. "What the fuck are you gonna do with this?"

I grab it, walk into the head, pop the cork, and start pouring out a hundred thousand dollars' worth of Lectra.

"Jesus Christ." Maart is behind me, crowding me, grabbing the bottle before I can waste any more. "You don't *pour it out*, dickface. We're gonna drink this later after you win!"

I laugh a little. And that reminds me of the girl. She laughed a little too and I liked the sound of that laugh.

Who is she?

Lazar's daughter—for lack of a better word— obviously.

But her presence here is a little bit disturbing.

I suddenly crave some alone time so I can think about her a little more. There are two sleeping compartments on either side of the main room with bunk beds. I share with Maart and Evard and Rainer will take the other one. So that's where I head next.

Maart doesn't follow. He knows my fight-day routine. Actually, it's not just a fight-day routine. It's more like an every-day routine.

At least when I can get it.

There are interviews scheduled in a few hours. I will have to attend so they can get photos of me before the fight, but Maart will do all the talking. So I don't need to worry about that and I can empty out my head and let my thoughts drift.

I like being alone. If I never had to be around another person, I'd be OK with it.

I slide the pocket door closed and my crew immediately begins chatting. This used to bother me—the idea that they would hold things in when I was around, but talk freely when I wasn't.

I hate it. I really do. But I've learned to live with it. I can't change who I am.

Maybe I could've. Twenty-two years ago, I might've been able to change, if things had gone differently.

But that chance slipped out of my control a long way back. And anyway, even if I could change, no one would stop seeing me as the killer they know me to be. So whatever.

I strip out of my traveling clothes and lie down on the bottom bunk naked. Then I close my eyes and think about that girl as my hand drifts down the hard muscles of my stomach. I pause, then reach for my already stiffening cock and start to tug on it.

I liked the way she looked in that window. She was a mystery.

I liked the way her face was lit up with the late-day sunshine.

I liked her pouty lips and I picture what it would feel like to have them wrapped around my shaft.

I breathe a little harder as the fantasy takes hold. My cock grows stiffer as the dream takes shape.

I liked her silence, too. I could hear it immediately. It's just like mine.

She is just like me. Damaged and broken. Hurt and sore. Used and discarded.

But that laugh—that was truly unexpected. I liked the way she laughed. I liked the small hint of joy in that outburst and I wonder how attached she is to Pavo.

I wonder if she will watch the fight tonight.

I wonder if she will still be laughing when it's over.

I wake up to the sound of Maart's voice.

"Hey, fuckface. It's time, OK? Interviewers have actually been waiting an hour already. But you looked so goddamned peaceful, I didn't want to wake you up."

My hand is still clutched around my cock and I realize I drifted off without finishing. My eyes wander over to Maart. He's naked with his back to me, all his scars on full display. I catch a glimpse of his cock dangling between his legs when he reaches to hang a newly pressed button-down shirt on a hook.

I swing my legs out of bed, stand up, cross the distance between us, then slip my hand between his legs to grab his balls as I bite his shoulder.

Maart hisses in pain because when I bite, I bite hard. "Jesus fucking Christ, Cort." I back off, allowing him room to turn. He looks down at my hand on my cock. His eyes lift back up to meet mine. I take his hand and place it around my shaft and he immediately begins to tug on it.

Then he reaches for my hand and places it around his cock. My hand covers his and his hand covers mine. And we jerk each other off like that.

I press my body in to him and he backs up until he's against the door. I bury my head into his neck and he does the same.

We don't kiss and we don't talk.

We don't need to explain ourselves.

We don't need to feel anything about what we're doing.

We just do it.

That's all there is to it.

CHAPTER THREE

ANYA

The muscles.

The tattoos.

The pure, raw power of him.

But most of all, those silver-gray eyes.

There is no way to get Cort van Breda out of my mind after that encounter in the reception hall. The way he looked at me. Like he was drawn to me.

But then… that sneer. If he had been closer, and Pavo hadn't been talking, I think I might've heard a growl.

Sick. Heart. That's what they called him in the *Ring of Fire* article. Two words with two periods. Like you have to pause between each one to get the full effect of how disturbing he is.

I was raised a certain way. I have been around certain people who had expectations of me. And if I didn't meet those expectations, there were consequences. I became intuitive. Instinctual. It was a survival mechanism.

And eventually, these instincts became habit. And those habits turned into something natural and innate. Something I did without thinking.

I read people.

I put very little weight on words, even though I have more words inside me than maybe anyone else on this godforsaken planet. Words don't mean much. I've lived with more than my fair share of empty promises, so I know this first-hand.

No. I look for something other than words.

I look at the eyes first.

The lips.

The eyebrows.

Are the shoulders tight and tense? Or open and relaxed?

Words never tell you as much about a person as body language. You don't need words when you can look a person in the eye.

But even this is not enough.

Not in the world I live in.

You need to see into their hearts. That's where the truth lives and this is how I process my world. This is how I get through it.

Pavo is still raging about Cort, even though he disappeared nearly half an hour ago now. "The fucking nerve," Pavo is saying over and over again. "The fucking nerve."

Pavo has described how he will win this fight tonight about seventy-five different ways. He wants to break Cort's bones. He wants a head injury. He wants to snap Cort's back and force him to watch, powerless, as he chops his throat and crushes his windpipe.

And as brutal as it sounds, it's a lot tamer than the plans he was making *last* night.

Pavo has just been sipping the Lectra today, but last night he was raging drunk on it and today he has to pay the price for that. Lectra is a weird drink. It turns you inside out for a while, and then, when it's gone, you flip back—but if you get in the habit of this, eventually you're never the same on the trip back.

When you're an addict, you're never yourself again. Ever.

You're always a little bit meaner.

A little bit darker.

A little bit closer to hopeless.

I've only sipped the blue liquid about half a dozen times. I was not high last night. As long as it is my choice, I will never drink Lectra with Pavo. It sexualizes you. Makes you crave things you never normally would. Erases inhibitions. Degrades common sense. Reduces what's left of your moral code.

And let's face it, no one on this ship can afford any more erosion of their moral codes.

Last night Pavo couldn't stop talking about cutting off Cort's dick. In fact, all he did was talk about what he wanted to do to Cort's dick.

I was forced to listen to him last night. It could've been worse. I could've been forced to do more than just listen to him, so whatever.

He spent most of the night jerking off in a corner, talking the entire time. Talking about Cort and how they were boys together. "He was my friend," Pavo said drunkenly. "Did I ever tell you that, nyuszi?"

I hate that nickname. *Bunny*. Gag. But when you're locked in a cabin with a psychopath on Lectra, you don't make a fuss about the small things.

"We were boys at the same training camp."

I didn't want to hear it. I don't go around forcing people to listen to my childhood stories, why can't he give me the same consideration?

But I was there. And try as I might, I could not tune him out completely. Also, I actually was interested in the parts about Cort, since none of this was ever mentioned in that *Ring of Fire* article.

"He was two years older. Prettier than me. Everyone said so."

Oh. So that's what this is about. Jealousy. Figures.

"We learned everything together. And he always thought he was better. Always faster. Always tougher. He took the slaps, the punches, the scarring without whimpering or sniveling. He was always better with the pain. But I was a good fighter. I still *am* a good fighter. I'm going to win tomorrow, nyuszi. You watch me. I'm going to pin him to the platform. Lie on top of him. Make him feel how hard the fight makes me. Then I will take it all from him. Everything he has will be mine."

That's how the spoils work for the fighters. They inherit the loser's training camp. This is a big deal for the men who own the fighters. They will lose all their up-and-coming prospects, but only in that particular camp. This is why they don't have just one big camp. They typically have dozens of smaller ones instead.

I don't know what Pavo will get from Cort if he wins. No one even knows where Cort's training camp is. No one knows where he stays. The *Ring of Fire* article said he owns no house, no fancy car, no ten-million-dollar yacht. These are all things Pavo has. He has been rewarded handsomely by my father over the years. He is the pinnacle of my father's stable.

Pavo also has wives. Many, many wives by this point in his career. You get one each time you win in the Ring of Fire. And Pavo has won thirteen or fourteen times now, Cort twice that many, so Cort should have a pretty large harem. The article didn't talk about that either.

If Pavo wins I will not go to Cort's harem. I will stay here on this ship. My father has already explained it to me. He will take a controlling interest in the *Bull of Light* and I will probably live on this ship for the rest of my life.

It's not a bad place, I decide. It could be worse. A lot worse, actually.

The *Bull of Light* is like a city. There are hundreds of people here. Women working in the laundry and the kitchens who I could make friends with. Men I could have sneaky affairs with. I could even get a job. I could work in the kitchen or the laundry too. Because Pavo is beyond delusional if he thinks my father will let him stop fighting.

We will not be playing house. He will fuck me constantly for a few days while he drowns himself in Lectra, hopefully get me pregnant, and then he will leave for Thailand to continue training and I will stay here. Pavo will have at least four or five more fights before they let him even think about trying to buy himself out.

The men in his class only fight once a year. And every time he fights there is the possibility that he loses. That means that I will not be safe if Pavo wins me. I am property and I suspect my ownership will change many times before they let me die.

By next year, I might have a baby with me. If Pavo loses the next fight, the baby and I would both go to the winner.

The obvious solution to this is to not get pregnant.

The other, even more obvious, solution is that Pavo loses tonight's fight.

Then I would go home with the Sick Heart.

I try to imagine that for a moment. Fully imagine how bad it might get. I would be somewhere far away. Not on a floating city with the possibility of some semblance of a life. My father would lose track of me. Lose interest in me too. I would become part of Cort's harem, wherever that is. I would eventually get pregnant, I would eventually have babies.

But this is his last fight. It is known. I would not be given away. Ever. I would be his, and his alone, forever.

Cort van Breda is nice to look at. I'm not even gonna pretend he's not. From a distance, though. I could look at him all day long if he wasn't such a looming threat. But to be with him all the time? Forever? To be left alone with him and his violence? Not even under the protection of my father?

He could do anything he wanted with me.

He could sell me. Leave me somewhere. Beat me. Starve me. Tie me up and never come back. He could lend me out to his friends. And he seems very committed to those friends, so I imagine that's a given.

No. The Sick Heart is a risk.

Going home with Cort van Breda would be orders of magnitude worse than staying here and being Pavo's. If Pavo wins, my father would not stay here, but he would come often. He is obsessed with this ship. He might even want Bexxie to stay here too. I could beg for that. I could make it happen.

In my world, this scenario—being Pavo's property, having his babies, living here on the ship with Bexxie nearby and only occasional visits from the men in control of me?

This is a fairy-tale ending as far as I'm concerned. Something right out of a fucking storybook.

Pavo *must* win.

Bexxie returns a little while later. Her face is flushed and her eyes are calm, like she just woke up from a long nap. "Look what I found." She plops down onto the couch next to me and offers up the program in her hand. It's for tonight's fight.

There is a picture of Pavo and Cort on the front, both of them shirtless, both of them looking like monsters. Inside there's a short welcome paragraph from Cort's father, a small writeup about my father and... a full-page picture of me.

"You look so pretty in that pic, Anya. I love it."

Looking at the dress I'm wearing, I recall posing for it now, but I didn't know they would use it as promotional material. And it seems like too much. I'm not really the prize. The prize is the ship. I'm just a trinket that comes with it.

"They want you downstairs for wardrobe." Bexxie leans into me. Her little hands grip my arm and she snuggles up against my breasts like I'm her mother. I lean my head on hers. "They're not going to let me watch." She pouts out these words. "Daddy says it's too violent. And that's stupid." She sits up straight again. "Why did I come all this way if I can't even watch?"

I'm glad she won't be watching. She's already seen way too much in her short nine years.

"*You* get to watch."

Get to watch? Hah. That's an understatement. I was already told I will be on the platform with them. I will be *forced* to watch. I will see every horrific thing the two fighters do to each other in perfect clarity. I will spend the entire time wondering which monster will take me home. Which one of the blood-covered animals in front of me will be my master?

Bexxie gets up and offers me her hand. "Come on. I'll walk you down."

I let her pull me up and then I let her keep hold of my hand as we exit the reception hall and head down the stairs. Several of my father's guards fall in behind us. I can't quite decide if they're doing this for my protection, or to make sure I don't run.

I would like to think of myself as a person who might run, but it's a ludicrous idea. We're in the middle of the ocean. Where would I go?

I roll my eyes internally. As if *that* was the reason. I have had hundreds of opportunities to run. Never happened.

I am not the kind of girl who runs.

Down on the main deck lots of people are milling about. It is massively wide. You could fit several houses side by side. But the front part of the ship is actually two long arms that extend outward like a forklift, if said forklift was a hundred and fifty meters wide. The topside is propped in the middle of the ship-sized forklift on massive robotic arms and ballasts.

I am not an oil rig expert, but our father is very excited at the prospect of winning a controlling interest in this ship, so he explained all this to Bexxie and me while we were traveling here.

The topside is a pre-fabricated oil rig minus the legs that anchor it to the ocean floor. Those have already been built and now this ship is carrying the working part—the power plant, the housing units, the office, the command center, the pumps or whatever they use to get the oil and gas up out of the ocean floor—so it can be placed on the legs.

A topside is a factory. And right now, the topside roof sits higher than the command center of the *Bull of Light*. So that's where all the important people will be watching the fight.

But the fight itself will take place on the *Bull of Light*'s helicopter platform, which extends slightly outward over the side of the ship's hull. That's where I will be too.

Bexxie leads me below deck. I don't even know where we're going, but she seems to, so I don't worry about it. We end up in a compartment that must be a salon, where a team of people are waiting to turn me into something else.

"I'm gonna stay with you," Bexxie announces. "We'll have mani-pedis together like the old days." Then she pouts. "I hope you don't leave. I don't want you to leave, Anya."

I don't have any say in that—and neither does she—so I don't encourage this line of thinking. I just sit down, close my eyes, and enjoy the moment.

I'm good at that.

And so is Bexxie.

I don't get to choose my polish. I don't get any say in how I look tonight. But Bexxie is more than satisfied with her gold and silver nails and toes.

After the mani-pedis are finished, I am directed to a flat table where they will wax me.

"I'll see you when it's over, OK?" Bexxie's bright blue-green eyes look at me with fear and I nod. "OK," she says. Then, without another word, she turns and walks out just as the team of body painters walks in.

The stylists undress me and point to the table. I lie down on it and open my legs.

I've never been Pavo's prize before, but I've watched two of his fights.

This thought makes me pause and wonder where his other girls are. He must have a harem of them by now as well. And children. How many children must he have? Dozens, maybe. He's been fighting for girls since he was twelve. Even if only half of them had two babies in those dozen years, that number is in the upper twenties. But it's not likely that they haven't been pregnant every other year. Some of the earlier prizes might not even be around anymore. Hell, even his oldest children are probably dead by now. Used up and thrown out.

And if he had boys, those boys started training for the fight ring by the time they were two or three. Most of his sons are probably dead, or they will be soon.

Cort, too, must have dozens of slave girls somewhere. He's been in more fights than any other man in the history of this sport. When he was younger, his father used to make him fight three or four times a year.

I hiss when they rip the strips of wax off between my legs. But that is a small pain and it's not enough to make me forget that I'm not really a prize, am I?

God knows, neither of them needs another girl.

They are here for their continued existence. They are fighting for their lives, they are not fighting for me.

The continued waxing makes me wince and hiss over and over. But soon that part is finished and when I get up off the table, the body painters immediately begin. I don't know how they will decorate me. I don't actually care. Not one decision about my life is mine to make.

I don't know exactly what Cort and Pavo will look like tonight, but I've seen pictures in *Ring of Fire*.

If a fighter has tattoos, they like to paint those in something that glows. If they don't, they make the designs up. The rest of their body is painted black. So when they are fighting in the dark, you can only see the glowing tattoos or symbols.

They reduce us to non-humans as often as possible.

How else would they live with themselves?

My body will be painted white with dozens of unsettling symbols in red. I don't know what the symbols mean—slave girls don't need to know that kind of stuff. But I do know they have meaning.

I will be the opposite of the men. My symbols will be invisible in the dark—the red will not glow. But the white will.

It's intriguing and I almost wish I could watch myself from a distance. See me the way everyone else will. Almost like an out-of-body experience.

I keep still as they airbrush my skin until it has a pearl shimmer to it. I reposition when they ask me to, lifting a leg or an arm. And then, when that paint is dry, the artists begin creating the designs.

Spirals and spinning circles. Black suns and pyramid eyes. Arrows pointing to chaos. Stars, and pentagrams, and upside-down crosses.

To honor Pavo, they paint a snake eating its own tail around my right breast.

To honor Cort, they make one side of my face into a skull. My eye is outlined in deep black. My cheek becomes a jawbone showing teeth.

My hair starts out in two long ponytails. But they twist them up and secure them on top of my head like horns.

When I look in the mirror, I am evil personified.

And it fits, I think.

Everything about this night is going to be evil.

A group of teenage boys dressed up in slave attire—shirtless with gold skirts—escort me through the halls when I am done.

Two flank me on either side. They are young, because they are only my height. The two in front and the two behind are older. Maybe fifteen.

The younger one on my left whispers, "I hope Pavo wins."

"Yeah," the one on the right says. "You do not want to know what happens to the girls Sick Heart takes home." I glance at him with frightened eyes. "I hear he kills them."

Then the other one says, "I heard the same thing. He kills them all."

"But don't worry," the one on my left says. "We're all rooting for Pavo. He's the favorite tonight."

"He's got a cheat," the other one snickers. "And everyone knows it."

"Shut up," an older boy in front barks. "Quit talking to her."

"It's true," a boy behind me echoes. "We all know that Pavo's team hid a weapon on the platform."

"You don't know shit," the boy in front says.

This whole time we are walking upstairs. But we stop at a large double steel door and then the two slave boys in front pull it open and step aside.

Immediately I am bombarded with the flashing lights of cameras. Dozens of men take pictures while reporters yell questions at me.

My two flanking escorts take my hands and lead me through the chaos. Disgusting, sweaty bodies reeking of the hot stench of oil and ocean push up against me.

"Just follow us," the one on my right says. "We're not stopping here. They want you on the platform right now."

The boys who were behind me are now in front, pushing the crowd out of the way. The camera flashes stop and darkness takes over.

There is no moon tonight. And every light on the ship has been turned off.

Everything around me feels both empty and full in the same moment.

Then we are climbing another set of stairs. At the top I realize we've already reached the *Bull of Light*'s helicopter pad. Two spotlights come on, but not regular spotlights. Black lights. And my skin glows an unnatural bright white under the purple haze.

Both of my slave boys squeeze my hands. Then they lean in and kiss me on the cheek that's not painted like a skull.

"Good luck," the first one says.

"Pavo for the win," the other one says, making a fist.

And then they leave me there, under the spotlights.

I breathe heavy and hard for a few moments, then almost fall into a panic when the spotlights go out. My heart shudders inside my chest. Because it's all happening too fast and I don't know what to do.

But of course, that's not really true. I only have one job here. I am to stand in the center of the round helicopter platform and not move until the fight is over.

But then what?

What happens to me after the fight?

Men in the crowd begin to scream at me from the topside. They are much closer than I imagined they would be and when I look up, I can pick out a few individual faces as the black spotlight passes back and forth across the crowd.

I scan them, wondering what they are thinking.

They begin to boo me when I don't move. They jeer and spew insults. And I realize I need to be in the center before anything else can happen.

I take a few steps forward and they cheer, clapping and whistling, calling at me.

The helipad hangs out over the side of the ship by just a little bit. Just enough so that when the helicopters land, there is no threat of the spinning rotors hitting anything on the command center. But this asymmetry, combined with the rolling motion of the massive ship, sets me off balance and I need to brace myself with feet spread apart to control the spinning in my head.

After a moment, I close my eyes, still slowly walking forward, and force myself to snap out of it.

Everyone is watching you, Anya. This is the fight of the year. If you ruin it, they will not forgive you.

I swallow hard, open my eyes, and find myself in the center of the platform, standing on the giant H painted on the concrete.

That's when all the lights go out and the drumming begins.

A slow, thumping beat at first. Like the footsteps of some giant beast coming towards me. The drummers are close, but I can't see them. I know it's not a recording. The ritual has started and this is part of it.

The beat picks up and becomes tribal, turning this modern-day miracle of a ship into a jungle island in the middle of a sea of darkness.

And when I look around, past the men eager for the blood that's coming, and truly take in the fact that there is nothing around us for thousands of miles and no moon overhead to light my way… I am lost.

But does it matter?

Haven't I always been lost?

The pace of the drumming picks up. It gets louder and louder. And then there they are.

First Cort, then Pavo. They enter the helipad from opposite stairwells that lead up to the platform and they do not look the way I expected.

Oh, there is a skull and there is a snake. But Cort is not the sum of his tattoos like I had guessed. He is a glowing yellow skeleton, each and every bone outlined in fluorescent paint. His ribcage. His pelvis. The tiny bones of his hands. And yeah, even his cock. A long, thick line of yellow dangling between his legs.

Naked.

Well. I didn't see that coming. But I'm not surprised. Everything about these fights is hypersexualized. That's probably why Pavo was so distracted by Cort's dick last night.

Pavo is painted as a snake. His face is the open mouth of a cobra, fangs protruding and ready to strike, his body covered in intricate neon-green scales that coil around his chest, and hips, and one leg. The rest of him is black, except, again, his cock—a thick line of green between his legs, swinging and slapping against his thigh as he walks towards me, because he is *hard*.

I roll my eyes.

They walk up to me without hesitation and each of them grips one of my hands.

Pavo squeezes tight. Like he's trying to crush the tiny bones.

Cort's grip is delicate. Like he doesn't want to touch me, but is being forced to do so.

Drones circle above us. The drumming is so loud now, I want to hold my hands over my ears. The men on the topside walkways cheer with enthusiasm.

"Are you ready, Anya?" Pavo asks. He steps out of the line we make, far enough for him to look past me, at Cort. Pavo's eyes find mine and he smiles. "He likes you, nyuszi. I can tell. I can see it in the way he looks at you." Cort says nothing and Pavo belts out laughter. "He likes you because… the two of you share a secret, don't you, nyuszi? You and the Sick Heart. You are more alike than you ever realized."

I narrow my eyes at Pavo and sneer my lip, confused, but also annoyed. *Just shut up already. No one wants to hear you talk.*

"Oh, you don't know?" Pavo snarls. The spectators are growing tired of waiting and their cheers become jeers once again. "You *really* don't know?" He shakes his head. Then he leans in closer to me, still focusing on Cort. "He doesn't *talk*, Anya. Not a fucking word from him in public in over twenty years."

My mouth drops open. Then I turn my head to see Cort's face. It's unreadable, his mouth nothing but a flat line, his silver eyes narrowed down into slits, staring straight into mine.

Pavo grabs my breast with his free hand and the crowd goes wild. "He is silent. Just like *you*, nyuszi."

I don't look at Pavo. Because right now I cannot take my eyes off Cort van Breda.

Is it true? Is he silent, like me?

"He doesn't talk," Pavo continues. "And neither do you." Then he laughs. "I can only imagine how that would work out should he win. But he won't win. Don't worry. You will be mine in the end, Anya. And I will *make* you talk. I will make you do all kinds of things with that mouth of yours."

Pavo is saying these words to me, but he's really talking to Cort.

Everything I know about Cort van Breda flashes through my mind. He does not do interviews. He stands there. Looks pretty in his Muay Thai shorts and his skull tattoos climbing up and down his body. He didn't say anything when he entered the reception hall earlier. He walked right past us and grabbed the Lectra bottle.

Maart talked for him.

Just like Bexxie talks for me.

I look back at Pavo, hoping he will say more.

But he doesn't say anything.

He just punches me in the mouth.

My lip splits and my whole body goes whirling backwards from the force.

The crowd erupts in cheers as I hit the helicopter platform and slide almost a meter from the force of Pavo's blow, my entire left side scraping against the concrete.

And when I finally gather my senses and look up... the fight has started.

Pavo and Cort are a flurry of arms and legs. Kicks and elbows. Pavo lands a flat foot right in the center of Cort's stomach and Cort goes reeling back just like I did.

He doesn't lose his footing, but he pauses for a moment as the pain in his gut sinks in. Then his eyes narrow down and focus on Pavo. Some of the spotlights from above weave around the platform, making me dizzy from the strobe effect. But there is one black light trained on Pavo and one black light trained on Cort. This presents a bizarre dichotomy, making the two painted fighters look like futuristic creatures straight out of the ancient world.

Pavo doesn't wait, he's already on the next attack. He pushes forward towards Cort, throwing a kick. But Cort counters the kick with an elbow and simultaneously hooks Pavo in the jaw with the opposite hand. Pavo stumbles, but Cort doesn't give him a chance to recover. He hits Pavo with a powerful uppercut that lands flush with his mouth, the same way Pavo hit me.

Pavo goes down. *Hard.*

The drumming around us is deafening. Almost drowning out the cheering crowd.

For a moment I think it's over. Pavo is struggling to get back on his feet. Cort turns his back to him, walking away.

But it's not over. Because one of them is still alive. And spoiler alert: That's not how this ends.

I have only been to two fights, and neither of them were at this elite level. They both involved Pavo, but that was years and years ago. One was the fight that ushered him into top-level status. The other one was at Pavo's local stadium filled with a crowd of regular Thai people. He did fight that night, but it was more of an exhibition. There was a referee, there seemed to be rules, and most of the fighters that night looked like kids.

There are no rules here, they're not even wearing gloves—not even wearing tape on their knuckles. And these two men haven't been kids for a very long time.

They will fight until they no longer can.

I get up on my knees, refusing to be a compliant participant in the outcome of this night. Cort is turning back towards Pavo when my movement distracts him. His head swings in my direction. Pavo disappears into the darkness, his spotlight now gone.

The crowd begins to boo and shout, making sure their objections can be heard over the pounding drums. They probably have money on Cort and my participation in the fight seems to be a clear attempt at aiding Pavo.

Cort doesn't seem to notice. His eyes are locked with mine. He puts a hand up.

Stop, that gesture says.

But I'm not going to stop. I turn, crouched, looking for Pavo in the darkness.

Because… he. *Hit* me.

That piece-of-shit coward hit me.

That baby living inside a man's body hit me.

That arrogant prick who thinks I will become his property *hit me*.

In front of all these people.

There is blood in my mouth.

My tongue has been split open.

I spit the blood out and suddenly… I am *enraged*.

And that's when all the spotlights go out.

The drumming continues in the dark, a wild, frantic beat that drowns out the shouts from the agitated crowd.

There are flashes of yellow and green, the leftover glow from the fighters' fluorescent body paint. But after a few moments, even that blinks out.

Someone runs past me. The wind flutters over my bare skin and I can just barely make out the slapping of bare feet over the drumming. I squint in the dark, trying to make out shapes. And holy shit, is it ever dark. No moon, no stars, every light on the ship is out. And if I wasn't rocking back and forth with the rhythm of an ocean, I would be utterly lost. The kind of lost that drives people to madness.

Then, just as suddenly as they went out, the spotlights come back on. But all three of them are targeting *Cort*.

And they are not black lights. They are bright and white and he is alone in a shower of illuminated brilliance in the vast sea of darkness.

Cort shields his eyes from the intense glare and that's when Pavo attacks.

He rams Cort like a bull. Knocking him down with a hard thump that sends a sick chill down my spine.

I get to my feet and take deep breaths as the white lights blink out and the black lights make them glow again, but leave me dark.

Pavo's snake winds around Cort's skeleton.

The drums have slowed, taking up a pace that conjures up images of being stalked. A beat that reminds me of the hunt. I crouch again, thinking, watching the fight.

Pavo is on top of Cort, but Cort hasn't surrendered. They are grappling. Fast-moving arms, and legs, and elbows, and knees.

I look around, thinking about the boy's words just minutes ago. *He's got a cheat. We all know Pavo's team hid a weapon on the platform.*

Pavo, the cheater.

Pavo, the deceiver.

He is vile, rotten, and wrong.

He has no sense of pride, or loyalty, or fairness.

He is nothing but scum and even my nine-year-old sister-in-name-only can see it.

So I know there is a weapon on the platform.

SICK HEART - JA HUSS

But where? The helipad is nothing but a flat plane. I stand up and begin walking in the hazy, leftover black light that leaks outward from the fight, squinting my eyes and searching for a shadow that might be a knife.

That's Pavo's weapon of choice. He uses knives as part of his training ritual with his boys. He cuts them. Slices marks down their arms every time they don't follow one of his insane directives. So they can never forget who is in charge. So they have to carry their shame with them for the rest of their lives.

I walk faster, ignoring the two men fighting. They are on their feet now, and the blows are vicious. They are grunting and they hit the hard concrete more times than I can count as I scan the helipad for the knife I *know* is here.

Except it's not.

There is nothing on this platform. It is bare. It is flat. It is empty.

So that means it has to be somewhere else, somewhere close enough that Pavo can get to it. There are only two choices. The stairwells. I jog over to the closest one, searching, my fingertips gliding along the smooth steel frame.

There it is. Fastened to the underside of a thick railing.

I pull, and it comes free with a rip of Velcro.

And then I turn back to the men… and walk into the fight.

CHAPTER FOUR

The worst thing about fighting Pavo Vervonal is his incessant chatter.

It's like this asshole has no respect for the value of silence. My very first goal in this fight has nothing to do with winning and everything to do with knocking out his fucking teeth so I can make him shut up.

"You like her, don't you?" He says this as I ring my arm around his neck and take him down.

But he's slippery, just like the snake painted on his body, and he maneuvers this way and that until he's out of my reach. On his feet, opposite me, crouched low with eyes fixed on mine. We circle each other.

"You want to take her home, don't you, Sick Heart? You're imagining the party that comes next, aren't you? The Lectra. You want to—"

I attack and cut him off. But his talking was nothing but a trick, a way to distract me as he planned his moves. I crack him in the jaw with my right elbow, but he dodges the follow-up move and my left fist crashes into his blocking forearm instead of his head.

But I'm no stranger to tricks. I've been fighting for my life since I was five years old. I hold the current Ring of Fire world record for the number of times I've been on the platform opposite an insane asshole just like Pavo.

And I have tricks of my own.

I've got him on defense and his eyes are assessing my elbows, and knees, and fists, and feet for their threat value.

He does it in that order. Because my elbows are always what takes them down in the end. And my knees are always looking for that weak spot. And my fists are always going for the knockout punch.

So when his threat assessment finally catches up to my offensive moves, he's expecting a kick.

But I don't kick. I simply sweep him off his feet.

He falls backwards, and even over the pounding of the drums, I can hear the crowd.

They are not rooting for me.

They *never* root for me.

They will put money on me, because I like to win. But in this fight, I'm not the favorite. At twenty-seven, the mere fact that I'm still alive is just luck to them. And just before luck runs out, it runs slow.

They came here thinking my luck has been running slow for years now.

This is it. Money on Pavo.

But fuck that. I'm not even down, let alone out.

Pavo responds to my sweep with a series of grappling moves that leave behind a rash of concrete burns on my skin when we finally get back on our feet, once again crouched and circling.

One of my ears is ringing, blood is seeping down my throat, and I'm pretty sure at least one rib is cracked because every time I inhale, a sharp pain makes me wince in the back of my mind.

Pavo attacks. He's rammed me twice now, and I know he won't do it again, even though he comes at me with all the intentions of a bull. He pulls out of it in the very last second, but I'm ready for him. I swing up, grab him in a flying arm bar, and slap him down onto the concrete so hard his breath leaves his body in a loud grunt.

He lies there, still. This is my chance. This is the moment that I finish him.

And I'm just about to do that—just about to chop him in the throat, break his trachea, and spend the next three minutes watching him slowly suffocate—when I see a streak of white out of the corner of my eye.

Anya comes towards me with a knife.

I stand up and back away a little, unsure if her loyalty to Pavo has turned her insane or if this was part of the plan.

I realize my mistake when Pavo grabs my ankle and pulls. He was down, but not out.

There is no way out of this move. But I break the fall with the flat palm of my hand and land on my side, forgetting to favor the cracked rib.

Pain leaks out of me as nothing more than a low grunt of acknowledgement. But on the inside, the sharpness of the injury takes me by surprise. And my head is filled with nothing but screaming.

Screaming.

Little voices in the dark. The smell of blood in the night. The cackling laughter of the man who took us.

And then... the instincts. My instincts. Once I realized there was nothing more to lose.

And then Pavo is looming over me, sitting on me, crushing my already bruised and broken ribs. His bloody mouth grinning, his dark eyes flashing, his overdeveloped sense of self-importance rearing up like a wild stallion who just won a whole herd of mares.

My legs kick up, knees connecting with his back the same time his fist connects with my face.

Stars shimmer in the night even though there are no stars tonight.

I push up with my flat palms, connect with his chest, and roll him over my head.

There is a sick *thunk* as his skull hits the ground, and I think, *That's gotta hurt*, but in a life-or-death fight it's not over 'till it's over.

I get up on my hands and feet, pausing for a moment to assess Pavo. He's lying face down and blood is streaming along the side of his head. But he's not out.

He rolls over, one, two, three full revolutions. And then he's on his feet.

They never go down easy. Not at this level.

Another flash of white. Fucking Anya and her knife.

Pavo grabs her out of instinct, wraps one arm tightly around her neck, catching the vulnerable part of her trachea in the crook of his elbow. She drops the knife, both hands reaching for his arm to pry it away as he begins to strangle the life out of her.

And then the sound of metal on concrete changes *everything*.

A weapon. On the battlefield.

The crowd had faded into the background, but now it all comes roaring back.

Pavo's eyes dart to the knife, but I'm looking at him. He throws Anya and she goes stumbling to the side, still grabbing at her throat and wheezing as she desperately tries to suck in air.

I lurch back, but I'm too late. I am cut and bleeding before the pain even sets in.

Pavo is very good with knives. His skill with them is impressive, even to me.

He doesn't cut me again. Doesn't even try. He throws that fucker right at my neck.

I dart to the side, and still that knife pierces my flesh as it passes by and hits the ground several meters behind me.

My hand reaches up to find the damage and is instantly covered in hot, sticky blood.

Again the sound of the crowd and the drums fades back in. They are going wild for him and my head is spinning a little. Did he cut me deep enough? Did he hit the artery? Nick it? Am I already dead?

I don't have time to think about it, because Pavo is attacking again. His kick is swift and there are twenty years of practiced force behind it when the length of his lower leg hits me across the hips.

But I've got twenty-two years of practiced checks behind my defense as well. I grab his leg. He immediately checks me, hooking his knee, pulling me forward. And then he jumps up, left arm circling my head, holding it tightly in place while his right elbow finds the side of my face.

Stars. I stumble backwards and let go of his leg.

His defense wasn't an original move. But it was effective. I have to retreat, taking steps, and steps, and steps backwards as Pavo advances.

"Finish it." They are chanting now. "Finish it. Finish it. Finish it."

Pavo is their winner. They are here to see him. Not because they love *him*, but because they hate *me*.

They want to see me fall. After all these years, all these fights, all those prizes—they are done with me. They want me *dead*.

I too am a sacrifice. Just like this girl on the platform with us.

His legs are battering me and I am blocking. One blow after another. And each time I block his legs, his elbows are there because he's high on the kind of adrenaline rush one only ever gets when they think they've already won.

The drums stop.

The final moment is nothing but the maddening crowd. They forget who they are in the outside world when they're at the fights. All those rules they live by fade into the background. They stop caring about their role. They stop thinking about the gifts they accept. And maybe—if they're very lucky and they win their bets—maybe they forget about the things they gave up to be here. Maybe they forget the price they've already paid.

And if they get lucky enough, *and* drunk enough, *and* they find a lover tonight who knows what they're doing—then maybe they even forget how much they still *owe*.

"I told you," Pavo growls, breathing hard, his eyes locked with mine as he spits blood on the concrete at my feet. "You will be mine in the end."

But he's not talking to me. He's talking to Anya. I can't spare the moment it will take to locate her, but I can hear her wheezing somewhere behind me.

Pavo still has bounce in his step. And now I see it. The blue ring around his irises goes fluorescent purple in the black light. The ring of Lectra addiction. He is fucking high. Which is not against the rules. There are no rules. You win any way you can.

But it's a risk. The Lectra can be a bonus. It can make you fearless. It can dull pain. And if this were chess, it could help you see a dozen moves ahead.

But this isn't chess. This is life and death and Lectra can also make you afraid. It can amplify the agony. It can pull you into a slow-motion dream world where nothing makes sense and every action comes with hallucinogenic tracers.

It affects Pavo the first way. That's why he drinks it before a fight.

But it affects me the opposite. That's why I don't.

"You had a good run," Pavo says, attacking me again, his perfectly executed kick crashing against my hips. He doesn't check me this time. Just backs off because he knows I'm not in a good place.

I'm playing defense. I'm dizzy and blood is streaming down the right side of my body.

His knife didn't hit the artery because I'd be bleeding out on the ground by now if it had. But he hit *something*. My rib is screaming and I can feel those kicks all the way to my kidneys.

The drumming starts again. A new beat. The death beat. The final beat.

Someone, probably my father since he's hosting this event, has decided that Pavo has won and has instructed the drummers to pound out the ending sequence.

And that's when Anya steps between us, knife in hand. Pointed at Pavo, not me. And she thrusts it into his side.

I actually laugh at the gall of this stupid girl and the gasp of the crowd is loud enough to hear in between the slow beat of the death drums.

Pavo grabs her, reaching for the knife in his side. I expect her to let it go, but she doesn't. She holds on to it. She's actually *fighting him* for the knife, her body glowing a surreal white in the blackness all around us. A ghost fighting the snake.

That fucking girl just saved my ass.

I'm up. Hurting, but up.

Pavo sees me, lets go of the knife, and pushes Anya so hard, she goes reeling backwards. Right in to me.

I catch her. Hold her.

"Nice." Pavo laughs the word out loud enough to be heard. "Using a woman as a shield."

No. That's not what I'm doing, dickface. My hand slides over her hip and finds the knife in her hand.

She releases it. And I step out around her.

Pavo doesn't even look at the weapon, but I know he sees it. "You're not gonna make it this time, Sick Heart. Not even that knife can help you now."

I toss the knife and it goes careening across the helipad as I smile at Pavo Vervonal.

Then I attack.

I will *not* win my last fight with a *weapon*.

Four long strides cover the distance between us. He comes at me with elbows and knees, but I'm done with Muay Thai tonight.

There is an advantage to living on this side of the world and that's why I stay here. And that advantage is Brazil and the art of capoeira.

I duck and feign. Hop out of reach. Block as Pavo attacks again with kicks and I wait for that look on his face. It's a look every fighter gets when they think they've won, when they haven't. This look is a tell of weakness. Because in the Ring of Fire, it's not over 'till it's over.

When he pauses, I swing at him and he blocks as I twist my upper body—left leg front, right leg back—and then I am turning. Right leg following the arc of the spin until my heel connects with the side of his head with a sickening *thunk*.

He goes down.

Then I'm on top of him because there are no referees on the platform to pull me away and let him recover, and this is just how it's done in my world. You can set your fucking watch to the sick ending that comes with each and every Ring of Fire fight.

I straddle Pavo, running through all my options in my head. And then my hands are on his throat.

I can hear the crowd because the drumming has stopped. Actually stopped. And they are calling my name.

But it's not the way they *should* be calling it.

And I catch Maart's voice. "Behind you! *Behind you!*"

I twist off Pavo—who is still unconscious—and drop into a low crouch as I find Anya standing just a meter away holding that fucking knife.

We stare at each other. And I don't know how it happens for her, but everything in my world suddenly goes silent. All I hear are the words that she's *not* saying.

Her face is a bloody mess. Her nose may be broken and her plump, fleshy bottom lip is split. Blood is dripping down her chin.

She says nothing. And now that I know she's silent, that makes sense.

But when you live in a world of sick hearts and dead voices, you only need eyes to say what needs to be said.

And hers tell me... she is *furious*.

There is nothing but hate in her gaze. And for a moment, I'm caught off guard. Because when I saw her earlier up in the command center, I would've never guessed she was capable of that kind of hate.

She walks towards me with the knife. The crowd is screaming. Pavo has lost. He's barely conscious. Low, primal moans from him and nothing more. They all know I've won and that means this girl is mine. Or she will be, once I put Pavo out of his misery.

Or will she? Seems Anya is beginning to have an opinion about how this night ends.

She stops less than one pace between us. Our eyes lock.

Does she want to kill me?

No.

She looks at Pavo and then she holds up the knife.

I shrug and make a little gesture. A little wave of my hand that says, *By all means. Be my guest.*

She pushes past me and then, without hesitation, she straddles Pavo's body, crouches down, and then, again without hesitation, she buries that knife right in his gut.

Oh, Anya. That's gonna be messy.

Pavo gulps air. Blood spills out of his mouth as his back bucks up, arching and twisting.

Anya stares down at him, and then rises up, leaving the knife right where she put it. She turns to me, wipes the blood away from her mouth and lets out a long breath.

I look down at Pavo, then back up at Anya. Tears are streaming down her face. They leave a track of blurry white body paint on her cheeks.

Then I shake my head and sigh as I pull the knife from Pavo's stomach and drag the blade across his neck, making sure to cut right through his trachea, because I'm ready for what comes next.

The blood pours out of him and suddenly he is lying in a pool of crimson scarlet. The drones hover just off my shoulder, barely ten feet off the ground, filming the entire death scene so that all my watchers tonight can replay it back in 4K ultra.

But this isn't enough. This ending had a twist, that's for sure. But it won't haunt them. And I need to *haunt* them. This is my real heat-of-the-moment payment. It's not the girls. It's not the money. It's certainly not the fucking accolades.

It's the ending.

It's the look in their eyes when I catch them by surprise.

And so far tonight, Anya is the only one who has made the news.

Yeah. I can't leave it like that.

When I look down, the knife is still in my hand. I hold the hilt in my fist and drag the blade down Pavo's body from neck to belly, splitting him open. And then I thrust my hand inside him, dig under his ribs, grab hold of the thick, still-trembling muscle, and use every bit of energy I have left to pull his heart out of his chest.

The entire *universe* stops to watch me.

The crowd says nothing. They don't even dare to gasp.

Oh, shit, they're thinking. *What will he do with it?*

I consider the optics of eating it. That would really give them nightmares. But I can't stomach the thought of biting off a piece of Pavo and the drones are too close to fake it.

So I just stand up and throw it as far as I can towards the closest group of people, and when it slaps into the blocking arm of *Lazar*, I look down so the drones can't see me smile.

"Sick Heart. Sick Heart. Sick Heart." They chant it now. Not *for* me. They don't chant *for* me. Their chant is submission and nothing more.

They know who's in charge on this platform.

I point to Anya and she sucks in air. Then I motion for her to grab Pavo's arm. She does this without hesitation and we drag his body across the rough concrete, leaving a river of black in the white glow behind us.

He is just meat.

We position him until he's teetering sideways on the edge of the helipad.

The silent night breaks and I hear him. Anya's father, that fucking prick, is screaming my name. My real fucking name. "Cort van Breda! Cort van Breda!" in his stupid Hungarian accent.

I know he's running towards us because his calls become louder. And then he's screaming at Anya, telling her to stop me. But neither she nor I look back at her father. We simply roll the body over the edge.

And that's the end of Pavo Vervonal. Because he disappears into the churning black water of an endless ocean of death.

"No!" her father screams.

Lazar is right behind us. Very fucking close. Close enough to push either of us over the side. And while I'm not afraid of death and I might be able to get on board with jumping off this ship at some point in time, I just won my last fight and I have more things coming my way than just this girl who saved my life.

So I turn on him. And I growl at him.

Maart and Rainer are already running across the platform with several of the mercenaries as backup. But I don't need backup. Not for this dumb fuck.

Lazar stops just a few paces off and when I reach for Anya's arm and tug her behind me, he backs up.

Then the lights come on and everything is bright and white.

I can't see for a moment, but Lazar doesn't understand that. He's never had to fight for his life. He's never stood under the black lights and fought to the death. He's never had the white blindness after winning.

He knows *nothing*.

But his face is red with rage. "You're sick! You know that? Someone should put you down! You're an animal. And you didn't win this fight. My daughter won this fight. This ship is mine, this prize is mine—"

The mercs grab him and pull him away, and now his threats are for them, not me.

"Jesus fucking Christ!" Maart reaches me and immediately begins to assess my condition. "Come on, you've lost blood."

I reach up to my neck and realize that the entire right side of my body is nothing but sticky red and it's only then that I recognize the dizziness for what it is.

I sink to my knees, suddenly weak. Like all the adrenaline that was keeping me going has been used up.

"No, no, no." Rainer has one arm and Maart has the other. "We're not passing out here, champ. That would never do."

They drag me off the platform and I let out a long breath as I close my eyes, thinking, *Maybe this is the end?*

Because what's left after this?

Who am I when the fights are over?

I dream about Lazar as I drift in and out of consciousness in the clinic.

I don't know why I dream about him. I've never met him before, but he looks so familiar. I can't place it, really. It's just some fuzzy nonsensical association thing that comes with dreams. Especially half-dead dreams.

Rainer is monitoring my blood transfusion as Maart stitches up my neck. Someone I don't know is trying to fasten a brace around my ribs, but when I swing at him, Maart yells for everyone to get out and leave me alone.

Maart. I reach up, grab his hair with a weak fist, and pull him down to my face.

I don't open my eyes. Can't really open my eyes. But I just want to kiss him.

He laughs and pulls back. "You're dumb. And you just got blood all over me, asshole."

"Where's my kiss, Cort?" It's Rainer.

I lift my hand and wave him over. But he flicks the tip of his finger against my forehead instead. "You're good. Just relax. You're gonna feel a lot better once this transfusion finishes. But"—he lowers his voice and whispers right next to my ear—"Anya's here in the room. I wasn't sure what to do with her, but I didn't want her going back with her father in case he got any ideas about keeping her."

Fuck. I sit up out of instinct and immediately the pain in my ribs feels like it might shear me in half. I hiss and wince.

"Fucking hell, Cort!" Maart objects. "Lie back down. I'm still sewing you up. Ten more minutes, OK? That's all I need."

But I tune him out as I find Anya's paint-streaked face across the room. She's sitting on a wheeled stool in the corner wearing a hospital gown. Frowning at me. Silent.

That's right. I almost forgot. She's *silent*.

I like that about her.

But why? Why is she silent? I really need to know that, so I sign to Rainer because Maart is still trying to stitch up my neck and isn't watching my hands. *Why is she silent?*

Rainer hesitates. "Uhhh, well... I dunno." Then he turns to Anya. "He wants to know why you don't talk."

She doesn't look at Rainer. Her eyes are locked on mine.

I sign to Rainer again. He grunts, walks over to her, grabs her face, forces her mouth open, and looks inside. She slaps at him, but Rainer is a huge dude and she's got no chance of resisting.

"Nope," Rainer says. "Her tongue is still there." He looks over at Maart. "She might need a stitch on it. It's still bleeding."

"I'm a little busy right now," Maart says. "So…" He looks up at Anya. "Probably not."

Anya grunts as Rainer releases her, pushing him away now that he's already retreating.

So. She's not silent because her tongue is missing.

They do that every now and then. If the girls object too much or they get caught trying to escape. Sometimes a slave will just see too much and that's the most efficient way to silence them. If they're not interested in simply killing them, that is.

But Anya isn't just any slave. She is Lazar's slave. And that means she's been with him since she was very young. She would've been taught to read and write to make her worth more at the auctions, so cutting out her tongue wouldn't silence her anyway. If Lazar had any concerns about Anya's loyalties, she would already be dead.

So why doesn't she talk?

I narrow my eyes at her and ask the question that way since she obviously doesn't know how to sign. *Why, Anya? Why don't you talk?*

She only frowns at me, but it's enough.

I nod and lie back down. Closing my eyes again as Maart complains about all the ways I'm fucking up his stitching.

"Here." Something cold presses against my flaming ribcage and I wince. "Evard brought you this. Figured you'd need it."

Oh, hell yeah. I almost forgot about the Lectra. I feel around without opening my eyes until my fingers wrap around the neck of the bottle.

"Don't spill it," Rainer cautions me. "There's no cork."

"Don't sit up to drink it, either," Maart objects. "I've got two more internal stitches, then I'll close, and you'll be done. Two fucking minutes, Cort. Just be good for two more minutes."

"OK, question." Rainer taps my shoulder. "You wanna drink the Lectra for the pain? Or you want me to give you this?"

I open my eyes and find him holding a syringe.

Maart scoffs. "No, Rainer. Don't give him that. He's gonna drink the fucking Lectra."

"Well, I know he's going to drink it. But he still has to walk all the way over to the fucking reception room. And those ribs are gonna hurt. The Lectra won't kick in for at least thirty minutes. One shot of this—"

"No." Maart is insistent. He's all practical like that when it comes to medical shit. It's a bad idea to mix opiates with Lectra. "We can hang in here for thirty minutes. It's no big deal."

But I point at Rainer and give him permission anyway.

Maart sighs. "Why am I even here? You never listen to me."

He knows that's not true. I always listen to him about the important shit. But this isn't about important shit. This is about getting fucked up.

My last fight. And I won.

I'm still here.

This night is going to be epic.

And tomorrow... tomorrow is a whole new beginning.

I don't know what that looks like, exactly. But it's been a long, *long* time since I had a new beginning, so I don't even care.

I relax a little as Rainer ties off my arm, pats my vein with his fingertips, and then slides that needle in and pushes those drugs.

I love that feeling. Not the drugs. I give no fucks about drugs. I take them because... well, this happens at least once a year and I need a way to get through it. And back when I was a kid, this happened six or seven times a year. Most of those fights were even deeper underground than this one.

No. I just like the way I can trace the drug in my body as it enters my bloodstream.

It burns as it travels up my arm. I like that feeling when it enters my heart. Then it exits and then suddenly that drug is everywhere all at once.

It's a weird, almost spiritual, experience.

Or I'm just fucked up and all this is just the delusions of a man on Demerol after killing someone.

I float for a few minutes as Maart finishes up. Then they help me sit up and I take my first sip of Lectra in over a year.

It even tastes blue. Something between too sweet and too cold. And I can feel that too. Going down my throat. Entering my stomach. Heating me up from the inside out.

I open my eyes and everything is blurry. But I can still make out Anya in the corner wearing her hospital gown. I sign a command to whoever is paying attention to find her some clothes.

But then I tell them not to let her wash the paint off. Not yet.

We're still playing our parts.

Reality comes much, *much* later.

Time passes—I don't know how much—but eventually Anya is wearing a loose white dress and I'm wearing a pair of olive-green cargo shorts and no shirt or shoes.

"You ready?"

Maart's words are blurry like his face. And I just smile.

Born ready, that smile says.

And the next thing I know we're in the reception room and people are clapping.

Liars. They are all liars.

They are not clapping for me. They clap to save themselves. Everything they do is done to save themselves. We all know that. And yet we still lie about it.

It's all lies to save ourselves.

But there's no saving us.

We are the evil everyone warns you about.

CHAPTER FIVE

ONE HOUR EARLIER

I'm stuck in the world of black night and glowing bodies long after the lights come back on.

Nothing really makes sense and I feel like I'm a little bit drunk on Lectra, even though I'm not. I think it's because something is bleeding in my mouth—my tongue and maybe my cheek. The blood is making me nauseous and the altercation between Cort and my father only adds to the sick feeling in my gut.

Did I win the fight for Cort?

Will I have to go with him? Or can my father keep me? Is there some rule that might save me from becoming another Sick Heart concubine?

I don't love my father. I don't care about him. But I do love Bexxie and if I leave… if I leave—

"Hey, you." A mercenary dressed in black body armor pokes me. "Let's go."

I look around and realize Cort is being helped off the platform. My father is on the far side screaming at Cort's father, Udulf.

I concentrate on this interaction for a moment. Focusing on Udulf van Hauten.

This is the first time I've seen him since we arrived and it's... disconcerting.

I *know* him.

I *remember* him.

And then I shudder with revulsion.

"Anya doesn't belong to Cort!" This is what Lazar is screaming. "He didn't win. It was cheating!"

I look around at the crowd, no one else seems to share his concern. And that means it's over. The bets are already being paid out and no one put money on me, so I am definitely not the winner.

The mercenary grabs me by the arm with a commanding grip that leaves no room for objection. I don't resist. I just try to keep up as I'm led down the stairs, across the upper deck, and then through a door and down more stairs.

I thought we'd be going up to the reception room for the party, but we're not. We're going deep into the belly of the massive ship.

I'm still naked and even though we pass dozens of men as we walk through the halls, not a single one of them lifts their eyes up from the floor.

Are they afraid to look at me? Because of my father?

Maybe they've just seen enough sacrificial girls to know I'm not worth leering at.

Or maybe they find me, and everything I represent, disgusting.

One—a dark, middle-aged man wearing an apron—crosses himself and mutters a prayer as we pass each other. Like I am the Devil's daughter.

The merc stops suddenly outside a door and knocks. "The girl," he calls.

The door opens and Rainer appears. He nods at my escort. "I'll take her from here. Thanks." The door swings wide open to reveal a small clinic—one bed hosting Cort, a small desk built into the side of the wall, and two of those rolling stools doctors use.

Maart is sitting on a stool, frowning as he holds a thick wad of gauze against Cort's bleeding neck with his elbow while he uses his hands to insert an IV. Cort's eyes are closed and I'm not sure he's even conscious.

"Are you waiting for an invitation?" I look up and find Rainer's scowling face. "Get the fuck in here. We're busy."

I walk forward and Rainer grabs a hospital gown off a counter, shoves it up to my chest, and then pushes me out of the way. The space is tiny and it's a tight fit with four people in it, even if one of them is on the bed.

"Put that gown on and sit over there," Maart commands me with a nod of his head.

I slip my arms into the gown and put it tight across my front as I walk over to the corner and take a seat on a second rolling stool.

Then there's another knock at the door.

"Get rid of them," Maart mutters.

Rainer opens the door and I try to peek around his muscular body, but he's massive and I can't see anything until he bends down.

It's the boy. He's holding a bottle of Lectra and trying to get a look at Cort. "Is he OK?" His voice is small and scared. "I brought him this."

"He's gonna be fine, Evard," Rainer tells him. "Just a nick. That's all."

"He's all bloody." Evard is not convinced. And when I look at Cort, I'm not either. Maybe he'll die of blood loss? Maybe I'll get to stay here on this ship instead of being sent to the harem? Maybe I can go home with Bexxie? Maybe—

"It looks a lot worse than it is," Maart says. He's not paying attention to Rainer or the kid. He's pulling a bag of blood out of a cooler on the floor and hooking it into the IV. "We got this, Evard. Go to bed now."

"Bed?" Evard's single word comes out both surprised and cynical. "I'm not going to bed! He's dying!"

Rainer is still crouched down. And now I realize he did that so he could look the boy in the eyes. He puts a hand on his shoulder. "He's not dying, Evard. He needs some blood, and some stitches, and his ribs will be fucked for a few weeks. But he'll be fine the next time you see him, I promise."

"No. I don't want to go back without him. Why does he do this? Why can't he just come home?"

Hmm. I wonder what this is about?

"Evard?" Maart has had enough of this. I can hear it in his tone. "Go back to the room and stay there. If you say anything else, you're gonna get three months on the Rock." Evard scoffs, but Maart adds, "Alone."

"That's fucking stupid," Evard yells. "He would never—"

"Wouldn't he?" Maart interrupts. And then he looks up from his work on Cort's body and his gaze slowly migrates over to the kid.

Evard has the good sense to slink back.

Hell, even I slink back and he's not even looking at me.

"Go," Rainer says, his voice still soft and calm. "He won't be happy if he wakes up and Maart tells him about this. You've already crossed lines here."

A long, tired sigh from the boy. Then he thrusts the bottle at Rainer. "Tell him I brought him this." Rainer takes the bottle and then Evard turns and walks away.

Well, that interaction was very interesting. Lots of little information nuggets to decode later. But not now. Because Maart begins to stitch up Cort's neck and this rouses Cort just enough to moan.

Rainer closes the door, sets the bottle on the small counter, and then turns to Cort. "You here with us, buddy?" He slaps his cheek a few times. "Cort? Can you hear me?"

Cort moans again, and his head turns, but he doesn't open his eyes.

Maart growls. "Stay still, asshole. I'm fucking stitching here."

Another bit of information gleaned. Maart is his... what? Medic? He certainly seems to know what he's doing.

Another knock at the door.

"Fucking hell," Maart says.

But Rainer is already opening it up. He whispers something, then opens the door wider. "This guy brought a brace for Cort's ribs."

Maart looks up from his stitching. "No. We don't need a brace."

"I'm sorry," the nurse at the door says. "Udulf commanded me to make him wear it."

Maart glances up from his work and shoots the delivery guy a death look, making him shrink back. Then he looks over at Rainer and sighs. "Put it on him then."

"Me?" Rainer laughs. It's a nice laugh. In fact, he's got a nice face. It's friendly-looking when he laughs. "Not my area of expertise."

Maart is really annoyed now. He looks at the nurse. "Put it on him!"

"Yes, sir," the man says. He squeezes past Rainer, but there's not just one nurse, there are two, and they both come in. And now this room is way too small. They shuffle around each other, one on each side of Cort's body, reaching under him to try to slide the brace underneath his muscular back as Rainer messes with the line feeding Cort a bag of blood.

But suddenly Cort wakes, his fist swinging at the strangers.

"Out!" Maart barks. "Now!"

Cort reaches over to Maart with both hands, grabs his hair, and pulls his face downward. I hold my breath and wonder what he will do next. Hit him? Headbutt him?

But no. Cort kisses him. Right on the lips.

Maart laughs it off with a joke about getting him all bloody and then Rainer is bending down to whisper in Cort's ear.

Suddenly Cort bolts upright, looking straight at me as Maart hisses objections. But Cort's steel-gray eyes are locked on mine and suddenly, I feel like I'm under a spell.

I can't look away. His hands are moving. Fast. And I realize that he is *signing*.

Pavo lied.

Sick Heart does so talk.

He just doesn't talk out loud, that fucking cheater.

I don't know why this surprises me so much, because people who talk are normal and people who don't aren't, but I am shocked. And disappointed.

I mean, it's only been like an hour since I realized he and I might be alike. But if he communicates, then he is *not* silent. And that means he's *not* like me at all.

"He wants to know why you don't talk," Rainer says.

I don't say anything to Cort van Breda. Not with my hands. Not with my eyes. Never with my voice. Because he's not getting that answer from me.

I do not communicate with anyone. Ever.

He's a dirty silent cheater, that's what he is.

He will never get a single secret out of me.

Never.

I watch as Rainer shoots Cort up with a syringe of painkillers over Maart's objections, and try to follow the silent conversation Cort's hands are having. It's not hard since both Maart and Rainer give clues with their voices, but Rainer actually signs and talks out loud, so that's super helpful with my limited understanding of sign language. Cort's signs are deliberate and defined, but Rainer's are slow and sloppy. Like he's skipping words.

Soon enough, Maart is done with the stitching and they start in on the Lectra. Even serious Maart gets in on the drinking goal. Cort sits up, flashing his talkative hands, and someone delivers a white dress for me.

Right. My dress.

This isn't over, Anya. Your nightmare is just getting started.

Cort is helped into a pair of cargo shorts, one arm around each of his friends as he steps into them. Is that what they are? Friends? I'm not sure. They might be lovers, actually. And if that's the case, maybe Cort does nothing with his concubines? Maybe he's not interested in them that way?

Not them, Anya. Us.

Because I'm one of them now. I belong to this man. I belong to this *killer*.

He dragged that knife across Pavo's neck like it was nothing. He gutted him like a dead animal. No thought at all went into his decision to kill tonight. And why should he think twice about it? According to the rumors—and the skulls on his body—he has killed dozens of men on nights like this.

"You ready?" Maart is holding Cort's head with both hands, staring straight into his eyes.

Cort sucks in a breath and nods the affirmative. "Then let's do it."

All three of them are in a much better mood now. Cort has been smiling non-stop since Rainer shot him up with those painkillers. And they have all taken at least half a dozen sips of the Lectra. I stare at the blue liquid in the bottle and notice that it is more than half empty.

"Hello?"

I look up and realize Maart is talking to me.

"Are you ready?"

I'm not sure what I'm supposed to be ready for, but since when did it matter if I was ready for anything that's happened to me in my life? I, of course, say nothing. But I don't change my expression, either. I'm actually thinking back to my laugh earlier in the day.

I laughed at Maart's threat to Pavo.

I don't talk, I don't use hand signals, and I don't laugh, either.

And now I'm mad at myself for doing that. For being so complacent. For not paying attention. For showing them something real.

No one gets anything real out of me.

Ever.

So I just stare at Maart like he is speaking a language I don't understand.

"I think that's a yes." Rainer laughs. "Come on, let's get the formalities over with so we can get this night started."

Rainer reaches for the door, but Cort puts one hand on his shoulder and signs something with the other one.

"Oh." Rainer looks over his shoulder at me, then offers me the Lectra. "He says you need to drink." Cort signs something and Maart laughs as Rainer amends his statement. "He says you need to catch up." Rainer grabs a marker off the small desk and draws a line on the bottle. "Drink it down to there."

I hold in my reaction. This is a test. Not the drinking part. Well, yes—the drinking part is a test of my obedience. Fine. Whatever. I'll drink ten thousand dollars' worth of Lectra if they want me to.

But the real test is my reaction.

My new master wants a reaction from me.

Cort's eyes are locked on mine when I find his face. And he probably thinks this Lectra will loosen me up. It will make me drop my guard. Make me compliant and easy. It might even make me talk.

That is a fantasy.

I will not smile.

I will not frown.

I will not glare at him.

And there is not enough Lectra in this world to change that.

Do they think I just woke up one day and said, "I think I'll stop talking?"

Fucking amateurs.

I grab the neck of the bottle and it goes down cold. So cold. Lectra is typically served at room temperature, but it's always like ice going down.

I don't stop until I'm certain that I have met the mark. And actually, when Rainer grabs the bottle from me, I see that I drank a little bit more than was required.

"Easy there, killer," Rainer jokes. "Save some for us." Then he winks at me. His eyes are neither dark, like Maart's, or blank slates of gray, like Cort's. Rainer's eyes are bright, bright green. They look like grass on a summer afternoon. His face reminds me of sunshine. The scruff on his chin has a glint of gold to it. And if I were someone else in this world, I would maybe think about liking him.

But I can't afford to like him. Even if he turns out to be as nice on the inside as he looks on the outside.

I can't afford to like anyone except Bexxie.

She is the only one I ever trusted. She is the only one who has had my back since the day she came to live with us. She is wise far, *far* beyond her nine years.

She is a survivor.

And now I have to leave her behind.

I sigh, heavy with sudden sadness, and look past Rainer. Past all of them like they are unseen ghosts.

Because this is over now. Nothing will ever be the same again and not even Rainer's bright green eyes can change that. So why bother looking at them?

Beauty is a trick. That's something I learned young. And all three of these men are far too beautiful to be anything but evil.

"Well, she's going to be a barrel of fun tonight," Maart says dryly.

Then they are pushing each other the way boys do, and not grown men. Cort is grinning and Maart is laughing as Rainer forces us all through the door.

The walk to the reception hall is long, but passes quickly. I know from watching Cort for the last hour that he is hurting. And he's drunk and on drugs right now so everything about this walk should make him slow. But it doesn't.

I hear just one tiny hiss when we need to brush past people in the hallway and a crew member's arm swipes the side of his bare ribcage. But aside from that, you'd never know he was in a fight to the death and had his neck cut open two hours ago.

He walks super-fast. He jogs up the steps. He never once wobbles or even breathes hard.

Either he is the definition of fitness and control, or he's so used to the pain, he's figured out how to get past it.

Or maybe he's all of that?

I begin to wonder about his life. Where he grew up—no. *How* he grew up. That's much more important than where. Who took care of him as a child? Where did Maart and Rainer come from? And that little boy? Who is Evard? One of his trainees? Evard wasn't allowed to watch the fight, but there he is, waiting for us outside the reception hall entrance. Two of those mercenaries stand on either side of him like he's under their charge.

The smile he beams at Cort is uncontainable. And his eyes are filled with love even though he says nothing when Rainer hands him the Lectra bottle. Like he knows his place in this entourage.

But then he spots me and smiles. "Hi, Anya. Bexxie wanted me to tell you not to leave without saying goodbye."

"Who the fuck is Bexxie?" Maart asks. All three of them are looking at me.

"Her little sister," the boy says. "She found me and we watched the fight together."

Well, that figures. That's totally something Bexxie would do.

Cort signs something to Maart and Maart looks at me. "Later. He says you can see your sister later."

Then Cort looks at me. Maybe expecting me to be grateful? I'm not sure. But this tiny sign of humanity isn't enough to make me react. Not even close.

"All right, you ready?" Maart asks Cort, pulling his attention back to the business at hand, which is the reception.

Cort nods.

"Then let's go."

The mercenaries open the wide double doors like we're royalty.

And I guess we are. For tonight, anyway. He did win the fight. My father does not get a controlling interest in this ship and Cort's father maintains his status.

All because of Sick Heart.

That is no small thing.

There are at least a hundred people in the room when we enter and they all begin to applaud. Not the barely-polite applause they managed outside, but a roaring, thundering applause that even comes with a few whistles and shouts.

And that makes me tired.

I'm so tired of the show.

So tired of the lies.

So tired of this life.

Why do I keep going?

That's the Lectra talking, Anya. You drank too much already and your night has barely started.

And that's how I get through the Lectra intoxication every time they give it to me. I talk to myself and no one else.

So this night should be so much fun.

I drift away in my approaching Lectra stupor, unable to even pretend to care what's happening around me. The little boy takes my hand and keeps hold of it. But I don't look at him. I don't look at anyone.

That's the Lectra taking over too.

It makes me want to float away. Just give in. And I will. Not yet, but soon.

The boy tugs my arm and I look down at him. "Don't worry," he says. "We're not staying here long. Cort hates parties. And we have better things to do than hang with these people. Here. Take a sip. It will make it better."

I look down at the bottle he's offering me and concentrate on breathing. Then I take it, knowing better, but not caring. The life that I know is over now. And I don't want to know what comes next.

The drink goes down cold and smooth. And then someone pulls the bottle from my lips, which are sticky now.

"Easy there," Rainer says. "You're good, Anya. You've got a long night ahead so it's best if you pace yourself."

A *long* night.

A whole life, actually.

I look past Rainer and find Cort with his father on the other side of the room. Maart is with him, doing the talking, I suppose.

Why does Cort pretend not to talk? He knows how to sign. All of them do. I bet even the little boy knows how. So what's the point? Did they cut out his tongue?

I've heard they do that to people sometimes. I've never personally known anyone who had their tongue cut out, but I don't live in that world. I'm in it, but apart from it at the same time. We had servants, of course. And I would not say that my father was kind to them, but he didn't go around cutting out tongues.

I watch Cort's father as he smiles, and laughs, and pats his *son* on the back. He's proud of him. That's very apparent. So I don't think he cuts out tongues either.

So why don't you talk, Cort van Breda?

It isn't rebellion. Because even though Cort had a very dark look to him earlier in the day, he doesn't come off as sullen or moody now. In fact, he's smiling, even laughing. He shakes the hands of the men his father lets close. Maart talks as Cort nods and even tilts his head a little in response.

Is he really interested in what they're saying?

Or is that just another layer to the lie?

Someone grabs my arm, a grip so tight, I wince and hiss from the sudden pain.

"You little fucking bitch."

I whirl around and find my father's face dipping down into mine as he growls out his words.

"You little fucking bitch. This is all your fault. This whole night is your fault and believe me, I will make you—"

And then, before I can even pull my arm from his grip or take a step back in surprise, he's on the ground and Cort is standing over him.

No. That's not Cort. That is Sick Heart.

"Whoa, whoa, whoa," Cort's father, Udulf, says. He steps in front of Cort, blocking my view of my father. "You can't touch his girl like that, Lazar. She belongs to my son now and you're going to need his permission to speak to her."

Lazar wipes the blood from his mouth with a fingertip. He stares at that fingertip with an air of astonishment. Then he gets to his feet, straightens the collar of his white button-down shirt, and glares at Mr. van Hauten. "Fuck you, Udulf. You cheat. He cheated. She helped him. You owe me. He was supposed to—"

"Come with me, Anya." I turn and find Rainer looking down at me. "I'm taking you back to the room."

He takes my arm, as if to pull me away, but I hesitate. Because Lazar was saying something and I'm pretty sure it was a clue. I'm pretty sure it was about me.

He was supposed to… what?

But Rainer's interference has changed the subject and suddenly Lazar is yelling, "You can't take her!" He is losing his shit. "She's mine! And we had an agreement!"

Maart steps up, places two hands flat on Lazar's chest, and pushes him back with such force, he stumbles into a crowd of men. "She is his," Maart growls. "And you better calm your shit down. Because if you raise your voice again, no one will stop him next time. You have been warned."

Damn. That Maart is scary too. He might not be the star of the show, but it is very clear to anyone with any sense of self-preservation that Maart is just as dangerous as Cort.

"Fuck you," Lazar spits.

"There is no such thing as an unfair fight in the Ring of Fire," Udulf says. His voice is steady, and calm, and low. But everyone hears it. Even me. And Rainer is pulling me towards the door. "And if your people hadn't planted that knife on the platform, then Cort's new woman wouldn't have picked it up and handed it to him."

That's not really what happened. I mean, there were extenuating circumstances. Like Pavo punching me in the mouth and splitting it open. I reach up to touch the cut on my lip with a fingertip. It's swollen and tender. And my tongue—thank God I don't need to talk, because it's swelling up quick. One whole side of my body is road rash from Pavo pushing me down on the concrete platform.

But it's not like I can object. Rainer has tugged me into the stairwell and we are going down, so I don't catch Lazar's response. But I do think about Udulf's words.

Cort's new woman. That's what I am now.

I sigh—internally, of course—and just float down the rest of the stairs, into some other part of the ship, and then I'm led into a room. The AC is on so high, it's frigid. And I don't realize until the moment I walk under the rushing cold air above the door that I am sticky hot with dried and cracking body paint, and sweat, and blood.

I just want a bath. And that's never going to happen. I highly doubt there are bathtubs where I'm going and there certainly aren't any on this ship.

Evard follows us in, leaving the door open. Then a few moments later, Cort and Maart enter as well. Maart kicks the door closed with the heel of his foot and he is holding another bottle of Lectra. Full.

"Want more?"

I look up from the bottle and find Maart's gaze.

Rainer, busy on the far side of the room with something, tsks his tongue. "I don't think she needs any more. She drank a lot and she's probably not used to it." He turns around with a small machine in his now-gloved hand. "Besides, it'll make her bleed more when we tat her up."

And even though I have been professionally uncommunicative for nearly fifteen years now, I am unable to stop the expression on my face.

Rainer points to me and his grass-green eyes brighten. "Gotcha," he says. But then Cort is signing something and Rainer laughs. "Spoke too soon, I guess. He has plans for you tonight."

Plans? What the hell does that mean?

Rainer buzz-buzz-buzzes the little machine in his hand and I realize it's a tattoo gun.

Cort is settling down on the couch, pulling the little boy into an embrace. His quick fingers sign something to him, and Evard signs back with a smile.

My mind wanders to all kinds of dark corners at this display, but then I push it aside, look back at Maart, take the bottle, and drink.

Plans.

Fuck Cort van Breda. Fuck him, and his friends, and his boy. And fuck his plans too.

Maart pulls the bottle away from my lips with a sigh. "All right. You're gonna really need to sit down. Over there." He's pointing at a chair. But then his gaze finds Cort, who is signing again. "Never mind," Maart says. "Sit next to Cort. He really does have plans for you."

Then the tattoo machine begins buzzing in Rainer's hand. Bzzz. Bzzz. Bzz. He points it at me. "Ready for your *mark*, Anya?"

I hold still, my head spinning and my vision going a little blurry.

"Goddammit." Maart grabs my arm, pulls me over to the couch, and then pushes me until I fall into the cushions next to Cort. "Just stay there."

"I told ya," Rainer says. "She drank way too much. She's gonna be hallucinating all night now."

Cort signs something and they all laugh. And that laugh lasts for an entire eternity.

It floats into my ears and gets stuck in my head. Bounces around in there and then... then I lose track of time.

I lose track of everything.

I drift in and out of consciousness. There are skulls all around me. Skulls everywhere. I reach for one and find the soft skin of a belly. And when my eyes look up, I find... him.

The sick heart.

The man with skulls all over his body.

I start tracing lines of teeth and jawbones. I trace the outline of an eye. Then a heart. Not a heart you draw, not a cute thing at the end of a note or an emoji on a phone, but a real heart. An anatomical heart with pipes or vessels protruding and spurting blood everywhere.

Then there is a keyhole in the middle of it. And I have that key. It's made out of a finger bone.

"Anya!"

I look up and see Rainer. Tattoo machine in his hand. Bzzz. Bzzz. Bzz. Black and red ink all over his gloves. And then I look down and see that I am practically on top of Cort.

I blink. Then the little boy is pulling me off of the rock-hard body of the fighter. He pushes me and points his finger in my face. "You're not handling this well."

That echoes in my mind and I think I laugh. It might even be out loud, but I can't be sure. I'm not sure of anything right now.

"She doesn't drink it like we do," Rainer says. His hand is buzz-buzz-buzzing over the skin of Cort's ribcage.

Maart laughs. He's sitting on the other side of me and I'm leaning in to him.

Cort snaps his fingers and it reverberates through my head. At the end of that snap, there is another tattoo machine. The little boy is kneeling at Cort's feet holding a little cup of black ink.

I feel like time is skipping. Like I'm losing hundreds of seconds at a time. Jumping from minute to minute like a stuttering old movie. Then Cort is dragging the needle across a finger on his left hand and I'm mesmerized by this. I watch, line by black line, as the image takes shape.

A skeleton key.

But that's when I notice all his fingers have keys on them. I get lost in that too, watching them dance as he draws and wondering... what the fuck do they open?

Then his buzzing stops, but Rainer's buzzing continues, and Cort is flashing his finger-keys in my face.

It's a sign.

The little boy is suddenly in front of me. "He wants to know where you want it." And his words come out slow and... shimmery. Like... *waves* of words. I want to laugh again. I can't tell if I do it out loud or just in my head.

Where I want what? That's my mind talking, not my lips. My lips don't talk. Not even the Lectra can make them talk.

Plus, I'm so fucking high right now, I don't even remember how to talk. I couldn't form the words if I wanted to.

"Never mind her," the boy says. "Do me."

I gasp before I can stop myself. And grab his arm. *No! No! Do not let him mark you, beautiful little boy!*

But Maart, who is behind me—or... no. I'm like... in his lap?—he pulls me back and I don't have it in me to resist. So I'm lying back on his chest and Cort has my foot in his hand and—

I kick and wiggle, because it tickles. I laugh again. This time, I'm very sure the laugh escapes.

This makes Rainer stop and smile at me. Next thing I know, he's looking back down at his work on Cort's ribcage and Cort is dragging his needle over my baby toe.

Then everyone is laughing. Maybe even I'm laughing? But I don't know what's funny.

Cort bends my knee and holds my pinky toe between his fingers, presenting it to me like something special and precious. They laugh again.

I have to squint to make out the shape. But it's moving all over the place like it doesn't want to be seen. So I give up and just shut my eyes with a long, audible sigh.

And that's three times that I know of. Three times I have made noises tonight.

I don't make noises.

Then the boy—Evard. His name is Evard, I remind myself—he's hissing, and moaning, and wincing, so I open my eyes to find Cort dragging a needle over the back of his neck.

But I can't keep my eyes open long enough to see the artwork, and then I just give in to the Lectra completely, my mind spinning as I breathe to the beat of Maart's heart, which is pounding against my back.

I am *fucked up*.

Maart's fingers are caressing a long, lazy pattern up and down the side of my thigh. I open my eyes again and find Rainer is done now and Evard is whining and complaining. Rainer drags him towards an open door on the other side of the room and pushes him through, closing the door, locking it with a loud click, as he turns back to us.

His grassy eyes find mine. And then he crosses the room with a smile and kneels in front of me. Right between my legs.

Then two hands that belong to two different people open my legs up and Rainer lifts the skirt of my white dress up and out of the way.

I catch one more look at those bright green eyes and then he dips his head down and begins to lick me.

CHAPTER SIX

CORT

Anya's entire body bucks up when Rainer licks her. She gasps, and I already know that making that little noise *bothers* her. Her silence goes way beyond not talking. She does not want to make any sound at all. Not a sigh, not a groan, and certainly not a moan.

Good luck with that, Anya. Good luck with that when Rainer's mouth is between your legs. When his tongue is working its magic against your pretty little nub.

She hasn't got a chance.

Rainer pauses and I grin at him. It has been a long time since we've done this and I suddenly feel great.

Last fight. Last fucking fight and I made it.

I'm done. *We're* done.

And after we finish celebrating here tonight I have just one more training camp and I will have earned out. I will have bought my freedom. And I will be able to take Evard, Rainer, and Maart with me.

Do I feel a little guilty about leaving the others behind? Of course. But I gave up trying to save the world a long time ago.

Saving everyone would mean a dozen more fights. At least. And if there's one thing I've learned about being on top it's this: Someone is always coming up trying to take your place and the best time to quit is when you're ahead.

If forced, I could probably win two, maybe three more elite-level fights. But anything more than that is just a delusion. And three more fights won't be enough to make any kind of difference. Hell, one loss is all it takes to wipe everything I've ever done away. I will lose everything I've ever loved and sacrificed for if I don't win.

Rainer and Maart can take care of themselves. They don't really need me. If I die, they will make it. Somehow. But I won't play with Evard's future like that.

Rainer looks at Anya with those questioning green eyes of his. Then he pauses and drags the back of his hand across his glistening lips. "You gotta tell me yes before I go any further."

Huh. This is new. But this Anya girl is very, very different than the kind of girls who end up in our room after a winning fight. When I look over at Anya I'm surprised she has her eyes open. She doesn't answer his question. Just stares back at him.

Come on, Anya. You know you want it. Just tell the man yes and he'll get back to business.

Maart, ever my trusty fucking mind-reader, pulls these words right out of my head. "Yeah, Anya. You have to give *permission*." He caresses her breast, rolling her nipple between his fingertips. She's practically lying on his bare chest. He didn't get tattooed tonight and neither did Rainer, but they lost their shirts hours ago.

Hmm. What will our little Anya do? Nod her head? Whine for more? Grunt?

No. I smile big. Because our Anya reaches down, places the flat palm of her hand on the top of Rainer's head, and pushes him back into position.

Maart and I exchange grins.

Clever girl. And horny. Though that might be the Lectra. But also so very, *very* committed to her fucking silence.

And I don't know why, but I love that about her.

Maart's turn. He wraps his arms around her, opens up her loose-fitting low-cut dress, and plays with both breasts as he dips his mouth down to her ear. "How about me? You want me to stop? I'm gonna need an answer if you want to keep going."

He's toying with her. Playing with her the way a cat plays with a captured mouse.

She stares straight ahead, eyes fixed on something on the far wall. One hand is still in position on Rainer's head, guiding him as he licks her pussy. He must hit her sweet spot because she bites her lip and closes her eyes for an elongated blink before opening them back up, wider than ever.

Maart pinches her nipple. Hard. And the pain is sharp enough to make her gasp again. "I'm waiting, Anya. I don't like to wait." He growls out the last few words as his left hand squeezes her breast.

She has very nice tits. They are large and firm and even though I know the meaning of the red-on-white symbols encircling her nipples, I like the way it looks. I like the way she wears it. I like the way she plays her part.

The sacrifice. That's what she was tonight. Lazar's sacrifice.

Here's something I bet our Anya didn't know. I was supposed to kill her tonight. I was told to throw *her* off the ship, not Pavo.

Udulf took me aside just before I went out on the platform and told me that's what Lazar wanted. And what did I care? What's one more dead girl? It's not like I get to keep them. And Udulf—well, he has no interest in a girl Anya's age. She's… not his type.

So I fucked up their plans by throwing Pavo over instead of Anya. Right now, somewhere on this ship, in some private space or compartment, or storage hold, there should've been a ritual to commemorate her death.

I smile just thinking about Lazar's panic as we were dragging Pavo's body towards the edge. Did he know I wasn't going to do it? Did he know?

Yes. He had to know. And he was panicked.

Why? Why this girl?

If my father is mad that I let Anya live, he didn't show it.

But he is the master of deception.

Still, without Anya he might've lost tonight.

Without Anya I might be dead.

So do I think he cares that she wasn't sacrificed in the end?

Probably not.

Maart slaps her breast and growls, "Fucking answer me, Anya."

Rainer stops eating her pussy and wipes his hand across his wet lips again. "You better say yes or we'll just throw you in the bedroom and go find someone else to play with."

"Someone more willing," Maart adds.

I hold my breath for a moment, wondering if she'll bow out.

I'm not gonna lie, I'd be disappointed if we had to go find someone else. I mean, she's already *here*.

Rainer has already gotten a taste.

Maart is practically in position.

She answers him, but not with sounds. She answers him with a hand. Again.

This time she reaches behind her back and grabs Maart's dick. He grins at me and shrugs.

And it's settled. She is in. So now it's my turn.

Rainer hasn't resumed his licking yet, even though he's still in position and Anya is still trying to encourage him with her hand on his head. "Now," he says. "Now you have to let Cort know you want it." His tongue darts out and the tip swipes across her clit. She hisses air through her teeth. "And if you don't want to talk, fine with us. We like your silence. Nothing worse than a mouthy woman."

Maart and I both laugh.

"But you better find a way to say yes in the next ten seconds, Anya. Because if you don't, we'll just jerk each other off real quick to quell the need and then go find ourselves someone with more spirit."

Anya looks at me and even though she says nothing—not with words, not with her eyes, not even with a crooked smile—I know the question inside her head.

You like men?

Don't we all like men, Anya? I sign that back to her and both Rainer and Maart chuckle.

And then Anya surprises me. She removes her hand from Rainer's head, twists her body towards me—creating space between her and Maart—and then she leans in, blue eyes locked with mine, and slowly… ever so fucking slowly… closes the distance between us until her soft mouth, all pliant and willing, touches mine.

She holds that position, neither kissing me nor not kissing me, and we breathe a lifetime of breaths in that pause.

Up until now I hadn't really felt the Lectra but it suddenly kicks in and my dick is instantly hard inside my shorts.

The dream-state is immediate and I kiss her.

I kiss her and she kisses me back.

And she tastes like blood.

Her tongue touches mine and I lean into it, pushing her back on top of Maart. Rainer is standing up, tugging his shorts down his long, muscular legs. Maart is desperately trying to unbutton his pants and get his dick out. I end up helping him as Anya and I continue to kiss. I lift up her hips as Maart pumps his cock, and then Rainer is helping me place her on top of Maart.

Rainer kneels down again and resumes licking her pussy while I play with her clit. Getting her wet enough for what comes next.

She bites her lip and closes her eyes when Rainer places Maart's cock at the tight entrance of her ass, and when Maart thrusts upward, she cries out. Her small protest tumbles over my tongue and gets lost inside my mouth as Rainer and I each slip a finger inside her pussy.

Anya is gasping and moaning as we slide in and out, feeling the length of Maart's cock inside her ass. Rainer keeps licking and every now and then his tongue caresses my finger. I shiver.

"Get on top of her," Maart whispers, his mouth right up next to my ear. "Get inside her. I want to feel you, Cort. I want to feel your dick inside her."

I want it too.

I continue kissing Anya as Maart lifts her knees up to her breasts and then I straddle their bodies. Rainer has my cock in his hand, squeezing it, sliding his huge palm up and down my thick shaft. Then he places me at the entrance of her wet pussy and I slide right in.

She moans. And it's not even soft.

But I moan too. And so does Maart. Rainer is standing on the couch now, his dick in his hand as he eases it towards my face. I pull back from kissing Anya, glance up at him, and smile. Then take his giant cock in my hand and play with the tip until he closes his eyes and moans.

Then I push Anya's face towards Rainer. She opens her mouth without objection and I'm fascinated as his cock disappears past her lips.

But that passive fascination doesn't last because Maart is fucking her ass. Thrusting his hips upward, desperately trying to feel me.

I take my attention back to him. His face is right there, just below Anya's right shoulder, and all I have to do is lean down.

His kiss is always rough. He always bites. And I laugh when he tries it, pulling back just in time so he can't draw blood.

And then... I begin to move.

Anya is full-on moaning now. Not even bothering to stop the "Ooooh, ooooh, ohhhhh," as she ruins her vow of silence. She shreds this vow of silence with moans.

But nobody cares. She certainly doesn't.

And so we just fuck like that. Me in her pussy. Maart in her ass. And Rainer in her mouth.

She comes quickly. Too quickly.

But we don't stop and she comes again. And again. And again.

And I get lost in the Lectra, and the sex, and the feeling of everything being just the way it should be.

It's a trick. It's the electric-blue liquid inside me. It takes over and it doesn't give up. Not easily. Not quickly.

This is the beginning of the end.

And I begin to drift.

My body is still moving the way it should. Maart is caressing my ass as he fucks her. Rainer is back on his knees between our legs, licking us. Licking all of us. Anya is clawing my shoulders with her nails. Orgasming. And every time I move the wrong way and the sharp pain of bruised and broken ribs forces me to come up for a breath of reality, the Lectra is there.

The Lectra takes care of that too. The Lectra… takes care of everything. Our naked bodies are the only things that matter.

But the Lectra takes you prisoner as well, if you're not careful. And I'm not being careful about anything right now because for the first time in my life I feel like a free man.

So I let the Lectra in. I let it grab a hold of my mind. And pretty soon it's asking me questions.

Let's go for a walk, Cort. Would you like to go for a walk with me?

Like no is even an option. When the Lectra invites you along, you go.

So I go. And find myself in a hazy room. Smoke, I think, because I can smell it—a mixture of tobacco, opium, and cannabis.

When I look down, I am tiny. Very small. Smaller than Evard, even. My body brown from the sun, and sweaty, and naked. The room is filled with men.

It's not just smoke. It's steam. Because I'm in a bathhouse.

I don't think I want to go there.

But the Lectra answers, *Since when do you have choices, Cort van Breda?*

Are you listening to me?

It's the Lectra talking, but no. It's not. It's a girl. Older than me. I *think* I know her name, but the Lectra is controlling me now, so I don't have time to remember it. I glance past the girl and see a man with blond hair. He's naked and laughing at some other boys, bigger than me, but only by a few years.

Are you listening to me?

I look back at the girl, but don't say anything.

She's pointing her finger in my face.

Go!

That's what she's telling me to do.

Run!

She's shaking me by the shoulders, trying to pull me to my feet. But my head is swimming with confusion.

I think it's the opium.

Or the Lectra.

Run!

And then the Lectra's grip on me eases and I'm on my feet. I'm on my feet and really am running. Hard. Fast. I'm naked and running through the bathhouse. Turning corners. Bare feet slapping on the slick tiles. Slipping.

Everything is slipping.

And then bam!

I slam into a man.

When I look up, I see Udulf.

My father. But he's *not* my father.

He wasn't my father then and he isn't my father now.

He's just… *breathe*… one of them.

I can't breathe.

No air is getting in and I'm gasping for it. Desperate for it.

But then I hear Rainer. "Cort! Let go! Let go!"

And then my eyes focus…

…and I'm back.

Both of my hands are wrapped around Anya's neck. Her eyes are wide with surprise and she's gripping my shoulders, digging her fingernails into my skin. I stop strangling her and she sucks in air like she hasn't taken a breath in years.

Maart is still underneath her. And we are *still* fucking. Her tits bounce and wiggle with the force of two men near climax.

Maart reaches that place first. He slips his dick out of her ass, pushes us off him, and then kneels on the couch so he can spray her breasts with his come.

I keep going. Trying to get deeper and deeper inside her. Trying to *own* her. She's still gripping my shoulders, her knees bent and legs lifted and wide open.

But then Rainer takes her hand and places it on his cock. He helps her finish him off, his hand on top of hers, fully covering it. Pumping back and forth as white come spurts onto her breasts and mixes with Maart's.

I lean down and kiss her, not even caring that both our upper bodies are now slick with the sexual release of other men. I bury my face in her neck, biting her earlobe until she pants and wiggles in protest.

And I like her struggle. I like the way she resists. I like the way her soft body presses against mine. I like the way she grips my hair, fisting it, pulling it so hard, my scalp burns.

I like the way her mouth finds mine. The way her tongue slides in and out of it, like she's fucking me instead of me fucking her. I like the way her pussy tightens against my shaft when she finds one more release inside her. I like the way she gushes. And I like the way she gasps when I come inside her.

I don't ask permission to do this.

I don't need permission.

I am not a little boy in a bathhouse.

I am Cort van Breda, Ring of Fire World Champion for ten years running.

I own this girl.

Anya Bokori is *mine*.

I don't know what happens next. All I know is that I'm wearing shorts again—still barefoot—and I'm cruising through the tight, nearly claustrophobic hallways of the ship.

I don't know where Rainer is. Or Maart. Or Evard. And even though I should care about that—about Evard, at the very least—I don't care.

The Lectra is one hundred percent in control.

It's telling me where to go and when I get there, it will tell me what to do as well.

People stop when I approach.

They press themselves into the walls, eyes downcast.

Looking at the floor.

Looking at anything but me.

I know I'm fucked up. That's the thing about the Lectra. It gives you glimpses. It gives you moments. But you gotta obey it too. You can't tell it no. It will spit in your face if you try.

So I go with it. I flow with it.

And pretty soon I'm not on the ship anymore. I'm walking the platforms of the Rock, alone in the middle of an angry ocean. Small and hungry. Beaten and bruised. Humiliated and sad.

And sick.

I am sick.

My heart is sick.

I am *heart sick*.

The girl who was telling me to run is gone now. I don't know what happened to her. All I know is that I woke up on the Rock.

There was nothing there back then.

He left me there for three months.

Three *fucking* months.

The Rock is where I learned to be silent.

The Rock is where I learned to live with myself.

The Rock is where I learned to accept my lot in life.

The Rock is where he *broke* me.

The Rock is where I put myself back together.

The Rock is where the nightmare begins.

The Lectra lets go and I find myself climbing the stairs to the event room.

There are mercs lining the stairwell, all dressed in black, carrying those giant guns. Knives strapped to their legs and ammo on their belts.

They would not have a chance against me in this tight stairwell. Not even with those weapons. Not even all of them at once. And they all know this. Because they don't look at me.

They don't dare fucking look at me.

I picture that fight in my head. Imagine myself jumping up, grabbing the platform of the stairs above my head, kicking five or six of them in the face and then swinging around to take out their buddies rushing up to help.

It would be a bloodbath. I would snap so many necks.

"Cort!"

I focus and find Maart standing at the top of the stairwell, just outside the open door to the observation room.

"Fuck, dude. Where the hell did you go?" He looks over my shoulder. "Where's Anya?"

Anya. Where *is* Anya?

"She left with you. Where'd she go? Lazar wants to talk to her."

Oh, does he? Too fucking bad for him.

"Cort? Where is she?"

Some time passes as I climb the remaining dozen steps up to Maart. And then he's talking again.

"Jesus Christ. Look at your eyes. They are bright blue, brother. You are *fucked up*."

I laugh, then sign, *I am so fucked up*.

"Where's Anya?"

But I'm not sure. I don't actually remember taking her with me when I left the room.

"Never mind," Maart says. "We'll find her later, I guess. Everyone's waiting for you. Rainer has been covering. You ready?" He's got me by the shoulders and gives me a little shake.

Oh, I'm fucking ready all right. *Let's do this shit.*

We enter the room and pause, taking it all in. I spy my father, but he's so far away it feels like a journey and a trek to talk to him. So I let people surround me. People I don't know. People I don't care about. Maart, of course, does all the talking for me. I'm not even paying attention. This is pretty much the best part about the silence. I can just tune them out.

But then that reporter is in my face trying to ask me questions.

"Cort." She's past middle age. Too much make-up and some of it is smeared. There are dark smudges under her eyes and her cheeks are pale now and not rouged. "What did it feel like to disobey your father tonight?"

"Come on," Maart says, positioning himself between her and me, kinda pushing her back a little. "Leave him alone. He's not going to answer you."

"Why not, Cort?" Her eyes are locked on mine. "Why can't you answer me? Is this some kind of vow? Did you take a vow? Did you know that Anya was silent too? Is that why—"

"That's enough!" Maart is all out of patience. "Get the fuck back." Maart grabs my arm and tugs me along through the crowd.

There are a lot of women here now. Whores. They are all whores. No respectable man brings his wife to a Ring of Fire fight.

A little head of blonde hair slips through the legs of the men like a sneaky little dog. Anya's sister. She is definitely not supposed to be here. But no one has ever accused Lazar of being a respectable man. I want to grab her for some reason, tell her to get the fuck out of my party, but she's too quick, too good at the game she's playing, and I lose her in the crowd.

I look around for Evard. I kinda remember Rainer kicking him out of the room after the tattooing was done and the fucking was about to begin. After a few minutes of blindly following Maart through the crowd, I find him in the corner. The little girl is too. He's smiling. Laughing out loud, actually. And they've both got a glass of electric-blue Lectra in their hands.

I'm just about to head that way when Maart grabs my arm again. "This way, big shot. Your father is waving us over."

My *father*.

Isn't it time for that charade to be over?

One more training camp on the Rock. Then I will never have to see these people again. I will never be beckoned with a wave from across a room. I will never go to one of these parties again.

Maart and I push our way through the crowd and I spy Lazar. He's sitting on the same long, silver couch that Anya was lounging on earlier in the day, glass in one hand, but he's not drinking Lectra. That shit is bring-your-own-bottle and he gave that bottle to me. But that can't be the reason why he's not drinking it. Surely he can afford hundreds of Lectra bottles. And even if losing this fight did set him back enough where he would second-guess a decision to gulp down a hundred thousand dollars of liquid sex, one of the other men in the room would accommodate him. Surely he has one friend in this room who wants to ease the sting of his loss.

So why, Lazar? Why aren't you drinking Lectra tonight?

Are you sad? Did you love Pavo? Will you miss him? Are you mad that I kicked his lifeless body over the side of the platform?

Or are you thinking about how I didn't kill your daughter?

Why did you let her live this long if you just want her dead now?

What has changed for you, Lazar?

He spits at me when we pass him. And that spittle lands on top of my right foot.

I scoff.

Maart tightens his grip on my arm, tugging me along, leaning in to my ear to whisper, "We'll get him another time. We have a couple hours of this, then we're out of here. The helicopter is—"

But I tune him out. I'm really not interested in the details of how and when we leave the ship.

It takes a few more minutes to push our way through the thick crowd of men and their whores before my father finally comes into view again. He throws his head back and laughs at something.

He won big tonight. Big. So he's very happy.

And even though it's been over a decade since he laid a hand on me, I still feel that old, familiar anger when he smiles.

I get tunnel vision and all I see are his teeth.

Like he's a predator.

And he is.

"Play nice," Maart reminds me. "Two hours. Tops. Just stand there, OK? Can you do that?"

He's having doubts that I can do that. Obviously.

Maart has good instincts.

"There he is!" Udulf beams. His eyes are glassy, his irises ringed blue from the drink.

And of course, at the most inappropriate time, the Lectra claws at my mind and brings up a memory.

Not just any memory. The bathhouse. That's the Lectra's favorite.

I am small. Very small. And there are a lot of little boys around me.

We are all terrified.

None of them have faces. Not even the little girl who wants me to run has a face.

She just has hands.

Every time I drink the Lectra, this is what it shows me.

And the men.

Two men. No faces.

And blood.

Blood on the bathhouse floor.

The rest is… fuzzy.

"Cort! My son!" Udulf grabs me. Hooks his arm around my shoulder. We are the same height, but he feels small and weak next to my muscular body. At twenty-seven, I might be on the other side of my prime fighting days, but I am still the most dangerous man in the room. At least for tonight.

I like it that way. That's why I tore out Pavo's heart on the platform.

I want them to fear me, yes. But more than that, I want them to *hate* me. I want them to hate me the way I hate them.

So that's how I do it.

I *will* fight. I don't have a choice. But I will give them nightmares too.

They will relive the last moments of Pavo's life over and over again when they sleep. They will wake up in a cold sweat, dripping with adrenaline under their expensive silk sheets. And they will be terrified.

They will *be* Pavo.

Because when their long, privileged lives are over, the Devil will stand before them, ready to claim their souls, and they will tremble.

Because they are the losers in the end. Not me.

And then... just as I think those words, something weird happens.

The Lectra takes hold again. I am back in the bathhouse. The little girl has already told me to run. I am running. Feet slapping on the wet tiles. Slipping around corners. Breathing heavy. Screaming when they catch me.

They are all screaming.

We are all screaming.

And then I see a face...

But it's not a face.

"Hey, you still with us, buddy?"

I blink and I'm back. Me. Strong, tall, muscular, *deadly* me.

I'm not that little boy. I haven't been him for a very long time.

I am the Ring of Fire World Champion.

I am the winner.

I am free.

I blink again and then Lazar is suddenly in front of me. And all I see is his stupid blond hair.

The Lectra takes over my fists and they are pounding him as the room erupts into chaos.

The next thing I know I'm running down the hallways of the ship. Maart, Rainer, and Evard are all following me, yelling for me to stop.

But I don't stop.

Time skips and then keeps skipping and a helicopter is landing outside. It makes the air thump.

I pass by a glass wall and glance at my reflection. I am covered in blood. Not just Lazar's blood, but the blood from Pavo. And probably Anya's blood too, because the next thing I know, I'm in a room. A closet, actually. And Anya is on the floor at my feet. Bloody. Not fresh blood, all dried up and crackling on her skin.

She is asleep.

No, she is not asleep.

She is *unconscious*.

I remember now. I took her out of the room with me after we had sex. Maart and Rainer were in the shower. I think I passed out. Anya did, for sure. But then I woke up and she and I were alone.

So I picked her up then and I pick her up now. I walked her out of my room then, and I walk her out of this closet now. I hid her then, but now... I reveal my plan.

"What are you doing, Cort?" That's Rainer. And he's asking that question in a reasonable way. But when I don't answer and just keep walking, his tone changes. "What the fuck are you doing, Cort?"

"Is she... *dead?*" That's Evard. He's panicked. He doesn't understand what I'm doing.

And neither do I.

Not really.

But I'm gonna do it anyway.

"Cort." That's Maart. "Cort, you have one more camp on the Rock and then we're done, brother. Do *not* fuck it up now. Do you hear me? Cort!"

I ignore him. I carry Anya's unconscious body in my arms, trying to find my way back up to the deck.

And I do find my way.

I *always* find my way.

Then the helicopter is there and I'm carrying my new limp, unconscious prize towards it. My father is standing in front of the door, shaking his head. I don't have any idea how much time has passed since I beat the living fuck out of Lazar, but it's been a while, because the sun is rising.

"What are you doing?"

I don't hear Udulf's words. The spinning rotors are far too loud. But I can read lips like a fucking champ.

Still, I don't answer him.

SICK HEART - JA HUSS

"Cort. What the hell? Lazar is already pissed off enough about how things ended last night. You can't have her. I need her." He reaches for me—for Anya, actually—one arm extended to bar my entrance to the helicopter. "Cort! I'm talking to you! Put her down!" I check him with my shoulder, climb in, drop Anya onto the seat, point at the pilot and shoot him a look that says, *You had better take off now, motherfucker. Or I will kill you and make a scene you will remember well into your next ten lives.*

We lift off the ground. Udulf is still reaching for me when I kick him back with one flat foot to the chest and he slams into the concrete.

The same concrete where I killed Pavo to the song of pounding tribal drums just a few hours ago.

And I salute that fucker.

Good game, that salute says.

Good game, asshole.

But it's over now.

And I have declared myself the winner.

CHAPTER SEVEN

My dreams are blue.

They are always blue on the Lectra. But the blue is nothing more than a day on repeat.

That's how I dream on the drink. Everything repeats.

I am profoundly thirsty when I'm startled awake by a deep keening noise, followed by a series of sounds that could be whistles or some kind of alarm.

What fresh fucking hell is this?

I push my ratty hair out of my face and open one eye to find a water-stained concrete ceiling. Then I close it again and just lie there, not even wondering where the hell I'm at, or what the fuck that noise is, because the whole thing is blue Lectra and that's just the way of dreams when I'm in the blue...

Mmm. No. Wait.

I open both eyes and squint at the ceiling again.

Then I'm awake. Fully awake and sitting upright staring at... what the hell am I looking at here?

It's a bird. For sure. It has wings. Large, long wings that—holy fucking shit. I scramble backwards when it attacks, a massive curved beak snapping at me. It calls out. That low keening is the call of this… *thing*.

And this thing sounds eerily human in my hazy, post-blue Lectra state.

I get to my feet and start kicking at it, wanting to yell, forcing myself not to. I pick up a wrinkled and weathered magazine and throw it at the giant albatross. It flaps and flutters. This room is far too small for it to stretch out its wings, which must span at least a dozen feet.

And a good south wind sprung up behind;
The Albatross did follow,
And every day, for food or play,
Came to the mariner's hollo!

Huh. I study it for a moment, Samuel Taylor Coleridge's verse lingering in my head as it cranes its neck upwards, opens its beak, and calls out.

Something answers back.

Oh, shit. I whirl around. There are more.

I pick up another discarded magazine, roll it up, and this time I thrust it, like a fencing sword. The massive sea bird wants to put up a fight. And then there's another noise and I see why.

There's a chick resting on a pile of old clothes in the corner. I use the term 'chick' loosely, because when I think chick, I see a tiny newly-hatched chicken in my mind's eyes. And that baby chicken and this baby albatross have absolutely no shared characteristics aside from the wings and the beak.

This baby is as big as Bexxie's blond cocker spaniel back home. It is fluffy, and white, and takes up a good portion of the available space in… OK. I push the hair out of my eyes one more time and take stock. Where the hell am I?

A small dirty room made entirely out of concrete blocks. I look around, one hand still thrusting forward to ward off the angry albatross's parental instincts, and get a glimpse of a door that says 'generator room' in Portuguese on one side, and another door mostly blocked by the bird. But there is a view of the ocean behind it. And... I'm swaying.

Am I still on the ship?

No. I don't feel like I'm on a ship at all, but the view outside is confusing me.

I stab at the bird with my magazine. The massive wings open, spanning the entire width of the room. The tips actually push up against the walls on either side, because there's not enough space.

It doesn't give up its position in front of my escape route, so I do that another dozen times until finally it sidesteps its way over to the chick and I can slip past.

Outside I stop short. Because I was right. I am not on a ship. Not even close to being on a ship. There is nothing around me but ocean for as far as the eye can see. And I am on the top floor of a platform.

A platform I vaguely recognize as an oil rig topside. Minus all the things typically on a topside that makes them habitable. There is a large, faded H painted in the center of the platform's open space. A helipad.

There are more birds out here as well. Several albatrosses as well as large formidable gulls are flying overhead, their wings gliding in and through the wind without flapping.

There are a few more nests along the edge of the tiny building I woke up in, and each nest hosts another sizable chick.

One of my flying enemies dives at me as I run towards the center of the expansive, empty platform to put some space between me and the chicks. When I get there I stop, turn in a circle, and see nothing in any direction but water.

My heart skips. Literally skips inside my chest. And then it begins to beat fast. Fast. Faster.

Calm down, Anya. Remain rational and do not overreact. He did not drop you off on an abandoned oil rig. That simply doesn't happen. Your life is not a movie, or a book, or some other fiction worthy of such drama.

I tell myself this kind of shit because there is still a slim chance that I'm not on an *abandoned* topside. It's still possible that this situation works. It is still possible that my life isn't one long string of *fiction-worthy drama.*

Right.

I snort.

And it's a real snort. Not an implied one. Because a flock of albatrosses—who, by the way, don't even live in the part of the Atlantic where I was located yesterday—always make their nests on the top floor of a fully working, commissioned topside oil rig.

I take a deep breath and let it out. Force the fear and confusion to go with it. And I think rationally. Because that's all there is left to do.

So where the fuck am I?

Albatrosses don't live over the Atlantic Ocean. It's a stupid, pointless fact to know, I get that. But it's true. They live far, far down in the southern hemisphere or far, far up in the northern one. They do not live in the *tropics.*

And I cannot be that far away.

I just can't.

It doesn't fit.

It's hot, and windy, and everything *feels* tropical. Yesterday I was somewhere off the coast of French Guiana. The ship was heading towards the Gulf of Mexico. And I don't know how I got here, but it was either a helicopter or a boat, which logically means that I cannot be that far from yesterday's position.

These birds are out of place. Not me.

I press my lips together and nod. I'm going with this last part. Because if I find out I'm stuck on an abandoned topside somewhere down near *Antarctica*, I might not recover from that revelation.

I snort again. Because either way, I'm probably going to die here. I'm clearly alone with no food, or water, or shelter—unless I want to share that tiny building with the overgrown fluffy killer in that nest.

Get it together, Anya. You are already losing your mind and you've only been awake for three minutes.

I rally, scan the area, find a stairwell, and head that direction. The birds—both the giants and the gulls—follow in the air, occasionally swooping down at me so I don't forget that I'm an unwanted interloper.

The stairwell is partially protected by a framework of metal that encloses the ten steps down to the landing where I get my first look at the level below. I pick out a sound of clicking at the far end of the platform, which is out of sight.

Click, click, click. It's a constant rhythm.

But really, it's not click, it's... *snick.*

Snick, snick, snick.

And for some reason, it's a familiar sound. Something I recognize. And this gives me hope. My feet skip down the stairs in a hurry, and I slip because they are slick with algae. I slide downward, my back hitting the sharp edge of the metal steps, and I grab at the handrail before I fall too far.

I let out a breath as I come to a halt. That's gonna bruise.

But then my mind is back on the snicking noise. I don't stand back up. I simply scoot down the steps until the far end of the platform comes into view.

And there it is. The noise. It's exactly what it sounded like.

A man jumping rope.

And if I were a person who laughed out loud, I would do that now.

It is Sick Heart. Jumping rope.

But Cort is not *just* jumping rope. He's doing little fighter tricks with that thing. I know, Pavo does this shit too—*did*, I remind myself, because he's dead now. I stabbed him in the gut and Cort van Breda slit his throat and sliced his belly open to steal his heart last night in the fight.

This memory makes my stomach roil. Then I gag. And if there was anything in there, I would hurl. But luckily, it's empty.

I take a deep breath and forget Pavo's death. Instead, I think about all the ways I've seen him jump rope over the years. It was a major part of his training. He was very good at it and so is the Sick Heart.

He's turning in a circle.

One foot, skip. Two foot, skip.

One foot, two foot, skip, skip—he stops.

Because he sees me.

And then he starts again.

Skip, skip, skip.

Snick, snick, snick as the plastic jump rope clips the concrete with each revolution.

No hello. Of course there is no hello. Because we don't *talk*.

And that right there, that's some advanced-level irony.

He's wearing the same shorts as he was last night.

Was it last night? I have no idea. I drank way too much Lectra.

I kinda-sorta remember having sex with Cort and his two friends, but that's seriously only *kinda-sorta*.

He's also still covered in blood. Pavo's blood. His blood. Probably even my blood. And because his body is sweaty, the dried flaky bits are actually becoming liquid again.

The whole thing is horrifying.

But then I look down at myself and realize I'm also playing a major role in this horror show. My white dress and my body are both also covered in blood. When I reach up to my lip, there is a thick, crusty scab over the place where Pavo split it open. And my tongue feels so thick inside my mouth, I have trouble working my jaw.

Pavo.

I sneer his name inside my mind.

He punched me in the face. That asshole was going to kill me. And Lazar was going to let him.

The snicking stops and I realize I'm still looking down at my disgusting blood-covered body. So I look up and find Cort is signing something at me.

Oh, Sick Heart. No, no, no. You can just go fuck right off with that shit, OK?

I don't speak sign.

I don't speak anything.

SICK HEART · JA HUSS

And I am certainly not going to suddenly give up on a silence I have been perfecting for over a decade to communicate with the likes of you.

Except I am communicating with him, because I say all those things with my eyes and Cort van Breda *speaks* eyes.

Because he laughs.

And then he points to something out of my line of sight and his skipping resumes. He turns in his little circle. Snick, snick, snick. Keeping his back to me.

I stay on the stairs. Just sit there as the ocean below me crashes against the steel pillars below, sending up a salty mist that irritates the wounds on my body, making them sting.

But he doesn't ever look at me again. Just... jumps his rope.

Eventually, I get up and walk—carefully, very, very carefully so as not to slip again—down the remaining steps and enter the level.

This is a gym. That is very clear. There are containers lining the perimeter. Multi-colored, but mostly an ugly red, or green, or simply rust. The beams above have lots of hooks where things might hang at some point. But only one heavy bag hangs now. And there are no mats. But it *is* a gym.

I look towards the ocean, wondering if there are people on the lower level, but I don't need to go explore it to know that there aren't. I can *feel* the emptiness. Emptiness and I are old friends. Even suffocating in a crowd of thousands, emptiness and I would recognize each other immediately.

The skipping stops and when I look over at Cort, he is pointing again.

I am now in a position to see what he is pointing at. It's a line of chalkboards affixed to a wall to my left. Not a wall of containers, but a real, cinderblock wall. There is a door in the middle and when I study the space, I realize it's a building. And inside there might just be promising things. Living quarters, toilets, and showers. A kitchen. There *must* be food here. There must be water.

My stomach growls at the mere thought of eating and I suddenly wonder—in a very serious fashion—how long I was out. Because I am starving, and parched, and my muscles are weak and achy. Very, very achy.

Cort walks past me and over to the line of chalkboards. He stops in front of the one with the name ANYA printed in neat, white chalk capital letters at the top.

He points at my name. Then he points at what's written underneath.

Jump rope. It's a command.

I say the words over and over in my head for at least a thousand years before I realize he actually expects me to jump some fucking rope.

I shake my head before I can stop it. And then I am fuming. I am pissed. I am nothing but anger.

Because for fifteen years I have perfected the art of non-communication. I have withstood beatings over this choice to not speak.

They have spit on me.

They have slapped me.

They have burned me.

They have *raped* me.

I have bled buckets of blood and endured volumes of hate and insults for my choice.

And after less than thirty minutes of being stuck with my new owner—and yes, that's what he is. A fucking slaveowner. Let's not mince words here—I have just shaken my head *no*.

He laughs. Out loud. The way I do not.

And he reminds me with that laugh that I am his slave, and he is my owner, and if he tells me to jump rope in the middle of the ocean while my body is still caked in yesterday's blood, and my stomach is rumbling with the pangs of hunger, and my throat is dry with the lack of water, then I will goddamned *jump that fucking rope*.

And not only that, I will *like* it.

He picks the extra jump rope up off the ground and holds it out.

I walk over to him, snatch it from his hand, and proceed to jump rope.

I don't even remember the last time I jumped rope. I might, in fact, have never jumped rope. It's probable that at some point, once, when I was very small, I did this. But it's equally probable that I did not. I just think I did because that's the kind of thing a normal little girl would do, and I have always wanted to be just a normal little girl, and I never was.

So my display, especially next to his, is pathetic and sad.

He one-foot, two-foots his way around his circle again. I am doing some weird double-bounce thing with my feet that I can't quite explain.

Every time his circle comes back around to me, he's laughing with his eyes. And he lets this go on for a good long while.

And even though jumping rope is something children do, it's no joke in the cardio department. I am huffing, and wheezing, and barely able to breathe by the time he stops his stupid rhythmic snicking, walks over to me, takes the rope from my hands, drops it on the ground, and points to my eyes. *Watch*, that point says.

Then he does a slower version of his snicking. He snick. Snick. Snicks. Which makes absolutely no difference to me at all.

He stops again, doubles his rope up, holds it in one hand like a whip, and then begins twirling it. Not jumping, just twirling it. Then he hops. He points to his feet. And I notice he's hopping every time the rope says *snick*.

He stops, picks up my rope, doubles it up, and hands it to me. He signs something that I assume says, *Your turn*.

I hesitate. Because… what the actual fuck, ya know? What is the point of this life?

It's a real question. What is the fucking point if I am to be stuck on an abandoned oil rig with a killer who wants to teach me how to jump rope?

He begins twirling his whip again, hopping at just the right moment, pointing at me to follow along.

I swing the rope, listening for the snick, and then hop. Not at the right moment, but I don't care. This is me doing what he says as far as I'm concerned.

His rope is back in both hands now, and he skips while I hop alongside my whip.

We do this for a little while and I'm huffing pretty good. I'm so out of breath, a sharp pain shoots up my side. This makes me remember something and I stop to just stare at him.

His ribs. Jesus Christ. Pavo *broke his ribs*. That whole scene with the nurses in the clinic trying to get a brace on Cort. His resistance.

He's jumping rope with broken ribs.

He stops and signs something at me, which I ignore, but then, even though I don't want to, I *need* to. I point at his ribs. At the new tattoo there. A skull, of course. A wraith-like skull that represents the death of Pavo Vervonal.

Cort looks down at his body, confused, then back up at me, smiling. And he keeps jumping.

So I hop. Out of breath and wheezing. Not even jumping rope. It's so fucking sad, my hop. But I do it anyway. Because that's the point. Isn't it? The point is pushing through the pain. The point is to keep going because they want you to quit.

And the secret… the secret is to keep *one thing* for yourself and let them steal the rest.

Cort van Breda must have decided a long time ago that he will keep his pain.

They can't have his pain.

And they can't have my words, either.

That's why he skips.

And that's why I don't talk.

It's impossible to tell time on the platform. There are no clocks, of course. But also, we're on a middle level and there is no real way to see the sun.

I do my pathetic hop for what seems like several more eternities, but is more likely twenty minutes. And

Cort shows off with the fanciest jump-roping I could never imagine. He skips, he jumps, he hops, he kicks, he double-skips, he double-jumps, he double-hops—but not the way I did—he double-kicks. He crosses his arms in a figure eight, he double-crosses his arms in a figure eight. He somehow travels the length of the fucking platform doing all these things, like he's dancing with that rope.

And he is.

Cort van Breda—Sick Heart himself—is having a love affair with his jump rope right in front of my face and he has absolutely no shame.

He's also not even out of breath.

He is dancing back my way when he suddenly stops and points at me. I'm still twirling my rope like a whip off to the side and halfheartedly hopping the way he showed me. But mostly I've been watching him.

He walks over to me. His body is glistening with a mixture of sweat and dried blood and he smells like… filth. Like *dead filth*.

I would take offense to that smell, but I'm pretty sure some of it is actually *me*.

He takes both handles of the jump rope of out my hand, then holds each one in a single hand, offering the rope back to me.

Right. I guess I knew I would have to jump rope for real at some point.

I take the rope and skip. And to my surprise, I don't double-hop. I don't even trip. I go six or seven whole revolutions before I mess up and have to start over.

Cort beams a smile at me. Like he's proud. Like I am a small, slow child who just needed a little extra practice and encouragement.

He signs something at me. I'm internally annoyed and start jumping again. But he puts his hand out, catching my rope, and stops me.

His steel-gray eyes look straight into mine. Then he takes my hand, pulls the jump rope handle out of it, and positions my fingers into a series of signs. And it's not like he's trying to teach me anything. Because he goes way too fast. He's just making a point, I think.

I don't answer or acknowledge him in any way. But again, I don't think he's waiting for it. He hands me back the rope, and then turns his back and walks away.

I watch for a moment. Well, no. I'm practically studying his back. Because he doesn't walk far, just over to the wall where he drops his rope on the ground and then reaches his arms up over his head, like he's stretching.

Hundreds of muscles pop out of his back. He is so well-defined, he looks like an ancient stained-marble statue of Adonis, but with a much finer physique. His back piece tattoo is large and intricate, a design that must have taken several years of fights to complete because even from here I can count a dozen skulls.

My eyes drift down to his ribs and I study his newest addition. It's a cross between a skeleton and a wraith. It's Pavo, I realize. In death. He won't be going to some better place. If such a place exists. No. Pavo Vervonal is going to *Hell*. And if you are given some kind of incorporeal body to live in for eternity, Pavo will be a skeleton wraith.

So it's perfect.

Then I remember that I got a tattoo last night as well. I look down at my baby toe and the experience washes over me. Like someone has suddenly pulled back the Lectra amnesia and in an instant, everything is clear again.

I bend down to touch it. To trace the fine, tiny lines of the star. It's a messy star. The kind of star little kids draw. The kind of symbol that says, *Good job*.

And, weirdly, it matches one he has on his lower stomach. In fact, he's got several stars like this on his body. They are filler, taking up space between his skulls and skeletons. Like the way most tattoo enthusiasts use smoke, or flames, or tribal designs.

And then, because I know Cort can't see my face, I smile.

It is the first real smile since... well. I have to pause at that. Because I smiled yesterday too. That moment when Cort took the Bokori bottle of Lectra from the bar.

Hmm. Two smiles in two days. And both of them are because of Cort van Breda's actions.

His feet are suddenly in my field of vision and when I look up I realize I'm in a very submissive position.

I immediately stand back up. But I don't look him in the eyes.

He bends down and studies my toe. Then he taps my ankle. I realize too late that it's a signal to lift up my foot. But he's already got it off the ground and I'm stumbling backwards. One strong hand grabs my wrist, and I am suddenly balanced again.

His fingers trace the star on my toe as well. And then he is still.

It's a weird stillness. Because he is just staring down at my foot and all I can see is the top of his head and the points of his knees. His thumb caresses my toe and the whole thing is suddenly weird.

What is he doing? Why is he just staring at my toe?

His shoulders curve in and he sighs. Then he looks up at me. It's a startling look. A vulnerable look. He signs something at me, but in the same moment, he is frowning.

My expression is flat because I've been doing this a long time and that's just instinct. But if he didn't look away, if he didn't let go of my foot, stand up, turn his back, and walk off—then... *then* I would've responded.

Because the way he looked at me? That look was something *worthy* of a response.

But just as quickly as it came, the moment disappears. It is utterly erased.

He makes me jump rope.

I have no concept of time. But while I'm jumping, he is working the heavy bag hanging from a steel beam. It's the only bag on the whole platform even though there are hooks for dozens and dozens of bags on the ceiling.

I get better at skipping as I watch him. My feet seem to grasp the new movements. And even though I can't go more than one or two dozen revolutions without messing up, that's actually a good thing, because I need recovery time. I haven't exerted myself so much since... well. Never.

Cort does punches. Punch, after punch, after punch. Fast ones, slow ones, combinations. What have you. I'm no punch expert. But it feels like he works through a sequence. Some predetermined course of practice that he's been doing his whole life. And the entire time he is distracted. At least, that's how he comes off to me. Thinking about other things. Like this is just mindless busy work to him.

Eventually he stops and walks over to me.

We are both disgusting. Nothing but sweat and blood, some of it his, some of it mine, some of it Pavo's. And it strikes me then that we're both pretty sick people. There is an ocean of water beneath our feet. One dip and we could wash this blood away.

But we don't. We didn't. And it's weird.

He points at me. Rolls his hand.

I get the meaning. He wants to check my skipping. So I skip. Because I can now. And I don't mind it. There are a lot worse things in this world than skipping rope.

He nods. No smile, no thumbs up, no pat on the back or star on the toe. Just a nod and then a point.

Keep going. That's what that nod and point mean.

I learned a long time ago that people would put up with my silence as long as I don't play dumb. If they can get their point across, and I do as I'm told, eventually they get tired of punishing me for my silence. So I keep going.

And he starts kicking that bag. I have no clue what these kicks are called, but he does lots of different types of them. Front kicks, and back kicks, and side kicks, and jump kicks. He does spinning kicks, and then he's flipping and I actually stop skipping to watch that part of his show.

Because that's what this is.

He's putting on a show for me.

And that's when I realize that he's working out in front of me for a reason. And I am jumping rope as busy work. I am jumping rope so he can make me do two things at once.

This is pretty clever on his part. I get a little lost as I imagine that this is how he runs his training camp. I picture men like him. Younger, though. Maybe teens. All jumping rope like me. All watching him dance with it, then fight the bag with punches and kicks.

They soak him up like a sponge. And so do I.

This is how we spend our day.

At one point he shows me where the water is, hands me one of two plastic cups, and we drink.

I pause many times. I lean my back against the steel beam closest to me and slide down it, resting as he continues his routine. He never seems to get annoyed with my breaks, though I am careful not to take advantage. I rest, catch my breath, then get back up and continue.

He does the same, only for much longer stretches. He works that bag hard. And then he slides his back down the far wall and watches me.

I let him. I mean, it's not like I could stop him, but I could turn my back and send a message. But I don't.

And I find that I don't hate him.

I find that these long, easy periods of skipping, and drinking, and resting, and then doing it all over again are a comforting routine. Something I can count on.

This is a gift, I think. Day one with a new master should be filled with anxiety about my future. And it's not.

Perhaps he is instilling a false sense of security in me. Perhaps this is some elaborate, evil plan and tonight, when it's dark, and I'm too tired to fight back, perhaps he will rape me.

But I don't think so. And a girl like me doesn't get this far in life by being afraid of a little coerced sex. That's fucking ridiculous.

I'm not afraid that he will fuck me tonight. So his plan, if it is a plan, is working. I am, if not at ease, then resigned to my fate.

But all things must end eventually. And this easy, predictable day is no exception.

The sun is finally visible on the left side of the platform because it is low on the horizon. It is May right now, so I approximate the time to be perhaps five-thirty or six o'clock when he takes the rope from my hands and sets it down in a little pile next to his. Then he points to the stairs and we meet up over there and begin to climb.

The birds attack.

I had forgotten about the fucking birds.

They are huge. The wingspan on these albatrosses is easily four meters from tip to tip. They are like pterodactyls, something out of place and out of time. But Cort waves them off like this is just part of the fun of living on an abandoned oil rig in the middle of the ocean, and they are not persistent.

We make our way to the other end of the upper platform, behind the small building that I woke up in this morning, and he points to the back wall.

That's when I notice the hose. It is draped over a large hook. The nozzle looks like something you'd clean the bottom of a boat with. And I see what's coming.

I hesitate. He takes my arm—not harshly—and drags me over to the wall. Then he points at me. I've deciphered about two dozen of his points today. And this one means, *Don't move.*

It's gonna sting. I already know that. But I'm sweaty, wearing yesterday's paint and blood, and I don't really care how I get clean at this point, just get me clean.

So I strip off my dress, toss it aside, and stand with my back against the wall and my eyes closed.

Yes. It fucking hurts. And even though I don't want to wince, and hug myself, and cower from the cold water, I do all that.

He makes me turn around and face the wall, and then he sprays my back too. The whole thing takes maybe... five minutes? My body is red and stings all over when he's done. But I am clean.

Cort walks over to me, his body still smelling of death and filth, still covered in sweat, and blood, and paint, and he hands me the hose. I look at it, and then him, and realize he wants me to hose him down next.

This is the moment when I realize everything I thought I knew about Cort van Breda was wrong.

Maybe I understand the Sick Heart. I get the fighter inside him.

But Cort? The man inside him?

No.

I was wrong.

I could hurt him with this hose.

And he either doesn't care, or he doesn't think I will.

I won't.

CHAPTER EIGHT

CORT

When I first introduced Anya to the jump rope her face was a mixture of sadness, confusion, and many years of lowered expectations.

I'm pretty sure she thinks that no one can read her, but I can read everyone. We might be silent for very different reasons, but the outcome is the same.

Silence lets you hear things that aren't said.

Silence lets you see things unseen.

Silence gives you space.

And space is a gift if ever there was one.

My first trip out to this Rock was when I was around five. Udulf had just acquired me and I was not in the mood to comply with anything he had in mind for my first night at his estate.

I ran. I hid. And when they found me, I kicked, I screamed, and I bit.

It didn't stop him. He did with me what he had planned to do with me.

He beat me senseless that first night. He beat me so hard, and for so long, I just passed out. And really, that was a gift as well. Because I have no solid memory of that night. Or anything that came before my first trip out here to the Rock. The only thing I have left of the life that came before Udulf is the Lectra dream.

And that's not reality.

When Udulf dropped me off on the lowest platform of the Rock that first time, I stayed for three months. Alone.

There was no food, but there was water. And that was so cruel. You can die in three days with no water. It takes months to waste away from starvation. Even a small boy can last many weeks without food.

It was good water, though. Bottled. Sealed. Clean. A hundred cases at least. I had so much fresh water, I bathed in it. The rig had only been decommissioned for a few months when I arrived. It was still clean. And you could walk all the way down the steps to the water without slipping on slick algae and breaking your neck if you weren't careful.

All the housing containers had been removed but there were still leftover things inside the permanent building on the middle level. Clothes, and blankets, and even a deck of cards. And there was the kitchen, of course. Bathrooms, too. Those were built into the frame of the topside for electrical reasons, and couldn't be disconnected.

Food, on the other hand, that was hard to come by. There was no leftover food on the rig and it would take me weeks before I successfully caught my first fish down on the lowest platform using a steel beam as a spear and a discarded net that was stuck on the rig's frame, just above sea level.

But that wasn't what kept me alive.

The bird kept me alive.

Just one bird back then. One wayward albatross who should've been on the other side of the world. His wing was bent in a weird way and he didn't fly very well. I don't know how he got here, since the natural habitat of the royal albatross is sub-Antarctic and this rig is equatorial, but he *was* here. And he *could* still fly— just not well enough to go home.

I think he knew I was in the same position. So we were in it together.

I gave him water and he brought me food like I was his chick.

Little fishes. Little disgusting fishes that he spit out and I swallowed whole, so I didn't have to chew. And even though I could've talked to the bird, I didn't. Not at first. He didn't say anything either. It was like we both knew there was no fucking point. We were stuck here and that was that.

I liked it. I won't admit that to anyone, but I liked it out here on the Rock. It was my first real taste of freedom. For the very first time I was in charge of my life.

Udulf came back months later, expecting me to be dead and only there to drop off another disobedient house boy who was actually thrown off the rig and disappeared into the dark, choppy water without ceremony before we left.

By that time, I didn't want to leave.

That bird, he was the only family I had left.

That was the last time I cried.

And that is how I learned to be silent.

When I finally got off the Rock, I was taken to Udulf's training camp. Apparently, in Udulf's world, you are either a house boy or a gym boy, and he had decided that I was a gym boy.

His camp back then was nothing like my camp right now. And it would take me ten long years before I had won enough fights and killed enough boys to earn my own camp.

But on that flight from the Rock to the shore, Udulf had come up with a new way to separate the wheat from the chaff, thanks to me. Every boy from then on would do three months on the Rock. Alone.

He lost a lot of boys that way. But they were disposable, weren't they? And anyway, that was in my favor. Because if any of them had come back, they would be formidable opponents.

Pavo Vervonal was the first to make it off the Rock, but by that time, I was nearly eight and he was just five. He followed me around like a sad, lost puppy when they brought him back but he was sold just a few months later so I never thought about him much. I don't know if Lazar was the one who bought him originally, it doesn't matter. The point was, Pavo had earned his place as wheat and that fight last night was nineteen years in the making.

It's hard to believe that it's over.

Almost too good to be true.

Anya is staring at me. Then her eyes drift down to the hose in my hands. She looks disoriented and confused.

I would not call her clean, but the blood and the paint has been stripped off her flesh. She is red now, not pale. And for the first time, I take a good long look at her body.

Her breasts are firm and her nipples are bunched up into tight peaks. Her hips are wide and her waist is narrow. Her hair is blonde, but looks brown now that it's wet.

She is pretty. Even like this, and without recalling her from yesterday when I had just arrived on the ship, I can see her beauty. I can see why Lazar kept her around long after her usefulness wore off.

He could've sold her. And she would've fetched a lot of money if her buyer wasn't put off by her silence.

But Lazar kept her long past her, for lack of a better word, usefulness. And then he chose to put her up as a sacrifice.

Why? Was he really so sure that Pavo would beat me and she would not be killed? Or was it something else?

Anya steps forward, reaching for the hose, and I have to shake myself out of my introspection. It happens to me out here. I lose myself in the open sea, and the wind, and the birds.

There are a lot of birds now. Not all of them albatrosses. Lots of gulls too. And is it irony or fate that this old rig has turned into an unsanctioned breeding colony of vulnerable wayward seabirds?

I don't know. But I smile about it anyway.

I slip my shorts down my legs and stand still. Most of the paint and blood has melted away with the sweat from the day's workout. But it has left filthy, disgusting streaks down my legs.

Anya turns the hose on and it hits my body at full force, making me take several steps backward and grab at my ribs.

She turns it off and shakes her head. Like she didn't mean to do that.

I sign to her. *Go ahead. I'm OK.* She doesn't understand the first part, but everyone knows the sign for OK.

The hose hits me again. This time, she has figured out the mechanism for pressure, and while it's still strong and it still hurts, it's nothing I can't handle.

I place both my hands on top of my head and stand there, naked and with my eyes closed, as she washes me off.

When she's done, I coil the hose back up, hang it on the hook, and then nod for her to follow me. It's not the best way to get clean here on the Rock, but it's the only way to fully enjoy what comes next.

We go down to the training level, but this time I take her in to the building. It's dark, so I prop the door open with a large rock, sign for her to stay put, and then I turn and walk forward down the hallway.

There isn't a whole lot to this building. It's got the switch for the generator, which lives in the small building on the top level. A lavatory with about a dozen urinals and a few stalls, minus the showers, since the living quarter containers that used to populate this rig all had private bathrooms. A clinic that is mostly stocked. And a small kitchen that was only used for the construction crew, because when a rig is running it has a proper mess container.

I find the switch, kick it on, and the whole place comes to life with a rumble.

Back in the hallway I flick on the lights and find Anya standing in the open doorway where I left her. She looks me up and down, and I do the same. Like we're both just now noticing the other is naked.

We are also both still wet. And she is shivering a little. I should probably give her a towel, but it's not really necessary.

I beckon her with a crooked finger and then disappear into the kitchen. She follows me, standing in a new doorway now, just watching as I take things out of the cupboards and hold them out for her to see.

I'm not your fucking cook, these gestures say. *I will cook for you tonight because you're new. But I'm not your fucking cook. So take notice of where I find these things and what I do with them.*

I think she gets it because she unconsciously sneers her lip as she watches my hands.

I show her how to wait for the water to run clear when I turn on the tap. I show her how to make rice in the small cooker. I show her the pre-packaged dehydrated meat. And then, when everything is cooking, I nod my head and make her follow me down the hallway again.

There is one more room to show her today. The best room. The whole reason why we hose off first.

And when she sees the tub, and when I turn on the water and it begins to steam, she sighs. No. She fucking *moans*.

I chuckle out loud.

It's not a bathtub, it's a therapy tub. Meant for athletes, not spa days. But the end result is the same. Warm, pampered muscles after a long day of work.

Anya leans against the door frame as the tub fills and I go searching through cupboards for soap and shampoo. We don't keep anything fancy here and for a moment I wish we did. It was a long day for her and she didn't complain. So I want to make her feel better—or at least understand that what I do here has a purpose and it's got nothing to do with torture. Luxury soaps and lotions are just an easy way to do that. But Anya doesn't seem to care that the toiletries are industrial-grade.

I hold out my hand. She pushes off the door frame and walks towards me, accepts my help as she walks up the four wooden steps, and then squeezes my hand as she swings her leg over and lowers herself into the hot water.

I climb in after her and we settle on benches placed opposite. The water hits her mid-waist so I have a very nice view of her breasts. If this bothers her, she doesn't show it.

And why should it bother her? She is a Bokori house slave. An old one, for sure. So she probably hasn't been touched in a while. But she was raised naked. Like me.

They do that to strip us of any lingering sense of self. To make us into things to be used. To take away our humanity.

And once it's gone, it doesn't matter what happens next. It doesn't matter if the nicest man alive buys you, takes you into his home, treats you like a person, gives you plenty to eat, and never even looks at your body like it is just a thing to be used.

It does not matter how good it gets after that first *shattering*.

You don't come back from that. You are dead inside. And you are a killer on the outside.

Anya Bokori is a killer. And so am I.

She straddled Pavo Vervonal last night and thrust a knife into his gut. I practically cut off his head five seconds later and then ripped his body open and tore out his heart.

There is no happy ending for us.

A tub of hot water on a rock in the middle of a dark ocean with birds that look like they came right out of Jurassic Park flying overhead, ready to pick apart your half-dead body and feed it to their chicks— this is about as good as it gets.

Anya washes herself quickly. She soaps up her hair and dunks under to rinse it off. And in less than three minutes she is done. Her blue eyes find mine, filled to the brim with questions.

She looks at me like she doesn't know what to do next.

I'm more careful. My ribs are actually screaming at this point. I overworked them today and every time I draw in a breath, a sharp pain shoots through my upper body.

I point to my eyes, then her. Then close my eyes. Then open them and point to her again.

She gets it. And she sighs, maybe letting down her guard a little. Because she slouches down, her foot bumping against mine, and closes her eyes.

I watch her, fascinated, as I wash up. And then I do the same. I slouch down and stretch out my long legs, then decide to prop my feet up on her bench, brushing them against her hips.

I peek, just to see if she will object to that with a sharp look. But she doesn't open her eyes. Instead, she props her feet up on my bench. Brushing them against my hips.

And then it's my turn to sigh.

The buzzing of the rice cooker down the hall wakes me and I sit up, a little bit disoriented. Anya is as well. She rubs her eyes and breathes heavy as she tries to make sense of her surroundings. Like she was in a deep sleep and it came with a dream that had nothing to do with me. Then she looks at me and her gaze is one of understanding.

I get out of the tub, grab a towel from a shelf, wrap it around me, then go looking for clothes. I find us t-shirts and shorts and take them back up to the tub room.

Once we're dressed, I take her into the kitchen, scoop the rice and meat mixture into two bowls, give her a fork, and signal for her to follow me out onto the training platform. We sit on the hard concrete and lean up against the wall. *Normally I like to eat up top.* I sign this to her one-handed as we both shove the food into our mouths. *But the birds will steal the meat right out of your bowl since you're new here.*

I don't think she understands, but I don't care.

If it really were just me out here tonight, I'd be signing things to the General—that's the name I gave my old bird buddy. I'd be filling him in on the last eight months of my life. So having Anya here instead, this is like a bonus, even if she doesn't talk back.

The General never really did either. I mean, I always gave him points for trying, but while his vocabulary is interesting, it's not very big.

I've done a lot of research on the albatross over the years. They are monogamous birds. They find one soulmate and that's it. Just one. And even though they live solitary lives when they're not breeding, soaring over the ocean for months and months at a time without ever touching solid ground, they meet up every other year to raise a new chick.

The General is somewhere around thirty years old right now. And he'll live another thirty, if he's careful. So I guess I did win in the end, didn't I?

I do have a family. A rather big one, actually.

The General has raised ten chicks on this rig with his mate, who I call Seeker. I don't know where he found her—and it's entirely probable that they were mated before he got lost and she actually found him after he disappeared—but either way, they live here now.

Ten chicks over twenty-two years. It's not a bad record for an albatross.

And every single one of those chicks has left the nest, has found their own wayward mate, and has come back here every other year to meet back up.

This rock of death is an unsanctioned breeding colony for the largest flying bird on earth.

This prison, this punishment of a place, is also home to something a little bit... *magical.*

And that's only one of the many reasons I love it.

Dinner is over too soon. I catch Anya staring into her empty bowl, wishing for more.

I explain that things are scarce here at the moment. And even though she doesn't know any signs and I get the feeling that this vow of silence is something she takes very seriously, she nods her understanding. Frowning though. It comes with a frown.

I take our bowls back into the kitchen and dump them, wash everything up, and put it all away. Then I go back out to the platform and find her standing near the edge, looking out over the dark ocean.

Night out here can be one of two things: deeply terrifying or indescribably peaceful. I know what my first night on the Rock was like and even though Anya's position is much more advantageous, it's got to be unsettling.

I walk over, tap her on the shoulder, and motion for her to follow me. Then I open up one of the huge shipping containers to reveal stacks and stacks of sleeping mats. I hand her one, then grab one for myself, and direct her to follow me up the stairs.

It's night now, and there are at least a dozen albatross chicks sleeping on makeshift nests and another dozen adults with their heads under their wings, also sleeping. There are twice that number up in the air somewhere. Most are far, far away. Out hunting so they can bring food back for their mates and their chicks.

They're quiet at night. And they don't even look up as we walk past them, out towards the southern edge of the platform. I lay down my mat and Anya does the same. Then I ease my aching body down, trying to be mindful of the ribs, and let out a long breath.

I overdid it today. I think it's because I was still high on the Lectra and the drugs. But all that has worn off now, and every time I breathe, that sharp pain is there to remind me of what happened yesterday.

It's easy to forget. At least for me. I'm so far away from that ship right now—so far away from everything that reminds me of who I am and what I do—that it's just too easy to forget.

But Anya isn't me. And she has not forgotten.

Anya sits down on her mat, but she doesn't lie back. She hugs her knees and stares off into the distance. There is a shipping lane about fifty miles south of here that I sometimes like to watch. And on the north side of the platform I can see the city lights of São Luís, the capital city of Maranhão. If I were in a pensive mood, I would imagine I can see my base camp, which also lies in that direction. But I'm not pensive tonight. I'm content.

I point to the barely visible sliver of moon out of habit, glancing over at Anya to make sure she sees this. She does, but she's not interested. So I put my hands behind my head and look up and study the stars. I don't know a single constellation name. When I'm out here, I often wonder what they're really called and how to figure out which one is which. But of course, wondering things out here does me no good. There is no internet to look things up. And when I'm back at home, I don't have time to watch the stars. No one gives a fuck what stage the moon is in. The sky is just the space above us so I have never bothered to learn the names of the things up there.

Anya sighs and lies back just as one of the birds wanders over to me and sits down next to my head, snuggles in to me and then tucks her head back under her wing and falls quickly back to sleep. I catch Anya smiling out of the corner of my eye when another one wanders up and does the same, pushing her large body against my broken ribs until I wince. Then all the adults are wandering over. They have missed me.

Anya sighs and this makes me turn my head so I can see her face over the large back of an albatross.

What does she think of all this?

Does it scare her? To be out here so alone? Among these giant birds that could, if they wanted to, rip her to pieces with their massive beaks?

Or does she like it the way I do? Does she feel free and safe?

I would ask. I want to ask, actually. But she won't answer, so I don't bother.

I just look at the sliver of moon and settle back into life on the Rock.

And then, before I even realize it, I'm out.

There is no hope of sleeping past sunrise on the Rock.

The gulls scream the moment the sun first peeks out over the horizon. They circle and squawk, soaring above us and diving down to poke at us, and Anya is on her feet, waving her hands in the air to ward them off.

The albatross who huddled with us all night are gone now, either tending to chicks or out looking for food. But the damn gulls—they prefer to steal their breakfast. And now that I'm back, they remember how to do that.

We pick up our mats, go back down to the training platform, and there they are, dozens of gulls waiting patiently near the door to the kitchen. I chase them off, but this is a losing battle. The albatross don't come down here. They prefer the open air of the top platform. But gulls are a different kind of bird altogether. They don't breed here, thank God. They would quickly take over the platform and there would be no way to get rid of them once that happened. But they are curious, and smart, and will steal anything they can carry unless you're diligent.

I don't need to be diligent in the morning. Because there will be no breakfast.

Anya follows me over to the container and we drop our mats inside, then I close it back up. I can hear her stomach growling and I know she is expecting food. Maybe even coffee. Which makes me internally chuckle. But bringing her to the Rock with me wasn't in the plan and even though we have food, when we left here last year, we only rationed enough for me when I came back. So there isn't enough food to feed two people for the length of time that we will be here.

So. One meal a day and that's still pushing it.

I go over to the jump ropes, pick them up, and then hold one out for her.

She doesn't take it.

I drop it at her feet and shrug. She *will* skip rope today. She will do a lot more than that too if she wants to eat tonight. But she can pretend she won't for a little while, if that makes her happy.

I start skipping. My ribs are still screaming and they will continue to do that for at least a month. But it is what it is. A few broken ribs aren't enough to interrupt my training schedule. I casually make my way down the length of the platform, then back again.

Anya has gotten herself a drink of water and she's dragging her finger over her teeth. I stop skipping and stare at her, shaking my head a little.

She doesn't get it. And I suddenly understand that she might have the willpower to withstand my rules and decide I need to make a point here in the interest of saving time.

So I walk over, take the cup of water out of her hand, dump it out so it splashes up her legs, drop the cup on the ground, and point to her jump rope.

Her expression never changes.

And… we're back. Petulant Anya has decided she is too tired to jump rope, or she is too sore to jump rope, or she is too hungry to jump rope, or maybe she is just too fucking *good* to jump rope.

She picks up the cup, fills it with water, walks back over to me, brings it to her lips.

I take the cup, dump it out, throw it on the ground, and point to her jump rope.

She picks up the cup, fills it with water, walks back over to me and throws it in my face.

Cold water hits me in the eyes and runs down my chest. I look at it. Then back up at her. She is still defiant. No expression. Just a flat line of a mouth.

I grab her arm. Hard. Hard enough to make it blanch. She tries to pull away, but there is no hope of that. Her arm is a spindly thing and my hand is so large in comparison, I almost completely encircle it. If she wants me to leave fingerprints on her skin, I will. And there's no one here to stop me.

I pick up her rope with my other hand and shove it at her.

She refuses to take it.

You get one chance with me. If I were talking, I'm sure this little rebellion of hers could be squashed with one or two harsh threats, but I'm not talking, and she never talks, so the easy way isn't an option.

I drag her over to the stairs. She resists, of course. But now I'm fucking pissed.

I drag her down one level, throw her on the ground, and then shut the squeaky chain-link gate and clamp the combination lock closed on the latch.

She just looks at me from the floor. Unmoving. Disbelieving.

I sign at her, my hands and fingers moving quickly. *Believe it, princess. This is happening. And I'm only going to do this once. Do it again, and you will go in the ocean.*

She doesn't understand the signs. But she gets it. Because she stands up, rushes over to the gate, wraps her fingers around the chain link, and rattles it.

I turn my back.

One chance. That's all you get with me. I'm not fucking around.

I leave her there, climb back up the stairs, and start my workout.

And you know what the nice thing about her is? She's *silent.*

There is no screaming, there is no kicking, there are no hysterical threats.

She is easy to forget.

So that's what I do.

I forget her.

CHAPTER NINE

All night those birds bothered me. They nipped me with their long, thick beaks, they flapped their wings at me, they stretched their necks and threatened me, eye to eye, until I rolled over, covered my head with my hands, and just didn't move until morning.

I know how this sounds. Birds are out to get me. I am insane.

But these aren't just any birds, they are one meter tall and four meters wide when they open their wings. And when they decided that they didn't appreciate the fact that I was sleeping in the middle of their nesting grounds, they held it against me.

Stupid Sick Heart couldn't even wake up once to control his flying beasts. And they wouldn't let me get close enough to shake him awake.

I didn't sleep. Not a wink all night.

And when I figured out that he wasn't gonna feed me breakfast, well—it was a breaking point for me.

Call me naïve. Fine. I guess my expectations for being one of Sick Heart's concubines were unrealistic.

Because I thought that position would come with an actual place *to live*. A place with a bed, and a roof, and food.

That dinner last night was pathetic. Barely a cup of rice. Probably more like half a cup, if I'm being honest. And a few meager scraps of rehydrated meat? Are you fucking kidding me? After I burned... what, two thousand, three thousand calories jumping rope yesterday?

And then no breakfast? Just, *Here's your rope, Anya. Get busy.*

Well. Fuck you.

I rattle the chain-link gate. But he's gone. Cort van Breda is already skipping his stupid rope. I can hear it on the concrete above my head. Snick, snick, snick.

It has been a long time since I had the urge to scream, but I have that urge right now. I want to open up my throat and wail. But I can't.

Because I'm silent. And I will stay silent, goddammit.

My voice is the only thing on this body that is mine and mine alone. Even my baby toe has been claimed with this monster's mark.

He will not get my voice. Ever.

I look around the platform and realize it's a lot like the one above. Except there are a lot more containers. In fact, there are so many containers, they form a steel-box perimeter around the entire level. Front-facing and locked up tight, with no space between them at all. So I have no view of the ocean. But I don't need a view to understand that it is very close.

The stairs go down another level at least, but from the sound of the ocean, I decide it's probably not a level. More than likely, it's the base of the topside.

The wind is strong today. Even with the containers forming a makeshift seawall, it finds a way into the space, whistling and whipping my hair around my face. And every once in a while, the waves are big enough to splash against the containers and a puddle of seawater seeps underneath them and stains the space around them with dark wetness.

I try to open the containers, but they are all padlocked. Then I go back over to see if there is a way to climb over the gate. I'm not at that stage yet, but it's good information to have.

The gate is not scalable. It fits snugly to the top of the frame. Not even room for a finger to squeeze through.

So I slide down a steel beam in the center of the space and wait.

I sit. Quietly. Straining to hear the workout going on above my head.

I am good. I am calm. I am silent. I am compliant.

But Cort van Breda doesn't come back.

It's times like this that I wish I did speak. Because I could call up—*Hello? I'm sorry for overreacting. But I'm hungry and your birds didn't let me sleep last night. I can't breathe through my nose, my lip is split, my entire body aches, and I don't understand what's happening.* And a reasonable person would at least listen to me.

But I can't say any of that and Cort isn't acting very reasonable today.

So I sit. And I wait.

There is water down here. A steel spigot that sticks up from the floor, connected to dubious-looking rusty pipes which lead up top. Is this water potable? I have no idea. But by late afternoon, I no longer care. I turn it on, stick my mouth underneath the spigot, and gulp it down. It's not salty, so that's something.

Then I wait some more.

Surely, once his workout is over, he will feed me. I get it now. One meal a day. I can deal. It's fine.

But he doesn't feed me. The sun sets and I sit. And he never comes.

The sound of his workout faded a long time ago. And the curious gulls who kept me company for most of the afternoon disappear.

I know where they are. Up top, begging for food or trying to steal it out of his bowl.

My stomach cries. It twists, and gurgles, and whines for something to take the edge off. But Cort never comes.

He doesn't come at sundown. He doesn't come at dinnertime, he doesn't come in the morning.

He leaves me here to rot.

At least, I don't *see* him come. At some point in the night I drift off, defeated by utter exhaustion. And when I wake up—no, Cort isn't here. But he *was* here. Because in a little pile on the first step outside of the gate is a jump rope.

My hands are small, but not so small that fitting them through the hole of this chain link fence doesn't come with pain. Nonetheless, I'm able to press my arm forward just enough that the tips of my fingers are able to reach the rope and pull it through to the other side.

Message received, Sick Heart.

I start skipping rope.

It takes him several more hours to appear at my gate. And then he spends at least five more minutes signing things at me—furious fingers flitting through the air, his eyebrows knit into anger and frustration, his mouth tight, his breathing heavy. I have no hope of keeping up with all his signs, but he doesn't seem to care if I understand his words. He wants me to know one thing and one thing only.

I've pushed his button and he's pissed.

I roll the events back in my mind as he continues his silent rant, trying to figure out where exactly I crossed that line. Of course, throwing water in his face was definitely over the top. But that wasn't his breaking point. It was before that. And that's why he poured the water out.

Finally, his fingers shut up. Then he opens the gate, points at me, frowns at me, hisses his silent words at me with his fingers, and then he points upward.

Finally.

I push past him, go up, and if I think that he might feed me, or give me a drink of water, or do anything other than instruct me to *jump rope*, I'm mistaken.

I jump rope and watch Cort van Breda dance with his. One foot, two foot, skip, skip, skip. Figure eight, straddle, cross, scissor, scissor, spin. He does things with that rope that I can't even begin to describe.

He does have a rhythm, I will give him that. And watching him really isn't that boring. In fact, there is no way to not watch him. And it's not because he's the only thing on the platform. There are at least a dozen gulls getting up to things. And one huge albatross is wandering around poking his beak at the door leading to the kitchen, like he's thinking about grabbing some breakfast.

Nice try, buddy. If anyone's getting breakfast around here it's me. I'll fight you for it.

But even with all that distracting me, Cort has my full attention.

We don't jump for long. Not like the other day. He stops, walks over and takes my rope, then drops them both into a pile near the kitchen door. He chases the albatross until it unceremoniously steps off the platform and glides away in the wind.

Then he turns back to me, his steel-gray eyes burning into mine. I feel very small when I become the center of his attention.

He snaps his fingers and points. And then I follow him down the line of containers until we stop in front of a green one. He opens it up to reveal—well, I don't fucking know what that thing is. It's a metal-frame contraption. And it's holding a huge punching bag on a chain.

The whole thing is on wheels and under his direction, I maneuver inside the container and get behind it so we can push it out. There are dozens of punching bags stacked in the back of the container, but I don't have time to think about that, because Cort and I are taking this one over where the other bag is hanging from the ceiling beam.

He pretty much does everything else and I realize this thing is a crane used to hang heavy bags. It lifts the bag up, then Cort climbs up the contraption, slides the bag's chain onto a hook, and then hops off and lowers the crane.

For a moment my stomach sinks. Because I'm thinking he's gonna make me do this. This is my punishment. He's going to make me hang punching bags all day.

But when we push the crane back to the container, he slides it inside and closes the door. Then he opens another container, drags out a mat, and positions it underneath the new bag.

Then he looks at me and smiles. And that's when I realize my punishment is going to be way worse than hanging bags.

He walks over to the new bag and then demonstrates a few punches and kicks and points to it.

I huff. Right. But I'm too hungry to argue. If I piss him off today and he decides not to feed me, I don't know what I'll do. It's been a long time since someone starved me. I'm not used to it anymore. In fact, I might have let myself go over the years. I might've forgotten what it was like to be a girl in this world I live in.

I might've gotten... *soft*.

I can't afford to be soft. Not then, not now, not ever if I want to survive. So I suck it up and start kicking and punching.

Cort watches me for a little bit, his arms crossed over his skull-covered chest, his gray eyes mostly looking at my hands and feet and not so much my face.

I'm expecting him to correct me because I have no idea what I'm doing and this is painfully obvious, but he doesn't. He watches, then he walks over to his bag and begins his own workout. Which looks nothing like the one I'm doing.

I slowly position myself so that I can watch him as he goes through his moves and still keep punching and kicking my bag.

This is when I realize I'm doing it all wrong.

I squint and try to decipher his punches. He's got a combination of them. Hooks or whatever. I'm not sure what they're called. But I copy him. Not hitting the bag hard, because that actually hurts. I'm pretty sure you're supposed to have gloves on. Or tape or something. My knuckles are bright red after only a few minutes. So I don't put a lot of effort into the force. Instead, I just concentrate on the form.

When he moves on to kicks, I do the same thing. I watch him and notice something important. Most of the time he's not connecting with his foot, but with his knee. I try to copy him again. And maybe it's far from perfect, but by the time he steps away from the bag, I have better form than I had when I started a few hours ago.

He pays no attention to me at all. His gaze is directed towards the sky, distracted by something. I use this moment to study him. His body is slick with sweat, his breath still coming out quick and with effort from his workout. He runs his fingers over his head and turns to me. I have an urge to smile until I see the look on his face.

And then I hear the helicopter.

I whirl around, looking for it. But Cort has me by the arm and he's tugging me across the platform towards the stairs. He's not careful as he leads me back down to the prison level, and when I realize he's going to lock me in again, I decide this is my limit.

No! I scream it inside my head. *I don't want to be left down here. I spent a lot of calories this morning. I need food!*

He shoves me hard enough to make me stumble and fall, then he locks the gate and disappears back up the stairs.

Now the helicopter is loud. Directly above us. It lands, but the rotors don't wind down.

I wait, wondering what this could mean. Did someone come for me? Is it Lazar? Did Ring of Fire decide that I won the fight and I don't have to be here with Cort?

Oh, I hope so. Please, please, please.

And when I see Cort's father, Udulf, appear at the top of the stairs, I become even more hopeful. It's true. I won that fight. I am not the Sick Heart's prize. I'm going to get on that helicopter and fly away from here and I'm never going to see Cort van Breda again.

But then I read the expression on Udulf's face. It's an expression I recognize. It's an expression I know well because I grew up with a man who looked at me that same way once upon a time.

And this is when I realize my rescue fantasy is just that. A fantasy.

Because Udulf is looking at me like I'm *his* prize.

Like I'm *his slave*.

Like he is going to take me off this rig, but I definitely won't like what happens next.

CHAPTER TEN

Fuck him.

I sign that right in Udulf's face. *Fuck you.*

I've made it twenty-two years in his hellhole. I'm at the end now. I've *earned* this. And he's going to come here and tell me he's taking Anya for himself?

Fuck you. I flash my fingers in his face.

"Stop it." He bats my hands away, snarling. "Use your voice, Cort. I'm tired of these games."

He's tired of the games? This motherfucker *invented* the game. He's pissed because I found a new way to play and my success forced him to play along. He would never admit to knowing sign language in public because it is the language of slaves and then everyone would know he learned it to talk to *me.*

But he does know it. He understands every fucking word I sign.

"Where is she?"

I point to the lower levels, then flash, *You're not taking her. She's mine.*

He scoffs. "You don't even like girls."

That's not even true. I like girls just fine. And I'm keeping this one because she's my last fucking prize and I want her secrets. I want to know what's going on inside that head of hers. I want to open her up and see what's inside.

He's not getting her. And anyway, I sign, *She's too old for you.*

His chuckle comes out with his words. "That's not what I want her for."

Then what *does* he want her for? Not to have sex with. He and his ilk—they are some seriously sick fucks. Anya's sex slave days have been over for quite a long time now.

This is intriguing, now that I think about it. Because Lazar kept her around too. Why? And now my father wants her for himself. Why?

What is so interesting about Anya Bokori that these two powerful men care where she is and who she's with?

Why did Lazar keep her for so long, only to offer her up as a sacrifice at the fights?

Why is Udulf here? He hasn't come out to the Rock in more than a decade. Why now? Why *this* girl?

He's walking down the steps towards the lower levels. He pauses at the training room. Not one bag. Two. But then he keeps going, clutching the dubious metal railing as he descends. Those expensive shoes of his are worse than being barefoot on the slick algae-covered metal steps. So he holds on tight.

If the 'copter wasn't above us on the roof, I'd push him over the edge, jump in after him, cut his throat, and wait for the sharks. Then I'd watch. I'd watch until they ate every last bit of him.

Take a deep breath, Cort. You're almost there. You are two days into your final sentence on the Rock, then you have one more round of training, and you're out.

Obligations fulfilled. Free.

I barely understand the meaning of the word. But Rainer, Maart, and Evard are part of the deal and we'll figure it out. That's all I know. Once we're fucking free, we'll figure out how to deal with it.

Udulf stops at the landing and looks down the steps. Anya is waiting at the gate, clutching the chain link tightly, and for a moment her face has the look of hope on it. But she must recognize my father's expression and come to a sobering realization, because that look of hope turns into despair.

Udulf just stares at her. I can't see his face because I'm behind him, but this is abnormal behavior.

What is it about this girl?

Udulf turns abruptly. "Open the gate. I'm taking her with me."

I glance down at Anya and watch her panic in real time.

My head shakes out a no. And then my fingers tell him to fuck himself.

He's so lucky. So lucky he and I have never been somewhere alone together. His mercs didn't follow him down here, but they're on that helicopter. My father goes nowhere without his bodyguards. And he certainly doesn't take meetings with me without them.

"Cort." He sounds tired as he turns to face me. "Just... open the gate."

It's not gonna happen. I point to my chest with one hand and sign the word for 'mine' with the other. Then I jog back up the stairs to finish this conversation in private.

"None of them are yours," he calls after me. "They are all mine."

It's mostly true. He's taken every single woman I've won in these fights. Oh, he wants me to fuck them. I always have to fuck them. Because he wants them pregnant with my seed inside their bellies so he can breed more little fighters just like me.

But this wasn't just any win. This wasn't just another fight.

It was my *last* fight. My last prize.

I exit the stairwell on the training level and walk to the middle of the room. By the time I turn, Udulf is just reaching the landing. I sign to him, *She's mine.*

He doesn't follow me onto the mat. "You really want to fight this battle?"

I nod.

"Why?"

Why do you? I sign.

"Because what's yours is mine. You paid for three extra people, Cort. Not four. She's not going with you. You know this. And you're not getting off this rig for months. You still owe me *that*."

He's stalling. I can tell. But why?

She's mine.

"This is the hill you will die on?"

I scoff. *Try it.*

He huffs a laugh. His eyes dart upward, towards the top level where the helicopter waits. "You would lose."

I might. I might not. But one thing's for sure. I *would* take him out with me.

He runs his fingers through his hair and I know I've won. He only does that when he's internally negotiating. "Tell me why. If you tell me why, then I'll leave her here. But I will collect her at base camp when you return."

I narrow my eyes at him. Did he give in too quickly? Did he not bring enough backup to fight this war with me today? Or do I just scare him?

I would like for it to be the last one. But I don't know. I try hard to scare people. That's why I do the things I do during the fights. Fear is everything in our world.

But I am not so full of myself to believe that Udulf is really afraid of me. He's never been afraid of me, even when he should've been. If he were afraid of me, those mercs would be down here with him. They would have automatic weapons trained on my chest.

Udulf laughs. "This is a problem for you? Is it a secret, Sick Heart?"

Fuck you. I think it, but I don't sign it. He's gotten more silent words out of me today than he deserves. And I just want him gone. So I tell him what he expects to hear. *I want to fuck her.*

Udulf laughs. "Since when?"

Twenty-eight more days, I sign.

"Oh. Until Maart comes." He draws in a deep breath as he considers my answer. Does he believe me?

Maybe.

He thinks Maart and I are lovers. We're not. We fuck. But I fuck a lot of people. He's no one special. Not in that regard, anyway.

We're friends. Best friends. I love him, but more importantly, I *like* him. And he's had my back since I was nine. He's the only reason why I'm still fighting.

I have been in thirty-five Ring of Fire fights. But the prizes were small at first. Extra protein for a year.

New training equipment. Hot baths. Girls—not the girls I won in the fights, girls for camp. And boys too, also for camp. In fact, I already won Maart, Rainer, and Evard in fights before this. But that wasn't their freedom. It was just the right to bring them to camp.

But I fought for Maart again three years ago. His freedom is guaranteed, as long as I win mine. Rainer came next. Then Evard. And now me.

Once I serve this last sentence and do the final training, we're free.

It's so fucking close I can taste it. And Udulf knows this. So now he's asking himself, *Why? Why would Cort risk all that over this girl?*

I don't know yet. I just know she's worth something. Something more than I've paid for her, that's for sure.

But if this man, this pseudo-father, this master of mine wants to believe that I want Anya to ease my craving for Maart as I serve my last sentence, then fuck it. What do I care?

Yes, I sign. *I earned this.*

His mouth lifts up on one side in amusement. Then he takes one last look down the stairwell where Anya is surely waiting at the gate.

She knows things. Lots of things. Or maybe just one thing—something very important. That's why Lazar wanted her dead, but not just any kind of dead. He wanted to get something for her before he let her go.

But what? The ship? That can't be it. That ship is worth billions. No human on this earth is worth billions. Not even Udulf is as valuable as that ship.

Even if that's true, why did Lazar let her live this long? Why didn't he kill her after he kicked her out of his bed?

Slave girls in our world rarely make it past age eleven. Twelve-year-old girls are practically unheard of. They use them up and throw them away. And by throw them away I mean they kill them.

They do the same with the boys. Even at the gym, even at camp—we are disposable. We fight, and we either win and live, or lose and die.

That's how our world works.

I walk back over to him and pause. Waiting for him to make a decision.

"You didn't *earn her*, Cort." Udulf and I have the same steel-gray eyes. I've always hated that about him because people really think he's my father. I don't know if he is. I don't know who my real father was. I don't think I ever knew that. All I have left of the time before Udulf is the Lectra dream.

But I find myself praying at night sometimes. Praying that Udulf is *not* my father. Because if he is, he's so much worse than even I understand.

But those eyes…

"Fine. Keep her until you get back to base camp. Then…" He lets out a breath. "Then I will pay you one last visit and I will collect her. But"—he points a finger in my face—"I need her alive. Do you understand me? I'll wait you out and give you this… *gift*. You have been a good boy." He places his hand alongside my cheek and a shudder of revulsion shoots through my body. Udulf mistakes it for… something else. He pats my cheek and continues. "But she had better come back to me alive, Cort. Do you understand me?"

I brush his hand away and lift my chin up in response. It's a yes, but not a nod. He didn't earn a nod. He didn't earn any of this today. He's taking from me right now. He doesn't belong here.

"Calm down," he says, tugging on his shirt collar as he looks off to his right where half a dozen albatrosses are gliding in circles barely ten feet away. "I'm going. I hate those fucking birds." And he starts climbing the steps.

All of this bothers me. He can read my mind these days.

Like it or not, Udulf van Hauten knows me *intimately*.

I follow him up and stand on the platform with my arms crossed, flanked by my giant white guardians as Udulf's helicopter lifts off.

I stay that way until it's long out of sight. Then I walk back down the steps to get Anya. She's waiting for me at the gate, her blue eyes locked with mine, filled with questions she will never ask.

Why? Why don't you talk?

If it were something as simple as she saw too much, she'd be dead.

That's not it. That can't be it. It's something else and I need to know what that something else is.

I need her secret.

I open the gate and wave her forward. Then I follow her up to the training level. She pauses there, waiting for instructions. And I'm not being mean when I think this, but Anya Bokori is weak. So fucking weak.

She cannot be something special. She simply doesn't have it in her.

I have locked eight-year-old boys on the lowest level of this rig—barely ten feet above an angry ocean—for *days* at a time, just for being little dicks. They got one cup of water a day, if they were lucky. And they didn't cave. They didn't cry. They didn't beg. They didn't give up.

Anya had to skip a little rope and miss a meal and she throws a tantrum? I should've just let him take her. She's going to be trouble. And I *don't* want to fuck her.

I don't need her here to ease my loneliness, because I don't even understand the meaning of that word. I *like* it here. I fucking *love* it here. I hate it when I have to share this place with others.

I point to the bag. She doesn't balk at all. Just walks over to it and starts punching it like a stupid girl. No, that's not even true. I have eight girls at my camp who punch *like girls*. And half of them can knock out a full-grown man.

Anya's punches are *weak*.

And yet she's here, Cort. Why? None of this was in the plan. You were allowed to fuck her, you were allowed to tattoo her, and that's all you were allowed to do.

But you brought her with you. Over everyone's objections. Why?

I don't know. I really don't.

Anya whines and when I look over at her, she's cradling her hand. Her knuckles have split open and they are stained with blood.

Fucking great. I walk over, grab her arm, and tug her into the little building, then lead her into the clinic. I point to a stool in the kitchen and she sits. Then I hunt down a roll of wrap, a mostly used tube of antibacterial ointment, a bowl of hot water, and a clean rag. I place it all on the counter, grab another stool from the other room, slide it over to her, and then start washing the blood off. I'm about halfway done wrapping her second hand when I feel a soft tap on my shoulder. I look up, surprised.

She motions with her hand. It's not a sign. She's making shit up. But I've gotten good at interpreting made-up hand signals. She's asking me why.

Why what? I sign back. And even my signs are irritated. Because she draws back at their quick sharpness.

She points up.

I point to her. *You tell me.*

She sighs, then lowers her eyes and doesn't look at me again until I'm done with her hands.

But when I get up and put the wrap stuff away, I find myself smiling.

She talked to me.

She didn't use her voice and those weren't really words.

But she talked to me.

Me.

CHAPTER ELEVEN

ANYA

His care in tending to my wounded knuckles doesn't continue back out on the training floor. I don't know this man very well, but here's something I've picked up on. Sick Heart is a control freak. Also, he likes a tight schedule. In other words, he's not very flexible. His world revolves around things he can predict.

I continue fighting with the heavy bag as I ponder this. It's not surprising. The world he lives in can't be much different than mine. I mean, he's got a lot more than I ever did. And he could do a lot worse than this abandoned oil rig as far as time-out space goes.

When Lazar was unhappy with me—back when he cared about such things—he would leave me in a dark, windowless room until I was so weak from hunger and thirst, he had to either let me die or bring me back.

But this place. I pause my punching and stare out across the ocean. It's peaceful today. No wind, either, which makes the endless flat, blue surface of the water appear deceptively innocent. Of course, under the

171

smooth water there is a whole world of natural-law violence.

But this rig. It's not fancy, but it has food, and water, and it's safe. As long as Udulf stays away. And I don't know what Cort promised him to make him leave, but he didn't stay long. I got the feeling that there is no love lost between the two of them.

I could get used to life on this rig.

A hand slaps the bag in front of me, pulling me out of my introspection. And when I jerk my gaze to Cort's face, I realize he's telling me, without words, that we are not done here and I need to keep going.

I sigh, but continue punching and kicking the bag.

I expect Cort to go back to his training, but he lingers, watching me. Then his hand reaches out, just as I'm about to hit the bag again, and he grabs my fist. Blood is seeping through the wrapping over my knuckles. Cort frowns at it, like I've just disappointed him. Then he sucks in a deep breath and slowly exhales as he points to the center of the platform.

I follow him across the mats and then he turns to face me. He does a couple of punches, moving his feet, and then he pauses and points to me.

I scoff and shake my head. Not because I'm trying to be difficult, but there is just no way I can imitate what he just did. His movements are fluid, like a dancer. Even if I had known that there was a pop quiz coming, I would not be able to do what he's asking. It's all blurry. I need a slow-motion step-by-step.

He sighs again, maybe frustrated, maybe tired, or maybe he's thinking, *Why didn't I just let my father take her away earlier?*

That gets me moving. I don't want to be here, but I don't want to be sent to his father. That man is scarier than Lazar. So I make an attempt, punching the air with my fist and hopping a little with my feet.

His laugh is loud and immediate. And when I look over my shoulder at him, he's scowling and shaking his head at me.

I drop my fists and frown back. It's not my fault he's asking me to do things I can't.

He demonstrates again. But it's still too fast and while I can see that he's punching with his left hand and taking a step forward—and this seems like a very simple thing—when I try it, none of it works. My punch is late, my feet are in the wrong place, and I actually lose my balance and his grip on my upper arm is the only reason I don't fall over.

He shows me again, this time breaking the movement into six unique parts. He holds up a single finger.

One. Got it.

He does it and points at me, but when I try it's... not good. He stops and shows me again. And this time I break this move down into three parts. A baby step forward, a punch, and a bounce back.

I say that over in my mind as I try and when I look up at Cort, he's smiling.

I suck in a deep breath of air and turn my head away so he can't see me smile back.

I do that again, and again. Baby step forward, punch, step back. And he corrects me each time, adjusting my hips, or my chin, or my fist.

Then he moves on to the second move. This time it's a step back with a punch using the opposite hand. Like I'm retreating from an approaching opponent.

This one takes me longer because the opposite arm and leg are doing different things. I don't get it down all the way, but Cort must get bored, because we move on to move number three.

This one is mostly pivoting my hips while throwing a cross punch. I don't have to take any steps forward or backward while I punch, so it's easier.

Or so I think. Because suddenly Cort is behind me, once again pressing his chest into my back. And when his hands grip my hips, a chill runs through my body at his touch. He directs me to punch and moves my hips, keeping them within some pre-determined parameter. One hand remains on my left hip as his fingertips trace down the length of my right arm. He wraps his hand around my fist and then he does the move for me. His body becoming my body. His hips moving my hips. His hand throwing my punch.

I get lost in this, my mind unable to process the intimacy of it. And it's dumb, I get it. He's not coming on to me. We're not dancing. This isn't emotion.

He's teaching me how to *fight*.

When he backs away, I suck in a deep breath and force myself to continue the move without him, even though he's wiped my mind of everything but his missing touch.

I do this move over and over as he watches.

Then he points at me. One finger. And he does the baby-step move. I follow along and do it as well. Then he flashes three fingers at me. Which is the hip-pivot cross punch. So I do that. And when he flashes two, I'm ready to take that step back.

He claps. It's a slow clap. One you see in movies when people are being mocked. But I don't care because he's smiling at me. His eyes are bright and I really think I've made him happy.

He has taught me something.

It's a pretty useless thing, if you ask me. It's not like I can use any of this to protect myself. It's not like I can say, *Hold on, hold on. Let me get my hips in the right position before I hit you with my weak, girly cross punch.*

He flashes his fingers—one. Two. Three.

And I do them. Baby-step punch, retreat punch, hip-pivot cross.

He claps again, then holds up four fingers. Moving on, I guess.

This time it's a baby-step advance with a one-two punch. And number five is a baby-step back with a one-two.

I suck at those. But he doesn't stop to make me practice. Just ends the sequence with number six—a mid-air foot switch.

Yeah. I can't get that one.

But again, he doesn't care. Just goes all the way back to number one and makes me practice those moves, holding up fingers so I can't get a pattern going.

And if someone had asked me last week if I would enjoy learning how to box, I would've laughed out loud at the absurdity of their question, today I find it… fun.

Maybe it's because after about an hour, I can do these three simple moves on command and I start envisioning myself actually using them in a situation. But more than likely it's Cort.

Even though I've been acting like a spoiled brat for two days, he's actually pretty patient when he's in teacher mode. And he smiles a lot.

So far, the Cort I've come to know is a broody, scowling jerk. So this is a new side to him. Perhaps even a real side to him.

He rolls his hand at me to keep going, then turns his back and walks over to the door that leads inside, disappearing without any more explanation.

I do keep going. Even though the Anya of last week would've taken this opportunity to slack off because there is no one around to make me work, I suddenly decide I don't want to be that Anya anymore.

Before the fight with Cort, that was the only girl I knew. There was no other life for me. There was no future for me. Not a good one, anyway. Not one that involved being alone with a brand-new version of Sick Heart on an abandoned oil rig where I have his complete and captive attention.

He doesn't seem interested in having sex with me. And even though he did lock me down on the lower level after my tantrum—and left me there for almost two days—he didn't beat me to drive his dominance home once I surrendered.

And this leads me to believe that Sick Heart here has… well, a heart. Or at least a very well-developed sense of fairness.

I wonder what his life has been like. Did he start out in one of the camps? I don't remember the *Ring of Fire* article saying anything about his early years. But he's been fighting since he was a very small boy. So I bet he did live at the camps. That's better, I think. Because if he had been a house boy…

I let that thought trail off because I don't want to imagine strong, commanding Cort van Breda as someone's beaten, helpless house boy. Especially Udulf's.

Cort grips my arm and pulls me out of my introspection. He's shaking his head at me. Signing things. You know, the most important thing I've learned about being silent is this: Most of the time you don't need words to understand people. Like right now, for instance. Because he's telling me that I wasn't concentrating and my moves are sloppy.

He looks a little frustrated again. Like maybe he's thinking I'm a waste of time. I might not have understood every word that transpired between Cort and his father, but I heard enough. The rest I can deduce. Cort's ownership of me is dubious at best. Udulf didn't retreat, his absence is only temporary.

I don't belong to the Sick Heart.

I belong to Udulf.

This makes me shudder as my skin prickles up with the thought of what will happen to me when my time out here on this rig is over. I can think of a few possibilities. None of them are good.

I think I was supposed to die at the end of the fight between Cort and Pavo. And I lived instead. That's not good either. When the men in my world make a plan for someone, they make it with a goal in mind.

So if I was supposed to die, and didn't, then I messed up someone's plan. And I will pay for that sooner or later.

Cort points to the stairs and for a moment I think he's going to take me back down to the prison level. But he points up and when he moves towards the stairwell, still holding my arm, I follow willingly.

I want to eat, but the kitchen is on the training level. But the hose is on the top level. And I can barely stand the stench wafting off me, so a shower—even a harsh one that stings my skin—is worth the wait for dinner.

When we reach the top he leads me around the birds and past the old mechanical building to the fire hose, but he stops and frowns at me, then points to the cistern mounted on the roof. He's tall enough so that when he reaches up, he can tap the water line clearly visible through the semi-opaque white tank.

Well, shit. I frown. There's not enough water for a hose down, I guess. I don't know how long we'll have to be here. But it must be a while because the cistern is huge and I would guess that there are a couple hundred gallons left. There are six of them, actually. But the rest are already empty.

Still, a couple hundred is a lot if you're just drinking it. But that bath the first night—that must've used up fifty or sixty. Plus the hose down.

There will be no more baths. And no more hoses, either, from the looks of it.

I huff, irritated. Why did he bring me up here if we can't even wash?

He shoots me a crooked grin, but I don't find it charming. I smell. Bad. And now that I know I can't get clean, I'm noticing the pain in my stomach from not eating. I frown deeper.

Cort tugs me over to the wall and then points up to a shower head.

My mouth makes a little o. And then I smile. When I look at him he's… what? What is that look? Smugness? He's definitely feeling smug.

But his hands are flashing at me. So I watch, carefully, trying to understand what he's telling me.

I think he's saying it needs to be quick. That makes sense. He keeps pointing to the showerhead, then him. Then me. He holds up one finger. Then two.

Meaning—I'm not supposed to be here. I am eating his food, and drinking his water, and if we're not careful, we're going to run out of both.

I nod, understanding, then I wave him towards the shower in a *Be my guest* gesture. It's his water, not mine.

But to my surprise he leads me over to the shower with him. Then he pretends to take off an invisible shirt and points to mine.

Oh. I see.

I don't even bother fighting this. I take the shirt off. Because this is not my shirt. These are not my shorts, this is not my water, that is not my food, and let's face it, this is not even my body.

For every moment of my life, someone has owned me.

At some point these men—these monsters who run my world—were given dominion over me. Over all of us. We have no rights.

Not even girls like me. Girls who lived under a king's roof. Who ate a king's food. Who drank a king's water and wore a king's clothes. We are nothing and no one.

We are disposable.

I came to terms with that reality a long time ago.

I am not a girl. I am not a woman. I am not even human to them. I am nothing to them.

But that's not all there is of me.

There is one piece left. One sacred piece of me that they can't have. No matter how hard they try, they cannot take my silence.

She is all I have left. The spirit of me inside my head. The one who can't talk, or walk, or do anything but go along for the ride.

So when I take the shirt off, I immediately go for the shorts. And then, moments later, I am naked.

When I look up to meet Cort's gaze I find him once again frowning. I sigh and look down at my feet.

He takes my hand again, but instead of leading me over to the shower, he just… holds it for a moment. A long enough moment to make me look up and see what the hell he's doing.

His eyes are locked with mine. He does not look down at my body. And then he flashes his fingers at me with deliberate intent, his pointer and middle fingers snapping down on to the pad of his thumb.

No. That's what his fingers say. *No.* He signs it again. And his eyes are angry now.

I don't know what he wants from me, so I just shrug and resume looking at my feet. He stands there for another long moment, then he sighs.

We seem to do a lot of sighing.

Are we frustrated? Or tired? Or giving up?

I don't know.

Maybe for me, it's all three.

CHAPTER TWELVE

I have seen monsters in my day. Hell, I've become one.

I fight the king's fights. I kill the king's enemies. I accept the king's prize and I live under the king's rules.

I do the king's bidding.

It's a bad lot in life, no doubt. But it's nothing compared to what some do for the king. And I'm starting to get the feeling that Anya was one of the *some*.

She has done things and she will never forget them.

It would be easy to assume Anya is one of the strong ones. She has made it longer than any other slave in her king's house. What is she? Seventeen? Eighteen? She might even be as old as twenty. That's an amazing accomplishment for a sex slave.

She is not a whore. There is a very definite difference in these two things in the world of kings. Sex slaves are children and whores are women.

She might be turned in to one, if Udulf has his way. Pimped out to other kings. A prize, perhaps? For some favor. She might even make it to a breeder. She

SICK HEART - JA HUSS

has a nice face, a perfect, athletic body, and she's smart enough to keep her mouth shut.

But that's not really Udulf's style. He doesn't like to put his trophies on the shelf. He does not admire them. He uses them.

He will use her. Any way he feels fit.

I slip my shorts down my legs, turn towards the shower, and put Anya out of my mind. *She is not your problem, Cort. You have your circle. You fought hard for them. They have fought hard for you. You drew a line, you made your choice, and now you are weeks away from freedom. Mere weeks. After twenty-seven years, you will finally, finally have your own life.*

And I refuse to feel guilty about the ones I'm leaving behind.

I am no one's savior.

I am no one's hope.

And maybe Anya did help me that night on the ship, but I fought for her too. She is alive because of me. She is here, out of Udulf's hands, because of me.

But she saved you too, Cort. And she might have a secret you can use.

No. I'm not getting caught up in her. I'm done with this shit. I turn the water on. Then I push her underneath it and step in next to her, wetting myself down, but just enough to coat our bodies with the water. Then I turn it off again, take her hand, squirt some shampoo into her palm, and then do the same for me.

We wash ourselves in silence. Me gazing one way, her the other. Pretending the other doesn't exist.

I grab the dried-out bar of soap I brought up here last night and rub it over my skin. The scent reminds me of a hospital, which makes no sense, because I've never been to a real hospital. Every medical procedure I've ever had was done by Maart.

This makes me smile. I flip the water back on to rinse, but also to hide the smile.

Maart. He's not a doctor, but he has saved my ass more times than I can count. Saving him back is the least I can do.

And Rainer has had my back in more underground training centers than I can count. You don't start out fighting in the Ring of Fire. There are no cheering fans in the early days. You are dropped off at the event and if you win, you're picked up when it's over.

And trust me when I say this—when you're in a third-world country, fighting a local rising star, the natives aren't very happy when their ticket out dies.

I owe Rainer.

Evard never did anything for me but bring me a bottle of Lectra and then judge my bad behavior the next day.

I actually chuckle at that, then remember that Anya is behind me. I step out of the water and point for her to take my place. She is not looking at me, so I push her underneath the water.

I'm done, so I walk over to the pack I brought up and take out two towels. It's still hot out tonight, but the sun is low on the horizon and the unbearable stuffiness has subsided until morning. By the time I'm dry and dressed in a clean pair of shorts, Anya is done. I shut the water off, throw her a towel, then point to the pack and walk away.

I don't want to think about her.

She is not my problem. Hell, she's damn lucky I talked Udulf out of taking her today. That will have consequences at some point. So the way I see it, she owes me. And I fully plan on getting her secrets before Udulf comes back. All of them.

In the kitchen I start the rice in the cooker and then lean against the counter, wishing I had started cooking before washing up so I didn't have to wait for it.

To waste time, I go out onto the training floor, kinda looking for Anya, but not finding her. So she didn't follow me down here. She probably senses my uneasiness and wants to stay as far away from me as she can. That's how I'd be feeling if I were her.

And wasn't I her once upon a time? Didn't I walk around like that? Afraid of everything. Every too-loud noise. Every strange face in a crowd where all others were known. Every hushed whisper of my name in the night.

My call to duty.

I shudder with the thought of it. No. Not the *thought* of it. The *memory* of it.

I don't like thinking back on it. And I think this is why I don't like this girl.

She's pretty enough to look at. But I learned early—very early—that beauty is deception. If there is one thing you do not want to be in this world we live in, it's beautiful. If you're beautiful, they notice you. It's never good to be noticed in this world we live in.

I turn to the empty wall of the small building housing the kitchen, the clinic, and the toilets and in that moment, I wish they were all here with me. Because if Maart, and Rainer, and Evard, and the others were here, this last punishment would be over. And even though I like it out here—I really do—I don't want to be here with this girl.

She bothers me. There is something about her that is very, very wrong.

And I can't put my finger on it. I don't want to put my finger on it. But at the same time, I want those secrets she hides behind her silence.

I know I earned my freedom. And Udulf admitted that I paid for myself and three people—Maart, Rainer, and Evard—just not four. Not Anya. So he's not backing out.

But still. I have no guarantees and nothing to hold over him if he changes his mind. If he should find some unpaid bill. Some debt on my balance sheet.

Knowing Anya's secret would go a long way in guaranteeing that in four months this whole life I've lived will be nothing but the remnant of a nightmare.

When the rice is done I drop in the freeze-dried protein, stir it up, and then split the ration in half with a sigh. I'm losing weight. It shouldn't matter. There are no more fights in my future and plenty of feasts coming up, but just the idea of losing muscle mass triggers a panic inside me that isn't easily tamed.

The Rock gets stocked with food once a year. When the training camp beings. We bring as much as we can and then we ration it to make it last. But I always come out here by myself at least once at Udulf's command. So when we leave camp, there needs to be just enough to get me through until the supply ship comes again.

Anya wasn't supposed to be here. There is just not enough food for both of us.

But whatever. It can't be helped. I'm not going to let her starve.

I take the two bowls, climb the stairs up to the top platform, and find her sitting on the edge, feet dangling over. There's a low, steel-beam railing that lines that side of the helipad with just enough room to slip your legs underneath and dangle them off the edge. And it's funny that she chose that spot, because that's where I like to eat too.

The steel beam is wide enough to be a table. And when the kids are out here, they will all fight for a spot at the beam when it's chow time.

I smile at that, then push the thought aside. They're not my problem either. They're all just like Anya. Lucky as fuck that they ended up with me and not someone like Pavo.

I slide my legs under the beam about two feet away from Anya, then push the second bowl of chicken and rice in front of her.

She doesn't look at me, but she starts scooping the meal up to her mouth with her fingers. We have forks, but I didn't bring them on purpose. Life on the Rock is that of a heathen and Anya Bokori is just going to have to get used to it.

We eat in silence, but the meal is so meager, it's over in a matter of minutes. I think I am hungrier when I'm done than I was when I started. I think Anya is too, because she looks down at her bowl with longing.

I sigh. Loudly. Because it would be nice if she could see this for what it is. Kindness.

There is enough food here to last one person exactly twenty-five more days. She's lucky I give her anything.

She gets to her feet—not saying anything, of course—and then picks up my empty bowl and walks off. After a few minutes, I get up and follow her because she probably won't think about bringing the sleeping mats up. But when I get to the stairwell, she is already on her way up, mats in hand.

I smile at that. She doesn't smile back. Just hands me a mat and then follows me back up to the helipad.

The birds are back. The gulls are loud on the platform below us, but the albatrosses are here on top, dropping off the last meal of the day for the chicks, who are several months old and as big as medium-sized dogs.

Some of them—the ones without chicks this year—follow me across the platform. They don't beg much if it's just me out here. It's like they know I don't have any food to spare. In fact, they will often drop slimy little fish at my feet like I'm their chick and they're in charge of my wellbeing.

Anya lays her mat down in a spot near the center of the platform, but I walk over and pick it up before she sits down, pointing to a spot as far away from the nests as we can get.

Again, if the kids are here the albatross know their limits. They are outnumbered and a couple dozen brats under the age of twelve is nothing but annoying. But if it's just me—or just me and Anya—that's a temptation they can rarely resist. They aren't mean. Not to me, anyway. But they are pests and once they get a little attention, they want more. So it's best to stay out of their way.

She doesn't motion or make any move to contradict my change-of-location decision. Just plops down on top of her mat and pulls her knees up to her chest with a sigh.

I sit down too, then lie back. Tired, not exhausted—you can barely call what I did today training—but tired in another way. Weary, I guess.

And Udulf's visit has left behind a bad taste. A lingering sense of doubt that I would prefer not to think about.

Usually, when I'm out here alone, I will cheat. I talk to the birds. And the moon. And the sea. I talk a lot, actually. It's only when others are here with me that I keep the vow of silence I came up with that first time. And maybe, if Anya had been chatty, we'd have spent these weeks together getting to know each other. I probably would've cheated with her here, telling myself she doesn't count since she's not one of us.

But she's not chatty. And now, after a few days of thinking about it, talking to her feels like submission. And isn't it?

I imagine she had everyone in her king's house under her spell of silence. That little sister of hers probably talked for Anya the way Maart talks for me when I'm in silent mode. And don't I do it for dominance? So yeah. Fuck Anya. I'm not talking to her.

I point up at the sliver of moon out of habit, my arm straight out, my finger an extension. It is three days past new. I shut one eye, still pointing, like the moon is a target at the end of a rifle. This is a nightly ritual even when the kids aren't here.

And then Anya lies back on her mat and points her finger at the moon too.

This pisses me off. Because she doesn't know why she's pointing at it. This is not her ritual, it's ours.

I drop my arm, sigh, and turn my back to her.

Why did I bring her here again? I'm having trouble remembering. Probably because I was high on the Lectra.

Oh. Ooooohhhh. I chuckle a little under my breath. Because I get a flash of Rainer between Anya's legs that night. And her lying on top of Maart. And… yeah. That's why I brought her.

Fucking her again, though? That feels like a *really* bad idea.

She taps my shoulder and I turn over to find her sitting up, pointing at the moon.

What? I sign.

She points again and I realize she's asking for a sign.

I make a little c with my thumb and forefinger, put it up to my eye, then gesture towards the moon. My sign devolves into a point, because that's how we do it here, but that's just a personal embellishment.

Anya mimics my motions, then lets out a long breath.

Life would be so much easier if she would just talk. Then I could cheat and ask her all the questions. I could maybe even… seduce her into giving up all the answers.

But no. This one has to be special. Silent. Frustrating.

But then I realize she did it again. She communicated with me. Asked me a question.

So maybe I can ask her one back?

I take her hand and she pulls back instinctively, a look of shocked panic on her face. I put up a hand. *Sorry*, that gesture says. *Didn't mean to startle you.* Then I take her hand again and form her fingers into the sign for 'A'—a fist, but not a punching fist like I showed her earlier today. Then I make the sign for 'n,' 'y,' and another 'a.' I point to her. *That's you*, I sign.

She nods, getting it. And then she does it back for me.

Only—and I laugh—she does it with my hand. The way I did it with hers. Then she points to me.

I shake my head, still smiling as I point to her. *That's you.*

She smiles too, lies back down, stares up at the moon, and makes the sign. Then she puts her fist up to her heart and signs her name. When she looks at me, I find her very serious. She reaches for my hand again, then puts it over my heart and points to it.

Sick Heart. I don't know how I know that's the name she wants to learn, I just do. She's not asking about *Cort*. She's asking about Sick Heart.

I sign it. Not spelled out like names usually are, but two words. Sick. Heart.

That's how they say my name out loud too. Two words.

Sick. Heart.

She frowns and makes a heart with her fingers in the air.

I shake my head and show her again. Because that's not it. That's the other kind of heart. A romantic heart. Follow your heart. Hearts and flowers.

The heart in my name is the organ. The thing that beats. The thing that breaks. The sick thing inside me that has kept me alive all these years.

But how to explain that to someone who can't sign?

I point to my head. My brain. I make the sign for it. Then I point to my foot, make the sign for foot, then do the heart sign again.

Her mouth makes a little o shape. Like she understands. But she doesn't.

I mean, sure. She gets it, I guess. But she doesn't understand why I use that clinical sign for my name and not the romantic version. She can't understand that because I don't even get it.

It wasn't something I decided. That name was given to me along with the knowledge of how to sign in the first place. I just don't remember any of it.

I don't remember learning ASL. It's just something I've always known. And that only makes sense in one way.

Those early memories are so terrible, I've blocked them out. And that's bad. Because I can remember plenty of horrible things in my early years. Yet I don't know how I got my name.

I do know my name is not really *Cort*. That was the name Udulf gave me. Just a throwaway name when he finally gave in and sent me to the training camp for good. Up until then, he called me Sicko.

Just thinking that name sends a chill up my spine.

How did he know? I mean, how did he figure out the *sick* part? Did he—what, look that sign up online and then turn it into… an endearment?

Sicko.

I shake my head, then notice that Anya is moving her hands around, her fingers gesturing and making signs that aren't signs. At first, I want to correct her. Tell her no. *That's not right. That's not how it's done. You don't know what you're talking about.*

But I stop myself and just watch her. I watch her talk without words.

She *can* talk though, right?

I lean over and she stops, suddenly, when I enter her personal space. She holds absolutely still as I touch her lips with two of my fingers. Then I kiss her, opening my mouth to give her some tongue. And yeah, her tongue is there. Responding and pressing against mine.

I knew this. I vaguely remember checking her that night of the fight. But I needed to be sure, because if she *can* talk, and she *wants* to tell me something, why not just… do it?

No one is here. No one is going to know. She won't be punished, if that's what she's afraid of. So why keep this charade up?

I pull back from the kiss and look into her eyes. They are dark in the moonlight, but still vaguely blue. *Why?* I ask.

And she is smart. Because she throws that sign right back at me. *Why? Why me? Why don't you talk?*

It's an easy explanation and I'm sure I could get her to understand if I put a little effort into it. Talking to her, here, in this place, would be cheating. This is just a rule I live by on the Rock. It gives me direction. It gives this place meaning and gives this training definition, and all my kids need that.

Just like I needed it.

Just like Anya, apparently, needs it too.

And sure, maybe I would've cheated if she talked. But she doesn't, and I didn't. And I won't. Not now. I've made up my mind and once I make a decision about something, it's done. I don't have the luxury of second chances and regrets. My life is all about instincts. All about moving without thinking. All about predicting what my enemy will do before they do it. And then meeting them there, halfway, before they know what's happening.

But this feels like an explanation Anya hasn't earned. So I just turn over and say nothing.

A few seconds later I feel her fingertips on my back.

I look over my shoulder, scowling now, then sign, *Leave me alone*. I'm tired of her. I'm tired of this day and Udulf's visit this morning is finally sinking in.

He's up to something.

He won. Right? He got to keep controlling interest in his precious ship, he got my prize money. Why does he give a fuck about Anya Bokori? What made him get on that helicopter and fly out here after three days?

He's never done that before. It's been more years than I can count since he's set foot on this rig. At least a dozen, but maybe even more.

And damn, I don't normally allow myself to wish for things I don't have while I'm on the Rock. It's just pointless. But I'd give anything for a sat phone right now. Not that Maart or Rainer would know anything about what Udulf is doing, but I could set them on a mission to find out.

Anya pokes me again.

I sign, *What?* and make a scowling face so she knows I'm pissed.

Her hands make a gesture that is actually a word, but I'm pretty sure she's not saying 'pie.' Still, her middle finger is slipping across her palm. And I can't help myself, I sit up to try to figure it out.

Then she does the sign for moon again, pointing to it.

Calendar? I ask.

She throws her arms wide, frustrated. And I'm thinking, *Yeah. Me too, babe. Me too.*

Then I get it. *How long?*

She sighs and nods.

How long will we be here? I lie back and point to the moon, then hold up three fingers.

It's not what she's looking for. This is the number of days we've been here, not how many we have left. But that's one of the rules too.

Never think about how much time you have left in Hell.

Only congratulate yourself for time served.

CHAPTER THIRTEEN

ANYA

I think about four things after he turns his back to me for the final time.

One. That kiss. Jesus. That kiss. I'm pretty sure he didn't enjoy it the way I did, because I have a sneaking suspicion he was checking for my tongue again. And that means he's probably irritated with me for the silence. But it was so unexpected and so—well, nice—that the feeling of his mouth on mine lingers long into the night.

Two. His name. There is something about the heart part, but I don't know what it is. I drew in the air and that made some kind of sense to him, because he went into that anatomy explanation. But I'm not sure if he just thinks I'm too stupid to understand that was the sign for 'heart,' or if there was a much bigger, more involved explanation to it.

Three. He's not very patient. I mean, he has signs of patience at times. But that comes and goes in bursts. He was patient for a while down on the mat. But once he felt I had the moves down, he went back to his own business. And even though he showed me some signs tonight, the role of teacher tired him out pretty quick.

Four. He's frustrated that I'm not talking. Like I'm a lot of effort and he's short on effort right now. Plus, I think that visit from Udulf means something bad. I'm not staying with Cort after we leave here, that was pretty clear. And I'm not saying this bothers him—the part about me, anyway. But something about that is bothering him.

So his frustration concerns me. Am I a liability?

I don't want to be a liability. And he's clearly not interested in anything sexual. I suspect that Sick Heart here isn't into strangers. Maybe if his friends were here, he might think about another sexual encounter. But only because of them, not me.

My stomach grumbles. And this is no ordinary grumble. I'm in a serious calorie deficit right now. I know all about this. It might've been years since they used starvation as a punishment, but when I first came to Lazar's estate, there was another girl there, several years older than me. She knew the ropes and taught me, much the same way I taught Bexxie when she first came to live with us. Her name was Diona and she was the one who showed me how to track the hunger pangs so I knew how much food I could go without. Not how much I needed to survive, but how much I could afford to give up. She was a rebellious girl who thrived in high-drama situations. So she was always looking for a way to beat Lazar and the older woman who controlled us on the day-to-day.

Diona disappeared shortly before I turned eight and after that I told myself, *Do not be like Diona. Just exist, Anya. Do what they tell you, and live. Buck the system and you'll end up like all the other girls who got too old to meet Lazar's sick, twisted desires.*

My stomach rumbles again. And it feels like I'm eating myself from the inside out. Technically, you can go a very long time without food. But you become too weak to do much after only a week. And I'm on the tail end of day three. Did I even eat that night of the fight?

No. Not that day, either. I was too nervous.

I need more food. But it's pretty clear that I wasn't supposed to come here with Cort. And whatever food he has, it's only enough for him.

He has to be as hungry as I am. He's much bigger, he's been training hard since we arrived, and his food ration was as meager as my own. He's been splitting it equally. But he had that extra ration that I went without when I was locked on the lower level.

He could—hell, if he was smart, he would—lock me down there again and keep my food ration for himself.

He could also start feeding me every other day. Or every third day. Feed me just enough to stay alive, but not much else.

I do not like the pain of hunger. It's a gnawing, biting, burning feeling that hollows you out. I need to be nice to him. And I was trying tonight. I tried to get him more interested in me.

He would prefer me to talk, even if he himself doesn't say a word. I'm in his world. I should bend to his rules.

I should talk. I know this is the easiest way to stay safe. But... I don't know what I would say.

Or, rather, I'm afraid I do know what to say. I'm afraid that if I open my mouth and utter any words at all, they will be all the wrong ones. And I know what happens to girls who say the wrong things.

And anyway, how do I know that Cort won't just tell everyone? I don't.

And if Udulf figures out I talked to Cort, then he will expect me to talk to him as well. And once I talk to him, I'm positively sure everything will begin to unravel.

I've been holding things together with my silence for a long time now.

More than ten years.

But everything seems to be changing at once and this is a very dangerous thing.

Deciding to talk now would be a fatal mistake.

So no. I will not be talking to Cort.

What I will do is be nice. I'll be pleasant. Submissive. Demure. Get him to see me as a sexual thing again. Take his mind off my limitations and play up my assets.

This pacifies both my anxiety and my growing hunger pangs. And I settle into sleep with thoughts of that kiss.

Because that's how I will take control of my future.

The kiss was just the start.

When I wake up in the morning Cort's mat has been picked up and I am surrounded by curious birds. Mostly gulls pecking at my hair, like they might pull it out of my head and use it for their nests, but a few albatrosses linger in my vicinity. They are huge birds, so massive, they look fake. When I stand up, their heads are well above my waist. And when I take a step forward to go down to the training level and find Cort, hopeful that we will have breakfast this morning, one of them extends its wings and flaps at me.

That wingspan is so wide, I have to take seven steps to get safely around it.

I take my mat down to the training level and find Cort already jumping rope, his back to me as he does that fancy footwork, traveling down the length of the bare concrete. But when he turns to find me watching him, he stops abruptly and points to the building behind me.

Is he pointing to the kitchen? Hope surges inside me. Did he make breakfast?

My stomach growls so loud just thinking these thoughts, if he wasn't all the way across the platform, he would've heard it. That rumble comes with a dull, gnawing pain.

But when I turn, I realize he was pointing to that small chalkboard mounted on the wall of the kitchen building. My name is still written in white chalk across the top and underneath that, it says, *Jump rope.* Underneath that it says, *Practice drills one, two, and three.*

Not one word about breakfast.

Or lunch. As if.

Or dinner.

I sigh, then glance over my shoulder to see if Cort is watching me. He's not. He's got his back to me. Just jumping his way back down the platform.

I don't know if I can do jump rope today. I don't know if I can do any of this today. I know it's only been four days since I last had a nice meal, but my stomach hurts. Bad.

Rally, Anya, the survivor's voice inside my head says. *Rally and do what you're told. That's how you get out of here intact.*

But then what? What happens to me when we leave this rig?

Nothing good, that's the only thing I know. There is nothing good in my future.

Stick to the plan, Anya. Make him see you as an asset, not a liability.

I'm not sure it will work, but I don't have any other options. I haven't seen a boat around here, so it's not like I can escape. And even though I can see lights off in the distance at night, they are tens of miles away There is no hope of swimming anywhere. I don't even know what country I'm in. Or if this rig is considered part of a country. Perhaps Udulf van Hauten's oil rigs and giant ships are all their own country?

I suddenly notice that the *snick, snick, snick* of Cort's jump rope has stopped. And when I look up, he's watching me. I turn my back to him, pick up my jump rope, and start my day, stomach burning and rumbling, mind a little bit foggy, and my prospects— well, they seem nonexistent at the moment.

I don't do anything fancy. I don't even try to do the single hop. I just can't seem to manage it this morning. I feel like my mind is swimming in the ocean down below and then, without warning, I find myself on the ground, a sharp pain shooting through the back of my head.

My vision goes blurry for a moment and when I force my eyes open, Cort is hovering over my face. He snaps his fingers in front of my eyes when I try to shut them, then he picks me up and carries me inside the little building, setting me down on a small bed in a dark room.

I turn over, ready to fully appreciate this bed, but Cort snaps his fingers again. And when I open my eyes, I see that there is blood on them.

Shit. I reach up, touch the back of my head, realizing I actually hurt myself. I fainted. From lack of food.

Asshole. I scowl at him. Point at him. Accuse him.

He sighs—his default answer with me, it seems. Then he gets up and walks across the hall, leaving this room dark. He flips on the kitchen light and I catch a glimpse of him pulling out the rice maker.

Oh, my smile is sweet. He's going to *feed* me. And all it took was a head injury.

That's cynical, I know. And he deserves a little more credit than that. Because I've fainted from lack of food before and, trust me when I say this, no one carried me to a bed and started making me food afterward.

So I am grateful.

He prepares more than rice too. It only takes a few minutes for me to realize he's making fish. I'm sure it's some disgusting dried fish that has been on this rig for months or even years, but I don't care. I'll eat anything right now.

He comes back, flipping on the light in my room, and then busying himself at a counter on the far wall. That's when I realize I'm in the clinic where he wrapped my hands yesterday.

Cort comes at me quickly, supplies in hand. He slips my feet off the bed and pulls me up to a sitting position, making me turn so he can see the gash on the back of my head. He sighs again.

He's mad, I think. He's mad that he has to feed me. And even though I'm happy about this now, I know everything comes with a price. I will pay for this later. Some way, somehow, this extra meal will come back to haunt me.

Cort presses his hand on the top of my back, right between my shoulder blades, urging me to lean forward. Then he pours something over the wound. Peroxide, from the smell of it. This bubbles against my scalp and he's not very careful about any of it, so the foaming liquid spills down the side of my head and drips over my arm and on to the floor.

He's certainly no Maart when it comes to bedside manner. I saw how Maart cared for Cort after the fight. He was very concerned and careful.

Cort stops pouring and then his fingers are probing the wound. And then he actually mutters, "Fucking hell," under his breath and I turn my face up to him with a smile.

He points at me. Signs something at me with angry fingers—it's probably *Fuck you*—and then pushes me down so I can't look at him.

He takes my hand, places my fingers against a thick wad of gauze over the wound, and applies pressure. I hold it there as he walks over to the counter and starts banging drawers open and closed, looking for something.

What does he need?

When he turns around, he's holding a little white package and a hemostat. I side-eye him, asking him questions with my gaze even though that is totally against all my rules.

He signs something at me—probably *Shut the fuck up, Anya. You're a giant pain in my ass today*—and then tears open the little package and pulls out a needle attached to a suture.

Oh, hell no. I stand up, forgetting about the gauze I'm holding and the pressure I'm supposed to be applying, and feel the blood drip down through my hair. He grabs my arm, shakes me, pushes me down to the floor on my knees, and then tells me to bend over the bed.

He's going to sew that needle through the skin of my head.

He pushes me, further making his point, and so I comply. He sits down on the bed next to me, then pushes my head into his lap.

Hmm. I don't know what to think about that. It's not sexual. Like at all.

But it could be.

I snicker a little and he pinches the inside of my arm, making me hiss. Because that fucking hurt! When I look up at him, he's not messing around. There is no sly smile on his face. That was not a flirt. He's not amused, or charmed by me in any way. He's all business.

So when he points to his lap again, I bend my head down and rest my cheek against his thigh.

He dabs the gauze, then without any warning at all, he stabs me with that needle and begins sewing up my head.

Everything about this is gross—the feeling of the needle, the smell of my own blood mixed with the cooking fish across the hall—and for a moment, I think I'm going to puke.

Cort stops. Like he knows this is coming. But he doesn't pull me up, or hand me a bowl to hurl into, he leans down and *growls* at me. Daring me to throw up on him.

I stop breathing through my nose and swallow it down, keeping my eyes tightly closed as he continues to sew up my scalp.

Finally, he ties it off, gets up, finds a pair of scissors, and cuts me loose. Literally.

There is no, *How are you, Anya? Hanging in there? Feel better now?* No, none of that. He simply drops his equipment onto the counter and leaves, walking across the hall to mess with the food.

I start wondering just how out of the ordinary this type of thing is for Cort. Cooking for someone. Taking care of someone. He doesn't seem like the type. I mean, isn't that why he has that entourage around him? This morning definitely feels like a Maart job.

I watch him get out a bowl, fill it with rice and the steamed fish, and then he pauses and looks down at it, staring at it for a little bit longer than should be normal.

I furrow my brow, trying to read his mind. What is he thinking about?

He doesn't want to give you this food, Anya. Isn't it obvious? There's not enough to go around. And if he gives you this extra, small, meager meal, it means one of us goes without food later.

I want to be that tough girl. That one who says, *You know what? I don't need that food. I can take care of myself.* I've always wanted to be that girl. But I'm not that girl, and I am desperate for that bowl of rice and fish, so I'm not even going to pretend.

Cort turns and looks at me. Then one final look at the bowl and he sets it down on the counter.

I sigh. He's not going to feed me after all. He's decided I'm not worth it.

But then he grabs another bowl. Scoops more rice into it. More fish too. And then he gets two forks, grabs both bowls, and nods his head to me as he walks down the hallway. Not to the door that leads to the training room, but towards the back of the building where the tub room is.

I get up—still slightly dizzy, my hair sticky with blood and a little bit foamy from the peroxide—and follow him.

We end up in a large open room with couches and maybe a dozen small tables with chairs. Hmm. A dining room? Or a living room? Or something in between?

There's a long shelf on one end filled with board games and puzzles. Monopoly. Life. Trouble. Even a beaten-up box of Hungry, Hungry Hippos. There are books too, maybe a hundred of them. No *War and Peace*, no *Moby Dick* or *Wuthering Heights*. There are classic editions of Winnie the Pooh and Beatrix Potter. Tattered paperbacks of Goosebumps and Babysitters' Club.

I am so stunned at the change in scenery—so surprised at the comfy feeling that floods through me at the sight of this room—that I just stand there in the doorway, looking around like a dumbass, forgetting all about the pain in my stomach and the newly stitched-up wound on my head.

Cort bangs a fork on one of the tables, and when I look over at him with a start, he's pointing to the chair across from him. I walk over, unsure how to process what I'm seeing. What we're doing.

What are we doing?

I sit and Cort shoves one of the bowls at me, then slides the fork across the aged varnished surface of the table. He starts eating immediately, eagerly shoveling the rice and fish into his mouth, and I realize he's just as hungry as I am.

Well, of course he is, Anya. He's twice your size and he's working out like a… well. Like a fucking fighter. While you've been halfheartedly skipping some rope and throwing a few punches.

I look around again, still trying to fit the pieces of this place together. What is this? Do they keep kids here? Did he grow up here? Are those his books? His games?

Maybe, but… the Babysitters' Club? That doesn't make sense. Bexxie had those books on her shelf. And before they were hers, they were mine.

The sudden appearance of Bexxie in my thoughts makes me startle and a gasp escapes past my lips. Bexxie. Shit, I forgot all about her. I *left* her. I mean, I knew I was going to leave her, no matter what happened at the end of that fight. But I always thought I'd have time to say goodbye.

The painful rumbling in my stomach fades, the wound on my head forgotten. Bexxie. I left her alone. And I didn't even give her a hug to let her know she was loved.

Cort taps the table with his fork again, but I don't look up at him. I'm suddenly very, very sad. And I don't know if it's all the new stuff I'm dealing with, or the hunger, or the rough stitching of my head I just endured, but it all becomes a little overwhelming. And then the tears leak out of my eyes before I can stop them.

It's not any of those things. It's Bexxie. Because I am suddenly very, very, *very* sure that I will never see her bright, smiling face again. And that might be the most tragic thing to ever happen to me.

Cort sighs, clearly frustrated with me. When I look up, I see a blurry version of him through my tears. He's slouched down in his chair, leaning back, his elbow propped on the chair arm, his fist under his chin. Like he's about ready to throw me over the side of this rig and make me take my chances in the ocean.

And can I blame him? So far he's had to wrap my bloody knuckles, stitch up my head, share his water and food with me, even though we don't have enough for one person, let alone two a at this point, and now I'm sitting here—surrounded by his reluctant kindness—and all I can do is *cry*.

CHAPTER FOURTEEN

What the fuck?

Like, literally, what the actual fuck is wrong with this girl?

I seriously want to slap her. What is her problem now? I've fed her, I stitched up her head, I brought her into the kids' room so she can eat at a fucking table and relax a little, and all she wants to do is *cry*?

I don't get it. I mean, I get girls, OK? I have eight of them back at camp and only one of them would even think about crying in front of me. And she's only four years old, so whatever.

But Anya is a grown-ass woman. Grown women don't *cry*. Especially when I'm going out of my way to not only keep her alive, but keep her comfortable. She's not even eating that food. I'm about to take it from her, eat it myself. Fuck her. Does she have any idea how dearly we'll pay for this extra meal in two weeks?

No. She doesn't. But she will. She's not gonna like that day. At all.

She is weak and I don't know if I can take much more of this.

I don't like weak people. I don't want to take care of her. I don't want to take care of anyone, actually. Maybe Evard, but only on certain occasions. And Anya Bokori is no Evard. She is no one to me. Just a way to piss off Udulf and hopefully get some secrets I can use later to fuck with him or Lazar, if either of them ever forgets who they're dealing with.

But she tires me out. Just thinking about all the stress that's coming—and how she's adding to it—pisses me off. I don't even feel like getting my ass up out of this chair to train, that's how weary she makes me.

So I just... sigh. And stay where I am. Staring at her blotchy face as she wipes her cheeks and works her way through her silent breakdown.

I understand some of it. I do. I've been through the same shit. I was a house boy for a little while, so I get that part. It's all very traumatic. But she's old now. It's over. She's here, she's being fed and cared for— what more does she want from me?

Why did I even bring her here in the first place? Why? I don't even like her.

I mean, maybe I *could* like her. If she wasn't such a stupid *girl*. If she would just do what I tell her without comment. Her silence isn't really silence, anyway. It's filled with all kinds of judgment and expectations.

And who the fuck is *she* to judge *me*?

Her eyes dart up to mine. She lets out a hitched breath, then reaches for her fork and begins to eat.

She eats slowly and takes small bites. I know she has to be hungry. She did go two days without food. I refuse to feel bad about that. It was punishment for being a brat. I have a pre-schooler who is better behaved than Anya. All I wanted her to do was jump some fucking rope. Just keep busy so I could concentrate on myself.

Why is she so dramatic?

She doesn't look at me again, just continues to eat her food. And I should just get up and go out to the training mats. Just get on with my day and leave her here.

But if she's not going to train today—and I don't think it's a good idea, not with the head wound—then what can she do?

Leaving her alone isn't an option. Most people have a hard time with solitude, especially out here in the middle of the ocean. She needs to be kept busy. I learned this a long time ago when I first started taking kids into my camp. They're OK if you keep them busy. You have to take their mind off the past. They need to forget where they came from and only think about the present. That's the only way you get through this shit.

But they are mostly boys, and they are all fighters, and Anya is not only a girl, she's a *weak* girl. I don't know how she's made it this far, to be honest. She would've been knocked out of my world by the time she was six.

Girls don't last long in the gym. There is no *female league* in the ring. You fight whoever they put in front of you. And sure, chances are you're going to get a girl or two. Even I've fought three of them over the years. So if you're a little girl in a training camp you got there for one reason and one reason only. You're not pretty enough or compliant enough to be a slave and you're worth too much for them to kill you without seeing if they can make their money back first.

And if you're a girl in a training camp and you make it to your tenth birthday, you got that far for another reason. The early years are mostly about following directions. But of course, you have skills. At least the beginnings of them. You can take a punch and deliver one back. You've had more black eyes than you can count, two of your ribs always scream when you take a deep breath, you don't smile much, if ever, and your thoughts are mostly consumed with revenge plans that will never pan out.

If you're a girl in a training camp and you make it to sixteen—and I have one that age at my camp—you are a certified badass. You forgot all about your sex. There is no difference between you and the boys you train with on the mat. This is your life and you either like it, or at the very least accept it. You have killed at least ten people to get to this point. And you have no regrets. You dream of making it all the way.

But if you do make it all the way—age twenty or so—you are cold, and demanding, and jaded, and I use them as teachers to keep the little ones in line.

I have three over the age of twenty. We all came up together. Me, Rainer, Maart, Cintia, Ling, and Sissy. That's the only reason they're still alive. We fought for them. And we fought hard. And their loyalty to us is absolute.

But I don't feel too sorry for the girls, because they have it easy compared to us. If you make it to twenty and you're a boy, they are just a younger version of me.

They are out fighting for their own camps. Trying to live long enough to buy their way out, just like I did. But no one makes it. That goalpost is so high and so far away, I can't recall a single fighter in my lifetime who has actually bought their way out.

I will be the first. And even though, at this point in the game, I can't see many ways in which I fail, there are ways. These men who run us can do anything they want. Even rip this reward out from under me for no reason whatsoever.

I'm trusting Udulf to keep his word. But that doesn't mean he will.

Almost no boys make it to twenty. They have even fewer chances than the girls because no one underestimates them in the ring. I've seen the boys when they get face to face with one of my girls. They smile, thinking it's gonna be easy.

But there are no rules in the kind of fighting we do. There are no refs, there are no tap outs, and the only way you get off the platform is by killing your opponent.

So the very first thing I teach my girls is how to go for the balls. There is no weak spot on a female the way there is a man.

Sure, you can hit them in the face. That stuns a girl who hasn't been hit much. But my girls know exactly what to do when a boy, or a man, hits them in the face. So they have no weakness, other than their smaller size and weight, when they step in that ring. And smaller size can always be used to their advantage if they have the right ajarn. And my girls have the best teacher on the planet.

I'm not saying I've got a perfect record when it comes to the girls. I don't take a lot of them, for obvious reasons. And most of them die fighting before they are ten. But the ones who make it to Anya's age—you do not fuck with those women.

I feel a little bad about leaving Cintia, Sissy, and Ling behind when Maart, Rainer, Evard and me walk away with our freedom, but they'll be OK. None of the twisted fucks like Lazar want women like them at their age. They are good for running camps and that's what they'll do for the rest of their lives. Cook, and clean, and teach.

It's the best I can do. I cannot afford to fight for their freedom. I don't have three more fights in me. Hell, I don't think I even have *one* more fight in me. I won't ever admit it—not out loud anyway—but if Anya wasn't on the platform that night, Pavo would've won.

I let out a long exhale, then look over at Anya and see that she's done eating. Her crying is over now, her face wiped dry and her eyes waiting for me to tell her what comes next.

What does come next?

I could just take her back out to the training floor and make her do busy work, work on those moves I showed her yesterday, but it's probably the wrong choice.

So I get up, walk over to the long shelf, and pull out a puzzle.

It's an old one. A black-and-white picture of the Eiffel Tower in Paris. Hell, I think this puzzle has been here since I first started bringing kids out to the Rock. And it's got to be missing a couple dozen pieces by now.

I drop it on the table in front of Anya and point.

I have every intention of leaving her here to do it herself while I go back outside, but then I think, *Shit. How long has it been since I sat down and did a freaking puzzle?*

When was the last time I took a slow day?

So instead, I sit back down, grab the box, take off the lid, and dump out all the pieces. And when I look at Anya, she's not looking at me, she's looking at the table. At all the little jagged edges. And she's smiling.

I smile too, unable to stop it.

She's pretty. A lot prettier than any girl I've been with in the last few years. I don't get to keep the girls I fight for, they go right to Udulf. What he does with them, I have no idea. So it's been a while since I've found myself wanting to stare at the face of a girl sitting across from me.

She looks up, meets my gaze with bright eyes, and I suddenly feel like this is the right way forward.

Make her happy, Cort. Why not? Be nice to her. Feed her better than you have been. Go a little easy on her, even. Because she has no future. None at all. She will probably be dead in six months, or sold as a breeder. Because unlike Sissy, and Cintia, and Ling, she is desirable. Not what Udulf is looking for, the sick fuck. But most men don't have Udulf's twisted sexual preferences.

He's going to sell her. Barter her. Use her in some business negotiation. And that will be that.

So why not? Why not just make her last days happy?

I start flipping pieces over, separating the edges from the middle pieces. Anya does the same and soon enough we have two piles. Then she keeps going, separating them into black, and white, and shades of gray.

I work on a few edge pieces and watch her busily building a section of city behind and to the right of the Eiffel Tower. That's kind of interesting. Most people would do the famous landmark first, but she is concentrating on some random group of buildings in the background.

I continue with the outer edges and eventually both of us are standing up, taking this stupid puzzle seriously.

I finish the edges and she still hasn't touched the tower. So I go for that next. We work quickly and efficiently and pretty soon she's grabbing the pieces I've put together and fitting them into the big picture.

Even though the puzzle is five hundred pieces, it doesn't take us long to finish. And, astonishingly, none of the pieces are missing.

Anya looks down at the completed picture and smiles. Has she been to Paris? Is she having a memory right now?

I've been to Paris a few times myself. Though none of those memories are anything I'd ever want to remember. They were all for fights. In the early days, when the stakes were smaller, and the rings were just gyms, and not helipads on massive billion-dollar ships.

When I look up, Anya is watching me. She points to the puzzle, to the spot she was concentrating on in the beginning. I squint my eyes and lean down to see it better. It's blurry, not meant to really be seen close up. Just something you put together from a distance.

What is it? I sign.

She places the back of one hand on top of her other palm, then presses them to her heart. It's not a real sign, but I think I get her meaning.

Home? I ask.

She smiles. No teeth, just upturned lips and bright eyes.

You come from Paris? I stare at the puzzle, missing her response.

Interesting. Both that she remembers where she came from and that she can pick out the building on a random puzzle in the middle of the ocean.

When I look back up at her, she's watching me expectantly, wondering what we will do next. I hadn't really planned anything after the puzzle. I figured it would take forever. But I don't think we've been here for more than an hour or two. So it's not even lunchtime.

I point to the shelf, then flash signs at Anya, giving her permission to make a decision.

She looks delighted, a spring in her step as she gets up and makes her way over to the shelf, carefully going through the other puzzles. But then she looks at the books and scoots down to pull one out, sitting back on her butt to page through it. It's nothing I recognize, but it looks like something a pre-teen girl would read.

The Country Club Girls. Never heard of it.

But I get up, walk over to Anya, pull the book from her hands, and toss it over my shoulder. She looks up, startled.

She can read that some other time. *We need to do something together*, I sign. *We're not going to read.* Especially not that book, I don't add. *Pick a game.*

She looks back over to the shelf, then crawls over there and pulls out Hungry, Hungry Hippos.

When she looks up at me, she's… smirking.

Seriously, I sign.

She makes motions with her hands, like she's actually making real signs, except she's not, and then gets up and takes the game over to another table and sits down.

Hungry. Hungry. Hippos.

I have never played this game, but I know it's annoying. Because the kids love it. They fight over that game. I'm secretly hoping that the marbles are missing, but I should know better. Five-hundred-piece puzzle and not a single missing piece, so no. All the marbles are there and Anya dumps them in the middle of the hippos, still smirking, but having enough manners to not gloat in my direction. She pushes the game towards the middle of the table and points to the chair across from her.

Bossy. I sit.

Anya has one hand over the marbles and the other already on the lever of the green hippo, ready to make its mouth open and gobble up a win.

Fine. She wants to play? I'll play.

She lifts her hand away from the marbles and then she's flipping the lever on the green hippo. But there are four hippos to play with here, and only two people. So I flip the levers on the other three, my large hands and long fingers reaching round to make it work.

Anya squeals at my cheating, swatting my hand off the pink one and taking over.

For about thirty seconds, we are children. Stupid, happy children. She even stands up, getting all serious about winning.

And she does win. Then, when it's all over, we do it again. And again. And again.

It is probably the most carefree moment I've had in… well, maybe ever.

After about a dozen games, we get tired of it. I go to the shelf next and pick Connect Four. This was always my favorite. I don't play games much, but Rainer loves them. And he will endlessly taunt me until I give in.

She wins the first game, but I let her. I kick her ass in the next five. And then she gets up and grabs Trouble. Another annoying game. Why does she like the loud ones?

We do this for hours. I pick Risk. She picks Perfection. I pick Clue. She picks Operation. And you'd think that the batteries in these loud-ass games would be dead, but no. The fuckers still work.

I pick Battleship. She picks Mouse Trap. We smile. I laugh out loud dozens of times. She huffs a little, her vow of silence too practiced to laugh back. But she is happy, anyone could see that—her hunger this morning a long-lost memory, the gash on her head and my haphazard stitching something from another lifetime. And it occurs to me, later, after I've made dinner and we're back outside, sitting along the beam eating our rice and rehydrated chicken, that I've never had so much fun in my life.

I've certainly never had a day like this out on the Rock.

I really do like this place, but when the kids are here, my thoughts are consumed with fighting. With skill levels. With the stress of who will be the next to die. And when I'm alone, I just slip into some quiet, somber life with the birds, and the moon, and the sea.

I've never spent time with a girl like this. For a moment I wonder if this is what dating is like.

Anya sighs with contentment when we lay our mats on the platform. Then she makes the sign for 'moon,' pointing at it, the way I taught her last night. But she uses three fingers and that's not right.

I grab her hand out of the air and she looks over at me, startled. Then I position her fingers into four.

We are on day four. She looks at her fingers, then the moon, and huffs a laugh, getting it.

The moon keeps time for us out here. That's how we measure the month.

She stares up at it, fully aware that I am watching her. But she ignores me for nearly a minute before she turns her head and meets my gaze. Then she reaches for my hand and, using her pointer finger, she writes 'thank you' on my palm, one letter at a time.

She goes to pull away, but I grab her hand back, then use my finger to write on her palm. *Why?*

She watches me spell out this word. But I know, before she looks up at me and shakes her head, what her answer will be.

Not even this day filled with food, and games, and smiles, and laughter, and a perfect night under a waning moon can make her answer that question. And for a moment, I'm conflicted. Do I even want to know?

It's not gonna be good. It's gonna be evil. People don't stop talking after amazing things happen. They stop talking because they have lost all control over everything else in their life and this one act of defiance is all they have left.

But Udulf and Lazar. There is something there. Something that feels like a threat. To her, for sure, but to me as well. Maybe even Maart, and Rainer, and Evard.

And if it were just me in danger, then fuck it. I'd fight my way through it. But when I asked Udulf for the chance to fight for Maart, and Rainer, and Evard, I tipped my hand. And now he knows what I find dear.

I will walk away from the rest of them, but not those three.

So I need to know what I'm up against. I can't afford to let Anya Bokori wrap her secrets in silence. Not if knowing them will keep me and the only family I have left safe.

But I know how to play people. I know how to get what I want when I want it. I know how to lie, and cheat, and steal with the best of them.

More importantly, I have the sick heart. I can turn that shit on and off at will.

I can stop caring. Easily slip in the skin of a cold-blooded killer. A very patient, very slow, very deliberate cold-blooded killer. And I do that now when I reach for her and pull her close, when I kiss her head and wrap my arms around her like a warm blanket.

I lie to her with these actions. Because they tell her she is safe. And she is not.

Not from Udulf.

Not from Lazar.

And certainly not from me.

I love three people in this world. And everything I do, I do for them.

But her guard is down. I didn't plan this day for that reason, but it *is* the final outcome. And of the many ruthless things I've learned over my twenty-seven years of life, the one at the top of the list is, *Give people what they expect.*

If I had tried this yesterday, she would've been suspicious. But after a long, soft, slow day she expects a long, soft, slow night.

So that's exactly what I give her.

CHAPTER FIFTEEN

ANYA

His arms wrap around me like a warm cloak, his chest rising and falling against my back in a slow, easy, predictable rhythm. I can feel his lips on the back of my neck, not kissing me, just… there.

My body stiffens as I hold my breath. And he feels this. He is in tune with me. Because his arms tighten a little, offering me comfort. *It's OK*, his arms say. *We're safe*, his slow breathing proclaims. And even though I know better, I exhale and decide to believe him.

I am safe, at least from outsiders.

But from him? I'm not so sure.

Today was good. I did faint from hunger and bang my head, but I got two meals today and my wound is clean and cared for. He didn't make me train. In fact, our day was pretty fun. The puzzle was a nice surprise, because my home base was there in that picture. And the memory of it was always sweet. It was always nice to go to that place in Paris. It would wipe away everything that has just happened. All the awful weeks that led up to Paris would be swept away and I would be rewarded with shopping, and bathtubs, and an older, careful woman who only spoke Hungarian. And even that was nice. As much as I hate to admit it, the Hungarian, like Paris, felt like home.

I don't have a lot of sweet, soft memories so what are the odds that, on this sweet, soft day with the killer called Sick Heart, I would find my home base in a puzzle on an abandoned oil rig?

I couldn't even begin to calculate those odds, but surely they are one in a billion. One in a trillion.

But the point is, this slow, sweet night isn't entirely out of place. One thing leads to another. That's how we got here.

So why am I so suspicious of him?

Hmm, Anya. Why indeed? He's a mentally unstable professional killer who just won you in a fight, plopped you down on a crumbling rig in the middle of the ocean, and has a creepy game room tucked away filled with things only children can appreciate.

It should make sense. He felt sorry for me this morning. That led to a break in his schedule, which led to extra food, and fun times in a game room clearly meant for the younger kids in his training camp.

That's all this is. It's very clear. It all makes sense. Up until the point when he asked me why. *Why don't you talk, Anya?*

I've been asked that question thousands of times. Hell, Bexxie alone has asked it a few hundred, at least. I've never answered any of them, so I'm sure as hell not going to answer Cort van Breda.

But it was a tell. A sign that he is playing me.

And he's good, I'll give him that. Because I would like nothing more than to melt my back into his chest and let him make me feel safe.

Instead, I just feel sad, all the good of this day wiped away from his deception. So I turn onto my stomach, breaking his tight hold on me, and just close my eyes to make it all go away.

I wait for a little before letting myself drift off. Wait to see if he will accept my rebuke, or fight it.

He doesn't fight it. He doesn't even seem to notice. Maybe he's even asleep. But I doubt it. He's a predator and they live in the night. They know how to use the darkness to their advantage.

But I have been hunted by predators far more dangerous than he is my entire life.

And I know how to be silent and slip away.

When I wake in the morning, Cort is over near one of the nests petting a super-sized chick. I don't move. Don't let him know I'm awake so I can watch.

He must've just woken up because his sleeping mat is in his other hand, like he was just about to take it downstairs to the training floor. He has a crooked smile on his face as one of the parents wanders up to him, extending its open beak towards Cort in what I might consider a threatening gesture. But Cort just gives the giant creature a scratch on the head, and the bird closes its eyes in grateful happiness.

I don't understand this man. At all.

He feels very human. But I saw him. With my own eyes. I saw him drag that knife across Pavo's neck, then down the length of his torso, then literally rip his heart out and throw it at Lazar before dragging Pavo across the helipad and throwing him off the ship.

And fine. I helped him with all of that. But my role in that night was circumstance. It wasn't something I do for a living.

He looks over his shoulder at me, like he can feel my gaze. He nods his head at me, smiling, then beckons me with a crooked finger.

I get up, grab my mat, and follow him down the stairs. We drop our mats off, then he goes inside the kitchen. I follow, holding my breath to see if we will get breakfast. And we do. Not rice—he must not be in the mood to cook, because he hands me a strip of dried fish.

I look at it dubiously. Yesterday I would've gobbled this up, no questions asked. But I'm not that hungry today. Still, if I refuse, he might not feed me tonight. So I take it, smile, and begin gnawing on it like jerky.

Cort finishes his food quickly, letting the long strip hang out of his mouth as he pokes around in the clinic, and by the time he points to one of two chairs, directing me to sit, he's done eating.

I sit on the chair and he maneuvers a rolling table between me and the other chair and orders me to put my hands on it. I do, and he sits and begins peeling off the old wrappings. Then he fills a bowl with hot water and salts, motions for me to place my hands inside, and gently rubs the dried blood away. When my knuckles are clean, he begins massaging my palms, the pads of his fingers and thumbs pushing into the muscles, kneading them and loosening them up.

This feels quite nice and I begin to question my conclusions about him. Maybe I was being overly cynical last night about his motives? Maybe he isn't a monster?

It's so hard to tell. It's so hard to know if I should assign malice to the things he does. That game room, for instance. It could mean he cares about the kids he trains. And that's probably everyone's first impression.

But I've seen things like that before. I've seen how tricky predators can be with children. Think about it. What better way to lure a child into the demon's den than to entice them with innocent, childish things? That game room could be the equivalent of a man in a white van asking a kid if they want some candy.

Nothing is what it seems. Not where I come from.

And I hate that. I really hate that. I wish I could just look back on yesterday and appreciate the puzzle and games as something innocent. I wish I could just enjoy the way he's touching me right now. But instead I have all this suspicion.

When I glance up at him, he's not looking at me, all his attention focused on my hand. He drops it back into the bowl of hot water and picks up the other one, repeating his slow massage. And I can't help it. My shoulders drop and I begin to relax a little.

He glances up at me, noticing the change in my posture, and offers me a small smile.

I look away. I'm not going to fall for it. I've seen too much to fall for it.

After about a minute, Cort takes the bowl away and places it in the sink. Then he comes back with a towel and pats my hands dry.

He motions to me with his fingers. *Stand up,* I think he's saying. So I do. And he turns my chair around so the seat back is facing him, then directs me to sit and rest my right forearm on the top.

I do this and he begins wrapping my wrist and hand with gauze, stopping briefly to add a thick wad of cotton padding over my knuckles. He motions for me to make a fist, and open my fist, and make a fist again dozens of times as he carefully winds the gauze through my fingers, over my knuckles and thumb in a figure eight, and around my wrist. It takes several minutes for him to finish and by the time he's done, everything is tight with tape.

He does the other hand as I watch, then he stands up, puts his chair back and begins to box the air, bouncing on his feet, twisting his hips, and making hissing sound effects as he punches. Then he points to me and I roll my eyes, embarrassed. But just as I do that his hand darts towards me and slaps my cheek.

I back up, startled. What the fuck?

He does it again, not smacking me hard or anything, but still. What the hell?

He pauses his bouncing and shakes his head. Then he brings one fist up to his cheek and points to it, then to me.

Oh. I get it. I'm supposed to block him. I put my hand up to my cheek but before I can even process anything else, he slaps me again, this time harder.

I back up, but he takes a step forward. So I back up again and hit the cot. This sends me falling backwards onto the thin mattress.

Cort pauses and shakes his head, then offers me a hand and pulls me to my feet. He leans into my face so we are eye to eye. Then he takes my left hand and places it against my cheek, gripping my fist firmly in his, like he's making a point.

I get it. He wants me to leave my hand there to protect my face, but then he just smacks me on the other cheek instead. I swing at him, backing him off.

He finds this delightful. Because he's smirking at me, bouncing from one foot to the next as he circles me in a fighter's dance. He points to his cheek. *Hit me.*

You don't gotta tell me twice. I swing, but he blocks me and dances out of the way, smacking my cheek again. Only this time, it fucking stings. Dick.

He's smiling big now, throwing fake punches at me with one fist as he points to his cheek with the other.

I just stand there. Why even bother? I'm never going to make it past his blocks. So I just leave the clinic and walk out to the training platform. Because if he took almost an hour to wrap up my hands, there is no chance we are going to spend today doing puzzles.

He follows me out, picks up our jump ropes, throws mine at me, and then he starts skipping down the length of the platform. Doing all kinds of crazy things with that rope.

I jump. And I don't complain. He fed me, wrapped up my hands, and let me rest for a whole day. I have no excuse today so I jump.

We do this for what seems like a very long time. At least an hour because I start and stop about a hundred times, so out of breath, so out of shape, it starts to become embarrassing. Because Cort is doing hops, and double jumps, and these high-jump things, and never once does his rope get caught in his feet.

Being around him on the training platform is nothing but a long lesson in self-loathing. I am not *un*fit. I sigh. I'm just not… *fit*, either.

This makes me chuckle a little and when I look over at Cort, I find him watching me. He finishes his skipping, takes my rope, as well as his, and tosses them both onto the floor near the wall. Then he points to the chalkboard with my name on it. It still has yesterday's schedule of drills one, two, and three on it. I don't even remember what they were.

But Cort directs me onto the mat and shows me again. Baby-step punch, retreat punch, hip-pivot cross.

Right. Got it.

I do them and he watches for a little bit, coming in to correct my form and then stepping back several times. Then he nods and gives me the signal to keep going and takes himself over to another mat where he begins some slow martial arts-type shit I haven't seen him do before.

His back is to me, so even though I don't stop my drills, I don't really pay attention to them, either. I pay attention to him. The way his back muscles stretch as he does a series of slow moves that look a little bit like tai chi. He has one massive piece of art on his back— two full-body skeletons doing martial arts. One of them has lost a leg, one only has a single arm. They are bleeding from the eyes and their mouths are x-ed out with black electrical tape. The one with two hands is signing something. I don't know what that sign means, I just know it's a sign. And there's an angel—a little girl with no face and soft, feathery wings—floating between his shoulder blades.

All around the two fighters are people watching. Dead people. Decaying people. All of them with x-ed out eyes.

It's a fight, of course. One of his, probably. He pivots on the mat so we're facing each other again. I am still moving my feet and my hands, but my effort is all very who-gives-a-fuck.

Suddenly Cort is coming at me, fist in front of him, punching the air. I back up, but he sprints and then he's slapping my face again. Only this time, he's not playing. It fucking hurts.

He dances a circle around me, jabbing, trying to hit me. Well, not trying very hard. More like threatening to hit me. Then he points to my fist and places his fist against his cheek, telling me to block.

Fuck that. I shake my head, letting him know I'm not playing a losing game with him again, but the sting from his next slap makes me gasp out loud. And that sting lingers as heat for many seconds as I just stare at him in pissed-off rage.

I flip him off and he laughs. Out loud. It's low, and deep, and for a moment it stuns me and I get lost imagining what his voice really sounds like.

Deep, I think.

And just as those words flash though my head he's got me by the legs and I am slammed into the mat so hard he knocks the wind out of me. I gasp for air, sucking in with a sick wheezing sound. He wraps his arms around my shoulders, pins me, knees gripping my hips, and places his head into the crook of my neck and whispers, "You better fight back, Anya. Because if you don't, I'll make you wish you had."

Then he's up. Bouncing back on the mat. Hands in front of his face like I am some kind of threat.

I get up on my hands, scooting backwards. What the fuck?

His words echo in my head. He said them in a soft voice, but they were not soft words. That was a threat.

He points to me, then lifts his finger in an upward motion, telling me to get to my feet. When I don't, he rushes forward and sweeps his foot just over the top of my head. So close, I feel the wind he creates against my hair.

I am breathing so hard, I'm gasping, still not able to draw in a full breath from the hard fall. But I scramble to my feet and quickly step away from him.

His eyes narrow on me. Like he's zeroing in on his target.

What the hell? I can't fight this man.

He dances forward and jabs at me, his fist coming so close to my face, I swear I feel the kiss of his knuckles against my lips. I strike, hitting him in the neck, and he laughs, bouncing backwards out of reach. Then he nods, and beckons me with his fingers. Daring me to do it again.

But before I can plan anything, he's already slapped my face again. And he's not playing. Because that shit hurts. And in the half-moment that I'm thinking those words, he slaps me again.

I rush him, swinging wildly. He doesn't back off. He covers his face with his fists and lets me land every single punch. Mostly I punch his hands, which is stupid, but I get one past them and hit his throat.

He starts coughing as he bounces backwards. Well, it might actually be a laugh and not a cough. But I did hit him.

He smiles as his feet stop and his posture straightens. His fists fall down to his chest and he nods at me.

I hold my breath, waiting for him to talk again. But he doesn't. He just points to the mat and quickly runs through my series of drills. Putting a lot of force behind the fake punches and a lot of effort into his feet.

Then he stops again and points to me, narrowing his eyes and growling. A clear threat that says, *Do not half-ass your work in my gym.*

I let out a long breath and salute him with two fingers.

Message received, Sick Heart.

Then I turn my back on him before he can say anything else and get back to work.

CHAPTER SIXTEEN

Anya came out here this morning thick with memories of yesterday's soft landing. Hazy with the kindness I showed her in the clinic as I wrapped her hands. Comforted with the extra food I put inside her belly.

I knew she would. That's why I turned my back on her when I started the kata. I have trained hundreds. I am not a fool. I know that when I turn my back the natural instincts kick in. Few people work harder when they can get away with working less and Anya is nothing special. It is only when you are watched—only when you think your effort might be rewarded—that you put in full effort.

Her face has to be stinging. I hit her quite hard a couple times. But she's the one who let her guard down, not me.

I return to my place on the mat and start my kata over again. She keeps her back to me through the entire thing, repeating her three simple drills. I watch her carefully for any sign of slacking, but even though she tires and her form becomes sloppy by the time I move on to my own drills, she doesn't repeat her no-fucks attitude again.

Sometime around noon I take her over to the bag and show her the punches I want her to work on. The padding I put over her knuckles will keep her from bleeding through the gauze and tape, but she will split those wounds open again today. She won't know it until I take her wraps off though. That's the important part.

Perception is ninety percent of reality. Thinking it's true makes it true. And if she thinks that padding is protecting her, then it is.

Her real test will come tomorrow when she knows better. But for today, she is blissfully unaware. The pain she feels when she punches the bag will be attributed to her prior wounds.

When I lead her over to the middle of the mat in the late afternoon her face is red, and sweaty, and she has been breathing like an asthmatic for several hours now.

But I don't care. We started this day with a lesson she failed. So she's going to get over that before we stop.

As soon as we're in the middle, I turn on her. My fingertips have slapped her cheek before she even knows what's happening.

But she reacts this time. A full day of focus has prepped her for this.

I reach out again, but this time she blocks me. It's a sloppy block that I could easily penetrate, but I'm not really *trying* to slap her. I just need to teach her that first girl lesson. Men *will* hit you in the face. There is nothing you can do about that. All you can do is mitigate.

I strike again, but her block is better this time. I bounce from foot to foot, dancing a circle around her. She's not light on her feet—there is no bouncing—but she hops a little, mimicking her bad form with the jump rope, as she tries to keep up with me.

I strike again, but this time she surprises me with an attempted left hook as she blocks. She doesn't connect, not even close, but I pause and smile down at her. Then close my eyes, bow, and straighten up.

She's scowling at me when I open my eyes again. I make a gesture of, *Your turn.*

She thinks about that for a moment, then gives me something between a nod and a head bow.

It's pathetic, but I'll take it. I close the distance between us with my hands at my sides, then clap her on the back, place both hands firmly on her shoulders, and turn her towards the stairs. But instead of going up, I direct her to go down.

She balks, probably thinking back to her punishment. But I just go first and make her follow me.

It was almost unbearably hot today, but I can't get Anya used to a daily shower. We'll run out of water, and unlike food, fresh water isn't something we can replace without a lot of effort to collect rainwater and I don't feel like collecting rainwater this time around. Salt water, on the other hand, is plentiful.

Anya follows me, her footsteps tentative at first, and when I pass the level where I locked her up, she pauses on the landing near the gate, unsure if she wants to follow me down. I look over my shoulder and wink, which makes her frown at me, her brows furrowed together in a look of confusion. Then I beckon her with a crooked finger and leave it at that.

Hey, if she wants to go to sleep tonight dripping with sweaty grime, that's her choice, I guess. But not me. I'll take a dip in the ocean over nothing any day.

I go all the way down the steps until I'm standing on a long, narrow landing about twenty feet above the water. Everything down here is slick with algae and when the tide is low, you can get a peek at what's underneath the surface. But it's not low now so all I can see is the thick tendrils of dark green algae waving at me, inviting me to jump in.

Anya comes up behind me and when I turn, I just barely manage to grab her arm before her bare feet slip on the slick surface and she goes down. She grabs onto me, gripping my forearm as she scrambles her feet, trying to get her balance.

I don't need to study her eyes for long before I realize she's afraid. What's that about? Me? Does she think I brought her down here to kill her? If that's it, she's just dumb. So what is it? She can't swim? She's afraid of heights? Maybe a little bit of all of the above?

All of this is very bad news for poor Anya here. But this day started with face-slapping. I gotta round it all out with an equally impactful lesson. Something for her to ponder as she lies under the moon tonight. Something for her to chew on. Something for her to learn from.

I smile at her, and she, being the insightful girl she is—i.e. one who not only survived a childhood of slavery, but somehow defied her lot in life as Lazar's fight night sacrifice—understands immediately that this is not a good smile.

Not for her, anyway. But I'm enjoying myself.

I wrap my arms around her, pinning her arms tight against her body. She grabs at them, frantic, afraid, and on the verge of panic. But my feet are already moving towards the edge of the platform. There is no time for a tantrum. No time for anything but the soft low words I whisper into her ear as I jump off the platform, taking her with me. "Hold your breath, Anya. Or this is gonna go bad real fast."

I don't know if she does that. Because we are already falling. And then we plunge feet-first into the ocean and the world shifts from sharp, sunshine clarity to murky, slow-motion blur.

We shoot down like a bullet. At least twenty feet under the rig. The sun is nowhere near close to setting, but it's lower on the horizon so the rays from above filter down from the surface at just the right angle to partially illuminate the dark water below the rig.

Anya is squirming in my arms. I have her restrained at the elbows, so her hands are free to try to pry at my grip. But I hold tight for a few more seconds, just enough for her to calm down and see what I need her to see.

It's easy to know when she does that, because she goes completely still. We are already floating back up towards the light, but it's a slow ascent. More than enough time for her to study the legs of the platform through the haze of bubbles and see the breathtakingly beautiful reef the ugly rig above is hiding.

Large bubbles float out of her mouth, like maybe she just gasped, and I allow myself a smile as we break the surface and I let her go.

She is coughing and sputtering. But she turns towards me, the shock of the drop replaced by the surprise of the secret reef. She's not sinking, and her panic is gone, replaced by delight. She smiles at me, frantically wiping at her eyes and trying to catch her breath.

I cock my head at her and then dive back down. She follows me. I swim around to the other side of the platform leg and watch her study a dozen different kinds of coral and aquatic plants that completely cover the steel underneath. Small schools of fish flitter around us, darting this way and that as bigger fish slowly pass by.

Anya reaches out towards a coral, but I grab her hand and pull it back, shaking my head at her. Some of them sting. And I'm not really sure which ones those are, so the general rule is that we don't touch them.

She looks back at the reef, then up at the surface. I know she can't hold her breath much longer, but she is reluctant to go back up.

It makes sense though. This silent world is familiar. That's why I like it. And when I first discovered that the rig's platform had actually created an artificial reef back when I was a kid, I felt like I had been dropped into a book. One of those boys' adventure books where they survive a plane crash or a sinking ship and end up on a tropical island with secrets.

I found my island's secret.

Finally, there is no way she can hold her breath any longer and she shoots up to the surface. I follow, and emerge just a moment later.

And then we just float there. Two inconsequential people immersed in a whole planet of water. I try not to see myself like that when I'm out here. I try not to picture this platform from space, a speck surrounded by the massive weight of the ocean. And then me, just dust, really, in the grand scheme of things. Because when I see this world for what it really is, that thought evokes a sense of overwhelming... *smallness*.

Our problems are so small from the perspective of the universe. But to us, they are often overwhelming.

I try to keep it all in perspective, but it's hard when you're surrounded by evil people who want to torture you for fun. Make you fight and kill for money, and ships, and women.

Anya puts her face in the water and just floats like that. Belly down, arms out, body undulating with the rhythm of the ocean. Like she's snorkeling without equipment. Every now and then she tilts her head to the side for a breath, and then she resumes her study of the reef.

I roll over and lie on my back, floating with her, my fingers twisted up in her t-shirt so she can't float away, my eye on the beams above, keeping it in perspective. It would be a mistake to assume that we are anchored to this platform just because we're underneath it. It would be very easy to float away. Too easy, actually, to float so far there is no chance of getting back. Even a very strong swimmer might not be able to fight the will of the ocean's path around a rotating earth.

But we don't float far. We just bob with the waves. Up and down. I let her gaze down, but I don't let her dive alone. No one dives alone out here. Ever. Not even me. That's why we keep a stash of food out here. Because fishing by myself is a risk Maart won't let me take.

Soon though. Soon, Anya and I will run out of protein and we will have to fish this reef. It's gonna suck, but it's at least ten days away, so I push that thought aside when she turns over on her back and floats face up with me, her fingers twisted up in the loose fabric of my shorts, mine still holding fast to her t-shirt.

And it's nice, I think. To float with her. To be with her. Just two people gazing up at a low, hot sun.

I turn my head and look at her. She's got her eyes closed. But her skin is getting cold and she's starting to shiver. So I grab her hand and we call it a day.

We have to climb a slimy ladder to get back up to the long, metal landing. I make her go first, just in case she slips. Also so I can look at her ass through the thin, wet fabric of her shorts, but mostly to keep her safe. She's sustained enough injuries over the past week.

We both have. It's time to settle into this now.

Once on the landing she begins to shiver for real, wrapping her arms around herself in an attempt to keep warm. The sun is on the other side of the rig, so we're in the shade and there's no hope of getting warm down here. But once we climb all the way up to the helipad, the heat of the sun is a relief.

She stands in the middle, face tipped towards the final rays of the day.

But I grab her hand and lead her over to a ladder on the side of the mechanical building. This one is not coated with algae, but the paint is pitted and flaking from decades of salt water and sun.

Once we're on top of the roof the wind is free to whip past us, blowing her t-shirt up like a balloon and making her scramble to keep it from flipping up. I shrug when she looks at me, embarrassed after partially flashing me her tits, and she sucks in a deep breath and points her face back at the sun.

I do the same, closing my eyes and opening my arms wide, letting the hot wind flow past me. I crack one eye open when Anya walks up next to me and smile when she does the same.

I'm not exactly tired. I would not call this a particularly strenuous training day. Most of the time I was distracted by Anya. But I'm tired in other ways, the way I was that day we spent inside. Weary. So I drop down to the roof and lie back, hissing a little when my back touches the sun-baked concrete.

Anya drops down beside me, sighing when she realizes how warm the roof is. I peek at her again. Her eyes are closed and her shirt drying from the wind. Less than a week on the Rock and her hair is already a tangle of unruly, blonde-streaked waves and her skin is already losing the too-pale look she had when I first saw her back on the ship. Her cheeks are pink, but her arms and legs are starting to turn a nice shade of golden brown.

I look back up at the sun and close my eyes, letting the yellow orb stain the back of my eyelids. This feels nice. The way yesterday felt in the game room. Comfortable.

Anya flips over on her stomach, hands under her cheek like a pillow, her head turned away from me. She looks like she's ready to fall asleep.

I turn over as well. Then my fingertips are pulling up her t-shirt, exposing the small of her back.

She goes stiff and sucks in a breath.

I drag the tips of my fingers lightly over her skin, tracing a pattern and making it prickle up in goosebumps.

She doesn't move.

I know what she thinks. She thinks I want sex. And maybe I do. But mostly I don't.

I have decided that I will not use sex to get her secret. It's not fair. I would be one of them if I did that, and I'm not one of them. I might kill for them on command, but I am not one of them.

So no, I'm really not thinking about fucking her. I'm thinking about knowing her.

And that is a far, *far* more dangerous thing. Because once I know her, I won't be able to unknow her, will I?

And I'm already about to walk away from almost three dozen people I know very well. I'm not sure I can add another one to that list and live with myself afterward.

But then she turns her head my way and opens her eyes. They are blue—I know they are blue—but right now, the sunlight plays tricks and turns them the color of the sea. Deep green one moment, bright teal the next. The corners of her mouth lift up into a small smile and she stares at me.

What does she see? The killer? The trainer? The game player? The diver? Which of these men is the one she likes?

Definitely not the killer or the trainer. Which is too bad. Because that's who I am ninety-nine percent of the time.

She frowns, like she's reading my mind. And she might be. You get good at reading expressions when people don't talk. You learn to see inside them. You learn how to know them without their consent.

But this is a dangerous path to go down so I slip my hand up her shirt instead. She closes her eyes, but opens them back up almost immediately.

Closing them is giving in. You don't have to be a mind reader or a mute to know that. And she's not the kind of girl who gives in without a fight.

But that's what I do best. I'm a fighter. So this comes off like a challenge to me.

I begin tracing bigger patterns over her entire back. Figure eights and spirals. Squiggly lines that start between her shoulder blades and end up in the small of her back, just above the waistband of her borrowed shorts. I keep my touch feather light and super soft. She winces and closes her eyes again, tensing her shoulders.

And this is a dead giveaway for ticklishness. So I poke her.

She giggles and draws back, opening one squinty eye to warn me with a half-assed glare.

I tsk my tongue and sloppily sign, *Don't warn me, girl. That's just another challenge*, with one hand.

She can't even follow two-handed sign language, let alone my made-up shorthand. So she squints her eye a little tighter, putting some threat behind her warning.

I almost laugh, but then poke her again instead.

She wriggles away this time. But I grab her and pull her back. Poking her a few more times just to prove I can. She twists and kicks and elbows me as she tries to get away. But in my arms, she is very small. And all I have to do is hold her tight to make her helpless. I don't even need to use both arms. So I have one free hand to keep poking.

She goes nuts. Like… this is the girl I want to see on the mat downstairs. That's how nuts she goes. Her back is bucking, her knees are jabbing, and she's laughing out loud.

God, she has a nice laugh. It's a little high-pitched, like it was that first time we met on the ship. But it rolls too. Smooth and easy. Something you want to hear more of, not less. And suddenly, that's all I can think about.

I want to hear her voice. Is it deep or soft? Hard or sweet?

I stop poking and rearrange my body so I'm just a little bit over the top of her, propped up on my elbows. I put one hand up and slowly sign, *Talk to me.* It's an easy sign and she gets it, because she goes tense again, then shakes her head no. But then she repeats my signs back with modifications, pointing at me, tapping her chin with a sideways hand, and then pointing to herself. *You talk to me.*

I already did.

She shakes her head and makes a sign for 'whisper.'

And now it's my turn to go tense and just stare at her for a moment.

Because she got it right. The sign is 'talk,' but if your other hand is cupped on the side of your mouth, it means 'whisper.' Like you're gonna whisper in someone's ear.

Did she just… I squint at her and she frowns in response. Has she taught herself sign language?

That's not possible. Not this fast. It hasn't even been a week.

Then whisper to me, I sign.

She shakes her head again. And then she touches my lips with the edge of her fingertips and slowly drags them up my cheek before pulling away.

'Kiss.' That was the sign for 'kiss.'

She wants me to kiss her.

I know this is a distraction. I know who I'm dealing with. A girl who has been silent so long, no one remembers her last spoken words. A girl who should be dead, but isn't. A girl who should be anywhere but here with me, but is. A girl who four days ago didn't know a single bit of sign language, and now knows enough to stun me silent.

So I should really know better.

I should push her. Keep going. Because I could *make* her talk. I know I could.

But then she leans towards me. And we're not that far apart, so that kiss she just asked for is now an absolute guarantee.

Our lips touch and just… linger there for a breath.

And so many things go through my mind in that breath. I want to resist her offer. Push her down, roll over, and forget where I'm at and who I'm with.

But that's just fucking stupid. I like this girl. A lot.

I want to kiss her.

And all those other thoughts earlier about not wanting sex… well. This seems like more than sex. So that's something I am interested in.

When our lips touch everything that happens next—whether it's today, tomorrow, or next year— everything that happens next is preordained. And there's no way to stop it.

I cup my hands around her face, my thumbs caressing small circles on her cheeks as her mouth opens and her tongue touches mine.

There is maybe one more moment. One more chance to stop the car crash that's coming, but it's such a small moment, so short and tiny, it barely exists.

And what comes next is pure lust.

I open my mouth, kiss her hard. Bite her lip, grab her breasts as I drop my full weight over her.

She kisses me back. But her kiss isn't urgent, like mine. It's soft. And even though we're stained with salt water, and sweat, and the wind, she tastes so sweet, I want this kiss to last forever.

Her fingernails dig into the muscles of my back and I hiss a little. Because she's not being gentle. The time for gentleness is over now and all that's left is sex.

She knows it as well as I do. Because she helps me get her shorts off. She's the one who takes off her shirt as I watch, my eyes drawn to her tight nipples and perfectly shaped breasts. The fading bruises on her skin left over from the fight just add to my desire.

This girl saved my life. And that's so fucking hot, I flip her over so she's on top of me, ready to show her how grateful I am.

She smiles and her eyes dance with mischief, or playfulness, or maybe just power. Her wild, tangled hair falls forward to brush against my chest as I pull her face down to mine and claim her mouth.

She's naked, but I'm not. Her fingertips are tugging on my shorts as we kiss, our tongues dancing as they twist together as she pulls my shorts over my hips. Her hand is between my legs, grabbing for my cock. It's hard and thick. And when she squeezes me and begins slowly pumping her hand up and down my shaft, I have to hit pause on this moment and close my eyes so it can't slip by without me noticing.

Anya's lips on my cheek make me open them again. She's leaning over me, her full, round breasts pressing against my chest. Her ass is up in the air a little, and I smack it, and grab it, and smack it again. Hard. I want to leave marks on this girl.

I want to leave *my* mark on this girl.

She must be a mind reader. Because her mouth dips down to my neck and she bites me. She doesn't nip me. No, she fucking *bites* me. Hard enough to make me hiss. Then she is kissing her way down my chest, her hand still on my cock, still working it, her thumb caressing small circles over the tip on the upstroke.

I sigh a little, so fucking grateful I brought her here. She was worth the fight. Worth the price, too.

Because I don't just like her, I *want* her.

Her lips reach my stomach and she licks my abs, dragging her tongue across the taut muscles. I put my hands on her head, ready to push her face down to my dick and put it in her mouth, but she pulls back a little, just enough to look up at me, and says, "Shhhhhhhhh," with that pouty fucking mouth of hers.

This is enough to calm me down. At least for a moment. Because shushing me is sound. And I want to hear all the sounds from this girl right now.

She scoots down a little more and I know it's coming, so I twist her hair around my fingers and promise to let her take her time.

It pays off. Because she knows exactly what to do with my fat cock.

She doesn't put it inside her mouth. Not at first. She teases the fuck out of me. Her tongue dances around the tip of my dick, her hand still squeezing, her thumb still massaging the head. And I give in.

Fuck it. I give in.

I just close my eyes and picture it all in my head as she licks me. Up and down my shaft. Over the tip, then down again. Her hand slips down to grab my hard, tight balls, squeezing them just a little as her other hand sends her fingertips exploring the sensitive skin just underneath. She places her mouth low on my shaft, then lets it slowly dip down until she's wrapping her lips around my balls.

I twist her hair a little tighter in my fingers, pulling on her scalp. But if she objects, or even notices, she doesn't say anything.

Then her mouth is moving back up, her hand once again squeezing my shaft, and then there it is. Her hot breath caressing the tip of my cock. Her tongue flicking over it. Her mouth open and ready.

I groan with anticipation, unable to stop my primal reaction to her seduction, and then I push her face down, forcing my dick inside her. She accepts my command and opens wider, letting it slip to the back of her throat, and I swear to God, I've had plenty of blow jobs in my lifetime, but this isn't a fucking blow job. She is making love to my dick.

I rock my hips forward, fucking her face a little. She responds by getting up on all fours, balancing on hands and knees as she devours my cock.

I slap her ass again. This feels good—very fucking good—but I want to push this girl down on the ground face first and take her from behind.

I breathe out, getting control of myself.

No. I'm not going to do that here. Not on the fucking concrete. That's how you fuck a whore and Anya Bokori is a lot of things, but whore is not on that list.

She pulls back, probably sensing my thoughts, and then straddles me, her hips slightly elevated, her hand on my cock, aiming it right between her legs. She is so wet, she drips down the side of my dick before I even get inside her. And then she leans forward, both hands smacking my chest with a hard slap, just to make sure I'm awake for what's coming—*trust me, Anya, I am*—and then sinks down. Forcing my cock inside her.

We both close our eyes and moan. And in this moment, I want to make all the promises to Anya Bokori.

I want to hold her.

I want to love her.

I want to keep her.

I want to save her.

She comes. Her head back, mouth open and moaning. Her fingernails digging into my chest. Her pussy clamping down on my dick. Her hips still moving. Her wind-tangled hair blowing out behind her.

And then I come too.

And I make all those promises with my fingers.

Knowing full well I will never keep them.

CHAPTER SEVENTEEN

ANYA

Things change between Cort and I after we have sex on the roof. I wasn't planning on fucking him ever again. I don't equate sex with intimacy. In fact, it's the opposite. Sex, to me, is transactional.

But lots of things have changed in my life since the fight and that trip down to the lower platform was some kind of... I don't know. The word that comes to mind is 'catharsis,' but that feels like a very strong word filled with drama and endings, so it doesn't quite fit. Because there's no drama here. It's actually the most peaceful place I've ever been. And this is definitely not an ending. Not even close. I feel like I was dropped into a brand-new life and all the things I relied on to survive no longer matter.

So it's really not a catharsis. Maybe more of a cleansing. Some kind of break. A pause between the old and the new.

I feel fresh again. Clean. Even though I'm literally covered in sweat and grime nearly all the time. But when Cort van Breda held me in his arms and jumped into the ocean and I saw that reef, something switched inside me. This whole new reality suddenly became real.

Some of that was probably fear, and the adrenaline from the jump, and the shock of the water. But most of it was the realization that I was somewhere... *else*.

Somewhere far, far away from Lazar. And even though I understand that it's not really that far away because we're stranded here like prisoners and he is just a helicopter ride away, the odds of seeing him again have suddenly dwindled down to near zero.

I don't belong to Lazar anymore. This is what hit me under the water that day. I might not be free, but I don't belong to Lazar.

It's not enough. I get that. I don't have any real power in this world and I don't control much. But I control myself. At all times. I can make certain decisions, I can avoid certain outcomes, and I can keep my mouth shut.

This won't last. I have no idea how long we'll be here, I just know it won't be forever.

One day Udulf will come and pick me up. He will take me home, or whatever. Sell me, maybe. I don't know what he'll do with me.

Cort and I will not be together. I understand this. He will go his way, and I'll go my way, and this pause in my life will just become another fairy tale story in my head. Something that never really happened.

But each morning when I wake up, I put the nightmare that is my life aside and only think about the reality of my new day. Which is training.

I jump rope for about thirty minutes. I do the drills I know, then learn a new one and practice that until I'm exhausted. And then Cort and I spar, or wrestle, or box. He has taught me how to kick, how to punch, how to use my elbows and knees, and how to block.

He still slaps my face every day. Well, he tries. The day after the roof sex he showed me four ways to block that slap. He made me practice relentlessly that first day and it's still something I practice as one of my drills. So now, on day thirty, I don't get slapped anymore. I have bruises all up and down my forearms from blocking, but it has been eight days since his fingertips even got close to my cheek.

Every afternoon we look at that tank on the roof and he decides if we can afford the water for a hosedown or a shower. And every few days, he decides we can. But on the other days we just jump into the ocean and swim around the reef, washing off the sweat but picking up salt from the sea.

We eat dinner with our bowls propped up on the beam and watch the birds, and the waves, and when it's dark, the lights far, far off in the distance. I think it's land. Like, *real* land. A coastline. And there's a shipping lane too. We're too far away to really make out the ships, but at night we track the running lights across the dark-blue horizon.

My skin burns, but then darkens to a golden brown as my hair becomes wild and tangled from the salty air and streaked nearly white from the sun.

Then, when the day is finally over and we're lying on our mats, Cort will point to the moon and flash his fingers. We are counting up, not down. And who knows where that count ends. Could be tomorrow, could be next year.

And when I think about this, I find that I don't care if we stay here forever. I know that's not possible.

We don't have enough water to last much longer. But if we could stay, I would stay.

I like this pause.

We haven't had sex again. We haven't kissed, or held hands, or even sent each other longing, meaningful looks. When Cort looks at me, his look is hard and filled with expectations. He's training me. I am a student to him right now. And at first, I felt a little hurt and maybe even a little used, but now I see that I am earning his respect. When he smiles at me now, it's because I blocked a punch or a kick. It's because he *didn't* get the best of me.

And that's new. Every man I've ever known has wanted *the best of me*. They want to take things from me. They want me to give myself to them.

But not Cort. He wants me to stop him. Everything we do is about me *stopping* him.

Sometimes, in the afternoon when it's raining hard enough for the water to blow in onto the training mats, we'll go inside and play a game. Or sometimes I will read a book and he'll just lie on the couch and stare at the ceiling. He never naps or even closes his eyes. He just stares up at that ceiling.

It rains a lot, at least once every day. In the mornings and then again later in the afternoon. Most of the nights are clear and we can see the stars as well as the moon. But there have been a few rainy nights and we've had to sleep on the mats on the training floor.

He doesn't like sleeping down there and I'm starting to get the feeling that Cort prefers to be out in the open as much as possible because when I tried to sleep in the game room, he just shook his head and pointed to the roof.

I don't know what that's about because we don't talk. We don't even sign anymore. He hasn't taught me any new ones since that moment he realized I was picking them up on my own.

I don't think he likes that I understand his language. And not because he's got some ego about the signs, either. I think it just took him by surprise, and I get the feeling that Cort van Breda hates surprises.

I didn't have to show him the signs. I could've kept that secret. But I wanted him to know. It felt like something he should know.

We ran out of food seven days ago. Unsurprisingly, no one came to pick us up or restock our pathetic pantry. But that morning Cort got up before I did and when I went down to the training level, he was messing around with a giant net. It was pretty obvious that if we wanted to eat, we'd have to get that food ourselves. We had nothing left. Not even a cup of rice. It was all gone.

We spent the entire day fishing with that heavy net, casting it out and pulling it in over, and over, and over again, hoping for fish.

We caught lots of tiny ones. And we didn't throw them away. But tiny fishes aren't enough and it doesn't take a genius to realize that there is no way to fillet a two-inch fish. You just have to eat it whole.

I want to hurl just thinking about it now. But that's exactly what we did that night. Cort ate like thirty of them. He was so full that night, he sighed and patted his belly in satisfaction. I only managed one and it was so disgusting I puked it back up.

The next day, we did it all again. It was easier that time because I settled into Cort's rhythm with the net-pulling. But my body was still sore from the day before. And that night, even though once again we only caught the tiny fishes, I forced myself to swallow five of them.

I clutched my belly that night, just like Cort. Only I was sick, not content and full.

It took two more days to finally net three large fish that could be filleted. And by that time, I was swallowing those little fish like a champ. I even ate a tiny fish that one of the birds dropped at my feet.

This made Cort smile like a boy. They do that a lot. And he eats them too. Every single time. I get the feeling this is something he's done for years. And I want that story. I want to know what's up with these fucking birds and how Cort van Breda—the Sick Heart himself—managed to tame them like he's Tarzan.

But of course, I didn't get that story. I will probably never get that story.

And tame isn't even the right word. Those stupid birds love him. Even the gulls. They don't feed him the way some of the albatrosses do, but they don't move when he gets near. They aren't afraid of him the way they are me.

We cut the meat of those three fish into strips and dried them in the sun. And that's what we've been chewing on for the past two days.

Today we are foodless again. And I'm not looking forward to more fishing.

But when I come out of the bathroom and go looking for my jump rope, ready to pretend fishing isn't happening, Cort isn't holding the net. He's just standing on the edge of the training platform, looking out to sea.

I walk over, wondering what's attracted his attention, and that's when I see the ship coming right towards our platform.

I gasp, and Cort turns to me, shaking his head. I'm not sure what that means. No, he will not let Udulf take me? Or no, there's nothing he can do?

But then I look back at the ship and realize it's neither of those. Because as the ship gets closer and angles the side of the hull up to the rig, I count twenty kids on deck wearing orange life jackets.

And then I see Maart. He waves to us.

No. Come on, Anya. Maart is waving to *Cort.* Not me. I saw those two together on the *Bull of Light.* There is something between them. Something more than just trainer and doctor, if that's what Maart is. And it's more likely that Maart's skills were built out of necessity and involved a lot of on-the-job training. He is probably half the reason Cort is still alive right now. Maart gives no fucks about me at all.

I saw the way he looked at Cort in that clinic back on the *Bull.* He was very worried about the blood loss and maybe he's just not used to having strangers in the clinic with him after a fight when he's putting Cort back together, but it might just be that he didn't care if I knew.

Maybe he wanted me to know that they are something more.

That bottle of Lectra was always going to be consumed, so they were always going to fuck me that night. But I get the feeling that Maart was sending subtle signals to me too. Making sure I understood that that's *all* it was.

Just fucking.

You're here today, gone tomorrow, girl.

But I didn't go. I wasn't sent away. Cort brought me out here to the rig with him. And now it's all starting to make sense. This is all a fantasy. Just a dream world. A temporary reprieve. And this place that has started to feel like home suddenly doesn't feel like anything anymore.

Because this is his training camp. And I don't know why we just spent thirty days out here alone, but I get the feeling it's all just... work.

I am just *work*.

Cort absently props an arm on my shoulder as he watches the kids jump from the ship. One by one, they jump, splashing into the sea below. Most of them have life jackets, but a few don't. The older ones, I realize. And by older, I mean like... twelve. Maybe. There are a lot of little ones, though. One very small girl is screaming her head off in Rainer's arms as he positions her over the side of the ship, ready to let her fall.

The ship is a platform supply vessel. Lazar was obsessed with ships and he owns several just like this one, so I recognize the class. This one looks like it's been around for a couple of decades and isn't freshly painted the way Lazar's ships are. But I don't care how rundown the ship looks. This means we're getting food and water today.

I'm already picturing a bath in the tub tonight when the tiny girl squeals again. The deck they're on isn't that far from the water. I don't know how long that fall is—twenty feet, maybe? But all the older kids—the ones with no jackets—are directly below her, like they're gonna catch her or something.

Cort shakes his head as he watches. And then he signs to me for the first time since we had sex on the roof. *She's afraid. But she's gotta get over it.* Then he quickly adds, more to himself than me, *If she can't make it through day one, she's fucked.*

Day one of what?

But I don't have time to think about that because Rainer drops the little girl and she screams. Like one of those super high-pitched toddler screams. But those damn kids below actually do catch her. And then I realize that some of the other jumpers are already clambering up the platform stairwell below us.

But I'm worried about the little one, and keep my eyes on her as she is maneuvered through the water towards the rig. She is *so* small. Barely more than a freaking baby. Definitely no older than three or four.

Cort taps my shoulder and points as the kids enter the training floor.

I expect them to greet each other. Some backslapping, maybe? At least a few hellos, but those kids say nothing. They don't even look at Cort. There is one older girl—pre-teen, or maybe an actual teen, wearing training shorts and a tight, black tank top— who takes charge and starts opening up the huge rusty shipping containers that line the back side of the platform with a set of clanging keys.

She swings the doors open, banging them against the containers next door, and then the next thing I know, the entire platform is swarming with kids. They are mostly small. The girl who seems to be in charge is the oldest as far as I can tell. One boy might be around her age. But all the others have to be under the age of ten.

Suddenly there is crying and when I look over at the stairwell, a sopping -wet Rainer enters the training floor holding the very small child who was just dropped out of the boat. She wails between hitches in her breath, totally out of control.

Rainer says nothing to her. He simply sets her down and gives her a forceful push towards the other kids, who are all very busy rolling equipment out of the containers. They work in teams and they work in silence. Not a single word is uttered. And when I glance over at Cort, he's just watching them, arms crossed over his chest, severe scowl on his face, and eyes a bit narrowed.

His camp. That's what he's thinking. And these little kids are his students. It's a weird place to have a camp and it doesn't make much sense to me, but my experience with training goes back one month. So what do I know about it?

I'm standing around doing nothing while everyone else works, and that makes me uncomfortable. But I don't know what to do. Cort is not paying any attention to me at all, so he's no help. And no one is talking.

No one. It's like we're all a bunch of mutes.

Even the tiny girl has mostly stopped her crying and is doing her best to drag a box across the mats, taking frequent breaks to swipe the back of her hand across her running nose.

Well, I could help her. It's better than standing here. I walk over to her and reach for the box. But the little brat attacks me with pointy little elbows and knees, snarling a little as she pulls the box out of my hand.

A sharp whistle makes everyone pause for a moment. I turn to find Maart glaring at me. "What the fuck are you doing?"

I just stare at him because what else can I do? I'm not going to communicate with him. I barely communicate with Cort.

"I asked you a fucking question."

I look over at Cort, but the expression on his face is blank. In fact, I don't even have his complete attention. He's mostly concentrating on the kids and how they are managing the equipment.

And then, suddenly, Maart has crossed the mats to where I'm standing, has got a hold of my upper arm, and is dragging me towards the building. I jerk my arm, trying to make him let me go—because his grip is tight—but he just grips me tighter and gives me a sharp jerk back. "Don't fuck with me today, Anya. I have a million things to do and none of them have anything to do with you. So right now, you're nothing but a waste of my time. Do you understand me?"

Again, what part of *I don't talk* does he not get?

He pulls the door open and tugs me into the hallway. Once inside, he lets go of my arm and gives me the same push that Rainer gave the little devil girl. I was just trying to help. Jesus, these people are all assholes. I can't believe she attacked me. I'm going to have bruises from those tiny elbows.

Maart pushes me again. Only now he grabs my shoulders and pins me against the hallway wall, his finger pointed in my face. "I don't know what the hell you and Cort have been doing out here for the past month, and I don't want to know. I don't fucking care. But whatever it was, it's over now. Do you understand me?"

Maart here is either eternally optimistic, or really fucking stupid. Because I am never going to answer him. I'm not going to nod. I'm not going to flash him an OK sign or a thumbs up. I am literally a professional non-communicator. And if he thinks some angry words and finger-pointing can get me to break, he's out of his mind.

What does he think? Lazar just said, *It's fine if you don't talk, Anya. I love it when slave girls defy me?*

No. That's not how it went. There were beatings over my silence. And much, much worse things that came after, when that didn't work. So Maart here, he's getting nothing out of me.

He scoffs. "You know what, Anya? I don't give a fuck about you. Those kids out there?" He nods his head towards the door. "That's who I give a fuck about. OK? In six months, half of them will be dead in the fights. You do not matter. *They* do. So I'm gonna give you a job and you're gonna stay the hell out of my way. You're gonna stay out of Rainer's way. You're gonna stay away from all those kids, and don't even think about getting close to Cort. Whatever the two of you have been doing out here, it's over now. Do you understand me?"

Wow. Is he *jealous?*

He is. He's pissed off because I was out here for a whole month. Alone. With Cort.

I almost smile. And he catches this.

"That's funny to you?"

The kids? No. That sucks. But kids die all the time in my world. Lazar has gone through… hell, I couldn't even begin to count the number of children who have passed through his house.

Maart isn't stupid. Because somehow, he reads this in my blank expression. He sighs, runs his fingers through his thick, dark hair, and then looks down the hallway. "You're the new cook. Normally, I make the oldest girl do it, but she's got a fight in four months and she could use the training." He looks back at me and shrugs. "She's good. But not good enough. It's probably not going to matter, but…" He blows out a long breath with that word. "Doesn't hurt to try. So you're the fucking cook."

The door swings open just as those last words leave his mouth and a bunch of boys are on the other side with boxes stacked on hand trucks.

"Perfect timing," Maart says. "Drop it all in the hallway, Anya's in charge of the pantry."

The boys don't say anything, just offload their boxes and leave.

Maart picks up two of the boxes and points to a third. "Pick that up and follow me." He goes into the kitchen, opens the door to the empty pantry, and drops the boxes. "Sort it out. Dehydrated and powdered protein goes on this side, carbs over there." He points to the shelves. "Pile the sacks of oranges on the floor in that corner where it stays cool. And anything else you find in these boxes, goes in there." He points to a cupboard with a lock on it. Opens it up to show me a smaller pantry.

Then he turns to the freezer and begins messing with a control panel on the outside. Something rumbles over our heads and then the panels lights up and begins beeping. I swear, I stand there open-mouthed, just picturing the things that will go into the freezer.

"It's going to take about twenty-four hours for this thing to get to the right temperature, but everything is packed in dry ice. So just put all the boxes marked 'frozen' in here and you can sort that shit out tomorrow. Make sure you check the pantry items for holes in the bags. We can't afford for any of this food to go bad. We have three fucking months on this damn Rock and we won't get a resupply."

I am momentarily stunned by that revelation. *Three months?*

"Anya!" Maart snaps his fingers in front of my face. "Get to work. I'll be back tonight when you're done and show you how to make dinner."

Then he turns and walks away.

Thank God. Maart is an asshole. But I don't actually mind the job. At least I'm busy. And the sight of all the food I unpack is exciting. The boys appear over and over again, dropping the heavy boxes of dried and frozen meats, rice, pasta, frozen French fries, potatoes, yams, dried fruits, and even a few boxes of treats. Cookies, some chocolate, and there are three bottles of Lectra.

Three hundred thousand dollars' worth of the Blue Devil.

I sigh just picturing my bowl of food tonight. Being the cook will be awesome. I'm going to make something amazing. There is some beef in there. I have spent the last thirty days eating just enough dehydrated chicken and nasty fish to get by and now the pantry will be *full*.

I don't even know what time of day it is when Maart comes back because there are no windows in this building, I just know it's been hours. I ran out of room on the pantry shelves a long time ago, but I have gone through all the boxes to check the contents, just to make sure none of the vacuum-sealed bags have any holes in them the way Maart asked. And they are now stacked neatly and precisely labeled on the far wall of the kitchen.

He pauses in the door to the pantry and looks it over. "Nice." Then he turns and looks at my stack on the other wall, nodding his head. His eyes meet mine. "Good job. Now…" He sighs, like it's been a long day. "We've got twenty hungry kids out there who need to eat. Plus me, Rainer, Cort, and you. So here's how it goes." He walks into the pantry, picks up a bag of dehydrated chicken cubes, and slaps it down on the stainless-steel counter. "You will rehydrate ten cups of chicken and make twenty-five cups of rice."

What? Oh, hell no. I am not eating rehydrated chicken and rice tonight. Is he crazy? I'm throwing those frozen hamburger patties on the grill and making bags and bags of French fries tonight.

He laughs. And when I look at him, I realize he was probably reading my mind. "Anya." His voice is low, not angry or stressed now, the way it was earlier. "I'm only going to say this once. We are on strict rations and these kids have a very specific diet. They will each get a bowl with one cup of rice and one quarter cup of chicken cubes. Do you understand me? You will not touch anything else in the pantry or the freezer without my permission. You will not be snacking on cookies tonight. There will be no steak dinner under the stars. For the next thirty days dinner is nothing but rice and chicken. Breakfast is one cup of cooked powdered eggs, half a cup of oatmeal, and an orange. There is no lunch. Got it?"

I don't react, but I die a little inside.

Maart pats my shoulder. "I get it. I don't know what the hell you and Cort have been eating out here for the past month, but I do know it wasn't enough for two. But if I catch you eating any food that the rest of us don't get, I will chop your fucking fingers off. Understand me, *Anya?*"

Dick. I shrug off his hand on my shoulder and then grab a giant stainless-steel pot from under the counter and bang it on the stove.

"Good. I'm glad we had this chat." Maart turns to leave, but then he pauses and looks over his shoulder, his eyes focused on something off to the right. "And I know I already said it, but I'm gonna say it again. Stay the fuck away from Cort. Whatever you've been doing, it's over now." His gaze finds mine. "There is no sex on the Rock. Ever. And aside from Rainer and me, there is no talking, no sign language, no communication period for the first thirty days. So don't even look at those kids. Cort can talk if he wants, but he won't. Everything he puts these kids through, he puts himself through as well. We have one mission out here and that's to teach them how to survive their fights. And if I think you're going to mess that up, Anya…" He pauses to narrow his eyes at me. "I will take you down to the ocean in the middle of the night, drown you, and leave your dead body there to be eaten by the fish. Got me?"

I get him. I make dinner the way he said. And afterward he tells me to wash dishes and explains that breakfast is served just before sunrise so it had better be ready.

There is no lunch on the Rock. Apparently that's the name of this place because that's what he keeps calling it. And everything is on a schedule.

He wakes me up in the middle of the night and takes me down to the kitchen, where I make the most disgusting version of eggs I've ever seen. The kids wake up just before dawn, grab their bowls, and I plop in a half cup of oatmeal, top it with this yellow stuff they are calling eggs, and then hand them an orange. Cort, Rainer, and Maart get a little extra, but not very much. I don't give myself extra. I'm used to feeling half-starved and to be honest, I have to choke down my ration of food every meal, it's so gross now.

Then they drop their bowls and forks into the large sink and I do the dishes. By the time I'm done with that, everyone is fully engrossed in their training. Groups of kids arranged by age fill the mats. Cort takes the very little ones who look to be maybe six or under. That's the biggest group. Nine boys and two girls, including the tiny elbow demon.

Rainer takes another group of four boys and one girl who look to be about eight or nine. This includes Evard.

Maart has the smallest group—the teenage girl who was in charge of the container keys the first day they arrived, another boy who looks to be about twelve, and two boys who are maybe ten.

No one pays any attention to me. But my name is still on one of the chalkboards. Every kid in camp has one and that's where they find their schedule for the day. Mine still says the same thing it did before all these people arrived, so I continue the schedule. I jump rope for about thirty minutes—and I'm pretty good at it now. I can't do all the fancy stuff like Cort, but I can do some of it. Then, if there's space on the mat, I'll practice my drills. And if there isn't, I'll try for a heavy bag. But mostly the space on the mats and the equipment is always in use and Maart is always ready to order me back into the kitchen.

Cort doesn't bother with me at all. He's with his group of kids every minute of the day. And at night, he keeps them all in a small section of the helipad where most of the bird nests are.

The baby birds are freaking huge now. They don't even qualify as babies in my eyes because they are bigger than most dogs. But they can't fly, so they are constantly being fed by the parents.

As far as the kids go, they don't communicate at all. I feel like I was dropped into an alternate reality filled with other Anyas. It's weird. They don't sign. They don't whine. They're like little robots who just go through a schedule with no emotion.

Except for one moment each night. When everyone is finally settled on their sleeping mat Cort, and Rainer, and Maart will point up at the moon, flashing fingers to count the days. And then all the kids do the same.

One moment, every night. That's it.

But we're going to be here three months. And if Maart thinks he can stuff me in the kitchen that entire time, he's insane. Because I like the training I did with Cort and I want to keep doing it.

So on the fifth day, after the kids drop their dirty bowls into the sink, I don't stay in the kitchen and do the dishes. I walk out onto the mat and stand next to the oldest girl. She looks at me, confused, then looks straight ahead again when Maart comes up to us.

"What the fuck are you doing?" Of course I'm not going to answer him. But I don't look at him, either. "Get off my mat and go do the fucking dishes, *Anya*."

I do not move.

"What the fuck is wrong with you? Are you trying to piss me off?"

Not really. But this moment is the most human contact I've had all week. I know that the kids appreciate the food I serve, but not hearing that little "thank you" when I feed them is really starting to annoy me.

In fact, I don't care for my assigned position here on the Rock and I would like to renegotiate.

So I reach out and slap Maart across the cheek as hard as I can.

CHAPTER EIGHTEEN

I only catch the last bit of Anya's slap. But the sound of it echoes in my head as everyone on the platform turns to look.

"Oh, fuck." Rainer breathes these words from a few feet away. I break away from my kids to interfere, but Rainer grabs me by the arm. "Oh, hell no. You will not save her from this. She just…" He chuckles a little and shakes his head. "Fuck that. If anyone else in this camp slapped Maart across the face they would be thrown off the platform and left to die. She wants a fight? She's about to get one."

I let out a long breath, but I hang back with Rainer as Maart's open hand strikes Anya across the cheek with enough force to make her spin and fall onto the mat as the breath rushes out of her lungs and she gasps for air.

Maart stands still, towering over her, his eyes narrowed and angry, his chest rising and falling just a little bit faster than normal. Anya chokes and then spits blood out onto the mat.

"What the fuck, Anya?" Rainer is pissed about the blood on the mat, not the fact that Anya probably just bit a chunk out of her tongue.

She pulls herself up, balancing on her palms, but she doesn't try to stand up. Instead she slowly raises her eyes up to Maart and glares right back.

That's a lot of words from a girl like Anya. But I don't think Maart understands that. He hasn't spent the last month with her. He hasn't learned that showing feelings of any kind is like a manic rant in Anya's world.

But I have. And her look says she's not done yet.

She gets to her feet—slightly unsteady, but she squares her shoulders and tilts her chin up in defiance. Daring him to hit her again.

He does the same. He won't hit her again. He would've never hit her in the first place. She's not worth a fight. She's not a student in this camp, she's a fucking cook. A dishwasher. Something to be dealt with. To Maart, Anya is nobody.

Well, she was. Until she slapped him across the face.

I have to bring a hand up to my mouth to hide my smile, but my girl has some balls on her.

She obviously has no idea who or what Maart is. Because if she did, she wouldn't have dared to touch him.

There is just one guy on the whole planet I know can kick my ass in a fight and that guy is Maart. He never made it into Ring of Fire because we planned it that way.

I was the one who would fight and he was the one who would put me back together when it was over.

Because I'm not fucking smart enough to treat broken bones and run IV lines and he is.

But make no mistake, Maart is one badass motherfucker. And there is no way he will let some princess of a girl get away with slapping him across the face in front of all these kids.

He has to do something. He *has* to.

If she slapped me like that, I'd have to do something too.

We all wait—practically holding our breath—as Maart considers his options.

He sucks in a deep breath and then glares at the kids and his words come out as a low, mean growl. "Get back. To work."

And just like that, the whole platform is on the move. Kids go back to their tasks, wrapping their hands or warming up for the day's training. Rainer lets out a relieved breath because if Maart was gonna make an example out of Anya, he'd want them all watching. Rainer goes back to his kids too, checking their wraps and play-boxing with Evard.

But I know better. Maart will never let this go. His eyes track around the platform, making sure every kid is doing what they should, as Anya stands in front of him, breathing hard and trying not to gag from the blood inside her mouth.

His gaze lands on me and I raise my eyebrows at him. And in that same moment he reaches for Anya, his palm still open and aiming for her cheek.

She blocks him, her forearm batting that potential slap away. I have to hide my smile again, because Maart never takes his eyes off me. And now he is saying things without words, just like Anya was.

He is asking me, *What the fuck did you do?*

And what can I say? All I do is shrug.

His head slowly turns and he studies Anya for a moment. Sizing her up. Evaluating her potential. "You wanna be a fighter, Anya? And don't you fucking dare hand me silence, bitch. You just slapped me. I have every right to throw you off this platform and let you die in the sea for what you just did. I am *ajarn* here." He leans into her personal space. "Do you understand me?"

I don't expect her to answer him with words, and she doesn't. But she nods her head and bows, just a little bit.

It's a slave bow, not a martial arts bow. But it implies absolute submission, so it works.

Maart lets out a long breath and looks over at me. I haven't moved, even though all my kids are busy. Anya has been forgotten as far as they're concerned. None of them are over the age of six, but every one of them—with the exception of four-year-old Ainsey—has been out to the Rock at least twice already. They know what's coming. They know that in six months they will have their first fight and more than half will lose.

Which means more than half will be dead when it's over.

They don't have time for Anya's defiance.

I don't give Maart any indication of what he should do about this situation. He's right. He can deal with her any way he wants. She disrespected him and he has every right to ban her from the camp.

But when he looks back at her, he grabs her face and turns it, trying to see inside her mouth to find the source of the blood. Then he sighs and points his finger at her. "I'm pissed. If you wanted to train, all you had to do was ask with respect and we would've talked it over. Get your ass in the clinic. I'll have to stitch that fucking tongue. I should just cut it off while I'm in there. It's not like you need it."

His insults continue as he follows Anya into the building, then taper off as the door swings closed behind them.

I turn back to my kids, ready to check hands, and find Ainsey—as usual—with a mess of wrappings around her knuckles.

She's not gonna make it. Knowing this is a curse. And every time I look into her eyes, I feel this heavy weight of guilt. This is why I baby her. This is why I kneel down, unwrap her hands, and then wrap them back up the proper way.

But I smile the entire time for two reasons. One. Anya blocked Maart's slap and he wasn't expecting that. And two. I have to wear this mask with Ainsey. I don't want her to know what's coming. I want her to spend these last few months with me thinking it's all gonna turn out OK, even though it's not.

By the time the kids are done jumping rope, Anya and Maart are walking back out to the mats. I pause and watch them as they make their way towards me.

"She's with you." Maart sighs out these words. Like he's tired. Or maybe just tired of her. I can only imagine the conversation that took place in the clinic.

Maart hates drama. And every time we get a new girl, he lets them know this. Maart is the complete opposite of Rainer. He is cold. He is calculating. He is serious, he is focused, he is intense. That's why Rainer has always been in charge of Evard.

Though Maart has warmed up to Evard over the past year, ever since I fought for his freedom and won.

Maart knows he's here for good. Unlike Ainsey. Her clock is ticking so loud, Maart goes out of his way to ignore her completely.

I'm not sure what he thinks about Anya. Especially now.

"What?" he asks.

I shake my head and smile.

"Just…" He runs his fingers through his thick, dark hair and sighs. "I don't know. I don't care what you do with her. Three fucking months. I can deal with anything for three fucking months." He gives Anya one final glare, then turns to me. "It was only three stitches, so if she starts getting lippy and whining about how she can't work hard today, send her back into the kitchen."

I chuckle. Yeah, ya know, I would actually love to see a lippy Anya Bokori. Because that sounds pretty fun to me.

Maart points at Anya. "And you will still clean those fucking dishes and make dinner. Do you understand me?"

Anya presses her lips together and nods, bowing her head in that slave way she does. I hate that slave bow. So I snap my fingers to get her attention, then point to the mat where my little band of misfit fighters are already doing drills.

Maart just turns away and walks off. I watch him, wondering what's really going through his head. Does he hate Anya? Does he resent her? Is he pissed at me for bringing her out here and putting a little kink in our escape plans?

I'm not sure. We haven't had time alone together since they all arrived. And our kids don't sleep in the same area on the roof. He hates the fucking birds and stays as far away from them as possible. I love them. Coming to the Rock is like going home for the holidays. These birds are my family. So anyway, I guess I'll have to make a point of finding Maart later to try to figure out what he's thinking. Because we don't need any tension. We've been living in a constant state of high alert our whole lives. This should be a fun time. A time to enjoy what we've built here and look forward to new things.

I turn back to Anya and bow to her. She is immediately confused and bows back. I put my hand on her shoulder to stop her and her eyes meet mine with zero expectations.

Sometimes she looks… lifeless. Like she's empty inside the way Lazar is. The way Udulf is. The way I would be too, if I stayed in this world much longer.

But then, other times, she's bright and the light inside her is so apparent, it makes me want to shield my eyes. She was like that in the game room. But the bright light has nothing to do with being happy. That light is about being alive. Because I could see it when she was puking up the tiny fish we caught in the net those first few days we had to work for our dinner. I could see it when I dragged her down to the lower level and left her there as punishment. I could see it when she helped me kill Pavo.

Anya Bokori is still in there. I don't know her story and the way this is going, I will probably never know her story, but I do know one thing. She's no quitter.

And she's no slave, either.

That's her first lesson today.

I put my palms flat together like I'm praying, then bow my head and raise my hands up until the front of my thumbs touch my eyebrows. If I was back at home, I would add a greeting, but this is a no-talking space, so I leave that out.

I point to Anya. And she does it just like I did. And when her bow is over, her light is back.

The both of us sigh at the same time, then I take her jaw in my hand and motion for her to open her mouth. She does, looking down—again, another instinctual slave gesture that she probably isn't even aware of—and I check her tongue.

Three tiny stitches across the side of her tongue where she bit it. Maart is a damn good stitcher, but inside the mouth everything scars. I think this is more of a reinjury than a new one. I have a vague recollection of her mouth bleeding back on fight night. Which means it's gonna scar good. And take extra-long to heal, as well.

It's still seeping a little bit of blood, but she'll live.

I walk over to Jafari, my tallest kid—which isn't saying much, he's six. But he's lean, and he's quick, and he's already done this camp three times because I got him young. So he doesn't need to be told what to do. And when I snap my fingers at him, then point to Anya, he just nods and walks over to her, his long, skinny arms already reaching up to slap her.

Anya appears confused for a moment. And then Jafari's little fist connects with the edge of her jaw and she snaps out of it, blocking his next attempt.

I look over at Rainer and catch him laughing and shaking his head.

But what else can I do? Jafari could kick Anya's ass if I let him loose. She should really be paired up with Ainsey if this were based on skill level. But Ainsey is with me, and anyway, she's too damn short.

I leave Anya and Jafari to it, and then walk over to Ainsey, who is pouting and sitting on the floor, playing with her toes. I kick her with the tip of my foot and she scrambles to her feet as I kneel down with palms up.

She starts punching my hands in her pre-defined pattern of jab, jab, cross. Over and over again.

The day passes like that. Jafari puts Anya through her paces and I pretend that I'm teaching my tiny one how to fight. I send Anya back into the kitchen a couple hours before quitting time so she can get dinner ready, and then I make my kids run up and down the stairwell until they are ready to drop from exhaustion.

I like them tired at the end of the day. Makes them sleep through the night. And that means I can steal a few moments to myself. That's the best thing about teaching the little ones. They like their sleep time.

After dinner, when everyone is settled on their mats, we all point to the moon and check off the day using the sign for 'six.'

The rules for the first month are strict. The food is bland, there is no talking, there are no trips to the game room, and every day is a lesson in hard work.

But we are all about milestones here. And Anya reached one today.

So a few hours later, once I know everyone is asleep, I get up, walk over to Anya, tap her awake, and instruct her to follow me.

She does this without any objections and we end up in the kitchen. She watches me open a bottle of the Lectra, pour two shots into a single glass, and then she follows me down the stairwell to the landing just above the ocean.

We sit on the stairs, shoulders touching, and then I turn and offer her the glass.

She is glowing silver in this moonlight. Her skin has darkened over the weeks and in the sun, she is a golden brown. But right now, she looks like something out of a Nordic fairy tale. Her long blonde hair is wavy and wild, her skin smooth and pale as the shimmering moonlight reflecting off the water turns her into a mythological creature of the sea.

She looks at the glass of Lectra for a moment. Then her eyes dart up to mine.

Half, I sign to her. And she huffs, and nods. Then takes the cup from me, downing half.

I drink the other half. One shot each. It's just enough, really. Just enough to give me a chill as it goes down, but then warm me back up once it settles in my stomach.

It's just enough to erase the tension in my shoulders and allow me to forget.

I lean back, my elbows resting on the step behind us, then kick my legs out and sigh. Anya does the same and we just sit there. Looking out at the sea. Watching the shipping lane off in the distance.

I'm not gonna lie, I've missed this.

We had a nice schedule going before the camp started. We were used to each other. At ease with each other. And even though it's been almost a week and everything about our schedule has changed, I realize that what we had, *didn't* changed.

When I turn to her, she's already looking at me. And when I kiss her, her mouth is already open.

I know this is the Lectra. But I don't care.

I kiss her back with force, angling my body towards her, then over her, until she's practically lying back on the steps. And before I can think too hard about it, or talk myself out of it, I slip my hand between her legs.

Why now? I can read her mind. *Why now, with all these people around us, when you haven't touched me in weeks? Why now?*

And the answer is because time is short. The answer is because she stood up to Maart. The answer is because I want to.

But the real answer is… because I like her. And I want her.

I know this is bad. I know this is using her. I know I will hurt her. And in the end, I will leave her.

But when she opens her legs, responding to—no, agreeing to my request—and I find her wet, I just don't fucking care.

I slip a finger inside her and she lets out a long breath. But it's not enough. I'm tired of her little offerings. I'm tired of her hidden sighs. I'm tired of her silence and I want to make her scream.

I pull her shirt up and over her head, then push her legs together and tug her shorts down.

Anya responds by going still and stiff. And I get angry. Because that's not what this is.

Do you want to stop? I sign.

She shakes her head no.

Then what the fuck, Anya? Do you want to go back up?

She shakes her head again.

Then what is wrong?

She sucks in a deep, deep breath, but doesn't answer me. Not with a shrug, not with a shake, not with a nod.

I pull away and lean back again, frustrated.

I get it. I do. The girl was a sex slave. But that was a long time ago, wasn't it? And we've done it before. Twice.

I sign this to her. And when she doesn't answer me, I take her hands in mine and start making signs for her.

I know you understand me. I know you can sign. I know you can talk. Tell me what's wrong.

Her eyes drift away, looking off into the distance at the shipping lane. And I'm just about to force her to look at me when she turns back.

And then her fingers are moving. Quickly and with confidence. And I am... *mesmerized*. So enthralled with the signs she makes—because while some of them are standard, most of them are not. They are weird combinations. It's like slang. Signs that only long-time users of ASL would even be able to comprehend, let alone make up on the spot.

And this is why it takes me almost thirty full seconds to realize what she is telling me.

I know who you are. I know what they did. I know what you lost.

I know why they call you Sick Heart. You're backwards. You are not Sick Heart, you are Heart Sick.

And I know who did that to you.

I pull back, unsure what that means. *No*, I sign. *That's not what I was asking. We've all lost people, Anya. I don't want to talk about that, I don't want to think about that, I just want to know why you don't want me to touch you.*

I do, she signs.

You pulled away.

She shrugs. *Nervous.*

Lies.

It takes her a moment to respond. And when she does, it wasn't what I was expecting. *Why did you bring me down here tonight?*

Ah. I get it. She wants to know where this is going. Well. The answer to that is… nowhere. But that's not what I tell her. I answer the actual question she asked, instead. *Because you stood up to Maart. You earned a place on the mat. You're on the team. It's a milestone and I wanted to make sure you got to celebrate it. Because now that you're on the team, you're on the team. In three weeks, you will fight one of those kids up there. And you will get your ass kicked, Anya Bokori. There is no way around that. Everyone here is better than you—except Ainsey, and she won't have to test through, she's too small. So I'm sorry, but you can't fight her.*

Anya smiles and then laughs out loud. It's that same sweet, unexpected laugh I heard the very first day we met on the ship.

And this reminds me of what we were doing before we got all sidetracked.

I want to *hear* her. So bad.

And this time, when I lean in and slide my hand up her bare thigh, she doesn't go stiff and still. She leans into me, her head resting on my shoulder, her legs opening to give me better access. Her hand slipping down the inside of my thigh where my cock is beginning to grow under my shorts.

I have doubts. And doubts lead to regrets, and regrets lead to mistakes, and I *know* better. I have spent my entire life carefully picking my way round landmines. Stepping gently. Speaking carefully. Fully understanding that this tenuous reality I have built is something so fragile, just breathing the wrong way could bring it all down.

But I like this girl.

I like her mystery, and her innocence—even though I am fully aware that it was stolen from her the moment she was born—and I like her anger.

Because that's what she is. Anya Bokori isn't some sweet, fair-haired, Viking-eyed child. She is unafraid. She is driven. She is dangerous. That's why she's still alive.

She is a threat. Lazar knows it, Udulf knows it, and now I know it too.

But... she's here with me. Her hand on my cock this very moment. And I understand what she's doing. I understand her power. But I don't care.

That is the kind of shit that comes later.

This is the kind of shit that comes now.

I reach down and place my hand over hers, helping her jerk me off. I look into her eyes and find them lit up silver. Shining with the waxing moon above us. Bright with the idea—or maybe even the anticipation—of sex. And searching me, like she knows I hold some secret that could change her life.

I search her like that too. I think she is the secret that can change my life.

She tugs on my shorts and I help her out a little by lifting my hips and sliding them down my legs.

Now we are both naked. Both bathed in the ancient light of the stars. Both stuck in between worlds like prisoners. Neither of us caring.

She climbs into my lap, her full, round breasts taunting me as they sway in front of my face, her long, wild tresses flitting against my arms and my shoulders. She takes my face in both her hands and stares down at me.

And then we blink and the moment changes.

It becomes urgent and heated as she positions her hips over mine. As her hand reaches down between her legs to grab me and place me at her entrance. As she sits down, forcing me to fill her up. I almost moan, that's how good this girl feels.

My arms instinctually wrap around her middle, pulling her close to me until her breasts are pressed up against my chest and our sick hearts are beating the same staccato rhythm. She releases my face and bends her head until we are bumping foreheads as she moves back and forth across my lap. Slowly and deliberately.

And I want to kiss her so bad, but her injury... So instead, I tip my head up, grab fistfuls of her hair, and hold her there. Capturing her essence and becoming her prisoner in the same breath.

There is this need that flows between us. I don't know what it is, but I feel it. And she feels it too. Because her hips begin to move quicker and with more determination. Her fingernails grip my shoulders, digging into the flesh. My hands wander across the smooth, pale skin of her thighs and then I grab her hips and drag her back and forth across my lap, thrusting my cock deeper inside her with each pass. She closes her eyes, and arches her back, and points her face up at the moon as her pussy begins to contract around my shaft.

And then she comes, biting her lip and silencing herself in a way that seems... sad. And practiced.

And in this moment, I feel nothing but hate.

I hate Lazar. He ruined this girl. *Ruined* her.

I fucking hate that man. I want to get him alone in a crowd. I want to stumble into him on a sunny day. I want to rip his arms from their sockets and slice his throat so deep his head falls off. I want to dig into his chest the way I did Pavo and take out his heart. Feed it to the scavenger gulls and watch them rip and shred it into pieces as they swallow him whole.

And then I come too. With this pale fairy girl on my lap. With this hate in my sick heart. With this dream of revenge.

Filled up with anger and loathing, I come too.

We stay like that for several minutes. Nothing but two broken bodies breathing heavily. Nothing but two lost souls with sweaty skin. Nothing but captured and wasted innocence.

But eventually, the spell wears off and she gets up from my lap, looking for her clothes. And I pull my shorts up, turning to face the stairwell.

And that's when I see him. Maart.

Watching me?

Watching her?

Watching us.

I can hear his sigh, even though he's way up on the top platform. And I can see his disapproval in the slight shake of his head.

You're going to ruin everything. That's what his head shaking means.

I'm going to ruin everything.

And I might. I just might.

Because this girl has awakened something inside me. Something I've been hiding away in a deep dark place for over twenty years.

I'm not sure what it is yet, I just know it's there. I've always known it was there.

I just never wanted to look too hard at the shadows in the corners of my memory. I have always thought it better to walk away and focus on the future.

But what happens when the future is now?

What happens to those shadows when there are no more distractions to keep them at bay?

What happens to me if I take a good long look at who I am and how I really got here?

This is what Maart is afraid of. And up until now, I have been too.

But Anya... there is something uncannily familiar about her.

She is my secret.

No.

She is my answer.

That's what Maart is really afraid of.

She is my answer.

CHAPTER NINETEEN

After Maart slapped my face so hard I bit my tongue, he took me into the clinic and gave me a piece of wet gauze to bite on while he got his things ready to stitch me up. The amount of blood that came gushing from the side of my tongue was crazy. And sickening. I threw up four times, unable to follow his simple direction of "Don't swallow it."

It took a while to fix me up, mostly because it wouldn't stop bleeding enough for Maart to see where he needed to stitch, so he made me lie down on the cot with my head elevated, biting on the gauze until, when he changed it, there was just a soggy splotch of pink.

I was hoping he'd say the stitches weren't necessary because he had already warned me that there would be no numbing. He was going to stab my tongue with a razor-sharp needle.

But that's not what he said. He looked at the gauze, then looked at me, then shook his head with an expression that looked a little like disgust and told me to lie on my side.

He scooted up very close to me on one of the doctor stools, my face in his lap. It was a weird position to be in. Clinical, I guess. But... I did have sex with this guy. And two other guys at the same time. So... not that clinical.

He wore gloves, but I could feel the heat of his skin against my cheek as he worked. The needle turned out to be so sharp, I didn't really feel it. So that was good. But I could feel the suture sliding through my skin and that was gross.

It was only three stitches, and once Maart got started he was quick and efficient. Silent too. I expected a lecture from him, warning me not to try that bullshit again, or something along those lines. He said, *I am ajarn here*. And I am no martial arts expert, but I have read enough *Ring of Fire* magazines to know that means the person in charge of the training camp.

But he didn't say anything until he started giving me instructions. "Try not to spit." He paused and narrowed his eyes at me. "This should stop the bleeding, but it's gonna swell. Good you're a mute. Shouldn't affect you at all." He paused again, waiting for a reaction.

I considered my options in that moment.

Maart has power here. He's not Cort, and from what I can tell, Cort is the actual one in charge. But they came from somewhere. These kids don't live here, this is just... what? Some kind of retreat, maybe? A breakout session. Or something. It's temporary, that's my point.

So Maart runs this place because Cort, for whatever reason, is silent here. Sort of. The rules these people live by are murky and seem rather variable if you ask me. But Cort is the champion, right? They serve at his pleasure. Maart is a manager. Like Lazar's top assistants. I didn't have to listen to them. Not technically. But it was very easy for them to make my life miserable if I didn't.

Maart is Cort's top assistant. Rainer too, but Rainer doesn't seem to care about power, and Maart does.

I bowed my head a little in submission. I didn't want to work in the kitchen. I mean, I don't mind cooking or the other stuff that comes with it, because I have the illusion of being in control of something. But we only eat twice a day. What about the eight hours in between?

Maart seriously thought I should just sit in the kitchen and do nothing? That's dumb. I had to take a stand to get my point across.

But now it was time to submit and beg. I lifted my eyes up, head still bowed, and begged.

He recognized this move immediately and sighed, blowing out a long breath that indicated he was tired of me. But tired is OK. It was when they got bored of you that you have to worry.

"Anya, we are not playing. We're here to save these kids. They will all have to fight the way we did when we were that age. And the Rock is a place where they truly advance. This is a proven technique. Thirty percent of our kids will live to see the age of ten. Five percent make it all the way to the Ring. And as pathetic as that sounds, we are the number one camp in the fucking world with this record. And now you're here, fucking up our good thing, and these kids will be the ones to pay for that, not you."

I lowered my eyes again. And this time my submission was real.

He placed a finger under my chin and lifted my head back up. "If I let you train with us, you follow the rules."

I was nodding before I could stop myself.

"You do exactly what you're told."

I nodded again.

"And you still have to cook and clean the kitchen, do you understand me? Because someone has to do it and in four months Irina will be fighting for her life. She needs this time. You don't. You have no idea what it's like to be a camp kid. And I get it, OK? Slave kids don't have it easy. But you have never felt the fear of walking into a ring knowing your opponent has been told to kill you in any way possible. No rules. No holds barred. Only one of you gets out alive. So you will cook and you will clean and maybe, if Irina wins, you can tell yourself you had a part in that."

And that was all he said. After that he took me out to Cort and Cort paired me up with a tall, skinny, dark-skinned boy who looked like he was maybe eight, but was probably the same age as the others in Cort's group, which was maybe six, and he was just tall for his age. I learned, through Maart's nagging shouts from across the platform, that his name was Jafari. And he was going to be fighting soon for real, so he was super focused on kicking my ass.

The rest of the afternoon was a blur. I just did what I could without any instruction. Cort spent the entire time babying the small one, teaching her how to hit his palms with her tiny fists. He was good with her, though. And that surprised me. Like he cared about her. And maybe he does. But he didn't treat any of the others that way. Not even the other little brown-haired girl, who was probably the same age as the boys.

It took me a while to realize why he was giving the tiny one more attention because she was always looking at her feet and her hair was always in her eyes. But then, at dinner, when I was plopping her rice into her bowl, she looked up at me and I actually gasped.

Her eyes were silver-gray. Cort's eyes.

She is his *daughter*.

And that's when I noticed that the boy who came with them on the ship for the fight—the one they call Evard—he has those same eyes too.

These two, and maybe more of them, are Cort van Breda's *biological children*.

And he was being forced to train them for the fights. Knowing full well that they were not going to make it.

My entire reality flipped with this realization and nothing would ever be the same again.

I was still thinking about this—maybe I was even asleep and dreaming about this—when Cort came to me in the night and took me down the stairwell for a sip of Lectra.

That's all it really was. Just a sip. One shot. But it was enough, and I guess that was the point. It was just enough to warm me up and make me sweat in the hot, humid night. Just enough to relax my shoulders and let out a sigh. Just enough to lower my defenses and let Cort van Breda be nice to me.

And he was nice. But I couldn't let my guard down. I can't ever let my guard down.

This was stupid. I had already let my guard down. I had already showed him my secret, he just didn't realize it yet.

And now, three weeks later—and with no more special night-time moments from Cort—I was starting to wonder if maybe letting go of the secret might be a good thing.

Maybe Cort and his band of fighters were the answer to my endless, unanswered prayers?

It was a very dangerous thought to entertain. Faith was a precious thing and trust… well, trust was both priceless and expensive. Because if you trust the wrong person in my world, you don't get a second chance.

"What the fuck, Anya? Are you even trying?"

I snap my eyes over to Maart. He's been lecturing us for the better part of the morning. Carefully watching each group. Not correcting us, just studying us. I have no idea what this means.

Meanwhile, Jafari's small, sharp, bare knuckles hit me right in the nose and blood rushes down my face.

Maart lets out an exasperated breath and walks over to Cort. I can't hear the whole conversation because Jafari and I are wrestling on the mat now. I'm trying to wiggle out of his hold. And even though I was a little embarrassed that a tall-for-his-age six-year-old could kick my ass a couple weeks ago, I'm so over it now. This boy is mean. Like, he's out for blood every time I step onto the mat with him.

So I'm mostly concentrating on trying not to breathe my own blood while I make attempts to eavesdrop.

I hear Maart say, "Don't even try…" And "She will test like the rest."

And that's that. Jafari and I will be matched for the test tomorrow.

This marks one month on the Rock for the kids, but two months on the Rock for me and Cort. That's what all that moon-pointing is about. We are counting the days that lead up to the new moon. What happens to us after the test, I have no idea. A belt ceremony? We don't wear those white uniforms you see on martial arts kids. So I'm pretty sure it's not a belt ceremony, but I'm also pretty sure there is a ceremony. Why else do we have Lectra? Not that these kids will be drinking it. I'm like a thousand percent positive that's only for the men. But we have cookies. And chocolate. And beef in the freezer. This food is here for a reason and I have not been allowed to serve any of it.

So I'm pretty sure there's gonna be a party and I can't wait.

I'm on my feet now and this is Jafari's worst nightmare. Because while I might not be tall in the grown-up world—coming in at only five foot three and a half—I'm a fucking giant compared to this six-year-old. I lock my arms around his waist, pick him up, and slam him down. The breath rushes out of him with a grunt and Cort comes in to stop the fight, which means I won.

I pump my fist in the air like an asshole and walk over to the sidelines where tiny Ainsey high-fives me with a crooked smile. She's my BFF now.

This entire world, and my place in it, is pathetic, and sad, and insane. I get that. But this is Fight Club, OK? It's every man for himself and fuck the rules. And besides, kicking Jafari's ass means I am making him better. When he fights for his life in a few months his opponent won't be eighteen years old. He or she will be six. And Jafari's gonna win that fight. He's gonna live because of me.

"Go clean yourself up," Maart barks. "And don't be late with dinner. I'm fucking starved."

No "Good job!" from him. No pats on the back. No encouragement of any kind. I've watched him with his own kids, and he definitely treats me differently. He only has four—Irina, the oldest girl who I have decided is probably thirteen, and Maeko, Peng, and Paulo, who are right about that age as well. Paulo probably a year or two older than the other two. Maart's four kids are serious fighters. They practically kill each other every single day during training. And Maart is forever calling out encouraging things. Especially to Irina, who I'm pretty sure is his favorite because while I've deduced that Paulo is the most accomplished, Irina is definitely the most ruthless.

Maart hates me. I'm very sure of that. He hates the way Cort looks at me, and the way Cort pays special attention to me on the mat, and most of all he hates that Cort and I were out here alone for an entire month before Maart showed up.

They have a thing going. I'm not sure how to explain it, but they definitely have a thing going. I haven't caught them doing anything, but we had sex together the night of the fight. And maybe I don't remember very much of it, but I remember enough to know that there were no inhibitions. Sex together was something these men did.

At first, I thought Rainer was gonna be the same way with me, but he's not. He's nice, always cracking jokes. But he's that way with everyone, so I'm nothing to him. He has five kids—Evard, who I am now one hundred percent sure is Cort's biological son, plus Raffie, Budi, Oscar, and Rasha, the middle girl in camp. They are all about eight or nine. Also tough as nails and ready to kill or be killed when on the mat.

I walk into the bathroom and splash cold water on my face to wash away the blood, then study the reflection looking back at me from the dirty mirror on the wall.

Bexxie would not even recognize me if she were here. My skin is bronze now. My normally blonde hair has nearly-white streaks running through it. It's tangled and wild from lack of proper care. There have been no more baths or showers. Only Cort, Maart, and Rainer are allowed to use the shower. They let us hose each other off every four days and the rest of time we just jump into the ocean and swim around until our caked-on sweat floats away.

But I like the way I look.

It's a wild look.

An abandoned look.

A look that says I'm a savage.

I think the savage life suits me.

Cort does pay attention to me on the mat, but after we're done training, he barely looks at me. At first, I was hurt. I mean, he took me down to the stairwell that first day of my real training and we had sex. So what the fuck, right?

But then I looked at it all logically. Sex in our world means nothing. It's just a physical act and nothing more. I knew this. I was hopeful that it would be different with Cort. But now I'm glad it's not. His cold shoulder forced me to concentrate on more important things. Like fighting.

I like it. I really like it. And I'm getting better.

So what if my sparring partner is six?

This makes me smile as I hold a rag over my nose with my head tipped back to stop the bleeding.

When that's taken care of, I go into the kitchen and start making dinner and spend the entire time fantasizing about what I might be allowed to cook tomorrow when we celebrate the end of our first test on the Rock.

CHAPTER TWENTY

The last night of the boring, disgusting if-I-never-eat-this-again-I-won't-miss-it rehydrated chicken and rice dinners is spent up on the top platform, as usual, but we eat all together tonight, instead of in small groups. The kids are sitting next to each other in a loose circle. Not talking or signing, of course. They want to, and they are so close now, they can taste it. But they are as disciplined as kids their age can be, so they feign patience.

They were told what to expect before they got here on the Rock. So there is a general excitement in the air, mixed in with their natural apprehension and nerves over the first test that will happen tomorrow.

One day. Twenty kids, ten tests.

Even Anya looks excited and I'm pretty sure she has no clue what's coming.

Oh, she's heard of the test. Maart and Rainer have been talking about it non-stop for the past four days. But she doesn't know what it means, how it will play out, or what happens after. So her excitement is more about anticipation than expectations.

I watch her as I force myself to choke down dinner. I cannot wait until tomorrow night. We will have a feast. I want beef so bad, I almost moan just thinking about it. Rainer is standing next to me. We're both leaning up against the mechanical room wall, while Maart keeps his distance and sits on the beam with Irina and Paulo, his two favorites.

We all know Paulo is gonna make it. He's like a mini-Maart on the mat. And Irina is great. For a girl. But the chances of her fighting another girl in real life are almost zero. She might be the only thirteen-year-old girl in the program alive at the moment.

It's going to be a boy. It could even be Paulo.

We hope not, but if it is, it's out of our hands and we just have to deal.

Rainer elbows me. "Stop it, she'll be fine."

I ignore him. I'm not really that worried about Anya. She seems to like the training. And she did well today. But Jafari is a little kid. There is no chance Maart is going to pair her up with Jafari. She knows him too well and that's rule number one. When you test, you need to be challenged.

Jafari is fucked too. Because he's been training with a much bigger opponent this past month. And that means Maart will probably make him fight one of Rainer's boys. Or maybe his girl Rasha.

But I'm not really worried about Jafari. He's going to do fine.

It's Anya. And it's Maart.

He hates her. He hasn't said it out loud, but I can tell. I know him. I don't need words to hear his thoughts.

"Jesus Christ," Rainer mutters. "Will you stop already? He's going to be fair. You know he'll be fair."

I shoot Rainer a dubious look, then sign, *You know who it is. Tell me.*

He smiles, which means he does know, then shakes his head, which means he's not gonna tell me.

Is it Budi? Please tell me it's not Budi.

Budi is a scrappy little Indonesian boy who was born into a Muay Thai camp and started training at the age of two. We didn't get him until he was five. Udulf isn't usually inclined to let me in on his selection process, but he took me with him to purchase Budi. He was my pick from over eighty boys who were bred at that camp for the fights and he is worth far more than the seventy thousand dollars Udulf paid for him. He will earn out that seventy grand by the time he's ten. He will make it to Ring of Fire. He might even earn his freedom, he is *that* good.

"It's not Budi."

I let out a relieved sigh. I know it will be one of Rainer's kids. Someone better than Anya and someone older than Jafari. I doubt it will be Evard. Maart goes easy on Evard because he knows Evard is out of here when we leave the Rock. Evard doesn't need to worry about fighting for his life. So Maart will pair Evard up with Raffie because Raffie sucks and there's really no way that kid lives through his next real fight. He's done.

So that leaves Rasha—our middle girl—or Oscar.

Anya and Jafari are in the same situation, I guess. It's going to be Oscar for Anya. He's better than Rasha. So he needs the challenge of Anya's much bigger size to take him to the next level. Rasha will wash out with Raffie.

I let out another long breath and start feeling better about tomorrow.

Anya will do fine. It's doubtful she will win, but who cares if Anya wins? She's not a fighter. Udulf is going to take her home with him the minute Rock camp is over. He'll probably be waiting at the village when we get there. And then… that will be that.

Easy come, easy go.

Hmm. I consider that for a moment. Because Anya didn't actually come easy. I earned her—hell, I earned all of them, but she was the only one I was allowed to take with me when the fight was over. And that part *was* easy, so—

"For fuck's sake," Rainer growls. "Stop thinking so fucking loud. Maart is gonna do the right thing. He always does the right thing for the kids."

That's true. Maart take his responsibilities as ajarn seriously.

But Anya isn't one of the kids. Anya, as far as he's concerned, is a total distraction. And possibly even some kind of trap.

He's suspicious like that. And he thinks that Udulf isn't gonna let us go. He thinks Udulf will fuck us all over at the last minute.

I'm not inclined to agree.

I've known Udulf my whole life. He might, in fact, be my actual biological father. And even though he's been tough on me, he's mostly been fair, if you take out the fact that he's been trying to get me killed in fights since I was five.

Wow. That's a really fucked-up thought that requires some serious self-reflection, but not now. Some day—some far, far day in the future—I will sort out all these feelings. But not now. I've been surviving on instinct my whole life, and even though we're close, we're not out yet. All the ways in which this life of mine is pathological can be thought about later.

I would not say I trust Udulf, but the few times he's given me his word on something, he's always followed through.

And anyway, letting us go isn't some favor. It was a transaction. I paid nearly twenty million dollars in collective purse money to buy our freedom.

This cost us dearly over the years. We might be the number one camp in all of Ring of Fire, but we're also the poorest. Because eighty percent of the winnings I was allowed to keep went to buying our freedom.

We scrape by. Barely. And there is a part of me that suspects that Udulf respects us for this.

We earned our freedom and he knows it.

Rainer bumps my shoulder. "Come have a drink with me." Then he pushes off the wall and heads downstairs.

I take one last look at Anya, then follow him.

We throw our dishes into the sink and Rainer grabs the bottle of Lectra we've been nursing since they arrived a month ago. It's the same bottle I opened for Anya.

Back out on the training platform Rainer points. "Up or down?"

I point down, not wanting to think about the damn kids anymore tonight. Or Anya either.

Rainer nods. "Sounds good to me."

I follow him down the stairs and we settle on the steps near the lowest platform. The ocean is a little testy tonight, the waves splashing against the rusted steel grate that separates us from the dark depths below. The air is thick with salt that settles on our skin and marks us as wild.

This is a wild place and I'm going to miss it.

Rainer and I pass the bottle back and forth, taking small sips. Not just because there's only a little bit left and we can't crack open the new bottle until after the first test if we want it to last, but because we can't afford to get drunk. Not on this shit. Not tonight.

But small sips are usually enough for me.

We don't typically have Lectra with us on the Rock, but this is not just any other training retreat. It's our *last* training retreat. We have been saving these bottles for years. Ever since I started paying for our freedom. And each bottle will be consumed before we leave here and then, we wil never drink this shit again. You can't even get it out in the normal world. And even though we're happy about leaving, and the Lectra is a way to celebrate our achievements—and the mere fact that we're alive—I'm torn about the whole thing.

Once we leave here, we'll never come back. What about my birds? Will they look for me? I have this horrible recurring nightmare that they will look for me the way they look for their missing mates if they don't show up at the predesignated breeding spots every two years.

I don't want them to look for me. I just want them to move on.

"God, Cort. What are you doing? You're being weird today."

It's funny that he can hear my thoughts. Even when I'm silent, around Rainer and Maart, I am never silent.

I sign, *Will you miss it?*

"This place?" He blows out a breath. "I dunno. Maybe some of it. But you can come back here if you want. We have the ship. I'm sure we'll be cruising by here all the time."

The supply ship, he means. That's where a lot of our purse money went. We're gonna run the platform ship and do supply runs for some of Udulf's other rigs. None of them are camps, like this one. They are huge drilling operations. And we had to do some serious upgrades to the one ship I could afford to buy to get those contracts.

I'm not gonna lie. This part bothers me a little. Because are we really free if Udulf is still giving us a paycheck? Are we just trading in the devil we don't know for the one we do?

But I can't picture it. I don't understand what a life out from under Udulf looks like. And I'm not trying to fool myself into thinking I love the man, because I don't. I've had a lot of feelings about him over the decades, but none of them were love.

Mostly, I hate him. This hate is coupled with self-loathing when I take the time to explore it. Because according to the most ruthless underground fighting ring on the planet, I'm the world champion. I'm someone to be feared. And yet I have lived under Udulf's thumb like a possession for twenty-two years.

I have never attacked him. And I guess that's part of the brainwashing, right? He gives me more than anyone else around me, but it's only ever *just enough*.

I get those pretty girls at the end of the fight. Like Anya. But then he takes them away. Like he will Anya.

I get the purse money too. But then again, he takes it away.

Weeks later, he'll give some back. And I can spend that any way I want. But it's only ever *just enough*. Just enough to make that payment on our future freedom, or the supply ship upgrades, or enough food and supplies to keep the training center going until the next fight.

I have never had *extra*.

And I get it. I'm fucking lucky. Because at the same time, it has been so long since I felt the hunger pangs of needing something that wasn't within reach that I've almost forgotten what it was like to be five years old in the world of men like Udulf.

It's another tactic, that's all. These provisions. It's a way to keep me in line. Keep me satisfied. Keep me docile.

And it has worked. It has one hundred percent worked. Because I just made the final payment on our freedom, giving credence to the idea that freedom is something you can pay for.

And it's not supposed to be that way. It's just not.

I sigh.

"I've been thinking," Rainer says, pulling me out of my thoughts.

I turn to him, suddenly aware that we've been sitting here in silence for a pretty long time.

"I've been thinkin' about…" He looks at me, blows out a breath. "Ya know what? Never mind."

Say it, I sign.

He doesn't look at me. But he does spit it out. "I've been thinkin'… I might stay behind."

What?

"Yeah. With the kids. We won't take on any more, but maybe Udulf will let me train the ones we have and—"

No. I make this sign so clear. *No.*

Rainer winces, then whispers, "I don't think I can walk away from them, Cort. I really don't think I can do it." He lets out a long, tired breath. "I don't think I can live with myself."

We saved the ones we could.

But he's shaking his head no. "We can—" He pauses. "I think I can do better than that."

And what will you do? I throw my hands up. *You can't take them all the way, not like Maart can. They'll all die in the end. Do you really want to hang out and watch that happen?*

"Do I want to watch it happen?" He signs his words as he talks. He's always done this for some reason. "No. I don't want to watch it happen. But at least they will have someone they trust at the end. And I think…" He pauses and lets the seconds tick off. "How do I put this?" He studies me for a moment. "You, right? You get in that ring and you beat the shit out of people and let people beat the shit out of you, all to save *us*. This is the literal meaning of going down fighting. But what do I do?"

Don't be stupid.

"No, really. What do I do, Cort? I keep them happy, mostly. And that has always felt wrong to me. Because I'm a part of their dark, evil world. And I haven't gone down fighting since we were twelve years old. You have been fighting my battles for me ever since. I'm too big. I'm too slow. I don't have that killer instinct the way you and Maart do. So you're right. They are all going to die in the end. And it will probably be over in three years. But I'll take those three years of fighting hard to the three empty ones I'll be living on that supply ship wondering… wondering if I could've made a difference. And that's not a dig on you, Cort. Or Maart. You've put yourself on the line for me so many times now, I lost count. And Maart too. You guys deserve this happy ending. But I haven't earned it yet. So I'm staying behind and there's nothing you can say to talk me out of it. I've already explained this to Maart. He's worried about you, by the way. He thinks Anya was a bad idea." Rainer sucks in a breath and holds it, then lets it out very slowly. "And Ainsey too."

I look away at the mention of Ainsey's name.

"I'll take care of her. I promise. I think maybe I can even talk Udulf into leaving her alone until she's older and out of danger."

I feel sick.

Rainer clamps a hand on my shoulder and gives it a squeeze. "I just want you to be prepared for this. I mentioned it to Udulf after you left the fight ship. It's been bothering me for a long time."

What'd he say?

"He said we'd work something out when we got back from the Rock." His green eyes stare into mine for a moment. Then he gives my shoulder another squeeze. "I'm not ungrateful. I hope you don't think that's what this is. I just can't walk away from it, Cort. That world." He looks over his shoulder, like it's coming up behind him. "I'm never going to get over what I am. What I've done."

I push him, making him look at me so I can sign, *What are you talking about?* Because, OK, maybe none of us are innocent, but if you're going to rank us according to guilt, Rainer would be down there somewhere with Evard. Present, accounted for, but a side note in the grand scheme of things.

"Look, I get it. You don't understand. You're never going to understand. And I'm OK with that. I'm just letting you know that I'm staying behind. That's all. And there's nothing you can say or do to change my mind about that." He gets up and points to the bottle of Lectra in my hand. "You can finish it. I'm done."

Then he turns his back on me and climbs back up the stairs.

I stay down there for hours just passing his words back and forth inside my head. They feel meaningful and deep. They make me sad, and angry, and, if I'm being honest, they scare me a little. Because who am I? What kind of man am I if I walk away from these kids?

And this, I think, is the issue. I'm not angry that Rainer is staying. I'm angry that I'm *not*. And I feel guilty for wanting out even though I've earned it.

I have often wondered about destiny. Like… was I only put on this earth to do Udulf's bidding? To rail against his world, but never be able to escape it? And let's face it, just because I will be allowed to walk away from the fights doesn't mean I'm actually free.

So I allow myself to picture a life of staying behind with Rainer and the camp. I allow myself to consider it. If I stop fighting, who will support the camp?

It's a trap. I know it's a trap. And Rainer will figure this out very quickly if he does stay behind. Who will pay for everything?

The kids. That's who.

We have three boys and one girl just about ready to enter the top-level fights. And Rainer will have to send them into the ring hoping they live—not just because he loves and cares about them, but because they will be supporting the camp from now on. And all the other winners coming up behind them.

And this isn't freedom. It's not even close.

He's gonna figure this out, but he needs to do it on his own.

I can't just tell him. He needs to see it, and live it, and then… he needs to regret it.

I get up and join my kids on the platform and sleep off Rainer's moonlight confession.

But it takes me hours to finally fall asleep. And my dreams are filled with little boys in bathhouses. Running. Screaming.

And the empty face of that girl.

That one girl and what they did to her.

No.

What *he* did to her.

The next day starts like all the rest until the first fight is called. My kids go first since they are the youngest. Ainsey sits next to me, her nose dripping and her breath rumbling inside her chest. She's sick. And that just feels like a very bad omen.

She's been tired and cranky for a few days, but this breathing stuff is new this morning. Even Maart was eyeing her at breakfast. But he doesn't have time to worry about Ainsey. Not today.

Twenty fighters. Ten fights. Ten winners, ten losers. And Ainsey.

One by one Maart calls up kids in pairs and they duke it out. Jafari ends up fighting Oscar from Rainer's group, and the whole time I'm wondering what Maart is up to. I really thought Anya would fight Oscar. So who? *Please, tell me it's not Budi.* He might only be eight, but he will kick Anya's ass.

Jafari loses, of course. But Oscar helps him up and gets off the mat while Rainer cleans up the blood.

I'm fixated on Maart because Anya is the only one left in my group. So I am watching his mouth as he calls Irina's name. But it takes me whole seconds to catch up with the fact that *she* will be Anya's opponent.

No.

Rainer intercepts me, pushing me back as I try to make my way across the mat towards Maart. "Let it go," Rainer says. "Don't you dare interfere. She *needs* this."

Fuck that! I sign. *Fuck that! Irina will kill her!*

Rainer leans into my ear just as Maart catches my eye from across the platform. Anya, seemingly oblivious to the fact that she is about to take the beating of a lifetime, is already in the middle of the mat, bouncing a little and shadowboxing, like she's got a chance in hell of making it out the other side conscious. "She needs this," Rainer repeats in a whisper. "Yesterday, after she fought Jafari and won, she walked off the mat and high-fived a four-year-old in celebration, Cort. She *needs* this."

I look at him, shaking my head. *Not Irina. That's not fair and you know it. Irina could give me a run for my money. Hell, she could kick your ass, easy. This isn't fair.*

"Life isn't fair," Rainer whispers. "Anya has two months. And I don't know what happens to her after that, but I do know this. It's gonna be a very dark time for her. It might even be the end of her. She needs this, Cort. And if you have any feelings for her at all, you will let her learn her lessons."

And by this time, it's too late. Because Maart has already started the fight and Anya and Irina are circling each other on the mat.

Irina toys with her like a cat playing with a mouse before the kill. She swipes at Anya, allowing her to block, building her confidence. And then that first kick across Anya's cheek is so powerful, Anya literally spins in place before falling over on her knees.

Irina backs off. Patient. No gloating from her. She isn't here to *fight* Anya. She is here to teach Anya a lesson.

You are nothing. You do not matter. Your life has no value.

We are all going to die, but you? You're going down sooner than later.

Anya is stunned, but she's already up on one knee. I want to tell her to stay down, but I already know Maart doesn't care. He has instructed Irina to keep this fight going for as long as possible. And that's exactly what happens.

There are no rounds in this ring. There is no resting. You fight until it's over.

And this one goes on for nearly nine minutes before Anya is unconscious on the mat, one eye swollen shut, the other one quickly following suit. Her lip is split in two places and every time she exhales, a little bubble of blood forms around her left nostril.

Maart and I meet in the middle of the mat at the same time. I am filled with rage, my breaths coming hard and fast. And I would knock him out right now. But a part of me knows… I'm not sure if I could.

And besides, I need him to stitch her back up.

He waits for me to figure all this out, his dark eyes daring me to be stupid.

And then I nod at him and we pick her up by the arms and drag her inside to the clinic.

CHAPTER TWENTY-ONE

I am not fully aware of everything happening to me. But I know two things.

One. I got my ass kicked by a ninja girl who is nearly half my age.

And two. I have swallowed so much blood, I am now puking.

Rainer's calm voice is in my ear, telling me to relax, I'm fine. Then Maart, snarling at me to stay still as he stabs my eyebrow with a needle and suture.

Cort is there too.

At least, I think he is.

Because someone is playing with my hair.

I drift after that. Maybe they gave me drugs or maybe I fell unconscious again. Hard to tell, probably doesn't matter.

But now I am lying on something very soft. So, so, so *soft*.

This is when I realize I'm dreaming. Because there is nothing about the Rock that is soft. It's all concrete and steel. So different from how I grew up.

Everything about that place was soft. My huge bed. My comfy chairs. The thick rugs under my bare feet.

I lived like a little princess for the past... what, ten years? No sleeping on concrete for Anya Bokori. No swallowing fish whole. No rehydrated chicken bits. No saltwater baths that never wash that sweat off, just add to it, so that each day you are stickier and filthier than you were the one before.

My life was clawfoot tubs filled with champagne bubbles. It was fancy dinners. Food cooked by a private chef. It was long rides on luxury jets and weeks spent wandering foreign cities with pockets lined with money. It was fresh fruit, and special dresses, and pretty hair and nails. Only the best for Anya Bokori.

But that was only half of it.

It was dank, wet tunnels filled with the smell of shit. It was iron locks on wooden doors and screaming kids behind them. It was bright lights over beds and strange faces watching.

It was sickness.

Even the good parts, if there ever were any good parts.

It was all just *sickness*.

I wake to the sound of a voice I don't recognize. A deep, throaty voice that rumbles into my head and weaves its way into my chest, and down my body, and then back up where it settles in my heart. It makes me want to leave the truth behind and keep this miserable fantasy going just a little bit longer.

I know it won't last. It always catches up in the end. But I figure it can pass me by for all I care, and go back to sleep.

A wet cough pulls me up from the depths. And for a moment I think it's me. I think, *Shit. Now you're sick, Anya. Lazar is gonna be mad if he has to take you to the doctor.* So I try to stop the coughing. But it keeps going—on, and on, and on—and it's so thick and wet, I clear my throat.

That's when I realize it's not me coughing. It's someone else.

"There she is." A cool hand flattens on my forehead. "Anya? Can you hear me?"

Who is that?

"Anya," he whispers. "Wake up. It's been almost two days. You have to pee. There's no way you don't have to pee."

I try to laugh, because that's true. I really do need to pee. But the pain that shoots through my face is enough to make me choke. And at the same time, the coughing is still happening.

"Can you open your eyes? Come on, Anya. Enough is enough. You need to come out of this.

Maart wants to call for a 'copter to take you to the mainland. And you can't leave now. Not yet." This last part comes out like a plea, which is so confusing, and this voice is not Rainer or Maart, so...

Oh. Ohhhhhh. It's Cort. He's talking to me.

I squirm, trying to open my eyes and sit up. But there is no way this is happening. My entire body aches. No, that's the wrong word. Every movement causes my muscles to scream in protest. And try as I might, I cannot open my eyes.

"Here," Cort says. "Lemme help."

I wince and then cry out as he helps me sit up a little. He presses a hot cloth to my eyes, wiping the sandy crumbs away. It's only then that I realize my eyes *are* open, but they are so swollen, just a sliver of reality gets past my lids.

I see him. His smile is fake, but I think that's because he's worried and not because he's about to lie to me. He lets out a long breath. "Fucking hell, Anya. You scared me. Maart wanted to take you back to the village and leave you with Udulf." He pauses, stares at me. "Do you know who I am?"

I nod. Then force a small smile.

"Yeah. Good." He smiles back. "I'm pissed at him, by the way. We fought over this. I didn't know he was gonna pair you with—"

I place a hand on his arm and he stops. I don't have the energy to sign anything, and I'm sure as hell not going to speak. But we're past that, I think.

The outcome of the fight doesn't matter.

I lost, and I don't care.

Because for the first time in my life, I feel... *alive.*

CHAPTER TWENTY-TWO

CORT

Her hand on my arm is a signal. She's OK. I don't know what's really going through her mind, but she's OK. That's all she needs me to know.

Anya's eyes migrate down to the limp body of Ainsey in my arms. I let out a long breath. "She's sick. *Again.* Third time she's caught pneumonia since she came to live with me last year. There's something wrong with her." I sigh. Because it all feels so pointless.

Anya tries to sit up, her distorted face registering a look of concern.

"No. She's fine right now. Maart gave her some antibiotics and she's actually breathing a lot better than she was yesterday. But he says there has to be a reason for it. Probably an undiagnosed heart defect and poor nutrition when she was little."

Even with both of her eyes swollen I can see the judgment.

"I know, I know. We've put her on a new diet. Her training is over. I don't know what else to do. I feel like a fucking failure."

I haven't said these words out loud to anyone. Not even Maart. And for good reason. Because the idea of leaving Ainsey behind is cracking my heart right down the middle.

Who knows how many of these kids in camp are mine? Just because they don't have the gray eyes doesn't mean they didn't come from the girls I won in the fights. I would never know. Because I don't know what happened to those girls after they were taken away.

So it feels like a copout to suddenly care about Ainsey because she has *my eyes*. It feels very fucking dirty.

And I'm starting to understand that the reason I didn't want to fight for Ainsey wasn't because I thought I'd lose, and then we would all lose everything. It's because then I'd have to face reality and admit that I left the others behind by choice. That I picked and chose who would live and who would die. And that all of this was my decision, not Udulf's or the people who run this sick world I'm a part of.

It was all just me.

I'm not gonna lie, not even to myself. Rainer's decision to stay and train them was a blow. It was a slap in the face. One of those genuine wake-up calls that ends up being a punch in the gut. Because how do I leave Rainer behind?

Two knocks on the doorjamb make me look over and find Maart standing there. "Hey."

"Hey."

His eyebrows go up. "So you're talking now?"

I sigh and shrug. "Seems like a more efficient way to communicate now that everything is falling to shit."

Maart's eyes migrate over to Anya. He squints at her. "Is she awake or not? I can't tell."

He can't tell because her eyes are practically swollen shut. "She's awake. I'm just about to help her to the bathroom."

I almost ask him to hold Ainsey while I do that, but before I can he says, "Good. I've got Irina making dinner." He nods to Ainsey. "Should we make her something? Or is she gonna sleep?"

I hate the coldness in his voice. I don't want to admit it's there. But it is. He resents Anya and he resents Ainsey because these two girls are fucking everything up.

He thinks Rainer is staying behind because of Ainsey. And he thinks Anya is making me question things.

He's not wrong, so I get it. I understand his judgment. But I don't like how it's changing my opinion of him.

Before Anya came, it was me and Maart. For so long, it's been just me and him. And yeah, Rainer has been here the whole time. And the girls back at camp. But Maart and I were a team. He's always had my back. And everyone knows you do not get this far into the game the way I have without a Maart at your back.

My success is his.

"I'll make sure she wakes up to eat," I say, finally answering his question.

He nods, then disappears down the hallway.

I push everything that just happened during our silent moments away and get to my feet, still clutching Ainsey to my chest.

Anya is looking up at me. "Come on." I offer her my hand. "I'll help you to the bathroom."

It takes several minutes just to get Anya standing. But I've been there. That first time you get up after getting the shit beat out of you is the hardest. But once you start moving it gets better. So I don't let her dwell on her slow pace. Just keep her moving out of the game room and down the hall.

When we get to the bathrooms, I help her sit on the toilet then linger for a moment. I put her in one of my shirts and no shorts just so when she got to this point, it would be easier to pee.

I sigh. The things I know and plan for. Makes me sick.

"I'll be down the hall, Anya. You get a bath today." I waggle my eyebrows at her, hoping for a smile. But she just nods and braces herself with one hand on the wall. "Right," I mutter, then leave to start the tub.

Ainsey is stirring in my arms and she starts signing to me. Begging for a bath too.

"You can talk, Ains. Fuck the rules, right?"

But she doesn't. Figures.

Everyone's strong after the weakest link breaks.

And today, I am the weakest link.

Once the water is running, I go back down the hallway and wait for Anya. Irina is busy in the kitchen. She looks over her shoulder at me a few times, wondering if I'm gonna bitch her out.

But I'm not. That's the first rule of camp. Both here on the Rock and back in our little training village. You do not *ever* apologize for winning.

Irina knows what she did was wrong, but it's not her fault. It's Maart's.

He's the one who told her to fight Anya. He's the one I hold responsible.

Anya appears, struggling to hold the door open. I help her into the hallway and then suddenly Irina is there. Signing to me.

I'm sorry. I'm sorry.

I hold up a hand. "Stop it. We've all been Anya, right?"

She is surprised at my voice, but she just nods, nervously looking at Anya, who is not looking back at her. She signs to me, *I will bring you guys dinner in the game room.*

Maart hasn't cleared Ainsey for a bath, so after I help Anya in, I take Ainsey back to the game room. She's crying and this makes her nose run, and that makes her cough, which makes her cry harder. So I settle down on the couch and pick up a book from the pile I've been reading to her over the past two days and eventually she settles and falls asleep.

And so do I. Because the next thing I know, Irina is helping Anya sit at one of the tables. Our games from last month are still open and Anya is sitting at the Connect Four table.

Irina moves it to the next table over, then hurries from the room as Ainsey and I take the seat across from Anya.

"Sorry. I fell asleep. Irina should've come and gotten me."

No big, Anya signs. And I smile. She looks better. A lot better. She notices me watching her. *Irina washed my hair.*

"Oh. Well, fuck. I missed out then, huh?"

It comes out... flirty. Which is not something I do, so... I don't know what to think of that. But Anya blushes. So apparently, she does.

Irina comes and saves us, putting a giant strawberry protein shake in front of Anya with a straw, a bowl of canned peaches and a peanut butter and jelly sandwich in front of Ainsey, and a bowl of rice and rehydrated chicken in front of me. She shrugs when I look up at her, then leaves without comment.

Ainsey is awake and excited about her peaches. She eats them with her fingers, getting the sticky juice all over me. Anya looks across the table at me, sucking on her straw. And even though her face is still swollen, she looks a thousand times better than she did just an hour ago.

Finally, once we're all done and the silence is getting awkward, I say, "I think your training is done."

Anya points to herself, then shakes her head, spelling out the words *F.U.C.K. Y.O.U.*

I laugh. I can't help it. "You know what?" I point at her. "I'm gonna get the story about you and sign language real soon. But first, why the fuck do you want to keep going? There is no fight in your future, Anya. You don't need to do this."

Her explanation is simple. *I like it.*

"Which part?"

She thinks about this for a moment. Then shrugs. *All of it.*

"The black eyes?"

She points to her eye. *Do you think this is my first?*

Fuck. "No. But... listen. I don't know why you're still alive or how you managed to do that. But you did, Anya." I reach across the table and take her hand in mine, trying not to notice her bruised and scabbed knuckles. "You did. You are. And you didn't use your fists to get here. If you try to fight a guy like Udulf using your fists, he'll always win. So whatever weapon you've been using to defend yourself, keep using that. Don't change what works."

She stares at me for a few moments. And at first, I think she's taking this to heart, but then she signs, *It's not working anymore.*

"What's not working? How did you get here? Why didn't Lazar kill you a long time ago?"

She looks away and draws in a deep breath. Then she straightens her back and signs, *I understand seventeen languages.*

"Really? Fuck. That's… impressive. And I guess that explains how you know how to sign."

But she's shaking her head. *No,* she signs. *You don't understand. No one taught me these languages. I just pick them up.*

"Huh. That's… like… genius-level shit, Anya. But what's that got to do with anything?"

I have heard things.

"Oh."

I don't understand everything right away. It's not magic. It takes me a few weeks. I have to be immersed in it. And then one day it just… makes sense.

She is signing all these words in a fast and furious pace that only someone who has been practicing sign language for years would be able to do.

"OK," I breathe, trying to put these pieces together.

So Lazar would rent me out…

"Oh, fuck."

A month or two at a time. They were told I was Hungarian, like Lazar. And I do understand Hungarian. I think that's my first language. But I never went to any Hungarians. They would talk in front of me. I was so small, anyway. They just did their business in front of me. Then Lazar would pick me up and make me tell him everything.

My eyebrows go up. "With words?"

Until I was seven. Then I stopped talking and just wrote it all down. She pauses, looking me in the eyes. *Udulf had me once.*

I think I stop breathing. "When?"

He was the reason I stopped talking.

"Why?"

Anya swallows hard and stares into my eyes. *He scared me.*

I feel sick. "Why?"

She shrugs. *I don't remember. I was so small. All I remember is feeling afraid. And his words did that.*

Everything I thought I knew about Anya flips in this moment.

She was with Udulf.

When she was seven.

"I was supposed to kill you," I say. "That night on the ship. Udulf told me that afternoon that if I won, I was supposed to kill you. That Lazar told him to tell me to do that. Did you know about that?"

She shakes her head. *But I am not stupid. I knew it was coming. I think Udulf found out about me. I think…* She stares at me, long and hard, with such intent in her eyes. *I think the fight between you and Pavo was a way to erase the bad blood between Udulf and Lazar and start something new.*

I don't even know what that means. "How do you figure?"

If you won, I died and Udulf's secrets went with me. And if Pavo won, you died and Lazar's secrets went with you.

"What?" I squint at her. Because I'm not sure I understand.

I'm tired of being silent, Cort.

"So... talk!"

No. You don't understand. I'm tired of keeping their evil secrets. I'm tired of being a victim. I'm tired of being a thing that has no mind of her own. I'm tired of not fighting back. I want to train because I want to fight.

She pushes her chair back, scraping it on the floor, and then picks up her shake and walks out. Stiff and limping, but alone. And without help.

I run all her silent words back and forth in my mind.

She is keeping Udulf's secret. I am keeping Lazar's?

How does that make sense? It doesn't. I don't have any of Lazar's secrets. And I highly doubt that Anya could be keeping a secret of Udulf's that would change anything. He's... *untouchable.*

It doesn't make sense. None of this makes sense. The entire sick world I live in is evil. And that's all there is to it. It's just evil.

I sit there at the table for a little bit, listening as things happen around me, just counting all the times that Ainsey's chest rises and falls against my own. Wondering where all this will finally lead.

Nowhere good.

I know I've been selling myself the lie for as long as I can remember, but that's all it's been. Just a lie.

There is no happy ending here. Even if we get out—even if Rainer does come with us—there is no happy ending. Because I will be leaving all these kids behind.

And what else can I do? Forfeit my life, my one and only life, to run interference for them?

If I thought that would save them, I'd at least consider it. But it won't save them. In six months five of these kids will be dead. In one year, at least ten. In two years maybe three make it. In five—none. Maybe not even Paulo.

There is no way to stop the fights. And they can call this Cort van Breda's camp all they want in that rag of a magazine. But this isn't my camp. This is Udulf's camp. I'm just a fucking employee.

No, that's not even right.

I'm lower than an employee.

I am a slave.

Eventually, I get up and when I take our dishes into the kitchen, I find Anya helping Irina clean up.

Part of me is surprised that Anya can forgive and forget so easily. But then again, she made it pretty clear that she was raised in violence when she pointed to her swollen and bruised eye and asked me if I thought that was her first.

Yeah. This whole world is sick.

And maybe it's better out there. In that alternative reality where the normal people live. But I don't think so. Because those normies are just living another kind of lie. They live in ignorance. They have no idea we're even here. And they don't *want* to know. They want us to stay the world's sick, dirty secret. Because if they had to admit that we're real, then they'd have to *do* something about it.

Or not do something about it, which is what I suspect would really happen. Ignorance is bliss.

I leave the kitchen and take Ainsey up to the helipad. Some of the kids already have their sleeping mats out. They are allowed to sign now, so some of them are busy having silent conversations. But most of them are playing hand-slapping games, a more elaborate version of patty cake that's popular back in the village where we live. They're allowed to laugh out loud now too, so plenty of them are doing that.

And their meals have changed. No more rehydrated meat. It's still frozen and not even close to high quality, but it's a helluva lot better than those dried-up chicken cubes. They get vegetables too. Not just oranges. Frozen peas and carrots. Berries too. They get protein shakes for breakfast now. That's what Irina fed Anya tonight as dinner.

Funny though, Irina brought me chicken and rice.

She's judging me, I think.

These rules I've had in place for nearly a decade suddenly seem very stupid. Why not let them talk? Why not let them laugh? Why not let them cry?

It's only one month a year where all those rules are strictly enforced, but still. A month of life is a month of life when you only get so many.

Why do I deprive them? Maybe I should've spent my time making them happy instead? Feeding them the best food, taking them nice places, letting them enjoy themselves.

But then Udulf would've closed my camp and they'd all just end up with someone else. With someone like Pavo.

I sit down on the concrete and lean my bare back against the hot cinder brick wall of the old machine building, closing my eyes and enjoying the last rays of sunshine before the darkness comes. Four albatrosses immediately start crowding me. This is kind of an evening ritual with the older ones, the ones who have been around a while, the ones who think of me as family.

Just thinking that word hurts a little.

Ainsey wriggles around until she's facing forward, at first reaching for the birds, who tolerate her and don't bite. But she knows they aren't pets and her attention soon turns to watching all the kids playing their games and talking with their hands.

She doesn't get up and join them. She doesn't belong here.

Why did I bring her in the first place?

It's a stupid question. In two months, I will abandon her to Udulf. And even though I keep telling myself I can live with that, I *can't* live with that.

God, Cort. You need to pull yourself together.

There is no way to save her. I can't risk another fight. I can't wait six or eight months to get it scheduled and train for it.

I can't do it.

Ainsey snuggles into my chest. She has no idea she is my daughter. No one has ever told her and no one ever will. She just loves me for some reason.

I hate that.

I hate that she loves me without knowing why when I will be the one to sentence her to death after I walk away.

A little while later Anya and Irina come up and lay their mats down over near the corner where Maart likes to sleep. Neither of them looks at me as they chat in sign language. They are not that far apart in age. Irina is only thirteen, and I still don't know how old Anya is. She could be sixteen for all I know. But I think it's more likely she is eighteen or nineteen. She's just kinda small, not that much taller than Irina, so I do see the logic behind Maart's decision to pair them up for that fight. But size has almost nothing to do with the kind of fighting we do. Anya could train for the rest of her life and she would still never be as dangerous as Irina.

Because every time Irina walks out onto the mat she is fighting for her life.

I'm sure Anya has done plenty of fighting in her own way. But she has never known that moment of fear when the only way to *not* be dead in ten minutes is to kill the person in front of you.

Budi walks over to us, holding out two mats. I nod and he sets them down beside me. Then he lays his mat down just a little bit to the left of the birds. They are warning him not to get to close, and he takes that warning seriously. Budi is not in my group, he's with Rainer because he's nearly nine now. But in month two on the Rock, they are allowed to sleep anywhere they want. And I guess he wants to sleep by me.

He lies back with a sigh, then folds his hands on top of his stomach and stares up at the darkening sky. The sliver of a moon is already rising and pretty soon all the kids will look up there and point to it, signing the number for 'three.'

Month two, day three.

A few other kids walk over and put their mats next to Budi's. And soon, I've got myself a collection of twelve little disciples. I feel like a cult leader. Like I'm leading these kids to their glorious demise.

It's not that far off the truth, either. That's the part that sticks with me. I am this bigger-than-life man with skulls on his body and a sick heart inside his chest.

I fall asleep to that thought, Ainsey tucked up next to me like a pillow.

And I think, as I drift off, that I'm not Sick Heart. I am *heartsick*. Just like Anya said. And I have always been heartsick. I just got the words mixed up back in the moment when it counted.

And then I just decided... to forget.

To become someone else instead.

CHAPTER TWENTY-THREE

The days and weeks go by fast as I recover from my ass-kicking. I join Maart's group. I don't exactly know why I end up in Maart's group. He didn't invite me in, but when Irina woke me up that first morning I went back to training, I just followed her down to the mats and started jumping rope with her. Then we did drills, and then we did heavy bag, and then the next thing I knew, I was in Maart's group.

Maart didn't even object, which was surprising seeing how he hates me and adding another person to his group threw off all the numbers. Now he had five kids, not four. But it all worked out because Maart started training Paulo one-on-one.

I learned though silent conversation that Paulo had a big fight coming up in a few months. But I guess the reality of fight club life never really sunk in until now. I knew that they have to fight for their lives, but I never imagined these fights took place with tiny children.

I knew it. But I didn't really comprehend it. Until now, this was just a fact floating around in my head. It didn't have meaning because Pavo was the only fighter

I knew and he was always big to me. Already a man in my eyes.

I can't picture these little ones fighting for their lives in a few months.

All these small kids.

And half of them here have already won at least one fight.

Half of them are little killers.

After I realized that I understood what I was up against. All the kids I would fight in the next test would be winners. Like Irina. She told me she had already won five real-life fights. She has one coming up too.

And that was... sobering. So I just buckled down and did my best. Which is pretty bad, but Irina is a surprisingly good teacher.

If Maart pays any attention to me at all, it is only to yell. He tells me I am worthless. I suck. I will never be a real fighter. I am wasting his time. And I've heard him telling Irina more than once that the more time she spends with me on the mat, the lower her chances are of winning the next time out.

I don't want her to lose. I want her to win. So I work harder to become a better opponent. So that she has to work harder too. So that when she gets to that next fight, she will win. And she will live.

It's a weird way to look at things, but this is the world as I know it. And it makes total sense to me.

Cort avoids me most of the time. He is constantly carrying Ainsey around, even though she recovered from her pneumonia and looks just fine as far as I can tell.

Word spreads through the camp that Rainer won't be leaving with Maart, Evard, and Cort when we leave the Rock. And that lifts the spirits of all the kids. But I think Maart is mad about this decision and I think Cort is sad.

So… month two looks nothing like month one.

Halfway through the morning of day six of week three Maart announces that we get the rest of the day off because it's raining so hard, there is no way to the keep the mats dry.

Rain doesn't bother us much. It rains at least twice a day and there have been plenty of nights where it drizzled constantly for hours and no one even bothered to go down to the training level to sleep. But this is a true tropical storm, so we all end up in the game room, spread out among the tables, playing games, or cards, or reading.

I choose a book, the one I was looking at all those weeks ago when Cort and I were still the only two people in the world, and I take it into the kitchen so I can be alone.

"Read it to me."

I look up and find Cort standing in the doorway. This is the first time he's talked to me since that day I woke up bruised and beaten. I smile at him. Because he's smiling at me. And he's shirtless, and dripping wet from being outside where he was tucking things into containers so they don't blow away in the storm. His dark hair is longer now. Two months with no haircut leaves the ends curling up a little, making it messy and wild. He notices my attention and runs his fingers through it, trying to tame the waves.

I look at the book and start signing the words.

"No. I want you to *read* it to me, Anya."

I scoff. Because that's a joke.

"I'm serious. Read it." He walks over to me. I'm sitting on a tall stool leaning my back into the corner. He stops just inches away, his wet stomach pressing against my bare knees. I stare at the skulls along his lower abdomen and notice the stars.

Tiny red stars. Drawn the way a kid might draw a star. With messy points and crooked lines. I touch one and he shivers, then grabs my hand and pushes it away. But I don't look up at him.

"I get it," he says, his voice a little bit frustrated and gruff. "You don't trust me. And why should you? But if you tell me the things you know—"

I place a hand on his stomach and push him forcefully away, then drop my book on the counter and exit the kitchen, pushing my way past the wet bodies of the children who linger in the hallway, sitting on the floor, backs up against the wall. I don't know why they're not in the game room, but I don't care.

Cort. Why do I even bother at this point, ya know? Of course he wants me to talk. He wants my secrets. If I would just tell him, he could... what? Make it all better?

He can't do that. *No one* can do that.

I'm not saying shit. Ever. I don't care if I'm ninety years old and living on a deserted island by myself, I am never speaking again. Ever.

"Anya." Cort follows me out onto the training platform. But I don't stop. I head to the stairs and have to make a decision to go up or down. I choose up, because even though the rain is coming down in sheets, the sea is angry today and I don't want to get that close to it.

"Anya, stop." He grabs my arm as I reach the first landing between the helipad and the training platform.

But I shrug him off and keep going. "Stop. It's fucking raining. Let's go down and talk about this."

Talk about what? How he wants to use me? I whirl around and flash fingers at him. *You do not want to know what I know. Trust me. You don't.*

"Fine." He throws up his hands. Rain is running down his body in rivers. "Keep your secrets then. I just want to hear your voice. And I don't want to wait until the last day. It doesn't make sense to wait until the last day."

I don't even know what that means, but even if I did, I don't care.

"Come back down. It's raining, and it's windy, and it's getting cold."

I don't care if it's raining. I don't care if I get wet. I don't care if it's cold. I don't care about anything these days. We live like savages. Our whole day revolves around fighting. Killing, really. Because that's all this leads to. Just killing.

I can take a storm.

"Anya."

I'm at the top now, and then so is Cort. He steps out in front of me. The rain has soaked him through. "Why are you running away from me?"

I scoff.

"What? What did I miss? I asked you to *read to me.*"

Fuck you, I sign, spelling the letters out in quick succession with alternating hands.

"What did I do?"

You want secrets.

"So? If you tell me why they're so interested in you—"

You'll what? Save me? You're not going to save me. We have one more month here and then I'm gone. Udulf shows up—

"But maybe I can stop him?"

Maybe? I don't have time for maybes. Leave me alone.

I turn away, but there's really nowhere to go up here except the old mechanical room, which is still home to several nests. The baby birds are massive now, almost full-grown, but they can't fly yet. They can, however, bite. Pretty hard. So I don't go in there. I walk over to the edge where Cort and I used to eat our dinner that first month and take a seat on the steel beam, the rain coming down so hard now, it stings my skin.

The crazy tropical wind is whipping my wet hair around my face, making it stick to my cheeks. But he was wrong about one thing. It's not cold. The air is thick and hot and so is the rain.

This is the tropics. Cold is relative. And this is the kind of cold that feels... comfortable.

In fact, this whole storm feels comfortable. Because I'm used to the storm. I don't mind the storm. I have been here for three months and it feels like I've never lived anywhere else.

One month. That's all I have left. One month.

That's all I can think about. Soon this will all end.

And even though I've been trying to convince myself that things will work out, they won't. I will never find a life like this again. I will never have a friend like Irina again. I will never work this hard, or care so much, or have so much to lose ever again.

This makes me so sad... I suddenly want to cry.

Cort sits down next to me. He doesn't say anything. The rain is too loud to have a conversation with words. But he takes my hand in his and starts spelling something out with my fingers.

It's OK, he spells, over and over again. *It's OK*. But it's not, is it?

Maybe for him. He's earned his freedom and he's leaving. So that's great. I hope he and Maart and Evard have a great life.

We all know Rainer is staying behind with the kids. They are very happy about that. And that's also super great. For them. Because they get to go back to wherever their real home is and things will mostly be the same.

But not me. Nope. I have no clue where I'm going when this is over. Not even a little bit.

I look up at Cort and frown as I shake my head. He's staring down at me with concerned eyes, truly wondering why the fuck I'm losing my shit.

I pull my hand out of his and start signing. *I don't think I can do it anymore.*

"Do what?"

Survive.

"Anya—"

No, I spell. *No! I don't want to talk to you. Just leave me alone.*

And then I turn my back to him and pull my knees up so I can wrap my arms around myself.

I wait, almost holding my breath, as the rain eases up and becomes a still consistent, but softer drizzle. But Cort doesn't get up to leave. Instead, he puts his arms around me and pulls me back so I'm leaning against his chest. "Do you want to hear my story then?"

I look over my shoulder, catching just a glimpse of his jawline. His chin is propped up on my bare shoulder and the scratchiness of his neglected week-old stubble suddenly makes me acutely aware of his body.

"Yes? No? You don't give a fuck?"

I think about my answer for a few moments, then finally sign, *Yes*.

He takes a deep breath and starts talking on the exhale. "I don't remember most of the early stuff. I was about four and a half, maybe, when Udulf started noticing me. And ironically, it was because I refused to talk. I had already learned sign language. I don't remember how, so don't ask. Some kid, probably. Some kid I was raised with. Or... I dunno, maybe a caretaker was deaf. Sounds about right." He scoffs. "That these sick fucks would assign a deaf person to care for the babies so they couldn't hear us cry."

God, that's the truth. I don't remember much of my early days either. I remember Paris, of course. it was always nice in Paris. But other than that—all those men I was sent to. They all just run together. There were yachts. There were private jets. There were beaches, and mountains, and green lawns in front of country estates.

But I wasn't a guest.

I was a slave.

And I was on a mission.

Every single time.

"Anyway." Cort pauses again, like he needs to build up his will. "I was one of the house slaves at first."

I picture that. Having been one myself, it's not that difficult. The boys had it much worse in my opinion. Lazar didn't keep a lot of them, and when I was small, he didn't have any my age. But I would hear them in the middle of the night when Lazar had guests. I would hear them screaming.

I turn my body, angling my bent knees between us, and look at Cort. His face is almost expressionless. And that's something I can relate to, as well. We learn how to turn it all off at a very young age. If you can't turn it off, you don't make it.

"I wanted to die back then. That's about the only thing I do remember. I had this overwhelming urge to just die. And because of this I made a lot of trouble for Udulf. That's why he brought me out here. I pissed him off and he dropped me off to die."

I exhale in surprise.

Cort nods. "Yep. I was about five. And I was done living. There was no point. Until..." His voice lifts a little. "Until I came out here and met these birds. Well"—he turns and scans the birds all huddled against the exterior wall of the mechanical room— "that bird, actually. See him? He's got a brownish beak. Their beaks get darker as they age. He's over thirty years old."

I look at Cort and make a face of *fuck you*.

He laughs. "I swear. These albatrosses practically live forever. And that guy over there, he was here with me that first time I was left on the Rock. He fed me fish."

Holy shit. Cort *is* Tarzan.

"That's how I stayed alive. Udulf didn't come back for months. In fact, I think he forgot about me. He only came to drop off another little boy my age.

"I was naked, and savage, and skinny. But I was still alive. My friend over there, he fed me. I had a lot of water. They left pallets of it when they decommissioned this rig." He pauses to smile. "I didn't want for anything. I taught myself how to fish. I swam around the reef. I would run laps around this roof. And…" He breathes out. "Every day I would jump off."

He's looking down at the sea when he says this, but then he looks at me. "I tried to kill myself *every day*. I wasn't unhappy, but I knew…" He shakes his head. "This wasn't right. There was something very wrong with my life. And if I didn't die really fucking soon, I was gonna figure out what all that wrongness was. So I jumped. Every day. But guess what?" He chuckles. "This rig isn't high enough to kill yourself by jumping. But I did try. I haven't jumped in more than two decades now, but you wanna know something weird?"

I nod my head.

"That night of our fight? That night on the *Bull of Light*? I had this overwhelming urge to grab your hand and run. Just run with you until we ran out of room and had to jump. And the only reason I didn't was because… I had *won*. I had finally reached my goal. We were free. And I was pretty sure that jumping off that ship *was* a death sentence. We would've gotten caught up in the wake or sucked under. And I realized that I didn't have it in me. I wasn't *ever* going to kill myself. My heart was not that sick and I was gonna have to ride this life out for as long as it lasted."

My hand crosses the distance between us and I place a flat palm over his heart.

He has a heart tattoo there with a big keyhole inside of it. But not the kind you draw as a kid. It's an anatomical heart. And I suddenly realize something, something I never paid attention to before. All the skulls have silver eyes. It's not easy to see because most of his tattoos are in grayscale. But once you see it, you can't unsee it. And that's when I realize… these skulls on his body… they don't represent the death of his *opponents*.

They represent the death of his *kids*.

Sick. Heart, I sign.

He nods. "Yeah. It's fucking sick all right."

I shake my head no. And change the signs around. *Heart. Sick*.

His mouth turns down and his eyes go distant for a moment. Unfocused. Like he's remembering something. Then he looks at me again. "There *was* someone else. I can't remember her. Not her face, but I know she was there. I just don't know who she was." He goes distant again, then refocuses. "It's stupid. Like…" He scoffs. Maybe it's even a laugh. "Like, I get it, OK? We all imagine that maybe this is all a mistake. Maybe we were kidnapped. Or lost. Or switched at birth before we left the hospital. We all want to think that we were dropped into the wrong life. That there is something else out there. Some other place where we truly belong. It's a fantasy. A very common one in kids. So I get it, right? But I'm telling you, Anya, I wasn't always this way. I just know that once upon a time my heart wasn't sick. Not until that girl got taken away. Before that, I was someone else."

I think I stop breathing in these moments.

He knows. He remembers. He just doesn't understand that he knows and remembers.

He is heartsick because of what happened to him.

And this is when I truly realize that his secret is my secret too.

Cort throws his hands up. The rain has stopped and the sun is peeking through dark gray clouds. Thin columns of light shoot down towards the water surrounding us. Like we're being cradled in the hand of God.

"But I haven't been him for a very long time."

CHAPTER TWENTY-FOUR

CORT

The storm quiets as Anya and I sit in the leftover drizzle. My chest feels tight, like I can't breathe, and I know this is because I said all those words out loud. It's been a long time since I thought deeply about life before Udulf and I don't even understand why I felt the need to bring it back up tonight.

Maybe because she understands me?

But even so, that doesn't make her special. We all come from the same dark place. We all live the same pointless lives. We all know that at any moment death is just right around the corner.

So why her? Why think about it now?

I've tried to piece my place in this world together as best I can over the years based on what I see around me. How these kids of mine come to the camp. How Maart and Rainer came to be. And Evard. Even Ainsey. They are both products of a Lectra-induced fight-night win.

They are the prize of a prize. Because when I win, I have to *breed with them* before the night is over. 'Them' meaning the girls put up as a prize. Like Anya. Udulf wants my bloodline and it's not like I'll be settling down and raising a little family for the Ring of Fire breeding program.

He takes it from me.

He take everything from me.

I don't know how many of those girls have gotten pregnant during the post-fight, Lectra-induced sex party. At least two, obviously. So that's one way you get born into our world. Breeding.

You can be kidnapped by traffickers, you can be sold by your parents, you can come from foster care, or an emergency-relief tent in some third-world country. So that fantasy of mine—that I was someone else, that I *am* someone else… it's not really wrong.

I got here somehow.

And even though I've been doing my best to not think about who I really am and where I really came from, it's always been there. In the back of my mind.

I am Udulf's son.

And he threw me away. Probably to save himself somehow.

Just like I will throw Ainsey away to save myself.

Anya gets to her feet and leans out over the edge of the helipad. I grab her leg out of instinct. This makes her look down at me and sign, *Just looking.*

Seventeen languages. That's pretty fucking crazy. No wonder Lazar kept her. I'm sure the people he sent her to assumed she could read and write. She's so pretty. These sick fucks like to keep the pretty ones as pets. Treat them like daughters. Which is a whole other level of sick evil.

The daughters don't go to school, of course. They hire tutors for them. But they don't really teach them anything of consequence. They learn a little math, they learn a little reading, they might paint or practice an instrument. But they do not teach the daughters foreign languages.

It's not like most people are even capable of learning seventeen languages. So she's a genius. And that's the real reason Lazar kept her all these years. She's too smart to let go. Too smart to even kill.

So why did he put her up as sacrifice for this fight?

Anya said, *If you won, I died and Udulf's secrets went with me. And if Pavo won, you died and Lazar's secrets went with you.*

This is what doesn't make sense to me. What secrets? And why get rid of her now?

Anya sighs. Then she starts backing up, her eyes trained on the horizon.

"What are you doing?"

She smiles, but doesn't look at me. I get to my feet. "Anya. What are you doing?"

She points to the sea, then looks me in the eyes. And in that moment, I know exactly what she's going to do.

"Wait, wait, wait, *wait.*" I step in front of her. "Why?"

She doesn't answer me. Just puts her hand out, palm up.

I look over at the edge. The steel beam is in the way. But it's a short leap over. Nothing insurmountable. I've jumped off this platform enough times to know that, at least.

Then I look back at Anya, take her hand, and the next thing I know, we're running.

And then... we're *flying*.

Falling. Plunging. Deep and quick—and then slow as the ocean suffocates us.

I push pause on life and just... open my eyes.

And she is all I see.

One beautiful blonde girl. Her perfect skin marred now with the scars of her fights. Her eyes open as well. And even though this water is not the kind you find near the shore—it's not the kind that glows turquoise in the sun, it's mostly dark green, cloudy and more like a lake today—even so, the blue of her eyes is so striking, I forget that I need to breathe.

Her hair floats around her face like she is a creature of this sea. A dark, dangerous creature of this sea that makes you want to give up everything and take your chances trying to tame her.

My sick heart changes in this moment. It doesn't quite mend. But the hole that once held the missing piece might... shrink a little.

Then we are rising again, our bodies naturally buoyant, seeking the air we need to live.

And when we crash through the surface together, I realize we're still holding hands.

She laughs. A real laugh. Even better than that first one I heard back on the ship before fight night.

She drops my hand and I almost reach for her again, missing her grip immediately, desperately wanting to hold on to her.

She wipes her eyes, still smiling, still laughing, spinning around as we tread the choppy water of a tantrum-throwing sea. Then she turns back to me, her face suddenly serious, and she says, "Don't ask me again. Don't ever ask me again."

I'm so stunned by her words—and so enthralled with her sweetness of her voice—I don't say anything back. I just float in front of her. Afraid I'll spook her and the magic of this moment will disappear.

"This is what I sound like." She stares into my eyes, so serious. "But it's the last time I'm going to talk to you. Don't *ever*. Ask me again."

Then she turns in the water and casually swims towards the underbelly of the rig, rising and falling on the large rolling waves like she really is a creature of the sea. Heading for the rusty ladder and leaving me behind.

I shake myself out of the stupor she put me in, then swim after her, overtaking her easily and then finally cutting off her retreat. "No. No, no, no, no, no."

She says a lot of things back to me in the language of her silence. She speaks to me in a language I'm fully fluent in by now, and that's fine. Because all I want is her attention.

I grab her face. Both of my palms flat against her cheeks. And then I lean in and kiss her.

Our lips touch and she tastes like an unsettled ocean of regret. Our lower bodies drift closer, our feet making small currents, treading water to keep us afloat.

She opens her mouth first and this causes a rush of satisfaction inside me. Our tongues tangle together, doing a little dance only they understand. It's not a light kiss, but it's not a heavy one either. Her lips are soft and mold against mine in just the right way. I grab her around the waist and pull her right up next to me, pressing us together, trying to make us one as we continue the kiss.

She reaches up and threads her fingers into my wet hair. And then she pulls back and shakes her head no.

"Why?" I whisper.

She doesn't answer. Just turns, reaching for the ladder.

"Hold on. Hold the fuck on. This is not how this night ends."

She turns in the water, eyes flashing. "Why? Because you didn't get sex?"

"What? No. What the hell, Anya? That's not fair and you know it. I don't care about sex."

"You seem to want to have it with me. Even though I know you're not supposed to be doing that. Maart told me. He told me I was fucking shit up and that was one of the examples."

"When did he say—you know what? Fuck Maart. This has nothing to do with Maart. This is about me and you. And the fact that after three months of complete silence, you just spoke to me. And that's it? 'Don't ask me again?' That's all you have to say?"

She shrugs her shoulders, her face blank. Emotionless. It's an expression I recognize. We all get it at times when we shut down. That's what she's doing. Shutting down so she can get past this conversation and not have to deal with something messy. "That's really all there is to say."

I stare at her for a moment. "What are you doing?"

She points her finger towards the sky. "Trying to go up there."

"That's where you're going. No. I want to know what you're doing. Why are you suddenly angry? Because I got you to speak?"

"I chose to speak. And now I'm choosing not to do it anymore."

"So you're what, failing at that on purpose? Because you're still talking, Anya. And fuck that, anyway. No. I have questions for you."

"No one gives a fuck about your questions, Sick Heart."

I narrow my eyes at her. "Don't do that."

"Don't do what?"

"Call me that name."

"Isn't that your name?"

"What the fuck is your problem? I didn't do anything. I didn't force you to talk to me. You chose to do that. So if you're mad at yourself—"

"I'm not mad. And trust me, *Cort*"—she sneers my name a little and I'm truly baffled at the complete one-eighty of her mood—"I learned to take responsibility for my own actions a very long time ago. I have no use for *blame*."

She turns, once again reaching for the ladder.

But I place my hand softly on her shoulder. "Anya. I'm not here to piss you off. I don't hang around with you hoping for a fuck. And if you're mad about talking to me, then…" I blow out a breath of resignation. "Then fine. Don't talk. But don't go up yet, either."

"Why?" She doesn't look at me when she says this. Just stares straight ahead at the rusted-out ladder.

"Because." I sigh. "Because you're the first person in a very long time who has made me *want* to talk."

She scoffs.

"No," I say, reading her mind. Because I can hear her thoughts like they are my thoughts. And they are,

I think. Because we are the same, somehow. "This has nothing to do with you talking to me, Anya. Whatever secrets you're holding for Lazar, I don't want them. I don't need them. That's not why—"

"Because you're out of here, right?" She peeks over her shoulder at me. "That's why you don't need them. You're *out of here*."

I let out a long exhale. "You know what? Five minutes ago, we took a leap of faith together—"

"Is that what you thought it was?"

"—and two minutes ago, you made the choice to speak. And you kissed me—"

"You kissed *me*!"

"You kissed me back. And who cares, the point is we were kissing two minutes ago. And now you're just getting all mean on me." I point at her. "I know how to read your silence. Even when you're saying one thing and thinking the other."

"Oh, do you?"

"You're being nasty because you want to change the subject. And anger is an effective way to do that. Trust me, I've been there. So I see *through you*, Anya Bokori."

She goes stiff, and even over the sound of the waves crashing against the steel pillars, I can hear her loud, deep breaths of frustration. Like she's counting to ten to calm herself down. Then she says, "You know what? That's the whole fucking problem." She turns all the way around and stares up into my eyes. "Everyone just sees right through me."

I point at her. "That's not fair either."

"No?"

"I'm trying to *know you*, Anya."

SICK HEART - JA HUSS

"I don't need you to know me, Cort. You're out of here."

"Ohhh." I draw in a deep breath. "I get it. I'm sorry. I should've realized quicker."

"Don't pretend like you know anything. Because you don't."

"You're hurt."

"I don't get hurt. That ass-kicking Irina gave me—"

"Not that kind of hurt, Anya." I place my hand flat on her breast. Right above her heart. It's thumping inside her chest. "This kind. You're mad because I'm leaving." She scoffs. And it occurs to me that this might be the longest conversation she's had in years. Maybe ever. "You're wasting it."

"Wasting what?"

"This." I point back and forth between us.

She frowns so deep. Her eyes go dark, and then they are glassy with the threat of tears. "There is no... *this*, Cort."

"Why? Because I'm leaving? What if I wasn't?"

"You are."

"But what if I wasn't?"

"You are. And you're fucking crazy if you think I'm going to take that away from you. And if you say another word about not getting out, I'll *never* speak to you again. That's a promise."

She wants to cry. I can see it. Hell, I can feel it. And this realization is like a punch to the gut. Because this is the moment when I truly grasp her hidden darkness. She wants to cry, not because I'm leaving and she's not, but because she thinks she has changed something in me. And she might become the reason I stay a slave forever.

"OK." I nod. "Fine. Topic over. But don't leave yet. Stay down here with me."

She makes a face. "Down here... *where*? We're clinging to a rusty stairwell in the middle of a rolling ocean."

I smile and point up. "There." Her face follows the end of my finger to the little catwalk-like platform welded between two pillars. "It's not much, but we'll dry off, at least. And we can stretch out and have privacy."

She shoots me a look.

"Shut the fuck up. I'm not trying to get in your shorts. If I wanted to fuck you, Anya Bokori, it would not be hard to change your mind."

She huffs.

"But I don't care about the sex. And I'm insulted that you think I do."

She lets out a long silent breath, then looks back up at the platform. "How do we get up there?"

I win. "Follow me."

We swim over to another rusty ladder on the side of a pillar and climb. This one is truly under the belly of the rig. And we have to climb all the way up to the top and then walk along a wide steel beam and climb down another ladder to the platform.

I have no idea what this rusty metal grate affixed to the side of the pillar was used for, but in years past, when I was out here alone, I used to tether my nets to it. Because net fishing isn't something that can easily be done alone.

On each end there is a platform that is shaped to the side of the pillar, so it curves a little. And when Anya and I lean our backs up against the pillar, we are looking out in slightly different directions, with slightly different perspectives.

"You don't have to talk," I say, breaking our silence. "But I would love it if you would listen."

She turns her head to look at me. And it's funny. Because I don't need her words to hear her talking anymore. She's asking me a question. *Listen to what?*

"I have this dream. Did I ever mention that? It's recurring and I've been having it since I was a kid. But here's the thing... ever since I met you, it's been changing. For as long as I can remember, the people in my dream are blank faces. Usually black blobs, but sometimes they are white blobs. The point is, they are blobs. At least, they were."

"What are they now?"

I huff a little air. "You."

"Me?"

"I know it's not really you. You're way too young." I pause, then say, "How old are you, Anya?"

She hesitates. "Eighteen."

"Liar," I whisper back.

"They tell me I am, anyway." I feel her shoulders shrug against mine. "How would I know?"

"Well... OK. Eighteen is too young. They tell me I'm twenty-seven and I'm pretty sure that's true. So you're nine years younger than me. You were born five years after Udulf took me into his house as a slave. There is no way you were there. So I know it's not you. But there is a girl there."

"And you think it's me... why?"

"It just feels like you."

"It's not me."

"Maybe not." But I say it like I don't mean it.

Because I don't mean it. I know that girl isn't Anya, but I also know, she is.

That's dreams for ya, right? They never make sense and they only ever give you a glimpse of the truth. Never the whole picture.

"That's like... projection," Anya says. "Or something."

"Close," I say. "It's called repression. It's when you rearrange shit in your head so you don't have to see the truth. And in my case, I have suddenly attached you to the face in my memory, even though it can't possibly be you." I pause to look at her. Then I smile. "I think it's because you are very fucking pretty, Anya Bokori."

She blushes, even though I know this is not any kind of revelation for her. She has lived in Lazar's clutches for nearly two decades. There is no telling how many times she has been used. And most of those people Lazar gave her to would have said something similar. But the blush is real.

"I want it to be you. Get it?"

She nods.

"I want it to be you, because if you were that person, then what I think happened... never happened." I sigh a little. "It means it was just a dream. I want it to be a dream."

"Yeah," she sighs. "You do want it to be a dream."

And... is that a weird response? Or am I just overthinking shit?

But before I can ask her about it, she says, "Don't you ever think about revenge?"

I turn my head to look at her. Then shrug. "Don't we all?"

"Then why not go get it? I've heard you're the most dangerous man on this planet, Cort van Breda."

I smile. "I've heard similar. But maybe I'm just holding out for the fairy tale ending, Anya Bokori."

She huffs. "Happily ever after?"

"Among other things."

"What's that look like?"

I pause there to think about it. Then sigh. "I don't really know. I guess I never thought it through, but just off the top of my head I'd say... a rescue would be nice."

"A rescue?" She scoffs loudly and turns her body towards mine. "Since when does the Sick Heart need a rescue?"

"I guess I don't. And I'm not expecting it. But it would be so sweet if, just once, someone would show up at the last minute—right before the bomb ticks down to zero, like in the movies, ya know? And someone—I don't know who. Someone I don't expect though. They show up and save my ass in the nick of time."

She's silent for a moment. Imagining the picture I just painted in her head. Then, she says, "You could just save yourself, Cort."

"I probably could. But I'd have to bite the hand that feeds me to make it happen. And then what? I'm on the run for the rest of my life? Hiding in favelas. Lurking in jungles. That's not an ending I can live with. So I don't know. I guess I can't answer your question. Or maybe I can, I just don't want to."

She looks down at her fingernails. Picks at them a little. "It's better that way."

And now I remember what she said. "Why do I want it to be a dream, Anya?"

She shrugs. Her shoulders bumping against mine. "Because then it's not real."

We're silent for a little while. I kinda wanna keep talking. I kinda wanna tell her more. I'm not sure why, because it's not going to do anything but drag us both deeper into the dark depths of this fucked-up world we're living in and then make us both remember what that fight was about earlier.

I'm leaving. She's not. And I guess we just have to live with that.

We stay on the platform, but we settle back into a world of silence. Like that little side-trip into the spoken word never happened. We doze off, leaning in to each other, and then wake up just before dawn and climb back into the real world.

Putting everything about last night behind us.

Because it's fight day.

CHAPTER TWENTY-FIVE

One by one the kids are called to the mat to test out of month two. I'm only half paying attention to who is winning or losing because I'm still busy thinking about last night with Cort.

Did I really speak to him?

I did. After all these years of silence, last night I spoke words. And I don't even remember what the first one was.

This blows my mind. Because in the early years, when I first stopped talking, I used to fantasize about what the first word would be. I imagined whole scenarios. And Lazar was a part of each and every one. I was going to spew the perfect words at him and make him sorry.

Today, all of that feels very juvenile. Just a child's dream of vengeance. I never did it, for one. I never spoke to him and none of my fantasy revenge plans ever came to fruition.

"OK. That's it. Good job, everyone. Welcome to month three." Maart pauses. "You have one day off and you're—"

Whoa, whoa, whoa. What the actual fuck is happening here? I stand up and take a few steps forward. Maart stops talking mid-sentence, his eyes fixed on mine. *What about me?* I sign.

"What about you?"

My fight? Where's my fight?

"You don't get one this time."

"Why not?" I turn to find Cort walking up behind me. "Why doesn't she get a fight? She's been training as hard as anyone else."

Maart sneers at him. "Because she doesn't *need* a fight. She won't be on a platform in a few months fighting for her life."

"How do you know?" Cort asks. I turn to look at him because his tone is dark and serious. And this is Maart. He doesn't speak to Maart like that. "You have no idea what's gonna happen to her when this is over. So why would you take this away from her?"

Maart's eyes track over to mine and he lets out a contemptuous laugh. "Am I stealing something from you, *Anya*? Because I thought I was doing you a favor. I'm not going to pair you up with little kids to stroke your ego." His eyes go back to Cort, narrowing down into slits. "Raffie sprained his ankle yesterday. So he didn't fight today. And you were so busy this morning coddling that useless toddler and dreaming about your night down below with that overgrown *house slave* that you didn't even notice Raffie didn't fight today. There is no one left for Anya to fight, so this is settled."

He pauses and I swear, the entire ocean goes still waiting to see how Cort will react to Maart's words. Because it's very clear that Maart is pissed. And it's also very clear that the reason he's pissed is due to Ainsey and me.

"What the fuck?" Cort's voice is low.

"What the fuck?" Maart repeats. "That's what I should be asking you. What the fuck are you doing?" Then his gaze lands on Rainer. "You're already fucking shit up, Rainer. Telling him you're staying behind. And whatever. If that's how you want to waste your one life, who am I to tell you no? But you've been going around telling these damn kids that you're staying behind to take care of them."

"So what?" Rainer asks. "Why do you care? In one month, you're washing your hands of the entire thing."

"Because this isn't over yet. And you two dumb fucks don't seem to get it. And that's fucking funny, coming from you, Rainer, since I'm the only one who seems to be taking this camp seriously. You're trying to make these kids into your best friends. And you?" He points to Cort. "You're trying to play Daddy to a little girl who won't—"

"That's enough!" Cort snaps. "We can talk about all that shit later when we're alone. Right now, we're talking about Anya's test. She did the work, she gets a fight."

Maart and Cort lock eyes as several long, awkward seconds tick off. "There's no one left for her to fight. Unless you want to force Raffie on to the mat." Maart looks at me. "But then again, maybe that's what you need. An opponent who can't even stand." Maart snickers. "Nah. He'll still kick your ass."

I step forward again. Because I get it. Maart hates me. He hates the fact that Cort brought me here. He hates the fact that Cort likes me because this reminds him that he's replaceable. I point to myself and then I sign, *How about you?*

"How about me what?"

Fight me.

Maart laughs.

All the kids gasp.

Cort says, "Fuck that. You're not—"

But before he can get all the words out, putting an end to my challenge, Maart says, "Fuck yeah. Let's go." And he whips his shirt off over his head and begins circling me on the mat.

Cort steps between us, arms wide to form a barrier. "Stop it. She's not fighting you. You would kill her."

Maart stops circling and straightens up out of his fighter's stance. "What the fuck is wrong with you? That's not a rhetorical question. What. The fuck. Is *wrong* with you? I've fought plenty of our kids and not a single one ever *died.*"

"She's not one of our kids," Cort begins.

But Maart cuts him off. "That was my fucking point. She's not one of us. She doesn't need a test. She won't be fighting for her life in a few months. She will go live in one of Udulf's mansions, or harems, or wherever the fuck Udulf keeps his women. And she will be fed, and fucked, and—"

"That is enough!" Cort yells it. And every single kid ducks their head a little, cowering from the anger and rage in his voice. "That's enough."

Maart walks towards him and pokes Cort in the chest. "Fuck you. I don't take orders from you, Sick. Heart. I'm not your underling. I am your equal. And you and I both know who the better fighter is, so don't you fucking tell me that's enough. I'll let you know when I've had enough."

Cort pushes him. Hard. Forcing Maart to take a step back. And then this fight is all but inevitable. Until Rainer steps between them, his back to Maart, his finger in Cort's face. "Step the fuck back and get out of the way. We have an uneven number of kids this time, so this is how it ends. If Anya wants a test, she fights Maart. This is how it's done."

"With kids who know what the fuck they're doing." Cort points to me. "She has no idea what she's doing. He's playing with her."

"Then I guess she should say no," Rainer says. He turns to me. "You have three seconds to make a decision. Do you want a test, or don't you?"

I nod yes before I can think about it. Because fuck this Maart guy. He's been on my case for two months now. Like whatever his problem is, it's all my fault. And I'm sick of it.

"There you go. Get off the mat, Cort. We're all hungry and ready to celebrate the end of phase two." Rainer pushes Cort backwards until he stumbles off the mat and is standing behind his row of kids.

And then it's just me and Maart. With nothing but a few feet between us.

He hunkers down into his fighting stance again and turns into someone else right before my eyes. Some ruthless killer version of himself. He turns into Cort the way he was that night on the helipad with Pavo.

He turns into an animal.

And I turn into his prey.

I put my fists up, mimicking his fighter stance, but without the two and half decades of practiced good form.

We circle each other for a few seconds, then, before I even understand what's happening, he's smacked me in the face. I grit my teeth, tasting blood. My tongue has mostly healed from the last time he did that, but it's like he knew he could split it back open with one well-placed slap.

And this pisses me off. Not that he cut my tongue back open. The fact that he *slapped* me.

Like I'm just a stupid girl. Not worthy of a real punch.

And I don't know what happens to me. But something does happen to me. Because I see red and my vision narrows down into a tunnel focusing only on my opponent. My whole body goes hot. My feet dance the way they've been conditioned to, bouncing on the mat like I really am a fighter.

And then, before I can think about it—before Maart can read my mind and counter what I'm about to do—I fake a punch and he ducks left. But I've already lowered my head. I ram his chest like a bull. Pushing him backwards, making him stumble. And then, like a fucking miracle from God, he's on the mat. On his back. Right in front of me. I drop to my knees as he laughs. And I punch him in the mouth.

I'm just about to smile and enjoy this one moment—this one time that I took Maart by surprise—when his fist crashes into my jaw and my whole world stutters.

And then it all goes black.

I struggle to swim up from the darkness.

People are saying my name over and over. "Anya! Anya!" Lots of people.

I recognize Rainer, Cort, and yes, even Maart. Then Irina. Even Evard. Hell, maybe all of them.

"Anya!" That's Cort. "Open your eyes." He pulls one lid open with a finger. "Look at me. Can you look at me?"

I nod, which makes my head swim. Then I look over at Maart and smile.

"What the fuck are you smiling about? I knocked you out, you dumbass."

Then I laugh and throw him my middle finger. And this, I think, is a moment worthy of words. "Fuck you. You fucking prick. You want to slap me? Like a goddamned girl? You think I'm just a *goddamned girl*? Someone to be tucked away in a harem house? Fuck you! You have no idea who I am. Or what I've lived through. Or what I'm *capable of*."

Every kid is laughing. So loud, Maart can't hear the rest of my curses. But I keep going. It's like… all those fantasy moments about what I would say when I finally started talking are playing out in real time.

"You're just a fucking bully," I continue as Cort pulls me to my feet. "And you're jealous. That's why you're being such a dick. You're—"

"That's enough!" Now Cort is yelling at me. I turn to look at him. "What the fuck, Anya? He just knocked you out with one punch. You want him to do it again?"

I throw him the finger too. Right up in his face. "Fuck you too. I don't need a big brother, OK? I can take care of myself." Then I look at Maart. "If you want to fight me, you better fight me. Because if you

SICK HEART - JA HUSS

slap my face like a fucking pussy one more time"—I spit blood on the mat—"I will cut your dick off in your sleep."

All the kids erupt in giggles.

But the three tough men go utterly silent. Just look at me like I'm some wild demon.

Then Irina has my arm and she's tugging me off the mat, leading me into the clinic to take care of my damage. The building's door has been propped open so we can hear Cort and Maart arguing outside as she cleans up my face in silence. Rainer is trying to play referee.

Most of the kids file past the clinic and end up in the game room. I figure that must be what Rainer was talking about when he said everyone was ready to celebrate the end of phase two. And then I get lost in the idea of that and what the next month will bring.

Who will I fight next time?

I look at Irina. She has a cut above her eye from her fight with Paulo just a little while ago. But their fight was mostly grappling on the mat. She smiles at me, giggles a little, then signs, *I fucking love you.*

Why? I sign back, not even sure why I'm signing instead of talking.

"Because," she whispers, looking over her shoulder nervously, "I have been wanting to say that to him for ten years." Her accent is thick Russian. And her voice is so much sweeter than I ever thought possible. "He slaps me all the time. It's insulting."

"Right? Fucking dick."

"Just punch me," Irina says. "I am no one's little sister. I don't need no fucking baby slaps."

"Yeah," I say, sighing as I push my wild hair out of my face. "Me either."

Irina points to herself. "I am *big* sister." Then she nods her head, pronouncing me fixed as she puts up a hand, palm out. I look at it dumbly for a moment. Then she takes my hand, slaps her palm with it, and then does some little wiggly things with her fingers. "Secret handshake," she whispers. "Phase three is good. You'll see."

Then she winks.

And walks out.

CHAPTER TWENTY-SIX

The night of test two out on the Rock is one of celebration. The first month is all about discipline. They can't talk, they can't laugh, they can't communicate in any way. They are their own worst enemy and they must learn to deal with that. They must learn to contain the fear. They must ignore the beasts lurking in the background, and never take their eye off the savage in front of them.

Because here's the hard lesson I want them to learn the easy way: No one is coming to save them.

I learned it early, but as Anya can attest, I never completely bought into it.

I need them to buy in to it.

It's one thing to have hope and be me. A man on the edge of the end and the end is gonna be sweet, not dark.

And it's quite another to be them.

Just getting started.

Udulf could walk into my camp at any moment and take any kid he wants for any reason whatsoever. He's done it seven times in the past twelve years and one of them was sixteen. Sixteen and she just disappeared one day with Udulf and that was that.

So they can make it all the way to me, all the way to the rim of that ring of fire and still, they will never be safe.

I cannot save them.

They must learn to save themselves.

It's a shitty lesson. And it's even shittier that they have to learn it so young.

But what is the alternative?

They break down crying?

They stop fighting?

They give in?

That is death. Even if they're still alive, if they break, they die. It might take a few months, but they are already dead when they break.

They must defy this life. Every possible chance they can, they must fight. And they must be smart about it. Like Anya. She is a fucking genius. And I'm not talking about all those languages, either. That silence. Yeah. It's brilliant. Because she gets one chance with every single person who knows she doesn't talk to stun them into their own silence.

Even if it's just for a moment, she has that one moment.

It's guaranteed to work.

She did it to me last night and she did it to Maart today.

"You want to slap me? Like a goddamned girl? You think I'm just a goddamned girl?"

No, Anya Bokori. I do not think you are just a goddamned girl.

I think you are some kind of mental ninja, that's what I think you are.

Month two is all about learning who has your back.

The kids never realize this until they are well into month three because all they are thinking about is death. And how to avoid it. If they failed their first test, they are stressing about the next one. If they passed their first test, they have just raised Maart's expectations. And that means he will do his best to make sure they fail the next one.

That's why Irina was paired up with Paulo this time. He kicked her ass. She looks a lot like Anya did last month at the end of her test. One eye swollen shut, her lip split, and she admitted to Rainer that her left ear is still ringing.

Anyway. The night of the second test is a party. A *real* party. They get free run of the game room, and candy, and then, just before bed, we show them their new sleeping quarters on the lowest level.

The entire perimeter of the platform is surrounded by shipping containers and up until now, they've only been allowed to open the one that holds their clothes. But tonight, we open all of them. And inside each one is a bed. A real bed. It's not big, just big enough for a small child, and the waterproof mattress isn't even as thick as the mats they train on. But it's a bed. They get a solar lantern, they get a set of sheets, and they get a pillow.

If you've never slept on a thin rice mat outside on a helipad of concrete for two months straight, you might not be able to imagine just how magical a pillow can feel. But these kids get it. And even though they're still not allowed to talk, they don't care. They're so used to it, they don't even miss it by now. It's just... life.

Maybe that's sad.

I've had rebellious kids tell me that in the past. Three of them, to be specific. About four years apart, so they didn't sit down and have some existential discussion about the pros and cons of deprivation. That was just who they were on the inside.

All three of them died early. They didn't make it to ten.

Ten-year-olds in my world are some of the wisest of creatures.

And here's the thing—those kids were right. It is pretty fucking sad when you wear deprivation like a badge. But what's the other option?

I watch the kids getting settled in their container rooms, waiting to see which of them will like the idea of solitude and which of them will go looking for roommates. Most of them have been out here before, so they know they're allowed to share a room if they move their own furniture.

And more than half of them do that. They get busy segregating themselves into groups, forming up teams. And the funny thing is, it never ends up the way you think.

The girls don't gravitate towards each other. Irina isn't sharing shit with anyone. She's always been comfortable being a loner. And Zoya, the little six-year-old in my group, is a lot like her. Her first act of independence was to color a sign that says 'KEEP OUT' in big, bold letters. And right now, she's dropping a pile of books and stuffed animals she stole from the game room onto her bed. Rainer's gonna be pissed about that. They're only allowed to take one book at a time and no toys or games ever leave that room.

Zoya is giving out no fucks. She's not hiding her booty, even though she knows the rules. She's displaying those books proudly. Like they are her trophies.

I predict she will go far.

Nine-year-old Rasha, on the other hand, is waiting on the edge of Paulo's container, her eyes begging for him to let her in. They are real-life brother and sister. I can tell he's pissed about it, but after about twenty minutes he starts flashing angry hands and fingers at her, and she bounces up and down in delight, clapping, then proceeds to drag her bed out of her container all the way across the platform and into his.

Rasha is not going to make it. She's not a terrible fighter, obviously. She's nine and still alive. But she's not ruthless. She is never going to be ruthless. She kills her opponents with tears in her eyes every single time and then she is depressed for weeks afterward.

It sucks. It really does. It sucks that her compassion will get her killed. It shouldn't be this way. But it is. And that's all there is to it.

Maeko and Peng room together. They've always roomed together. They are a lot like Maart and me. Or, well, how we used to be when we were that age. We would stay up late and choose our names for the Ring of Fire. I wasn't called Sick Heart back then. That was Udulf's name for me and it came much later, when I got in to the Ring of Fire. I called myself the Stray. Just thinking back on those days makes me smile. And Maart called himself the Badger, because even though he was super skinny, he just kept going in for the kill. He never quit. He would've gone all the way on his own. He never needed me. I needed *him*.

We made so many plans. We used to make up diagrams of our training camps. How many huts we would have. How many training rings. How many kids we'd train. And then we'd fantasize about what we'd do afterward once we won our freedom.

Buy a private island. Private jet. Private everything. Condos all over the world. Women everywhere hanging all over us.

We made a pact, too, to never let those girls come between us. I'd forgotten about that. Maybe because Rainer came along soon after and he brought Cintia, Sissy, and Ling with him. And we messed around with them when we got older, but girls, man. We didn't have time for girls. And the girls didn't have time for us.

The only thing we thought about was *living*.

I sigh. Because this is why Maart is mad at me tonight.

After he knocked Anya out, we had a pretty good argument in front of everyone. He was screaming at me, telling me I was blind.

But it wasn't just about Anya. It was Rainer, I think, who set him off. Maybe Maart felt like Rainer chose Cintia, Sissy, and Ling instead of us.

But Rainer... well, if he really does stay behind, we'd accept it. He's one of my dearest friends, but he's not Maart. It's always been me and Maart. And then along came this girl.

It's not even Anya he's pissed about. She's part of it, but that's not why Maart is so angry. It's Ainsey.

Ainsey. I shake my head as I watch her. She's dragging her bed across the platform. The steel frame the thin mattress sits on doesn't weigh a lot, but it's bulky. And every time she pulls, she scrapes the bed across the concrete about two inches. I don't know where she's planning on taking that bed, but she's gonna be here until morning at this rate.

I look around and find Rainer watching too. He's got one hand cupped against his mouth. Like he really wants to say something to her, but he's holding it back.

Then my eyes track over to Maart, who is also watching Ainsey from another end of the platform. He looks like he wants to say something too, but it's vastly different than what Rainer is thinking.

He blames Ainsey. For Rainer leaving, for me being distracted, for Anya being here.

And none of that really makes sense. I think he knows that, but we're so close and we have so much to lose. I sigh. It sucks when you have so much to lose. It's a terrible feeling. And it makes me want to go back to a simpler time. When we owned nothing, so we had nothing to lose.

Maart pushes off the wall he's been leaning on and walks over to Ainsey. I catch Rainer's look from across the platform, but I shake my head at him. *Leave it alone. Let's see what he does.*

Maart bends down, kneeling so he can look Ainsey in the eyes. I can see his lips moving, but he's talking too low for me to hear anything. Then he looks over at me, stands up, shakes his head, and starts walking my way. "Do you know where she's taking that bed?"

"No," I say.

"Upstairs." He points to the ceiling. "So she can sleep next to you out on the helipad."

I picture Ainsey trying to get that bed up the stairs and let out a soft chuckle.

"It's not funny," Maart snaps. "None of this is funny. It's bad enough you've got yourself all distracted by Anya, but this kid, Cort?" He points to Ainsey as the sound of another two-inch scrape fills the air. "She's gonna get you killed."

"You're being fucking dramatic."

"No." He shakes his head. "You're not gonna leave, are you?"

"What the fuck are you talking about? Of course I'm leaving. We've spent the last two decades working for this. I'm not giving it up."

"I don't believe you. Nothing about this last camp is right. It's all wrong."

I stare at him for a moment, acknowledge his fear—because that's what it is—and then say, "You know you always come first."

"Is that right?" He scoffs. Then he looks me dead in the eyes and says, "You should reconsider that."

"Reconsider what?"

"Putting me first."

"And why's that, Maart?"

He hesitates. Like he's not sure he should say anything more. But then he shrugs, giving in. "Because, Cort, I stopped putting you first the moment you took Anya off the ship with you."

Our eyes are locked for a few moments.

Maybe he takes off once we're officially out. Maybe running a supply ship isn't his idea of freedom either. Or maybe... maybe we're just over.

And when that thought enters my mind, I realize something. I'm not ready to let him go. "So you're out?"

He pokes me in the chest. Hard. "From the way I see it, I'm the only one still *in*. So maybe you should be asking yourself that question."

"You just said you stopped putting me first when I put Anya on that helicopter."

"Yeah. Because how fucking stupid do you think I am? You and her spend an entire month out here alone and you expect me to believe things didn't change?"

"If you want to know if I fucked her, just ask me if I fucked her."

He smiles and some of the tension releases from his shoulders. They drop a little. "Since when," he says in a low voice, "have I ever cared about who you *fucked*, Cort?"

I shrug. "That's why I'm confused. Why are you acting this way? She's not a threat to us—"

"Us?" He laughs. "Fuck you."

He starts to turn but I grab his upper arm. "Wait."

His dark eyes flash at me. "What?"

"What do I have to do to make this better?"

"Which part isn't good?"

"You know which part."

"Say it out loud, Cort. For once in your fucking life, say it out loud."

"You and me, that's the part that's not good. And I don't want it to be this way. If we don't stick together now then what was the point of all those years?" He doesn't say anything, so I keep going. "If we go our separate ways, Maart, then all those years turn into a business transaction. And that's not what it was."

"Wasn't it?" He cocks an eyebrow. "When we decided that I would stop competing and be your medic and trainer, wasn't that a business transaction?"

"Not to me, it wasn't."

"Hmm. Well, you never were the clearest thinker."

"So this is how it ends?"

"I never said it was over. That was you." He pokes me in the chest. "Stop using your sick fucking heart like a brain. It's not rational. It makes bad decisions. We both know this. And it's controlling you right now."

"Why do you say that? Because I care about my fucking kids? Because I don't want to see Anya taken away to Udulf's fucking harem?"

"*Your* kids?" He scoffs. "Which of them are *yours*, Cort? And which of them are mine?"

"They're ours."

"No. Not all of them. Ainsey and Evard only belong to you, right? And you're coddling that girl like you're her fucking father or something."

"I am. I'm sorry you don't like that—"

"Don't *like* it?" His eyebrows shoot up. "I give no fucks about your individual relationship with any of these kids. I love them all the same. Ainsey is no different than Irina. Do you think I want to leave Irina behind? Do you think I like watching these boys and girls work their asses off in a constant state of fear for over a decade, only to watch them be killed in a ritualistic fistfight to appease the rich and sick of this disgusting, evil world? Fuck you, Cort. Just fuck you. I do this because they *make* me."

"I'm not doing this for fun, either."

"No. Of course not. But you seem to think that you're better than me because you have that sick heart inside your chest and I don't." He points his finger in my face. "And that doesn't make you better, Cort. It just makes you softer. We both know I would've done better than you in the ring. But you're not smart enough to put me back together after the fights. So I gave it up to keep you alive. But I want to make something *very* clear right now." His eyes are seething with anger. "I would've gotten them *all* out. I would've fought for *all* of them. And the reason you have to leave Ainsey behind—the reason you have to leave Cintia, and Ling, and Sissy behind, even though they stood next to you all these years—is because you're too weak to accept the ultimate Ring of Fire challenge and pay the real price of freedom."

"The real price. And what the hell would that be?"

Maart huffs. "If you don't know, I can't help you. And if you want me to stick around after this shit show is up, then stay the fuck away from Anya. She's going to ruin everything and I did not spend the last twenty years working my ass off and making all these sacrifices just so your sick heart can bleed all over me in the end."

He stares at me with blazing eyes for a few moments, his chest rising and falling too fast, his hands balled up into fists, his anger so thick it seeps out of his pores. And then he turns and walks off towards the other side of the platform.

I let out a long sigh and then turn towards the stairs. Ainsey almost has that bed near the stairs. But I don't stop to ask her how she thinks she's gonna get it all the way up to the top platform. I just pass right on by, ignoring that ache in my chest, playing Maart's words over and over in my head.

When I get to the training platform I pause. Because I was gonna celebrate with Anya tonight. I was gonna grab the half-empty bottle of Lectra, take her up to the roof, get her drunk, and then maybe fuck her under the moonlight.

But not anymore, thanks to Maart.

Stay away from her. She's gonna ruin everything.

No, that's not true. He's the one ruining everything.

But I don't go looking for her in the clinic. I don't even go check on her. I just take the stairs up to the top platform and slowly walk out into the middle of the helipad.

No one is sleeping up here but me now.

Rainer and Maart both like the container bedrooms. They are a home away from home for them. But I have never slept in one of those things and even though I can already smell the rain on the wind, I'm not gonna start now.

I walk around the side of the little building, pass the water tanks on the roof, and end up on the other side of the line of supply containers, then climb up and settle back on the rough, rusty roof.

There is a sudden flap of wings and then the irregular, wobbly patter of large webbed feet walking on the metal. My very first friend settles in next to me like no time has passed at all. Like the last twenty years never happened.

I turn and look at the giant albatross. His beak was a light peachy pink when we first met and now it's patched with brown. His eyes used to be glossy black and now they're just a tiny bit duller.

"We're out of our prime now, buddy," I say, putting my hands behind my head and sighing up at the full moon. "The fights are over and it's all downhill from here. But make no mistake, that's a damn good thing."

He just tucks his head under his wing and goes to sleep. Because there's really nothing more to say about that.

It just is what it is.

I dream.

I dream about fights. And killing. And sick hearts. I dream about that fucking asshole, Lazar, and the time that came before my life with Udulf.

I dream of a tiny girl with dark hair, and gray eyes, and a pretty face, but no voice. Just hands and fingers for words. And in my dream, I call her Ainsey because she looks just like Ainsey. But her name isn't Ainsey. It's...

I wake to the sting of rain pelting my face before that missing piece can fall into place and I sit up, looking up at the storm. There are flashes of lightning off in the distance, but no thunder, so even though the threat feels close it's all very, very far away.

My friend, the General, has left. He never did like to sleep in the rain the way I do.

But the wind makes up for the lack of thunder and the temperature has dropped just below what would make staying out here comfortable. So I get up, climb down the container, and head back towards the helipad.

I stop in my tracks when I come around the corner. Because in the middle of the platform is a single child-sized bed. There is no child on top of it though, because Ainsey is sleeping underneath it, out of the rain. And my winged friend has joined her. They are snuggled up against each other the way I used to snuggle into him when I was small.

I walk over and I'm just about to pull her out of there and take her downstairs with me, but then... then I just crawl under there with them.

And before I can even think another word, I'm asleep.

The final month on the Rock always goes the quickest. The first one always goes slow because everything is new, and different, and honestly, even though it's hard for them, it's also fun. Training camp on the Rock temporarily erases what happens back in our village on the mainland and the reality of what comes after camp is still very far away.

In the second month all the kids are thinking about their first test and what they need to do for the second one. And they are busy laughing again. Playing their hand-slapping games and speaking in their silent hand signals.

But the final month is a mixture of reality, and fear, and acceptance.

That's why we give them the games. That's why we give them beds, and books, and let them be kids. Because in the third month the truth is far, *far* too real not to think about it.

And once your fighter starts thinking about their own death, they've already lost.

It's just a fact that most of these kids will be dead soon. And it's not like I ever just accepted this as fact, it's just… it's just a lot easier to give in to the inevitable than it is to hold on to the fantasy that someone will show up at the last minute and save them. Because it never happens.

I used to dream about that too. Even after Maart came along and we were partners. I used to imagine that someone from my past would show up and make it all better.

That girl. I used to dream about that girl with no voice who had the face of Anya a few weeks ago, but has now taken on the face of Ainsey. I used to hope for her to come back and say… I don't know… *I'm sorry I left you behind. It was all just a big mistake.* And she would take my hand and lead me somewhere… *safe*.

But it never happened.

I was about seven when I really came to terms with my situation. When I really understood that there was never going to be a *rescue*. When I truly accepted that at no point was anyone ever going to break into Udulf's training camp, take care of business, and lead me out of this nightmare.

And that the only way I would live long enough to grow up is if I fought for it. Literally.

So that's what I did. And that's why I have this camp on the Rock for my fight kids. It's a gradual lead-in to the final moment of truth.

Most of them don't get it the first time. Like… Ainsey isn't suddenly gonna understand that heroes don't exist when we leave here. If she makes it to next year, and there's another round of Rock camp, she *might* get it then. But I doubt it.

It takes most of them several years to come to terms with the truth. Just like it took me.

That's why I make them all come out here until they are fourteen. If they make it that long.

By then, they are hard. They are serious. They understand the lessons they learn out here can save their lives if they apply them correctly.

Silence is golden. Someone said that, I just don't know who. But I know it's true because silence has gotten me out of some very dangerous situations with Udulf and his ilk.

Quiet. Shhhh. Don't let them hear you. Speak with your hands, not your voice.

It's the secret language of slaves. I didn't know this until that night I accepted my fate. Udulf was angry because I would not talk. He was drunk on the Lectra and he was beating me, trying to make me tell him how I learned to speak with my hands.

But I didn't know. So I couldn't tell him. And I already knew that denying it wouldn't get me far, so I just said nothing.

It stuck.

Udulf never learned the lesson of silence because some time later, after his drunken rage was long forgotten, he was the one who told me about the secret slave language. And that conversation was the first one where he confirmed that the girl with no voice who left me behind was real.

That was the night he told me she was dead too.

And all my hope died with her and my heart turned sick.

And now it's all over.

Phase three on the Rock is history.

I look around the mat, on this last full day we will spend here out on the Rock as a group. I see that same sickness creeping into these kids too.

Budi has always gotten it. Someone told him early. Before he ever came to live with me.

Zoya, too. She's only six, but I see no hope of rescue in her eyes. She gets it.

Jafari is the only other kid in my group who understands. I think that fight with Anya did it.

Of course, Irina, Peng, Paulo, and Maeko got it a long time ago. That's why they're still here. But the rest of them... I look at each one in turn as they sit, lining the perimeter of the mat, listening to Maart give them instructions for the final test. Nope. None of the others understand what's happening just yet.

Evard doesn't count because as far as he's concerned, someone did rescue him. We rescued him. There will be no next fight in his future.

But that still leaves twelve kids who probably won't make it to next year.

Anya is sitting next to Irina. They are best friends now. Maart took over Anya's training for the past month. He treated her like shit every day on the mat. He yelled at her constantly. He corrected her relentlessly. And he made her sit out a lot because she was no match for the older kids.

But after dinner, he took her aside and made her train four extra hours each night. So she is actually a very good up-and-coming fighter right now.

I think he took her aside to keep me away from her.

And it worked.

Until now.

Because tonight I have other plans for Anya. I saved half a bottle of last month's Lectra and I will drink it with her tonight. Fuck him.

Finally, Maart is done talking and he calls the first two kids onto the mat. He starts with my group and nothing that happens with them is much of a surprise until he makes Jafari fight Budi.

Budi kicks his ass. Quickly and efficiently. And we have to pause things so Maart can go sew up a cut on the side of Jafari's eye.

Evard gets his ass handed to him too. By Rasha, of all people. Which makes me chuckle a little. Maybe rooming with Paulo did her some good because she has a new look in her eyes when she takes Evard down to the mat.

But things don't really get interesting until it's time for the teenagers to fight.

There are only so many combinations you can use with these four. And two have been done. Peng fights Irina. She is not an easy opponent, but he's a big kid and has at least twenty pounds on her, so he wins in the end. This means that Maeko should be fighting Paulo, but Maart calls Anya to the mat with Paulo instead.

"Fuck," I mutter under my breath. "Yet another ass-kicking for Anya. It's not really fair."

Rainer leans into my ear. "Shut up, you pussy. She made a big deal about being treated like an equal last test, so this is what she gets."

"He's doing this on purpose."

"Yeah. He's doing this to make her a better fighter and to cure Paulo of his fear of taking down girls."

"No. He knows it's our last night together. And he wants to make sure she's too fucked up to enjoy it."

Rainer almost guffaws at my statement. "Stop talking to me, you dumbass. Just watch the fight."

So I do. And to my surprise, Anya's got moves. Not amazing moves, like Paulo does. But she pulls off the same fancy capoeira move I used to take down Pavo all those months ago. She doesn't land it the way I did, so Paulo isn't knocked out. And he takes her down less than a minute later and almost breaks her arm, but still. I'm impressed.

And neither of her eyes are black. She has a bloody nose, but Paulo really does hate fighting girls so he mostly grapples when he has to fight them. Maart will berate him later for that and I'll probably have to talk to him too—just to drive the point home that you do not ever go easy on the girls in this business. They will kill you the first chance they get in the real fights.

But I'm relieved he didn't punch Anya in the face. She's had more than her share of that this camp and that means I can kiss her tonight and not have to worry about the pain.

Because yeah. I will kiss her tonight.

If I have to lose her tomorrow, I'm gonna make this a night to remember.

I am distracted by my thoughts and Paulo helping Anya up off the mat, but when I look over at Maart, he's already watching me. Anya and Paulo bow to each other, then him, and he refocuses on his students, bowing back.

Maart points at Maeko, telling him to meet him on the mat. He has an uneven number of kids this time around so he has decided to test Maeko himself. It's actually a long fight and I can almost hear everyone in camp reevaluating Maeko's future.

His moves are impressive. He has really improved this time around. His fight with Maart—even though he loses because Maart will never throw a fight with a kid—is his best ever. He is someone else now. Whoever he was when he got here three months ago, that kid is gone and this one takes his place.

I watch Paulo as this all sinks in and read his mind. Does he need to worry about Maeko? Should he be afraid of some future fight with him? Even if it's fifteen or twenty years away, the way my fight with Pavo was?

Fuck yes, he does.

The fight ends with Maart almost breaking Maeko's leg, but after they bow, Maeko is smiling as big as I've ever seen him.

He knows what just happened. He might even have a new hope that he will make it. And he probably will. That's why Maart singled him out.

Paulo, on the other hand, now has doubts. It's a bad way for him to end his camp, but what's done is done.

Maart finds my gaze from across the platform. He just stares at me for a few moments. Then he looks away and announces the end of Rock camp, phase three.

There is a lot of clapping, and pats on the back, and big smiles.

Tonight, they will eat well. We will cook up everything we have left and stuff our faces. Three different kinds of meats, pasta with sauce, frozen vegetables, and bread baked fresh this morning by Rainer and Evard is just where it starts. There will be cake, and ice cream, and chocolate, and everyone will get a tiny bit of Lectra.

And they will have earned it.

I find Anya in the game room a little while later. She didn't need any medical attention this time and she's reading a book when I walk in, like this is just another day.

I walk right over to her, grab the book from her hand, and hide it behind my back as she jumps to her feet and makes a grab for it. "What?" I ask her playfully.

She signs, *Give me my book.*

"This book?" I ask, holding it up above my head. Anya is short, like almost an entire foot shorter than I am, so when she reaches up to make a grab for her book, there is no hope of her actually snagging it. She puts her hands on her hips and glares at me.

"Anya," I say. "It's our last night. You're not gonna sit in here and read. You can take the book with you."

Her face remains expressionless, as usual. But I can feel her thoughts behind her blue eyes. She wants to ask me all the questions. *What will happen to me? Will I ever see you again?* Questions like that.

But even though I hear her silent words, I do not answer her unspoken questions. Instead, I toss the book onto the couch, take her hand, and lead her out onto the training platform. Rainer has all the kids gathered in a circle on the mats. They are sitting cross-legged, their attention on the story he is telling. I'm not sure what it is this time, but it's a story to help them understand what they just accomplished while also preparing them for what's coming next.

He finds my gaze and smiles at me as Anya and I walk towards the stairwell. Gives me a little nod to let me know he's got things under control here and we are free to go start our celebration without him.

I look over my shoulder, trying to find Maart, but he's somewhere else. He will probably have a problem with my plans with Anya tonight, but I don't care. He made his point and I considered it. And I've respected his feelings all month.

But this is our last night. I'm not going to waste it.

Anya and I come out onto the top platform, but instead of leading her over to the helipad I take her behind the building, past the showers, and ease between the containers towards the back.

I look up and then stop so suddenly, Anya bumps into me. She follows my gaze upward where Maart is standing on top of the container with the half-full bottle of bright blue Lectra in his hand. "What are you doing?"

He holds up the bottle. "What's it look like?" Then he nods his head to Anya. "Thought we might share."

I'm not sure if he means Anya or the bottle. Because we've obviously done both in the past.

"The bottle," he clarifies. "Unless you want some privacy. And if that's the case, then tell me to get lost."

I am not going to tell Maart to get lost and he knows it. I don't like the tension between us and this is our last night on the Rock. I want to spend it with him. He's my best friend.

But I want to spend it with Anya too. I feel like we've spent a lot of time together but it hasn't been nearly enough. I look to Anya. "You OK with this?" She's staring up at Maart with a weird look on her face. And I can say, after four months of silence with this girl, that I have seen every possible look on her face and I'm pretty good at deciphering them. But this one I'm not sure about.

Is she mad? Confused? Conflicted? The last one, I think. But conflicted about what?

She nods her affirmation and urges me forward with a light touch in the small of my bare back.

I meet Maart's gaze and shrug. "I guess we're in."

He grins back. And it's a wide grin. I have known him for decades and if you add up all the time we've spent in silence it would equal years. So I can read the meaning behind his expression. And I am not confused about this one.

He is up to something.

I reach up, hook my fingertips over the lip of the container, then pull myself up and turn to reach for Anya. Maart is reaching for her too.

I eye him, then Anya, to see if she will reject his offer of help. But this girl is nearly unshakable. She doesn't even hesitate. She takes both our hands and Maart actually chuckles as we pull her up in one smooth motion.

And then there she is. There *we* are. The three of us. Way too close. But I don't want to back up and leave the group. It would send the wrong signal.

What the fuck is Maart up to? I'm not quite sure yet, but he's staring intently into Anya's eyes. Then he points a finger at her face and in a low voice he says, "I have one rule tonight. And you do not get to say no."

She swats his hand away.

"No sign language," he growls. "I earned your words. So I want to hear you talk. Do you understand me?"

It's weird watching them because it's very clear that Anya and Maart have a relationship going.

Not the same kind of one I have with her.

Not lovers. There is no chance Maart would fuck this girl during training.

It's something else.

Something even more intimate.

It's mutual respect.

And of course, that's mandatory when you have a student-teacher relationship and spend hours together training one-on-one each night. But even so, I haven't been imagining them in a relationship.

Anya presses her palms together, like she's praying. She touches her thumbs to her eyebrows and lowers her chin. Her formal wai is the ultimate reverence typically reserved for monks. And ajarn.

Maart reaches out with the tip of his finger and lifts her chin back up. She drops her hands and waits.

"Well? Yes or no?" Maart asks.

"Fine." Her voice is small and soft. "I agree."

Maart smiles as his head slowly turns to me. Then he holds up the bottle. "Then let's celebrate."

I take the bottle and he turns his back to us, walking over to the other side of the container where he has a little plate of those little cornstarch cookies that are so popular in the rural towns of Brazil, some dried pineapple, banana, and guava, and some chocolate pieces in a stainless-steel bowl that's sitting on a chunk of quickly melting ice.

This is our thing. Every last day of Rock camp Maart, Rainer, and I come up here to the roof of a container and we get drunk on whiskey under the incredible blanket of stars that can only appear on the darkest of new-moon nights.

Maart has placed a blanket down on the rusty metal roof of the container, a thick quilt that feels very good on my bare feet when I step onto it. And it suddenly occurs to me that Maart has put a lot more thought into this night than I did. Because this isn't how it typically goes. We bring the bottle, we bring ourselves, and every once in a while, Rainer will produce cigars.

"What's all this?" I ask, panning my hand to the spread before us.

Maart grins at me, apparently in a very good mood. "It's our last night on the Rock. And we might come back here again one day, or we might not. I didn't plan on Anya being here. I thought it would just be us. But fuck it." He stares at her for a prolonged moment. "She's not bad to look at, though. Right? So I'm not complaining."

Anya walks over to him and raises her middle finger in front of his face.

He swats her hand away. "I said no sign language. If you want to tell me to fuck off, you will use words, nak muay."

Anya scoffs. "That's nak su to you."

Maart laughs. And so do I. Nak muay means fighter. Nak su means *warrior*.

Anya has proclaimed herself a warrior. And Maart must agree, or he would correct her. He's been so stressed this time around, it feels good to see him happy.

"So," I say, walking over to stand next to Anya. "You speak Thai too?"

We haven't spoken any Thai out here. So she didn't pick this language up from us.

She sits down and picks up a piece of dried pineapple, nibbling on it coyly. "I've been speaking Thai since I was seven."

I look at Maart to see if he knew this, but the expression on his face is some kind of combination between admiration and confusion.

"I understand seventeen languages," Anya explains, the tip of her pink tongue poking out to lick a sugar crystal off the pineapple. "I'm Lazar's spy."

Maart laughs and looks to me. "Did you know this?"

"She told me last month."

Maart considers this for a moment, his eyes narrowing down into slits, but he's not looking at me when this happens. Or Anya. So he's thinking about something other than us. But that expression disappears when he sits down next to her, reaches over her—letting his bare arm brush against her bare leg—and picks up a piece of dried guava. "Sit down, Cort. Stop overthinking shit."

I draw in a deep breath and hold it for a second. He's definitely up to something. Because it's not me overthinking anything right now. It's him.

Maart's dark brown eyes pierce mine, dragging this moment out for so long it becomes intimate. "Come on," he finally says, his voice soft now. And this breaks the awkwardness. "What are you waiting for, Cort? We got shit to celebrate." He holds up the bright blue bottle of Lectra. "Let's get fucked up."

I hate this. I love this. I hate this. I love this.

These two things cannot be reconciled. Ever. And tonight just proves it.

Because Maart isn't just any man. He is my best friend. Sometimes, he's more than that. He is my secret weapon and my greatest weakness.

And Anya isn't just a girl. She is a pretty girl. She is *our* girl. But she is more than just a pretty girl who is ours. She is a *reward*.

For a job well done. For a fight hard fought. And, whether I really want to admit this or not, she is my prize for walking away. For bowing to Udulf. For accepting his reality as mine. For giving in.

And that, I realize, is not how I want to win.

That is not the way of the warrior.

But it's far too late to do anything about it now.

So I take that bottle from Maart.

And I get fucked up.

CHAPTER TWENTY-SEVEN

ANYA

I know Maart fairly well now. We've spent the last month training together, one on one, every single night. He's had his hands all over my body while we grappled on the mat. And even though his touch never felt intimate or made my stomach queasy, now, when he brushes his arm across my leg to grab a piece of dried fruit, it is intimate and my stomach does something weird.

I don't remember much about the first night we were all together. I just know it felt good. And I was very drunk. It wasn't anything I relived in my head. I didn't play it all back, going from moment to moment.

Some of that is because I wouldn't be able to track those moments. I think I skipped most of them while it was happening.

But right now, time is not skipping. Time is long, and slow, and... I don't know. Maart's attention is somehow different. And I haven't even taken a sip of Lectra yet.

"Here," Maart says, putting the bottle of Lectra in my lap. "Ladies first. Drink up."

If I want to curtail what's about to happen, now would be the time to put a stop to it.

But I don't. So I drink. I take a long sip and Cort laughs, pulling the bottle away from my lips before I'm even done. "Slow down, killer." I love his laugh. He's been stressed this entire time. From the moment we got here he's been caught in some web of worry. But now he's different. He's calm and happy.

So even though I know that tomorrow is my last day with this man, I don't let that worry touch me. I don't let reality chase away our one night of dreams.

He drinks too, then wipes the sticky blue liquid from his lips and passes the bottle to Maart. They catch each other's gaze for a moment. Hold it.

And I want to know all the silent words passing between them in this moment.

Is it *I love you?* Probably. But it's also *Thank you.* And *We did it.* And, when both of them suddenly look at me, it's *She's pretty.*

I blush.

"Stop reading minds"—Maart laughs—"and drink."

I do. I drink. We all drink. We nibble on the sugared-up dried fruit, and then, suddenly, Cort is feeding me chocolate and I'm sucking on his fingers as I stare into those steel-gray eyes of his. Get lost in them. I know this is the drink catching up with me, but I don't care.

Maart is laughing, telling some story about their childhood. Some memory of a long time ago when it was just the two of them against the world and a girl called Anya maybe didn't even exist yet.

We lie back on the blanket—me in the middle, them on either side—and look up at the deep dark above our heads and marvel at the vast emptiness dotted with pin-pricks of light.

Our hands are wandering. Not doing anything sexual, not really. We're just touching each other the way you are compelled to do when you're on the Lectra. A fingertip across my upper thigh. A thumb caressing lazy circles on my cheek. My hand on Cort's scratchy face as he hovers over me. Kisses me.

Then Maart is there. Kissing Cort.

I get lost in that. The way their lips press together. The way their eyes close when they open their mouths. The way their tongues twist and then the way they both kiss me. Maart's mouth on my neck, trailing down to my breast.

We don't have clothes on and I don't even know how that happened. It just did.

Cort's mouth on my lips. His tongue twists with mine as Maart takes his kisses down my stomach. His fingertips parting the folds of skin between my legs. Pressing inside me. Making me gasp.

I see Rainer's face then. Laughing. Smiling. Joyful. Saying something about starting the party without him. The bottle. He drinks, his eyes lighting up as he watches Maart lick between my legs. And I sigh when Rainer's tongue passes over his lips, like he wants a taste of me.

And then he is tasting me. He and Maart are between my legs, holding them open as they kiss each other, then me.

My back bucks up from the pleasure and Cort's mouth is there, hard and demanding as he pulls my hair while he kisses my lips, whispering things into my ear as he bites my neck.

I understand seventeen languages, but I can't make sense of his words. They cannot make sense because I think he says, *I will rescue you,* and that's not right.

No one ever rescues me.

"Shhh," he's telling me. "Stop thinking so loud. Just enjoy it."

So I do.

Cort pulls me on top of him, positioning me over his hips, my long, wild, blonde hair dragging over his marked-up chest. And I get lost in those skulls—the big one on his right pec, the heart with the keyhole over his left pec, the little skeletons, and skull faces with gray eyes.

And the stars. I trace the stars as we fuck, his cock buried deep inside me. Maart behind me, pulling my hair as he wraps his palm around my neck. Not pressing hard. Not pressing at all, like he doesn't want to scare me, just turn me on. And it does turn me on.

He enters me too, momentarily fighting with Cort for dominance. But Cort's laugh echoes into the night and gets lost in the blanket of stars.

I turn my head and find Rainer sitting back on the blanket, jerking off as he watches us. He winks at me, says something in yet another language I don't understand, then comes in his hand.

Cort's thumb is swirling small circles against my clit and he and Maart fuck me and that's it for me too. I gush all over them. And then they gush inside me.

We collapse into each other, a heap of bodies drunk on Lectra. And that's when the buzzing of the tattoo machine starts.

Rainer is grinning wildly as he marks Cort up with yet another bit of ink. But it's not a skull this time. He turns the keyhole over Cort's heart into a lock.

Then he takes my hand and draws a key. A skeleton key, of course.

And he makes it fit the lock over Cort's sick heart.

CHAPTER TWENTY-EIGHT

CORT

The world is mine.

This is what the Lectra tells me.

It's all mine for the taking.

Finally.

We are a heap of sweaty fighters under the stars.

Warriors, all of us.

Champions in the dark.

My body is still humming from the sex, my mind is still blown from the ecstasy, and this is when the Lectra takes over. Pulls me into that other place. That other reality where I am small, and screaming, and running through a bathhouse.

I've been here before, I tell the Lectra. *You're gonna have to do better than this.*

And the Lectra says, *Challenge accepted.*

Everything in the dream changes and I'm suddenly in a shipyard, one small boy among dozens of small boys running between containers. But we scream. Oh, do we scream.

And our feet are bare. And they are bloody.

This is how they find us. We leave a trail of crimson scarlet in our wake. And all they have to do is follow it.

But I don't know this yet. How could I know that? I am only four.

I look up and the girl who is Anya or Ainsey, but is neither Anya nor Ainsey, is shaking me by the shoulders. She is older than me, years older. Maybe seven. She flashes her fingers at me quickly, efficiently, desperately.

Listen, her fingers say. *Hide! Run and hide and don't ever come out! No matter what happens, do not come out!* She shakes me again. *Do you hear me?*

No. I don't. Because she can't talk. She has no tongue.

But I do, of course, understand her. And that's all she really means.

So I nod. And I run again, weaving my way through the maze of shipping containers, never wanting to be inside one of those things again. Because I still smell like piss, and shit, and death from the trip across the ocean.

I run, and run, and Maart is there around every corner telling me, "Keep going. I've got your back."

And I do keep going.

I go. I climb.

I'm on the roof of a rusty green container, my whole body pressed flat so that the hunter men cannot see me from the ground.

The men are strong, and fast, and they catch her first. The girl with no tongue. The girl who talks with her hands. The girl who draws stars on the inside of the container in her own blood as we pray, with palms pressed together, thumbs against our eyebrows, that one day the men will open the door so we can run.

They catch her. And then…

I wake up screaming.

But only on the inside.

Because I know better.

And I know *why* I know better.

CHAPTER TWENTY-NINE

ANYA

"Wake up."

I turn over, my mouth a dry, sticky, gross mess, and see Maart's face pressed towards mine. "What?" I croak.

"Time to get up, princess."

I shield my eyes from the sun and look around. "Where's Cort?"

"Here." He hands me a cup of water. "Drink this. Cort's already downstairs with the kids. We're just finishing packing up and the boat is already here."

I let out a long breath, my head throbbing.

"Anya."

"I hear you."

"You're not moving."

"Give me a sec." I push my hair away from my face and sit up, then feel a little sick.

"If you're gonna puke, do it before you get on that boat."

"Oh." I groan. "Why did I get drunk last night?"

"Because it's fun."

I look down at myself and realize I'm still naked. "Oh."

"Here." Maart laughs and tosses my clothes to me. "You can take a shower. All the kids got a shower this morning."

I nod and yawn—"OK"—then look around again, this time actually seeing things. "Where's Cort?"

"I just told you. Jesus Christ. Get up." He doesn't wait for me to decide that, he just grabs my arm and pulls me to my feet. When I look up at him, he's smiling.

"What?"

"Nothing. Just… It was fun last night, right?"

"I barely remember it."

"Fuck you. You remember. Just say it was fun, Anya, and I'll stop bothering you."

I smile a little. I can't help it. It was fun. "Go away."

"It was fun, you know it was."

Then I frown. Because reality is suddenly slapping my face.

"What's that look for?"

I look at Maart and sigh. "It's over now. So who cares?"

He smacks my ass. "It's not over 'till it's over. And we've got a five-hour boat ride back home. Make the most of it."

I sneer at him, wondering what he's implying. But he doesn't bother to answer me. Just walks over to the edge of the container and jumps down. I pull my shirt and shorts on, then walk over to the edge too. He's got his hand out.

"Take it," he says. "I got you."

And even though I don't think his hand is gonna help break my landing when I jump, it actually does.

He gloats at me.

"Stop rubbing it in," I say.

"What am I rubbing in?"

"The fact that this is the first day of the rest of your life."

"Everyone's first day."

"Not mine."

"Stick with me, Anya. You'll see."

I don't know what that means, so I just ignore him and take my shower. I can hear lots of things going on down on the training platform, but I tune it out as I will my headache to go away.

When I go downstairs, I am surprised to find every bit of equipment put away in the containers. It looks like the first day I arrived here on the Rock four months ago and this is when the reality of my situation really sinks in.

It's over.

My life with these people is over.

I suddenly understand what it might feel like to fight for your life on the mat. Waking up that morning knowing you might only have hours left to live.

But there's one major difference.

They have a chance.

And I don't.

The boat is actually very nice and has a cafeteria. Most of the kids stay on the deck, signing, and laughing, and playing their slapping games.

Ainsey is attached to Cort's hip and even though I know Maart hates this, he doesn't even shoot Cort a scowl. Just lets it go.

If Cort leaves his base camp today—and he will. I mean, why the fuck wouldn't he?—then this is his last day with Ainsey.

I don't bother him and he doesn't come over to me, either. In fact, Maart is the one who hangs out with me all day as the ship crawls its way up the coastline of South America.

"Where are we going?" I finally ask him. We're sitting on the deck, our backs propped up against some cargo hold, just watching the scenery go by.

"It's a little village southeast of São Luís in Maranhão."

"No idea where that is."

"Brazil."

I make a little o with my mouth. "So why are you hanging out with me today?"

"We're sticking together."

"Are we?"

"We are."

"What's that mean, exactly?"

"You'll find out."

My stomach does a little flip at these last words. But I don't want to press him. I don't really understand Maart. There are times—plenty of times, actually—when I think he's on my side. But the few times when I think he's out to get me just wipe all those positive thoughts away.

He's… sorta terrifying. And not in the same way as Cort. I'm not saying Cort is dumb. Nothing about him leads me to believe he's just some dumb, low-IQ fighter. But he doesn't have that cunning look to him the way Maart does.

He's not calculating, and Maart is.

I don't know why Maart is in such a good mood. It might be because I'm finally gonna be out of his life. But I don't care. I'm not in a good mood at all. I don't want to be on this ship. I don't want to go to their village. I want to stay on the Rock and never leave. Just—collect rainwater and fish for food. Train all day and lie under the stars at night.

I'm never going to have a life as good as that again.

Snap out of it, Anya. Survivors do not dwell on the things they have lost.

And it's very clear that Cort is clinging to Ainsey today in order to avoid thinking about me.

Or, hell, who am I kidding? He gives no fucks about me at all. I am just a pretty girl he got stuck with. He made the most of it, and that's all it was.

This… is even more depressing. So I put all of it out of my mind and head down to the mess hall to eat my last meal. That's what it feels like, anyway.

I didn't eat much last night. We were too busy drinking—and fucking—to take part in the massive feast that the kids had. And this morning I was a little hungover, so I didn't have breakfast. But now it's nearly lunchtime and I'm famished. I ask for all the things in the food line. A grilled cheese, a cup of strawberries, two chocolate milks, a side of French fries, a green salad with ranch, and two bags of nuts to keep for later, just in case I'm in a situation where a bag of nuts saves my life.

But all too soon it is clear that we have arrived. And when I go up on deck I see that the ship is maneuvering sideways up against a large concrete dock. I look around, taking it all in.

Except for the dock, there is nothing here. Just a sheer cliff wall, the water below—the dark color indicating that it is deep and there is no beach down there—and then beyond the rock is a canopy of tall jungle trees.

Brazil. Not much different than other jungle places I've been.

Monkeys and birds chatter and squeal in the thick foliage as a gangplank is put in place so we can disembark. But even after it's firmly in place, no one moves to get off the boat.

I walk up next to Maart. He's leaning against a railing, watching Cort talk to the ship captain. Rainer is talking too, but his words are directed at the kids. "What's going on?"

"There's a ritual."

"What kind of ritual?"

"Going-home ritual." He says this like everyone knows what a going-home ritual is.

"What's it entail?"

He beams a smile at me. "Watch. And you'll see."

A few minutes later Cort is the first to leave the ship. He walks down the gangplank and then continues down the dock until he is standing on a large flat rock. He puts a hand up, whistles, and then Rainer walks Ainsey up to the gangplank and gives her a little push.

Ainsey doesn't need that push. She runs down that gangplank. She runs all the way to Cort.

Maart clicks his tongue next to me. But he doesn't elaborate on that noise, so I'm left to assume what it might mean. I know he's frustrated with Cort's attachment to Ainsey. We all know that. But what does he expect Cort to do? She's his child. And today he will be leaving her behind.

Cort bends down as Ainsey approaches. He puts up both hands, palms forward, and Ainsey punches them, like she's on the mat back at the Rock.

Cort laughs. I can't really hear him, he's too far away, but I know what it looks like from a distance.

Then I see Ainsey's lips moving. "Is she talking?"

"Yep. They get to talk again. And their first words belong to Cort."

Ainsey must have a lot to say because she talks, and talks, and talks. Cort laughs and smiles like she is the light of his life. But finally, he nods at her and points to the trees behind him.

Ainsey nods back and then, without any more discussion, she disappears into the jungle.

"Where's she going?" I absently ask Maart.

"Home," he says. "She's going home."

CHAPTER THIRTY

Ainsey's voice is sweet, so sweet, when she finally speaks to me.

"I did it!"

"You did it," I agree. I'm kneeling down so we're eye level. I put my hands up and she automatically begins to punch them.

"I didn't speak at all," she adds.

"I know," I say, pulling her in for a hug. "I'm proud of you."

"I'm so big now, right?"

My heart has never felt sicker. But I rally and smile. "Yep. You're big now, Ains."

She keeps talking now. Like she's got piles and piles of words collected up inside her that need to come out. She tells me about her time on the Rock. Just certain moments of it that were important to her, I guess. And then, finally, she lets out a long breath and goes silent again.

"Are you ready to go back home?" I ask her.

Her gaze wanders to the jungle behind me. She nods, and signs, and speaks all at the same time. And my sick heart melts into a big old goopy mess. "Yep. Yes. I'm ready."

"OK. Off you go then. Go find Cintia. OK? She's probably training. So just go find her and sit down on the mat until everyone is home. Can you do that?"

Ainsey nods. And then, without another word, she turns, walks off, and disappears into the trees.

Zoya comes next. She has stolen a book and a beaded bracelet from the game room. I eye both those things. "Do you have something to tell me, Zoya?"

She tilts her chin up, nods, and then says, "I should've taken more. Next time I'm taking a whole suitcase with me."

"Is that right?" I laugh.

"Yes." She is not laughing. She is dead serious. "Because every day is another sad fight. And if they make me fight for these sad things, then from now I will also fight for happy things."

She spits into the dirt at her feet. Salutes me. Sidesteps. And walks off into the jungle without another word. I don't even know where she comes up with this shit. It's not like she's sitting around on her ass watching TV and picking it up from old war movies.

It's always been like this. They are always different when they leave the Rock than when they got there. And I don't care how many times they get to do that, this is always true.

This ritual we have, these kids getting off the ship… they leave something behind out there in the ocean. They don't even know they do this, but every single time, without fail, a Zoya gets off that boat and meets me here and my world shifts.

This is a learning moment, and a teaching moment, and in this moment, I am both student and teacher. Trying to decipher Zoya's words and actions so I don't lose her underlying message.

But I don't have much time to think about Zoya and her new Zen attitude because all my kids are waiting to come ashore and speak their mind to me.

They do this one by one. Some of them have profound things to say, like Zoya. But most are just proud of themselves. Most just want to be told that I am proud of them too.

So that's what I say. Because they are still innocent. They are just kids. And even though they all know that ugly, evil, real-life monsters are coming to get them, this is not the day to think about that. This is the day to go home and let out that long breath they didn't think they were holding.

Jafari is the last of my students to meet me on shore. He's at least two inches taller than he was three months ago and if this kid makes it to fifteen, he will tower above me.

I rough up his hair. "I'm proud of you, buddy. This was a great summer for you."

He grins, tight-lipped.

"You can talk."

He nods.

"Or you can stay silent."

He signs, *Yes*, to me. And I wonder for a moment if I'm actually helping them at all or just justifying all the ways in which I am going to get them killed.

I can't bend down to look him in the eyes the way I did Ainsey because he's in that awkward stage of tall. So I just put both hands on his shoulders and say, "Jafari. I know that maybe you think silence is safety, but… there is no safety. You get one life, son. Just one. And you need to find the joy in each day. So if staying silent gives you joy? Hey, I'm fine with it. But if you're doing this to test yourself or for any other reason, then I would like you to reconsider."

He draws in a deep breath and on the exhale, he says, "OK, Cort," and gives me a nod. Then, without ceremony—no hug, no handshake, no look over his shoulder—he walks off into the jungle.

Rainer comes next. He and I greet his kids together. He is most proud of Rasha and this lightens my heart a little. Maybe I was wrong? Maybe Rasha does have it in her to go all the way? Maybe she will be the first girl to ever make it into the Ring of Fire?

I hope so. And that hope is both sad and good at the same time.

Life is a tradeoff.

You can make it all the way and lose your soul.

Or die fighting to keep it intact.

Who is to say one is better than the other?

I am most proud of Budi. He and I have always been a little team and when he walks up to Rainer, Budi greets him with laughter and some of his original hand-slapping moves. But when he looks at me, he bows. He bows low. And he holds it there just a few seconds too long, letting me know that this is his heart speaking now. With his eyes downcast, he says, "Thank you, Cort," in a small, low, voice.

I picture that day I first saw him in the Muay Thai camp on the other side of the world. He was a quiet, still, solemn three-year-old boy. Udulf wanted one of the loud ones. One of the showoffs. But I said no. I wanted Budi because of his smallness. Because even though his eyes saw everything, his mouth said nothing.

I wanted him because of his… *gravity*.

This boy has gravity. He is heavy and larger than life. He pulls things towards him and holds them close.

He is so much like Maart, my heart hurts.

But there is no time to dwell on all these thoughts running through my head right now. Soon he's gone too and Evard is coming towards us. He bows to Rainer. Then he takes one step to the side and bows to me. He says in his small voice, "It's not fair."

Rainer and I look at each other, then at Evard. "What?" Rainer asks.

Evard slowly lifts his head up to look at Rainer, then pauses to peer into the jungle to see if any of the kids are hanging around to spy. Finally, he looks at me and repeats it. "It's not fair."

My stomach tenses because I don't need to hear the accusation in his voice to feel it in my gut.

"What's not fair?" Rainer asks.

Evard is still looking at me. "That I get to leave and they don't. I think I want to—"

"Fuck you." I cut him off before he can get those words out, the anger in my voice surprising both Evard and Rainer. Even me. "Fuck you, Evard. Don't you say another fucking word. Do you understand me?"

He looks down at his feet. But he nods his head.

When I look over at Rainer, he's got his lips pressed together to keep his mouth shut. I know he wants to tell me to shut up. But he holds it in as Evard walks into the jungle.

Then Maart is there. And right behind him is Irina, so thankfully, there is no time to discuss this.

Irina is, without a doubt, Maart's current favorite. I try to think back, to recall if it was always this way, but it wasn't. Last year she was just another girl like Rasha.

She hugs Maart tight and long. And when she pulls back, she says, "You are a dick," in her thick Russian accent. She points her finger in his face. "You should not treat me like little sister. But I still love you."

She shakes Rainer's hand. It's been a few years since he was her teacher, so those bonds have loosened over time. But with me she stops and sighs. Like she is about to lose her patience with me. She pats my chest with an air of familiarity most wouldn't dare and leaves her palm right there, on my bare skin, over my heart. She nods her head to Maart. "He is ajarn. Fine. But you?" She huffs as she looks up at me, her blue eyes narrowing down into slits. "You are *leader.*"

Then she removes her hand from my heart, nods her head one time, and walks into the jungle.

"Fuck." Maart sighs, running his fingers through his long, thick, messy hair. "This shit feels very heavy today."

Rainer and I both look at each other, because he doesn't know the half of it. But neither of us fills him in on Evard's almost-act of defiance.

This is not the time for regrets. There is nothing else to be done. In a few minutes we're going to walk through that jungle and then it's all going to be over.

There is nothing to be done.

Peng comes next. Then Maeko. Then Paulo. Each of them pauses and has a small, whispered conversation with Maart. All three have tears in their eyes. They will miss him, and there's no way to hide that.

If I am the sick heart, Maart is the cold heart. He locks people out. He doesn't let anyone in to warm him up. He is cool, and even, and unshakable.

But today is not just any day. It is our last day. And if Irina were still here, she would pat his chest too and she would set him straight. She would say, *There is no cold in there. It is nothing but fire.*

I sigh and then, finally, Anya is walking off the ship. She looks nothing like the girl I met four months ago. Not even close. Her body is brown now, her skin glowing from the heat of the sun, her muscles tempered from the weeks of training, her hair wild from the rain, and the wind, and the ocean.

She is a goddess in her bare feet, and her borrowed denim shorts, and her tattered white tank top.

And even though, of all the kids that just walked off that ship, her future is the most precarious, she is smiling in a way I've never seen before.

She is happy.

"I just want to say"—Maart's low, soft words tear me away from the beautiful girl walking towards us—"that if ever there was proof that what we are doing is good, she is it."

I scoff. "How do you figure?"

Maart turns his head to look me in the eyes. "Just look at her, Cort. She is nak su. They are *all* nak su. We have raised warriors in this camp. We have taught them all the skills they need to survive. It's not their fault the entire world is corrupt. It's not their fault they are born, and live, and die in the shadows of the forgotten." His eyes dart down to the skulls tattooed on my body, then rise back up to meet my gaze. "And it's not our fault they were forced to fight their way into the next world. We. Raised. *Warriors.* Don't you *ever* fucking forget that."

Then Anya is walking up to us and, once again, there is no time to process all the words that are being dropped at my feet today. After decades of time that has flowed too slow—that has dragged on like torture—it is suddenly going all too fast.

Anya stops at Maart first and bows to him. Not the pathetic slave bow from months ago, but a proper, reverent, solemn bow with praying hands and thumbs at her eyebrows. She holds that position, but she's looking straight at him. "Ajarn Maart," she says. "Thank you."

He nods to her. Bows back. Then she moves on to Rainer and repeats her gestures of gratitude.

Then she is standing in front of me. And this is the moment when the full meaning of Anya hits me.

Maart was right.

She *is* a warrior.

But we didn't make her that way.

She was always a warrior.

A silent ninja.

A master of mental assaults.

A champion in the ring of survival.

We just taught her more.

We made her better.

But for what? To be Udulf's prize? His possession? His property?

Her eyes pierce mine and her silence is loud. *Don't you dare feel sorry for me. Don't you dare reduce me.*

So I don't.

I bow to her before she can bow to me.

The four of us enter the thick, jungle understory via a smooth dirt path. Our world becomes something made of shadows. The blazing sun is on the other side of the canopy leaves above our head. Monkeys swing through the trees and birds chatter and scream at us as we pass through their domain. We are walking single file because the path is narrow. So I am the first to walk out into the large, open clearing we call the base camp.

This place is home, but it is also a prison.

And it's weird. Because there are no walls around us. There are no guards here. I am not in cuffs. No one wears a collar.

But we are *all* in a cage.

It's an invisible cage but that's not why most people can't see it.

They can't see it because they don't understand what it means to be owned in this day and age.

There is no escape from these people.

There is no walking away.

There is no way out and that's not the brainwashing talking.

It's just the truth.

These men who own us, they are a global network. You can run. Lots of slaves and fighters have tried. But you can't hide. They find you in the end. Even if it's only to kill you and turn you into an example.

So no walls or guards are necessary.

425

All they need is that threat.

And I bought into it.

We all bought in to it.

The temperature difference when we leave the jungle is immediate. The still, humid air of the trees is replaced with the searing afternoon sun.

The path widens so Anya, Maart, and Rainer all come up next to me as we walk forward.

The first clue that this day is not going to go the way we planned is the silence.

The second clue is the stillness.

All our warriors are here. On my left I can see Cintia in the first of three large, covered training rings. She is bending down, whispering to Ainsey as we walk by. There are a few other kids with them, sitting on the mats in the background.

Sissy is in the second ring with our four older fighters—two sixteen-year-old boys, a sixteen-year-old girl, and a seventeen-year old boy who will be going to the Ring of Fire in the next couple months. They are what's left of my older kids. The ones who no longer go out to the Rock with us because they are past that.

The only ones to survive into adulthood.

No one is in the third ring, but when I look to my right, I see Ling leaning up against the porch of the small house she shares with Cintia and Sissy. The rest of the little kids—the ones not with Cintia—are sitting on the steps of the huts lining that side of the camp. Just watching us.

Rainer is the one who finally speaks as we make our way up the path towards the main house. "What the fuck?"

None of us answer him. It's pretty obvious what's happening because even from a distance of a hundred yards, I can count three of Udulf's mercenary bodyguards standing on the large front porch of our house.

"He's here," I say, more to myself than my friends.

"Yep," Anya breathes. "He's here all right."

"What are we gonna do?" Rainer asks.

"What do you mean what are we gonna do?" I answer.

"I mean, what the fuck are we gonna do? We're not going through with this. Tell me we're not going through with this."

"Shut up, Rainer," Maart growls. "Just... shut the fuck up."

It's a weird response from Maart. He doesn't normally talk to Rainer that way, but today is not any ordinary day. We are free men. I think. And we're about to walk away from this camp with a brand-new life.

It's stressful. Even cold-hearted Maart feels stress. So I let it go.

We walk the rest of the way in silence. We climb the porch steps in silence. We enter the house in silence.

Udulf turns from the spread of food and drink laid out on the dining room table, a look of happy surprise on his face when he sees us. "Ah. There they are!"

Yeah. There is definitely something going on here. And we're in the dark about all of it.

"Cort! My son!" He walks over to me and claps me on the shoulder. "You look... fabulous.

SICK HEART · JA HUSS

Fabulous," he repeats. "You always did thrive in solitude."

I'd like to point out that I wasn't alone on the Rock, not for one fucking second, but his words are just dressing. Just frosting. Just... fluffy air to fill the empty space in this room.

"And Anya." He moves on to her, taking her hand in his, even though she doesn't offer it, and bringing the tips of her fingers to his lips. He kisses them. Licks them. She tries to pull her hand back, but he doesn't let go. So she gives in.

It's a lewd gesture. One of disrespect. One that pretty much calls Anya a whore, in my opinion. He leers at her, looking her up and down like she is a sexual thing.

This is a tell with Udulf. We are playing some sort of game. Because Udulf only has sex with *children*. In his perverted, sick, twisted version of the world, Anya is much too old to sexually excite him.

He lets go of her hand, bypasses Rainer completely, and his gaze lands on Maart. Udulf laughs. "Well. Here you are. Are you still in?"

I look over at Maart as well. "In? In what? What the hell is he talking about?"

Maart ignores me. "You bet I'm in."

"What the fuck are we talking about?" I ask again.

"We"—Udulf turns to face me—"*we*," he stresses the repeated word, "aren't talking about anything. Yet. But Maart and I, we had a deal."

"What deal?" I look over at Maart. "What fucking deal?"

Maart draws in a deep breath. He glances at Rainer for a moment, but decides to skip whatever thought first comes to mind and concentrate on me. "You and I both know how we got here, Cort."

"Maart—"

"He got you here," Udulf interrupts. He walks over to Maart and stands next to him. "Isn't that what you're trying to say, Maart? Hmm? You're the... what do they call it?" He flips his hand in the air. "The wind beneath the wings, so to speak?"

"Maart—"

"You were never strong enough," Maart says.

"Strong enough for what? Because the way I see it, you're a free man today because I was strong enough in all the ways it counts."

"Exactly!" Udulf beams. "He is a *free man*. You are all three free men. And Maart has decided—"

"No." I shake my head. "Fuck that. You're not staying here. You're *not* staying behind."

"Behind?" Udulf guffaws. "He is out in front, my boy!"

"Maart. I'm not gonna say this again. What the fuck is he talking about?"

"The next fight, of course," Udulf says.

I ignore Udulf and lock eyes with Maart. "What. Fight?"

Finally, Maart speaks. "The final fight. The only fight that has ever mattered. The one fight you were too weak to even think about, let alone accept. The one fight that can free them *all*."

"No." I'm shaking my head. "You cannot be serious."

"The ultimate fight," Udulf says. "Listen to me, Cort." Udulf grabs my shoulder and squeezes. And he is very fucking lucky I have spent all of my twenty-seven years practicing restraint. Because I want to kill this man. I want to rip his head off and feed it to the fish below the rock. "You have no vision, Cort. Sick Heart. Whatever you call yourself these days. You have never had vision. Not like Maart. He has always known how to get what he wants."

"And what is that, Maart?" I ask. "What do you want that you don't have?"

Maart is silent for a moment. Thinking, I guess. His expression is one I don't exactly recognize, so I can't be sure how to interpret it. But finally, he says, "One life, right? We get this one chance to go through life. And this"—he pans his hands wide—"this shithole training camp is what you settled for? That forty-year-old platform ship? A fucking crumbling-down decommissioned oil rig? That's the best you could do, Cort? *Really*?"

Udulf laughs again. But I ignore him. "It took me twenty-two years to get this shithole training camp, that forty-year-old platform ship, and you just said yourself, right back there on the cliff, that the Rock was how we raised—"

Maart guffaws so loud, I stop talking. "For a man who prides himself on keeping silent so he can practice the art of reading others, you sure do miss a lot, Cort."

"What the fuck does that even mean?"

Maart nods his head to Rainer, who has been silent this whole time. "Everyone in the camp knew he was never going to leave."

"Even I knew that." Udulf laughs. He walks over to Rainer, claps him on the back, and says, "Rainer is a man who knows his place. He knows where he belongs. And that place is here. Well"—Udulf pauses to look over at Maart and smirk—"not here. Tell him, Maart. Tell him where Rainer belongs."

"What is he talking about?" I growl these words out at Maart.

But it's not Maart who speaks up. It's Rainer. He steps in front of me, blocking my view of Maart, and sighs. "We don't want to work on a supply ship, Cort. We don't want to drift for the rest of our lives."

I push Rainer aside so I can look at Maart again. "What did you do?"

"You say those words like they're a bad thing, Cort. But all I did was *elevate* us."

"Not true," Udulf says. "Not all of you. That's the price. There is always a price. And while you were never willing to splurge on the finer things, Cort, Maart and Rainer here have a different perspective on the meaning of a life well-lived."

I have a lot to say about that, but Maart speaks before I can. "You would leave them behind. You would never fight for them the way I would."

"What the fuck are you talking about?" I ask this question like I don't already know what he's talking about. But I do know.

"The kids," Maart says.

"You love them so much?" I say. "You love them so fucking much you will make a deal with this devil and take them to hell with you?"

"That's your problem, Cort. You think you're better than us. You think you've got some superior moral code going on here. But you don't." He nods his chin to Udulf. "You're not any better than him. How many people have died at your hands? Forty? Fifty? More?" He puts up a hand before I can defend myself. "Don't fucking tell me he made you do it. You could've bought yourself out a decade ago. But you stayed."

"I stayed to fight for you!"

"Thank you for that." Maart feigns a bow. "But now that I'm free, I can fight for myself. And I choose *you*."

I laugh. Like… a *real* laugh. "You want to fight *me*?"

"The ultimate fight," Udulf says. "The only one where no one—not me, not you, not them—none of us has any idea of how it will end. But we do know one thing, *Sick. Heart.*" He signs the words as he says them. "You will both die either way. Either your lover here kills you, or you kill him. This little bit of treason, this moment of backstabbing…" He shakes his head. "It won't be enough to erase the decades you two shared. If he dies, and you have to live on without the other… that's another kind of death altogether, isn't it? A slow one. An agonizing one. Like…" His eyes dart to Anya. "Like a knife to the gut."

"Why?" It's a question I've had my whole life but never had the guts to ask. "Why are you like this? Why do you want to hurt people? Why are you so fucking evil?"

Udulf smiles at me, his steel-gray eyes so familiar. "There is no such thing as evil, my son." I feel sick. Because it's in this moment when I truly accept that he is my real father. I come from this man's seed. "There is no judgment on the last day of your life. There is no Heaven. There is no Hell. There is only the game called life. You either play it, or you don't."

I scoff. "And this is the best you can do?"

He looks around, still smiling. "No. This is the best *you* could do. But I'm giving you another chance,

Cort. Don't you see? Don't you get it? Maart does. Hell, even Rainer does and he's pretty stupid. Because he's a free man, thanks to you, and he chooses…" Udulf shrugs. "Nothing." He laughs. "He chooses *nothing*. He wants nothing more than to stay the same. He wants his camp, he wants his kids, he wants his pathetic title of trainer. He wants to wake up every day and know that it will be predictable. And if that means walking away from you and sticking it out with Maart here, that's what he's going to do. But don't feel bad. Even if your big dream of freedom was more than just some worthless supply ship, he wouldn't go. He wouldn't. He doesn't have it in him. Freedom, my son, is highly overrated for most of the pathetic people of this planet. They say they hate the games we play, but what else would they do with their lives if we weren't pushing them in one direction or another?"

"Wow." I can only shake my head at him. "You, Udulf, you are the pathetic one. Not the people you control. They don't have choices, and you do. And you had better hope there is no Hell, because if there is, there's a fire pit with your name on it."

"Do you want the fight or don't you?" Udulf asks. I open my mouth to say no. I will not play this game with him or anyone else ever again. But he continues before I can answer. "Choose carefully, Sick Heart. Because if you say no, you walk out of here with no one. Just yourself."

"Evard—"

"Evard is staying," Rainer says. "He was trying to tell you that when he got off the ship. But you told him to shut the fuck up."

I step away from Maart, Rainer, and Udulf, trying to put distance between myself and them. Anya is standing off to the side as well, the expression on her face one of stunned shock.

I look Rainer in the eyes. "What the hell is wrong with you? He's free. You're free. We're all free. Why would you want to stay in this hell?"

"Because," Udulf says, "this hell is their home. It's all they know."

"I'm not gonna do it," I blurt. "Fuck this shit. You people can all fucking rot here. I didn't fight for my life for twenty-two years to just walk away with nothing."

"That's the whole point of the fight," Maart says, his eyes narrowed down into slits. "If I win, we're all free. I told you that, remember? Out on the Rock. I fucking told you, either we are all free, or none of us are."

"Oh, that's a nice touch," Udulf says, pointing his finger at Maart. "Freedom to choose. Everyone gets to choose to stay! I love it!"

He's fucking sick. I don't even look at him. I'm only looking at Maart. "If you win, I'm dead, you dumbass! Only one of us gets out alive!"

"That's right." Maart says this without feeling. If my heart is sick, his heart is cold. And that's exactly what he wants me to think.

I take a deep breath and calm myself down. "So you want to be the hero?"

"You never did."

"You're free to make this decision because of me, asshole."

"And you only got here because of me. You know that's true, Cort. So that argument doesn't work. You're too weak to think big. You've been in too many fights to see past your own survival instinct. You got

SICK HEART · JA HUSS

me out for the same reason you got Rainer and Evard out. You can't live without *us*."

"And that's how we know you're going to say yes," Udulf says. "The fight of the century. The Sick Heart against the one man who can beat him."

"Will beat him," Maart adds.

I huff out a laugh. "You people are all a bunch of deranged lunatics if you think I'll fall for this bullshit. I'm done. There will be no fight. I'm packing my shit, I'm getting on that ship, and I'm never looking back."

I start walking towards the door, but it opens before I get there.

I stop in my tracks, my heart suddenly beating so fast I can't breathe.

Because Lazar walks in holding Ainsey.

He smiles at me.

Like we're old friends.

Then he looks past me, at Udulf, and says, "I found one I like. This one will do just fine."

And then he *kisses* my daughter on the cheek.

CHAPTER THIRTY-ONE

Seeing Udulf again triggers something inside me.

Not some killer instinct, unfortunately, but memories. I'm trying to tuck them all down as this conversation happens between Maart, Cort, and Udulf—but when Lazar enters the house holding Ainsey, I lose control and things begin to... *slip*.

I am seven years old again. Everything on my body hurts and Udulf is the one responsible for all that pain. But I am a trooper. I am a survivor. I am a warrior. This man will not be the one to kill me. My death will not happen *here*.

We are in an unkept castle in the mountains of Romania. With its peeling plaster, uneven floorboards, and broken windows—this property has seen better days.

It's not Udulf's house. I don't know who owns this place, I just know it's not his. It's not even whole. It's a place they bring kids like me so they can do things to us.

Not just sex.

He could do that on his boat.

He could do that in his home.

He could do that anywhere he wants.

No. That's not what this place is for.

This place is for the things they can only do in old abandoned castles in the mountains of Romania.

But Udulf is alone. It's just him and me and he's got his computer open so he can play a movie on repeat.

It's a horrific movie.

I know they like to film it.

I get it. I've seen it all before. I am seven now and I've been doing this for years. Almost nothing can shock me but this movie *shocks* me.

It is mostly of Lazar and Udulf. Years ago, but not *that* many years ago.

To my seven-year-old eyes the man sitting on the bed with me is old. But to my eighteen-year-old memory, Udulf is probably only in his mid-thirties.

In the movie he and Lazar are much younger versions of themselves. They are in a shipyard and they are running between the containers. Laughing, mostly. But Lazar is also screaming threats to the children they are chasing.

Every few seconds another man or running child will appear. Just a flash. They are not important. They are not the focus of Udulf's obsession.

The two children he is obsessed with are caught. They are naked, they are filthy, their feet are bleeding, and the little one—the boy with the silver-gray eyes that so perfectly match Udulf's own—is cowering at the feet of the little girl.

His sister, I now know. She has those eyes too. She is what Ainsey will look like in a few short years.

I know what happens next.

Udulf played it for me dozens of times. He made me watch it with him for hours. He narrated the entire thing in Dutch, thinking I couldn't understand.

But the Dutch was already there in my head and all the things he said tunneled their way inside me like worms. They got stuck there with the images on the screen.

Udulf raped the little girl while Lazar filmed it.

Then Lazar skinned her alive while Udulf held the camera.

The boy just watched.

Silent.

He said nothing.

I didn't understand much that night.

I didn't know why they did these evil, awful, sick things to that little girl.

I didn't know why Udulf didn't kill me that night at the crumbling Romanian castle.

I didn't know why he kept me there until morning, but never put another hand on me. He just watched that movie over and over again on repeat.

And I didn't understand why he took me back to Lazar.

Not at the time.

Not for a long time.

The only thing I did understand were his words.

I had no use for words after that.

There was simply nothing left to say about this world.

Cort lunges at Lazar, Udulf's mercs point their rifles at Cort's head, Rainer grabs his arm and pulls Cort back just as his fist passes through the air in front of Lazar's face. There is screaming, and yelling, and the entire time I just stand there unable to move.

I just watch, the way Cort watched in that movie.

Then I snap out of it and drag myself back into the present.

What the hell just happened? I try to run it through in my head. But nothing makes sense. Maart, Rainer, and even Evard have chosen to stay?

Why? Why would they do that? They are free. They can walk out of here. Go anywhere they want. Leave these evil assholes behind. But they want to stay? Maart wants a fight?

All the men in the room are yelling and Cort is spewing threats at everyone. He tries to grab Ainsey from Lazar, but Lazar pulls her back. Then the mercs step in, grab Cort by the arms, and ziptie his wrists.

"Calm down!" Udulf is yelling. "This is part of the deal!"

"What deal?" Cort screams it, just as I say the same thing in my head.

"For losing," Lazar spits. "Anya won that fight. You cheated. You do not win by cheating."

"Fuck you," Cort spits back. "Pavo was a piece of shit who never stood a chance against me. That fight is mine."

SICK HEART · JA HUSS

"I agree," Udulf says. These words come out fatigued. "We've had this discussion *ad nauseum*, Lazar. The bookies paid out on Cort's win, so it has been settled. But as we discussed"—he nods his head towards Ainsey in Lazar's arms—"you have found yourself a new *daughter* to replace the one who died that night."

What?

What did he just say?

Died that night?

Who died that night?

I didn't die that night.

"Bexxie." I look up and find Lazar watching me. "*Bexxie*," he repeats, his voice filled with disgust and malice. "She paid for your treason with her life. And she went out bloody. Just. Like. Pavo."

I lunge at him. And I'm dead fucking serious about this lunge. The edge of my hand is already aiming for his throat, ready to chop his trachea and make him choke on those words, when one of the mercs grabs my hair and pulls so hard, I fall backwards on my ass.

"I have it all on film," Lazar says, his voice not even quivering from my threat. "I'll play it back for you some day."

"Someone had to be the sacrifice that night." Udulf's tone is mild, matter-of-fact. "And since it wasn't you?" He shrugs with his hands. "Well, she was the next best thing."

I lean over and throw up.

"What's my prize?" The whole room goes silent and everyone looks over at Cort. "If I fight, what is *my* prize? And don't say freedom," Cort snaps. "Because I already have that."

441

Udulf smiles. He smiles like a man who knows he has won. "Ainsey, of course." Then he nods his head to me. "I'll throw her in too."

"Not good enough," Cort spits. "My entire camp goes free."

"Oh, no, no, no," Udulf chides. "Maart has cornered that market. If he wins, your entire camp goes free. With the exception of the little one and Anya Bokori. If you win, you get them, and only them."

Cort laughs. "And what makes you think I would fight for just them?"

Udulf nods his head towards Maart. "Because he told me you would."

And Maart was right.

Because Cort agrees to the terms.

I spend the next thirty minutes locked in an upstairs bedroom as the entire camp packs up their personal things and are loaded into a bus. Everyone but Cort and all the girls, because Maart said they weren't worth his time and Cort could keep them until he lost and they could be sold.

I join them at the last minute, and then we're driven to a newly built compound that turns out to be Maart's new training camp.

I guess we all know when this deal was made. A long, *long* time ago.

Lazar wanted to keep Ainsey as a down payment on his 'new daughter,' but Cort refused these terms and threatened to pull out. So in the end, it was agreed that Ainsey and I were to be kept at the new compound and she would live in the barracks with the other kids until the fight is over.

It's a massive estate, a mansion with enough rooms to house the entire camp. But they have their own facilities, so instead it only houses me, Maart, Udulf, and Lazar.

The fight will happen in three days. And the whole time this was being negotiated, I could see the worry on Cort's face.

He trained every day, like the rest of us. But he didn't train hard. He worked out like a man who knew he would never have to fight for his life again.

Maart has spent the last three months working out like a man who would be fighting for his life in the near future. He has been sparring with four top-notch fighters. And he spent an extra four hours a night training with me. Which, OK, I'm not really a suitable opponent for him to spar with, but it was four extra hours a day.

It's so apparent that he is in much better shape, I feel a little sick.

And you could say, well, Cort has the advantage because he's got the experience. He's been in the ring dozens of times. He's undefeated and Maart hasn't had a real fight in over a decade.

But Cort's body looks like it's been fighting for decades. His bones have been broken, his muscles stretched and pulled past their limits. I'm not sure how many concussions he's had in his career, but I'd be willing to bet that number is significant.

He looks like a man who has been in the ring for decades.

Maart looks like a would-be champion about to rise.

It is the morning before fight day and I'm sitting at the dining room table with Udulf. He makes me take meals with him. To torture me, I think. To make me uncomfortable. But also because he's fishing for information.

He sits across from me, smiling as he chews on a forkful of scrambled eggs. "Tell me, Anya, who do you think will win?"

I, of course, don't answer him. He knows I'm not going to answer him, but so far, he's been patiently persistent.

I expect this patience to wear off at some point today, since the fight is tomorrow and I'm fairly certain he expects Maart to win and part of the deal was that Lazar would get me back if that happened. So Udulf here, he's got one more day to get answers out of me.

There isn't a lot in my life to give me joy at the moment, but watching him squirm over this almost makes the situation worth it.

"We all know it's going to be Maart. Does that disappoint you? I mean, surely you and Cort have gotten close. I saw the way he looked at you." He pauses to chew on a bite of sourdough toast, then continues. "I've been meaning to ask you… do you remember me?"

Do I remember him? As if I could forget the time Lazar rented me out to his good friend Udulf here so I could get his secrets.

But the funny thing is... nothing I came back with was secret.

Lazar was *there*. He tortured that little girl, then they killed her together.

So Lazar wasn't looking for secrets from Udulf.

It took me a long, long time to figure this out and the answer only just came to me that day we got off the ship and walked into Cort's village.

At first I thought he was looking for something else, but that wasn't it either.

Lazar sent me to Udulf to be *killed*.

Twice now.

And both times, I came out alive.

Why?

Well, that's a pretty simple answer, actually. The first time Udulf got a phone call. I didn't remember this until they started negotiating the fight between Maart and Cort the other day. It was a call from... someone. Doesn't matter. The only thing that mattered was the news.

Cort had won his fight.

He was officially in the Ring of Fire now.

On the night that Udulf was raping me and showing me a snuff film of Cort's sister—Cort van Breda was morphing into Sick Heart.

And this changed *everything*.

And, well. The second time Cort took me without asking.

Funny how that worked out.

What was Udulf thinking that morning he came to visit us on the Rock?

Did I remember how he raped the girl in the movie?

Did I remember Lazar skinning her alive?

Did I know Cort was the little boy who watched?

Did Cort know he was the little boy who watched?

Did I tell him?

So many questions had to be running through Udulf's mind during that short visit.

He left me there because he knew I didn't tell Cort and he knew Cort didn't remember.

So he left.

And he came back here, to Brazil. To Cort's camp. To talk to Maart and... probably Rainer, too. And that's when all this was set up.

"I remember you," Udulf says, sipping on his orange juice. "You were... what, eight? Nine?"

I was seven, but who's counting?

"Yes." He smiles. "You were... something. Very pretty. I'm sure you hear that all the time. Don't you?"

I sigh and push a piece of French toast into my mouth, chewing slowly with my eyes locked on his. These people are so sick. I never understood how they could live with themselves until Udulf's little speech at Cort's camp.

They don't believe in evil. There is no Heaven and Hell. There are no consequences. This is nothing but a game.

Well, I don't believe that. Not all of it, at least. There have to be consequences. There has to be more to the real world than just the tangible act of existence. Sick, evil people need to pay for their crimes at some point.

But here's the really interesting thing Udulf said. This is a game to them. They are players in a very literal sense. There are winners and there are losers and nothing else in between.

It's a good tip. One I will take seriously.

So when Udulf throws his napkin on his plate, and just before he pushes his chair away from the table, I decide to enter this game.

I lift up my juice glass and bring it to my lips. But before I take a sip, I say, in Dutch, "Of course, I remember you, Udulf." And then I switch to Hungarian. "I remember your midnight confessions." I switch to English. "How could I ever forget the man who masturbated to a movie of his own daughter being raped, and tortured, and killed."

He is so surprised by my spoken words, he laughs out loud before he can fully understand the threat behind them.

I try not to think of their full implication as well.

Men like Udulf and Lazar are the reason I believe in God. Because if there is a God, there is a Devil. And there must be a Devil, because these men work for him.

"She talks." Udulf's shock has worn off. He is delighted at my words.

"I do. And I know why you wanted me dead that night."

"Which night would that be, nyuszi?" Pavo's nickname for me rolls out of his mouth like flowing water, easy and smooth. "The first time or the second?"

"Both."

He smiles at me, a little bit tight-lipped, but he's mostly pulling off a pretty good I-give-no-fucks expression. "Are you going to tell me? Should I guess? Or were you just making an observation?"

"You don't want him to know."

He huffs. "What are you talking about? The films?"

Interesting. It's been eleven years and yet that memory is so fresh, his mind goes there immediately.

"Cort knows about the films. He used to enjoy watching them with me when he was small. He's an animal. He came that way. He will die that way."

"Maybe," I answer back. Cort is not an animal. He did not come that way and he will not die that way either.

Cort did not watch snuff films with Udulf. I know this for a fact because Cort does not remember what happened to him. He has repressed it. He has made up some other situation to account for it. The bathhouse nightmare is the stand in. It is bad, but it's something his mind can deal with. It's something he can understand. Watching your sister be skinned alive—nope. That's an experience that deserves to be forgotten. And if Udulf showed him a snuff film, the memory could come back. There was a chance.

And that would never do.

Not when Cort was *winning*.

Udulf watches me carefully. Maybe wondering where all this is going.

How many men on this planet own fighters in the Ring of Fire?

Eight? Ten? *Maybe* twelve.

It's not easy to turn a small boy into a grown-up killer so ruthless he makes it all the way to *twenty-seven*.

I know this now. I know this better than Udulf does. I've seen it all first hand.

They all want to be there. They all want the opportunity to win those prizes. They all want their stable of little boys in the camps and harems of little girls in their bedrooms.

And both Lazar and Udulf *made it.*

Udulf would never admit this, but Lazar gave it away that night on the Bull of Light.

They *need* these warriors.

They are nothing without them.

Lazar *mourned* the loss of Pavo. Maybe he's got another fighter on his way up, but I doubt it.

Udulf, on the other hand, had Maart in his back pocket.

His secret weapon to wield in a pinch.

And Udulf has definitely found himself in a pinch.

"Did you know that you were the reason I stopped talking?"

Udulf laughs, places a hand over his heart, his gray eyes dancing. Eyes that could be twins of Cort's, but aren't. Because Cort's eyes don't carry that kind of malice. "I must've made a big impact on you."

"Oh, you did."

We stare at each other for a moment. I have, obviously, learned the value of silence over the years. And he's an expert in it. So there is a long pause in our conversation.

Finally, he says, "Is there more? Or was that it?"

"I know who Cort is."

"Well, my Cort is a lot of things."

"Or should I say... I know who he *was.*"

Udulf's eyebrow lifts up.

"He was in that movie. That one you showed me."

Udulf's smile gets tight.

"He was running through a shipyard filled with containers. And those containers were filled with children. And those children were... what?" This is a real question because my mind is unable to comprehend how these devils think. "What were they to you and Lazar and the others that night? Just... *meat*?"

Udulf says nothing.

"Just a game?"

He forces a smile.

"Like a deer in the woods?"

"You're getting closer."

"You and Lazar killed a little girl in that film. It took me a while to piece together who she was. Because even though Cort has nightmares about that night, he doesn't really remember it. He doesn't really remember Lazar, either." Once again, we pause time and stare at each other. "But I do. How could I forget? You played that film on repeat for hours."

"Did you tell him?"

"Do you think I told him?"

Udulf laughs. "That last meeting at the base camp would've been a bloodbath if you had."

"I know how to keep a secret, Udulf van Hauten. And I have kept yours for over a decade now."

"Come now, child." He tsks his tongue. "It's not like you ever had a chance to tell Cort anything until four months ago."

I shrug. "I didn't tell Lazar I knew either."

"Of course you didn't. You're a *survivor*, Anya Bokori. You know when to hold a card close. You understand better than most that the moment of illumination is almost never the time to throw that card down." He flips a hand in the air. "But your opportunity is gone now. You missed it, nyuszi. You're never going to get close enough to Cort again to spill my secrets. He is no threat to me. He never has been. He's going to lose. He's washed up. Regardless of what I told Lazar, we all know that the only reason Cort won that last fight is because you helped him."

I nod. "Mmm. Probably true. On both counts. But I'm not telling you this as a threat. I just wanted to let you know that I've figured it out."

"Have you?" He tips his juice glass to me. "Tell me then. What have you figured out?"

"You… *men*." I use the word hesitantly. Because they are not men, they are all demons. "You have to control everything, don't you? Up to, and including, each other. And you use blackmail to do that."

Udulf's breath escapes as an involuntary huff.

"You do things. You film them. And then you hand that over to someone to hold over your head. It is a pact. A declaration of loyalty. And in this case, Lazar gave his over to you. That film you showed me that night. That was what you were holding over Lazar. It took me a long time to piece that together because you both look pretty guilty if you ask me. But even in your world, raping a child and skinning a child alive are two totally different things, aren't they?"

Udulf is silent for yet another moment. Then he laughs. "What do you want? A pat on the back? None of this matters, girl. It's all water under the bridge."

It's not. But I let that go and just move this conversation forward. "And Lazar had something on you too. Didn't he? What was it?"

"Again," Udulf says. This time with honest disinterest. "None of this matters. The secret Lazar was holding is gone. It has been... *cancelled*."

Cancelled. That word makes me sick and I have to swallow hard to keep the bile from rising up inside me. "Not yet," I say. "Because whatever else you may have done in your life, your secret was Lazar's secret too."

He shakes his head. But he knows I'm right.

"It's not even the rape. It's *who* you raped and *who* you didn't want to know about that. Because if Cort knew, then, at the very least, he would stop *fighting* for you. He'd probably find a way to kill you as well, but that's not even the point. The point is... you would have no fighters in the Ring. Would you? All your best fighters came from Cort's camp. And he is their leader. One word from him and you lose them all."

Udulf actually guffaws. "They all want to live, *Anya*." I smile at him for using my name instead of the derogatory nyuszi. "They don't really care about him. Just look at Maart. He will kill Cort tomorrow. And he thinks he will set the camp free. Fine. Let him think that. Let them all think that they have a *choice*. But then, you only have to look at Rainer to see how it will end up." He shrugs with his hands. "My boys, my camp. They are all mine. And that will never change because they are *slaves*, Anya. They are nothing but slaves."

I nod to move past this, but continue. Because I'm not quite done yet and he's getting impatient. "But that night of the fight on the ship. That night I was supposed to be *cancelled* too, wasn't I? Lazar wanted me dead because I knew his secret. You *told him* that I knew his secret. And even if I did know seventeen languages, and even if I was still able to spy for him, I was no longer worth the risk, was I?"

"Anya." He says my name sharply now. "I'm a busy man. What do you want? You're wasting my time and I'm tired of this conversation."

He already knows what I will say. But I say it anyway. "I want to *live*, Udulf."

His breath escapes slowly. Like he might've been holding it. And then he smiles.

"You want to live with *me*, you mean?"

I nod. "With you."

"I bet you would." He grins. Udulf van Hauten might be a sick, diabolical citizen of the uber-elite class who live in a world where there are no limits and his disgusting appetite for children is always satiated, but he is still just a man.

I am not his preferred flavor, but I am still a beautiful eighteen-year-old girl. And he is still a man with an ego.

I smile demurely as he gets up from the breakfast table, walks over to me, kisses my hand, and says, "I'll see what I can do."

CHAPTER THIRTY-TWO

My humble training village has been nearly empty for three days since Maart claimed all my fighters in his little coup and only left me Zoya, Rasha, and Irina.

This is all I think about in the time between his betrayal and the fight.

And I'm still thinking about it as my private, never-before-seen-or-photographed base camp is infiltrated by the other nine men in the world who own fighters in the Ring of Fire, and, of course, that pushy bitch of a reporter who tried to corner me for an interview back on the *Bull of Light* four months ago.

I didn't exactly agree to the interview. Udulf insisted. But I'm trying not to make waves here, since pretty much everything is on the line, so I don't kill her outright when she saunters up to me, sticks her microphone in my face, and tells her cameraman to roll film. "Tell me, Sick Heart. Did you ever think you'd be back in the ring after that disastrous last fight?"

"Disastrous?" She is enthralled by my voice, I can tell. She's never heard it. No one outside of my camp, and Udulf, of course, has ever heard it. Because I have never given an interview. Maart was always there to do my talking. And now he's not.

"I'm still here," I say, unable to hide the annoyance in my voice. "So I would not call it disastrous."

"Some say the only reason you won is because Anya Bokori helped you. Some even say she is the rightful winner of that fight."

I just blink at this woman. She is too old for that revealing red dress and heavy makeup. And if I were to touch her hair, it would be stiff and sticky from all the product. She is a shadow of the beautiful woman she was twenty years ago and I feel sorry for her. She was probably a whore. A very alluring one, for sure, but I can see the slave girl in her eyes. I can hear her history playing on repeat in her head. She probably started her life much like Anya did—a cherished toy as a child, a young girl just a little too pretty to throw away at the proper time, a woman to be used out in the wider world, and finally, when no one quite knew what to do with her, a reporter.

It's not her fault she ended up here. She was born into this. She doesn't even know better. But she *is* a grown woman. So she *should* know better.

"Anya Bokori's name wasn't on the playbill," I say. "She didn't give an interview for the *Ring of Fire* magazine."

"Neither did you."

She's got a point there. "And yet you pulled one together. Anya Bokori is a simple, stupid girl who managed to stay alive longer than most. But her time is up."

"Why do you say that?"

I'm tired of this woman, so I narrow my eyes at her. "Or maybe I'm wrong. Maybe *your* time is up." I look her up and down in a demeaning way, then find her eyes again. "I mean… you're getting a little old for this gig, don't you think? Maybe Anya Bokori wants your job? The future belongs to the young, isn't that what they say? And your youthful days are definitely over."

She huffs, then lowers her microphone, motions for the cameraman to stop rolling with a slicing motion across her throat, and says, "You're a dick, you know that? No wonder they don't let you talk. Good luck today." She looks me up and down the same way I did her. "You're gonna need it."

She's not wrong. I am going to need it. I haven't been training the way Maart has. I am not in shape. There is no way I could beat Maart in a fight today and my mind is swirling with anxiety about Ainsey.

What are they doing with her? Who has been taking care of her? Will they bring her today? Will they make her watch?

I think Rainer is taking care of her. I think they will bring her today. And I am positive they want her to watch me die. They want her to see it, be traumatized by it, learn from it. That's how they get us when we're young. It took me longer than I'm proud of to realize that, but it's not my fault. It's easy to deceive children. Way too easy.

I don't think they're doing anything to Ainsey. *Yet.* But if Lazar takes her home—and he will, if I can't stop him—then my little girl's life will end soon, and it won't be quick. He will go slow. He likes to go slow.

The rage building up inside me is so thick, I almost can't contain it. But the loud sound of a bus rumbles through camp. And when I walk over to the edge of the porch, I catch a glimpse of the front end through the trees.

The invited guests are already here. This is not a sanctioned Ring of Fire fight, so that guest list was fairly small. Only the other owners were invited, and that number is exactly nine, plus Udulf and Lazar, and the mercs, doubling today as drivers since Udulf wants to keep this little party as elite as possible.

Ego man, it never fails.

So they have a grand total of thirty. Plus the reporter and her cameraman, that's thirty-two. But I'm not sure they really count.

So this bus rolling up holds my camp.

I glance over at the nearest hut where Zoya, Rasha, and Irina have been staying. They are waiting it out on the porch as well, their eyes all tracking the movement over by the bus. They have a better view than I do, so they are more committed to their watching. But soon enough, I can see all my people.

Rainer comes first, his eyes automatically tracking to me on the porch of our house. He's holding Ainsey. But he looks away quickly, and when Ainsey's gaze lingers on me for an extra second too long, he whispers something in her ear. *Don't look*, he's telling her. *Don't look at him*. She turns her head, obeying.

Evard is trailing behind Rainer. He doesn't need to be told not to look.

Then the rest appear. My entire camp. Fifteen more kids under thirteen. Four teenagers. Three grown women. And Maart. Not a single one of them looks at me.

But it doesn't matter anymore.

I have what I need.

I know who I am.

Or rather, I know who I *was*.

CHAPTER THIRTY-THREE

ANYA

The next morning I am escorted back to the base camp for the fight in a limo sitting between Udulf and Lazar.

Nothing about this day is very clear to me. But I am very sure that the reason this fight is happening has less to do with how I helped Cort in the last one and more to do with some sick need of these two men to maintain control.

Udulf hasn't gotten back to me about where I will end up. Not that I expected him to. I expected him to go right to Lazar, have a little conversation about their shared secret, and part with their heads swirling with blood and delusions of grandeur.

The purpose of our little chat yesterday was to make him see me. Because before that talk I was just a slave girl who outlived her usefulness and after that talk I was something else.

I don't really know how the story goes between Udulf and Lazar—but I can take a good guess.

Once upon a time Udulf and Lazar were best friends. They grew up together. They went to school together. They shared the same interests, they shared the same goals, they shared the same sick desire for control.

And when they were in their early teens—before they had money to buy their own house slaves to abuse and fighters to find glory, before they were asked to join the ranks of their elite elders—these young men, and probably others just like them from similar families all over the world, played their own game.

Let's call it... Breed and Hunt.

Because that's what it was.

It was mostly just some really sick shit at first.

They raped their father's house slaves, got them pregnant, and then shipped them off somewhere private to have those brand-new baby slaves. Out of sight and out of mind until... those children were old enough to *run*. Then, they brought them back in containers and had a little hunt in the shipyards.

That's where Cort's sister comes in.

And maybe they took some of them home for later.

That's where Cort comes in.

But along the way they realized that not all these children were useless bags of meat to be killed in ritualistic fashion.

Some of them had survival instincts.

And this was a real opportunity.

I think this is how they started their stable of fighters.

I think this is how they got their harem of house slaves.

I think this is how it all began for Cort.

Maybe it's not one-hundred percent correct, but I'd bet my life that it's pretty damn close.

And my words to Udulf yesterday were just another part of that game. No one really cares what they did. No one is coming to arrest them. There will be no trial, no prison sentence, no consequences at all.

Because these men rule the world. They are untouchable.

And it doesn't even matter if Cort finds out the secret of his beginnings. He's already dead to them.

Today, he and Maart will fight. Maart will win. And Maart won't leave. Rainer has paved the way for this, so it's not even unexpected that Maart would stay. They would all stay. Maart and Rainer would take over Cort's base camp. Would continue the traditions. They would choose their own new crop of fighters. And then Maart and Rainer would be the ones sending little boys and girls onto the mat, or onto the platforms, or into some makeshift ring, and one by one, all these kids, along with thousands more around the world, would *die trying*.

And, since this is the most successful camp in the Ring of Fire right now, those older teens that are ready to enter the Ring would keep the legacy going long enough for all of that to pan out. And the younger teens—like Irina, and Paulo, and Peng, and Maeko— they would be right behind them. Ready for their chance.

It's kind of a perfect plan.

There are so many ways to keep the glory going in this scenario.

This is what Udulf and Lazar are imagining this morning. And the only reason why they bothered to keep all this stuff secret for all these years is because

Cort was *winning*. And Pavo was *winning*. And as long as they had *winners*, they were winners too.

If it ain't broke, don't fix it.

They brought in money, and power, and prestige. By luck or by chance, this whole Breed and Hunt thing somehow... worked.

But make no mistake—I can almost hear Lazar or Udulf whispering these words to one or the other in the past—as the undefeated world champion of the Ring of Fire, Cort van Breda was *dangerous*. And Pavo was coming right up behind him.

I don't know how Pavo came into this world. I have no idea what his story really was, but I'd bet money that it was very close to Cort's.

And these men who fight for their lives over and over again. These men who make it to the top of their game in the Ring... they are no joke, man. They are some dangerous fucking animals when the instincts kick in.

It's like those tiger trainers in Vegas. They put those beasts on stage for decades. Day, after day, after day. And they had this precarious hold over them. This sense of... *control*.

No one really knows why the damn tigers went along with that shit show as long as they did. Maybe they loved their masters? Maybe they feared their masters? Maybe they just didn't give a fuck?

Or maybe... *maybe* they knew they were tigers but they had been kept in cages their whole lives so they didn't really understand what it *meant* to be a tiger.

It's hard to read the mind of a beast, but one thing is for sure—control over something so powerful is only ever an illusion. And eventually, that illusion will be shattered.

This is what Udulf and Lazar were trying to prevent by keeping their shared secret.

Because if the tigers really understood how they got there and what was taken from them in the process... well. We all know how that ended in real life.

Udulf and Lazar are aging trainers standing on stage with fed-up tigers. And all that stands between them and the jaws of the beasts is a chair and a whip.

Will it be enough?

We're about to find out.

Our limo crawls up the dirt road and parks behind the bus that Maart and the rest of the camp came in on.

Lazar opens his door and slips out. I'm just about to follow when Udulf grabs my arm. I turn to look at him and we stare at each other for a moment.

He breaks the silence first. "I don't know what the purpose of our chat was yesterday morning, but it's not going to work."

"You don't want me?" His pause tells me he's not sure how to answer this. But I don't care how he answers it. "Whatever, Udulf. It makes no difference to me." Then I pull my arm away and get out of the limo on Lazar's side.

Lazar is wearing a cream-colored linen suit with a light blue shirt, mostly unbuttoned, showing off a thick patch of wild gray chest hair. He reaches into a pocket, pulls out a handkerchief, and dabs his head, mussing up his bleached-blond hair in the process. The jungle heat is overpowering and the humidity is thick enough to choke on, yet he wears this ridiculous suit in this ridiculous manner.

And this is the moment when I see him for what he really is, and not what I thought he was. It's a little bit sad, really. When the old still see themselves through the lens of the young.

Udulf walks around the car and joins us. He's wearing gray slacks and a white button-down shirt, but unlike Lazar, at least he has enough sense to actually button it.

Lazar looks every bit a Vegas tiger trainer.

And this fight is now his stage.

CHAPTER THIRTY-FOUR

CORT

We use the center training ring for the fight. Unlike the other two on either side, this one is elevated, more of a typical ring you find in gyms and event centers, but without ropes or a cage around the raised floor of mats.

There are no chairs set up so I can only assume that these assholes—these other owners in the Ring of Fire—do not expect it to last long enough to sit.

No one needs to tell me the odds. I know they are against me.

I have won too many fights.

I have earned my freedom.

And I'm setting a bad example for the younger fighters coming up behind me.

These owners need to set this record straight.

There is no buyout, there is no freedom. The last fight only ever ends one way.

This isn't some welfare scheme.

This isn't some stepping stone to the outside world.

This is a death sentence.

That's why the reporter is here. It's her job to make sure everyone knows where we stand when this is over.

Maart is already on the mats when I exit my house. Alone.

They don't even care that he's there. No one actually *cares* about this fight. They expect Maart to win, they expect the record to be set straight. They expect to drink and party in my house tonight. They might string my dead body from a tree to make it a little more dramatic, but unlike the fight on the ship, this one is not a big deal.

The reporter is only here to record my death for the next issue of *Ring of Fire*.

This fight is nothing to these men but a restructuring.

What happens in this camp, and others like it around the world, it's just... *business*.

Udulf and Lazar are both standing in front of the ring, smiling and laughing with drinks in hand, the ice in their crystal glasses rapidly melting. Patting each other on the back. Chatting up their peers and ignoring Anya, who stands among them, but is not one of them. All of them sweating in the sweltering heat as I walk towards the ring.

They don't even acknowledge me. This is just another afternoon get-together. A little bit exotic because it's my training village and none of them, save for Udulf and Lazar, have ever been here before. But this place is seriously not much to look at.

I glance over at the small hut, just behind the crowd of owners, and find Zoya, Rasha, and Irina standing on the porch. They will watch from there. Then I glance to the opposite side of the ring near the encroaching jungle, and see Rainer, and Evard, and all the other fighters. Only Sissy, Ling, and Cintia catch my eye and nod.

I don't nod back.

This fight looks nothing like the last one on the ship. There are no drums, there is no dark sky under a new moon, no body paint, no spotlights, no slave boys, no one in my corner at all.

There are no expectations here aside from death and rebirth.

But that's OK. I have lived with the threat of death for as long as I can remember. This is just one more day in the life of the Sick Heart.

I hop up in the ring and stand a few feet away from Maart and it takes several long seconds before the owners even notice the fight is about to start.

Insult, upon insult, upon insult.

Maart and I walk towards the center of the ring and bow. And while we are looking down at our thumbs, he says, in a low voice, "Finally. Something really worth fighting for."

And when I look up to agree, he punches me in the face.

CHAPTER THIRTY-FIVE

ANYA

Cort is his usual cool, collected self as he walks down the steps of his porch and makes his way towards the center training ring.

Everything about a fight day is significant. Every decision has purpose. And isn't that how they like it? These sick men who prey on children in the shadows?

But they do it in the light of day.

Oh, none of them are giving interviews about their pedophilic tendencies. Not to the masses, not even the *Ring of Fire* reporter wants to hear that shit. But these men are far, far, *far* too smug and confident in their untouchable status to hide their depraved, immoral, deviant behavior. And why should they? They are proud of it.

But it's always hidden in plain sight.

That's why the fight on the ship had the drums, and the dark moon, and the symbols painted on my body. That's why there were black lights to make us glow. That's why we were naked. That's why there were slave boys dressed in gold.

They thrive on that shit. It's like a secret handshake to them. It comes with a wink and a nod. And they all laugh and wink and nod back.

Take Cort's name, for example. Udulf's peers all know Cort was his biological child, just like we all know that Evard and Ainsey are Cort's children. And Udulf gave Cort a different surname because Cort is no one to Udulf. He is nothing but a slave.

He told me that himself just yesterday morning.

Cort's mother was of no consequence to Udulf. He has no idea who she was. Just some slave girl, maybe no older than a child herself when she gave birth. I'm not sure about that. But it doesn't matter. The only point is Cort's actual name. Van Breda.

It doesn't make much sense unless you have other clues, because 'breda,' as far as I know—and I'm pretty fucking good with languages—can't be translated into anything meaningful. It's a Dutch city, but that's not meaningful. You have to look at Pavo's last name to really see what they are doing here with the surnames. Pavo's surname was dripping with symbolism. It means 'bloodline' in Hungarian.

Because we are *bred*. Every single one of us.

I know Cort might think—or maybe *hope* is the better word—he might hope that these are not his people. That he is not one of them, but he is.

We are.

It is a plan.

And you only have to casually look at the name van Breda to see the connection.

Breeder.

That's what Udulf thinks of Cort. His sick heart is nothing but a breeder.

These people, they all love a good symbol.

But two can play that game. Or, as it happens, thirty-one. Because that's how many people live in this base camp. That's how many fighters, including Ainsey and myself, call this place *base*.

Thirty-one of us. Thirty-two of them. It's not quite one-on-one, but they could probably outnumber us two-to-one and it would still be in our favor.

I hear, rather than see, the first punch. Maart lands it sloppily on purpose.

This day is absolutely about a fight—but it's not the fight these men came to see.

My first clue was Maart's smiling face and little talk with me on the ship.

"We're sticking together."

"Are we?"

"We are."

"What's that mean, exactly?"

"You'll find out."

The second clue was learning that he made this deal before he and the kids came out to the Rock. This was always Maart's plan. This was why he caused all that tension in camp with Cort. This was why he got on his back about me and Ainsey.

He needed Cort to believe it was real when it mattered.

And it was real, so Cort did believe.

Until Maart dropped the third clue.

The third clue was the fact that he left the girls behind with Cort.

I mean, maybe Maart gives no fucks about Zoya or Rasha, but Irina?

Come on. Everyone saw through that.

He loves Irina. He wants her to be the first girl in the Ring of Fire.

473

Or he did, before he set this whole plan in motion.

Maart needed Udulf and Lazar to be the arrogant pricks they are.

He needed them smug.

He needed them proud and cocky.

He needed them to think exactly what they do right in this moment.

That this fight is nothing but a cancellation. Of no importance whatsoever.

He needed these men to think that the Sick Heart's time was up and that Maart was someone they could relate to. Someone like them. Someone smug, and proud, and cocky.

Someone who wanted to live and would do anything—make any deal with the Devil he could—to make that happen.

But that's not Maart.

Not even close.

So while all the devils are watching Maart and Cort pretend to beat the shit out of each other, several small children are crawling under the skirt of the platform. And the older ones, the ones I don't know—those women, the teenagers who are on their way up, these fighters who, by this time, have killed more opponents than they can count—don't bother sneaking around the side of the ring because this is the oldest trick in the book.

And these men—these arrogant men who are so full of themselves—have left their bodyguards all the way over by the cars because they are acting as drivers. And that is much too far away to stop what is coming.

Finally, these kids are in a fight worth dying for.

That night Cort and I jumped off the platform and sat under the rig we had that small conversation about revenge.

And Cort's words have stuck with me. Have haunted me.

Don't you ever think about revenge? I asked him.

Don't we all?

Then why not go get it? I've heard you're the most dangerous man on this planet.

Maybe I'm holding out for the fairy tale ending, Anya.

What's that look like?

I don't really know. I guess I never thought it through, but just off the top of my head I'd say... a rescue would be nice.

Doesn't everyone want a rescue?

Sure. I guess I can see the logic in that.

It's just all so unlikely.

If there's one thing I've learned in this life it's that no one is coming to save you and if you want the happily ever after you should just rescue yourself.

But it doesn't have to be that way.

Maybe the fairy-tale ending isn't about being rescued at all.

Maybe that whole lie is all twisted-up backwards?

This is what I'm thinking about when Irina, and Rasha, and Zoya creep up behind the unsuspecting slave owners watching Maart and Cort pretend to fight, and the little kids crawl out from under the mat platform, and the older ones walk straight around the ring and the slaughter begins—I just watch for a moment and appreciate it for what it is.

And when Udulf and Lazar break away and start running for their lives—the way Cort ran in that maze of shipping containers back when he was just a small boy—I pay no attention to Lazar.

I go for Udulf.

Because this is the Sick Heart's rescue.

And what comes next might not be anyone's version of happily ever after, but we don't care.

For the first time in our lives we're in a fight worth dying for.

CHAPTER THIRTY-SIX

Maart has me pinned to the mat when the slaughter begins, his fist raised, ready to strike. But he pauses. And smiles. Then hops up, pulls me to my feet, and says, "The ship is waiting at the dock. Meet you at the cliff when this is over." Then he turns, ready to go join in the fight.

But I call out, "Wait! Maart! How long were you planning this?"

He looks over his shoulder and grins. "Since day fucking one, haven't you?"

I hold my breath and shake my head as chaos erupts around me.

Maart comes back to me and grabs my shoulder. There are people dying ten feet away and we're having a *moment*. He looks me in the eyes and says, "It's fine. This day was never your job, Cort." He puts his hand over my heart. Presses it like he's making a point. "It has always belonged to me. And besides." He grins at me. "I've always been the brains of this operation. Go find your girl, Cort. She needs saving."

Then he jumps down into the fray and tackles one of the slave owners who is pointing a gun at Oscar. A shot rings in the air, but I don't have time to see how it ends, because Ainsey screams somewhere behind me, and when I turn, I spot Lazar running through the woods carrying my daughter like a football.

Something happens to me in this moment. Something changes inside me and I go from Cort the Sick Heart to Cort the father before I can even process it's happening.

Fuck that dude. Just… *fuck that dude*.

I jump off the platform, land, and then I am running into the jungle understory after him. Everything goes dark when I enter. The canopy above is so thick, almost no light gets past the tree tops, and this means that not much grows on the jungle floor. Ferns, mostly. Plants that suck nutrients from the ground instead of processing it from the sun.

So I can see Lazar ahead of me, weaving his way around the thick, massive tree trunks. Monkeys and birds scream as he passes, pissed off about the intrusion.

But even if the wildlife wasn't announcing his presence in my jungle, I wouldn't need to worry about losing him. Because there is literally no way Lazar escapes in that direction.

He's heading for the cliffs.

So I go slow, my mind whirling at the sudden change in fate. I can hear the fight I just left. Guns are going off. People are screaming. But as I go deeper and deeper into the jungle, the shadows around me begin to shift into something else. Another time, another place.

Same man.

I stop in my tracks as the memory suddenly comes back.

The shadow people suddenly have faces.

Udulf and Lazar.

And I'm not running through a bathhouse—though that did happen at some point in my unfortunate childhood, I was just too young to separate all the horrific experiences I lived through after my sister and I were put into that shipping container and sent across the ocean.

She was the silent girl. She knew the silent language and she taught me.

That's where I learned to sign. From the silent girls of the breeding camp I was born into.

There were dozens of children in the container with us. We were not the only ones. We were just the last ones out.

Stay still, stay back. She signed these words into the palm of my hand as we listened to the locks jangling on the other side of the metal door. *We will go last. After everyone is out. And then we will run.*

And that's what we did.

We ran. And they chased us.

And, of course, they caught us.

Lazar had my sister that night. Carrying her like a football, even though she was much bigger than Ainsey is now. Her legs were kicking and her arms were flopping. But he kept running, laughing, the entire time as he weaved his way around the maze of shipping containers.

I ran after him, yelling and screaming, but only with my hands. Because I didn't know how to use my voice.

Udulf was coming up behind me when Lazar suddenly stopped and turned around.

Lazar put my sister down and Udulf...

I suck in a deep breath and skip ahead.

Lazar pulled a knife from a holster on his belt...

I skip ahead again. Coming back to the present. To the jungle. And just stare down at my bare feet.

Then I start walking again.

That day ended a long time ago and there is no reason to unlock the rest of that memory.

Because it is nothing but blood.

The monkeys near the cliffs are screaming their alarm long before I exit the jungle and find Lazar standing at the edge, looking down, Ainsey in his arms, looking with him.

My foot snaps a branch on the dirt floor and Lazar turns, panic on his face.

And how ironic is this? Twenty-something years later we are back in that maze. Him running with a little girl in his arms. Me chasing him down. But this time, the end belongs to me.

"Don't take one more step, Sick Heart." Lazar has a knife pressed against Ainsey's neck. maybe even that same fucking knife he used to skin my sister in front of me.

For what? What possible reason could there be to skin a little girl alive?

Cruelty. Evil. That's the only explanation for these people.

Lazar is panting hard from his run, his chest rising and falling in an alarming fashion, like he's on the edge of a panic attack. "I will cut her fucking throat and throw her over. I swear to God I will."

I nod at him. Give him a tight-lipped smile. "Yep. I'm sure you would. But if you do that, Lazar, I will pull your eyes out with my fingertips the same way I pulled Pavo's heart from his chest."

He scoffs, so fucking arrogant, and then he presses the knife just a little harder against Ainsey's throat. His heightened threat trickles out as a tiny stream of blood. "I'll do it," he says again. His voice cracking.

And once again, I nod. "You've miscalculated here, Lazar."

He sneers at me. "How the hell do you figure? I've got the knife and a scared little girl who I happen to know is important to you. You would give up everything for her, apparently. You agreed to this day."

"Well," I say calmly. "Yeah. I suppose that part is true. But here's where you went wrong. She's *not* a little girl, Lazar. She is *nak su*."

Lazar's head tips back to laugh just as Ainsey's tiny fingers dig into his eyes.

He screams, stumbles backwards, and this is the moment when I really do panic. My feet are moving, my body crossing the distance between us, because they are falling...

Ainsey reaches for me as Lazar screams, and I snag her, pulling her with all my strength from his tight grip.

She comes free, but I hear the snap of her shoulder as I save her from the fall onto the rocks below.

Ainsey screams, her shoulder limp. But she's safe. In my arms. And even my dumb ass knows how to put a shoulder back in place. Her relief is immediate when the bone slides back in and we both let out a long breath of relief.

"Fuck," I say. Looking her over to see if she's hurt. "Are you all right?"

She holds her palm up and says, "High-five."

I just stare at her for a moment. Sad that she can adjust so easily.

Then vow to change that as soon as I can.

But I still high-five her.

Gunshots ring out on the other side of the jungle. "Shit. We gotta go." I pick her up, go back into the trees, and start making my way north along the cliffs, towards my ship.

A branch snaps behind me, and when I whirl around, I find the reporter and her cameraman, both with their hands up, like I'm about to rob them.

"It's just us!" she says. "We're just trying to get away."

I look her up and down with disgust. "Get all that on film, did ya?"

"That's my job," she sneers back at me. "I tell stories."

"No." I shake my head. "You *steal* stories. And you're not a part of this one, so you can't have it."

More gunshots ring out in the distance. More yelling. The reporter looks over her shoulder, very nervous about what's happening in that direction. Then she looks back at me. "I'm just as much a part of this story as you are. I see the way you look at me. I know what you fighters think of me. And fuck you, Sick Heart. *Fuck you*. This is my story too."

I shrug. "You're a footnote. Maybe. You're not coming with us. I don't care what you've been through, you're *not* coming with us. I will not be your rescue. You didn't earn it."

She flips me off. "Go fuck yourself. I can start wars with my footage. I can change the world with my stories."

"Then go do that, bitch. Don't waste your time telling me about it. Because I don't care." Then I turn my back to her and start running for the ship.

But she calls out, "Who do you care about, Sick Heart? That little girl with your gray eyes? Is she the only one who matters to you now? Is she the only one who gets a rescue?"

I slow down, turn and walk backwards, shaking my head. "You really don't get it, do you?"

"Get what?"

"The only way people like us get saved is if we rescue ourselves. And if a pack of disposable kids can come up with a plan to take on an elite cabal in the middle of a jungle, then you should be able to do it too."

Then I turn around again, and this time, when she calls my name, I don't stop.

I do not look back.

CHAPTER THIRTY-SEVEN

I catch up with Udulf at the parked cars. And everything about this moment is ironic.

There are ten limos. These powerful men all came in their fancy cars. Didn't even think to carpool, but whatever. All the mercs are doubling as drivers today but they are all back in the center of the base camp, fighting with a pack of warrior children.

Udulf is going from car, to car, to car looking for keys—desperately holding on to the idea that if he just searches hard enough, he's going to stumble into an escape plan.

I slowly walk up to him.

He's got a gun, so he's feeling pretty cocky when he points it at me. "Find me some keys. Now!"

I just scoff. "Like I know where the keys are? I don't live here, Udulf. I have been with you for the last three days, remember? I don't have any keys. So if you want to escape—" I nod my head to the road as I continue to slowly walk up to him. "You better start running."

Gunshots ring through the camp behind us and Udulf laughs. "I better start running? Do you think you're winning, you pathetic, worthless little whore?"

"So shoot me." I am still walking towards him. "Go ahead. If I'm no threat to you... if I'm just a pathetic, worthless little whore, what are you so afraid of, Udulf? Hmm?"

He scoffs. "What are you doing? You think you're going to fight me?"

Fight him?

I mean, everything about that is just stupid and his gun is only the first reason.

No. This moment with Udulf isn't about *fighting him*. I don't need to fight him. I just want him to see me. I want him to be thinking about *me* when he dies.

Because he *is* going to die today.

My eyes dart to the jungle behind Udulf just as Zoya slips between two ferns.

Udulf turns, automatically firing into the trees. But his aim is too high. Zoya is barely three feet tall. He realizes his mistake as his gaze finds hers. She is a fierce-looking girl, for sure. But not really a threat to a full-grown man. And Udulf knows this.

So he chuckles. And not some nervous chuckle, either, but like this is actually funny. "Her? That's who's gonna save you today, Anya Bokori?"

"Try again," Rasha says, coming out of the jungle from another direction.

Udulf looks confused for a moment, but still doesn't realize what's happening. "Two of you!" He guffaws. "Plus you!" He's looking at me when he says that.

And that's why he doesn't see Irina slip out of the jungle, come right up behind him, put her knife to his throat, and slit it open.

It's over so fast I feel like I missed it. And I have a moment of regret for not doing it myself. For missing out on the heat of his sticky blood all over my hands.

But Irina shakes her head at me from the other side of the road. She points her bloody knife at me and says, "You are mental ninja, Anya Bokori." Then she points to herself. "I am *real* ninja. And I am big sister here. Don't you ever forget that."

I have never killed anyone.

Not really. Cort is the one who finished Pavo off, not me.

And even though if you had asked me just ten seconds ago if I *wanted* to kill Udulf van Hauten, I would've said yes… ten seconds later I would've regretted it.

I am not a killer.

And now, I will never have to be.

So I accept Irina's unexpected rescue with a silent bow.

Irina bows back and then we all meet up in the middle of the road and look down at Udulf. He's not quite dead yet, still choking on his own blood. And I'm sure we're all thinking we should feel something about this… but we don't.

Zoya says, "I'm hungry."

Rasha says, "Should we go to the ship now?"

Irina tsks her tongue and huffs. "It kinda pissed me off that they *never* see us coming. What does a girl have to do to get respect around here?"

I say, "Me too. Let's go," and then I give Irina's shoulder a squeeze. "Being underestimated can be a good thing. Just embrace it."

Then we all enter the jungle, make a wide circle around the base camp, and jog towards the cliffs.

Irina stops us before we get to the path that leads to the rock where we got off the ship just a few days earlier. She whispers, "There are men up there, look!"

We all follow her pointing finger and, sure enough, we can see some of the mercenaries are on the rock. Shooting at the ship.

But someone is shooting back.

"Rainer," Rasha says. "And the ship security."

"There is no gangplank," I say.

"So what do we do now?" Zoya asks.

"This way," Irina says.

And we run again, our feet pounding on the jungle floor, until we run out of jungle. We stand there, on the edge of the trees, looking out over the water towards the ship.

"It's leaving," Zoya says. Her fierce calm suddenly cracking in panic. "It's leaving without us."

And she's right. The ship is moving. We are the last ones and—

"Warriors!" The yell cracks through the jungle and we all turn in that direction. "This way!"

The mercs hear the call as well and stop shooting at the ship.

They start shooting at *us*.

"Run!" It's Cort calling to us. He's running towards the cliff carrying Ainsey in one arm and pointing at the ship with the other. "Jump!"

And we do.

Because Maart might be our teacher, but Cort is our leader.

And when your leader tells you to jump off a cliff—you jump off a cliff.

We hit the edge of the rocky ledge at the same time, but Cort and Ainsey are about thirty yards down the shoreline.

And none of us hesitates.

We've been here before.

We've spent our whole lives living on the edge of a cliff.

So we jump into the deep water and we swim through a literal firefight as the ship security takes on what's left of the Ring cabal, bullets snapping the water around our heads.

Zoya gets hit in the shoulder, and we pull her, against the rolling waves, until the rescue boat picks us up out of the water.

I fall back into a pile of rope, thinking... *Huh. I got rescued twice today.*

And then I smile.

Because that's a happily ever after right there.

CHAPTER THIRTY-EIGHT

THREE MONTHS LATER
CIMA HOSPITAL – ESCAZÚ, COSTA RICA

It's been a helluva week.

Anya and I cling to each other as we wait in the children's ward reception for the nurses to bring Ainsey out. She had open heart surgery six days ago to repair an atrial septal defect, the cause of her frequent pneumonia, and today she is well enough to go back to the little apartment we're renting just a few blocks away.

We've been here for seven weeks and even though the small neighborhood is starting to feel like home and we've made friends with the hospital staff and the people who live nearby, the three of us are very ready to get back to the ship.

That won't happen for at least three more weeks because of Ainsey's recovery, but it's closer now and my sick heart is starting to feel better about things.

I'm starting to breathe a little easier.

Starting to let myself calm down.

Starting to feel normal, whatever that is, for the first time ever.

We got away that day back at base camp. But it wasn't clean. Oscar and Sammy, another one of my little boys, were both shot. Both made it to the ship and Oscar lived, but Sammy didn't. He lost too much blood and we didn't have time to find a match and give him a transfusion in the ship's clinic.

Peng died back in the camp and Maeko refused to leave him behind, so he carried him back to the ship while Paulo covered him with a gun stolen from one of the slave owners. We had a sea burial for Peng the next day and Maeko hasn't been the same since.

Ling and Zoya both took a bullet in the shoulder. Zoya is weirdly proud of this. I think we need to have a chat about that at some point. Rainer took one in his upper arm, Jafari actually drowned because he and Budi also had to jump off the cliff to get to the ship, but Lilith—my oldest girl fighter in the camp—pulled him into a rescue boat and brought him back.

Maart, Cintia, and Sissy didn't sleep for forty-eight hours, they were so busy trying to glue our kids back together.

And of course, Ainsey came down with another case of pneumonia less than a week later and even though we didn't have seventy-two thousand dollars for the surgery in a private Costa Rican hospital, Sergey, my oldest boy in camp, took a legitimate fight in Rio and earned enough for a down payment with his win.

Ainsey is going to be fine. She won't be training for several months, but even though Anya has pointed out that it isn't normal for four-year-olds to train, I have been having a hard time giving up the life. All of us have.

What does life look like without training? We don't know, but we're trying to figure it out.

The platform ship isn't really the money-maker we had hoped for. Udulf, Lazar, and every other Ring slave owner at that last fight—they are all dead. And with their deaths came a bizarre in-between world of uncertainty.

At least no one came looking for us.

I don't know why. Maybe they all knew I had bought my freedom. But that's not likely, so it's… luck? Maybe?

Or maybe they are afraid of us?

We did take down a lot of very important people. Plus almost all the mercenaries died too.

But whatever the reason, we're not taking it for granted.

The downside is that we have to find our own contracts now. And while that's not really a bad thing, it's definitely a lesson in the meaning of the words 'fresh start.'

The ship is the new home base. It's only rated to house fifty-two crew members and we've got a total of sixty-seven—all of us from camp, plus the ship's regular crew—but it works for now.

Money is tight, especially since Anya and I have been paying rent in Escazú for two months. But even with all these bitter setbacks—the deaths, the injuries, the open-heart surgery, the challenge of starting a new business and taking care of thirty other people at the same time… freedom still tastes very, very *sweet*.

"Here she is!" I turn to find a nurse pushing Ainsey towards us in a wheelchair.

I bend down and smile at my daughter. My *daughter*. It feels real now.

Well, not the part about her being my daughter. That's always felt real. The part about me being her father. That took some getting used to.

Anya bends down too. She touches Ainsey's cheek. "You ready to go home?"

Ainsey nods, but says nothing.

"She's got your eyes."

I look up at the nurse. "Yep. She sure does."

"No," the nurse says. "I mean, yes, of course, she has the same color eyes as her daddy. But otherwise her eyes are all Mommy, aren't they?" The nurse smiles at Anya and me. And we smile back.

Because, of course, Ainsey isn't Anya's daughter. But that's not a story we're going to tell. Ever.

"I mean," the nurse clarifies when we don't respond, "neither of you talk much." She points to Ainsey and Anya. "Not with words. But your eyes…" Her words trail off and she shakes her head. "They say all the things your lips don't."

Anya and I stand up, agree with the nurse, and then take our daughter home.

CHAPTER THIRTY-NINE

SIX MONTHS LATER
Lençóis Maranhenses National Park, Brazil

Stepping onto the shore of the park is exactly like stepping into the pages of a fantasy book.

It is a beach.

It is a desert.

It is an oasis.

There are almost no words to describe the beauty of this place because it's all very inexplicable. Deceptive mounds of pure, soft sand dunes hide hundreds, if not thousands, of small freshwater lakes.

But it's not the dark, dank, dangerous freshwater you normally find in Brazil. It's not the kind filled with piranhas, or worse, waiting to eat your toes if you just think about taking a dip. It is the kind of lake you find at the tippy-top of mountains.

Because these lakes are the color of a perfect Fijian beach. The seafoamiest green-blue you've ever seen in your life.

And it makes no sense. None at all. How do these lakes get here? Rain, I guess. But why doesn't the water just seep into the sand, the way it does on the shore?

I haven't looked it up yet so I don't know.

I might never look it up. I don't want to spoil the fairy-tale fantasy of it all. I just want to enjoy it.

We are on vacation. The entire camp.

Well, we're here for two reasons really. One, we've saved up enough from the supply ship runs and the legitimate fights that Sergey, Lilith, Ivano, and Kioshi—the four oldest kids in camp—have been taking in the nearby city of São Luís, and we've bought a small collection of nearly falling-down houses deep in the jungles north of Rio de Janeiro.

So we're leaving this part of the continent and we might never sail by Lençóis Maranhenses ever again.

We've told ourselves hundreds of times, at least, every time we did sail by, that we would come out here and enjoy it up close. But we never have, until now.

The second reason we're here is to say a formal goodbye to all the warriors who came before us. And even though I wasn't a kid in Cort's training camp, and never really did fight for my life, I still count myself as belonging to this camp and these people.

We belong to each other, really. All of us. And I feel the loss of the fallen warriors as acutely as anyone.

Besides, I do have someone to honor.

Someone I wish could be here, but isn't.

We bring rocks with us. Backpacks filled with rocks. We have collected them from all up and down the beaches of Brazil. We have collected them from the beaches of Central America, from the Bahamas, and Mexico, and even some from the forbidden land of Cuba. We wrote names on them and painted them up with pictures. And we have spent the entire day erecting small monuments around the lake we're camped next to, so that now, lying under the light of a full moon, we can see the shadows of the kids who died fighting.

I made Bexxie's monument myself. It's a tower of nine flat rocks. Alternating color. Black, white, black, white. I painted something on each one and wrote her name on top. And then I sat next to it and told her everything that happened since we last saw each other. I didn't leave out a single detail, even though she's not really old enough to hear the sexy parts, I told her anyway because this was the first time I have ever talked to her. It was the first time she ever heard my voice. And if I stopped talking, I wasn't sure I'd ever want to speak again.

I wasn't sure I'd ever get over the sadness.

So I just kept going and finally, the entire camp was listening to my tale. Even Maart was listening when I described the last breakfast I had with Udulf and how I had figured him out.

Irina pointed at me and said, "Mental ninja," and this made Cort laugh, and Cort's laugh made everyone laugh even though we had tears in our eyes.

Then… it was over and we were all ready to say goodbye.

Every lost warrior has been accounted for.

Not a single one of them has been forgotten.

And maybe some park ranger comes along in a month and kicks them all down, we don't care. We did this. And that's all that matters.

We are all huddled together in a pack. I'm in between Maart and Cort, kinda snuggled in between them, in fact. Maart's hand is resting lazily on my leg and Cort is absently playing with my wild hair.

I don't know what we are. A couple? A threesome?

Not sure.

Don't care.

We just are.

None of us have sleeping mats and we're not on the platform of the Rock, but the entire camp points up at the moon with a single finger at the same time.

We have locked the past up in the rock shadows of the fallen warriors around us, and that's where it will stay forever.

Because this is day one.

EPILOGUE

ONE YEAR LATER

The mood after Paulo's first professional fight is celebratory.

Sergey paved the way for Lilith. Lilith paved the way for Ivano and Kioshi. And they paved the way for Paulo.

This might be Paulo's first official win as far as the wider world is concerned, but they don't care.

They flock to him, just like they flocked to all the others. They are trying to write offers as they hand him drinks. They are begging him for attention.

His eyes find mine from across the room and I hear all the words he's not saying. *Thank you. I owe you. I love you.*

And I raise my glass to him and silently say it all back.

He nods, then starts paying attention to reps from the UFC and Jungle Fight as they have a bidding war, complete with lawyers furiously amending contracts on their tablets as the discussion progresses, at the after-party.

Anya slides up and hooks her arm in mine, leaning into me a little.

"Tired?"

She doesn't say anything, but I feel her shake her head. She's still not much of a talker, even when we're at home. But when we're out, she almost always prefers to speak with her eyes.

"Good. Because we've got big plans tonight."

She pulls back a little, smiling. "What plans?"

"You'll find out."

She smacks me playfully and then says, "Get me a drink, will you? I'm gonna go congratulate Maart."

I lean down and kiss her, enjoying the way she kisses me back. Then she turns and walks off and I wait, and watch her ass, as she makes her way across the room, parting throngs of people as she approaches, and finally lands in front of Maart.

She is gorgeous tonight.

Her blonde hair is sleek and straight. Her face has a little bit of make-up on it. And her strapless gown is the same shade of blue as her eyes.

Maart takes her hand. Kisses her lips. Plays with her hair. Smiles.

He and I are still close. We talk nearly every day and every few months we do more than that. But Maart has his gym in Rio and I have my camp out in the jungle, and, well… that's just how shit shakes out when you grow up.

We haven't grown apart, not really. We're still walking the same road, but one of us is slightly off the beaten path.

He likes the attention. He likes the lights, and the parties, and the hectic pace of Rio. And I still dream about my life on the Rock.

"Now that's a story."

I turn at the remark and find a woman staring back at me. Slightly familiar, but only slightly.

She shakes her head. "You don't recognize me, do you?"

"I'm sorry, I—" But then I do recognize her. The reporter from Ring of Fire. She still looks her age, but she's wearing a dark blue gown and a jacket, not even a hint of cleavage. And her makeup is subtle, like her updo hair. She has an air of sleek sophistication. "Huh. I can honestly say you were the last person I ever expected to see again."

She raises her glass at me. "I'm not gonna take that personally."

I actually laugh. "Good. So."

"Yep. So. I made it out."

"Did you change the world with your stories?"

She nods, smirking. "But not so anyone would notice. If you know what I mean." She pauses to chuckle. "I did my part, Sick Heart. That's all I'm gonna say in public. I did my part."

I raise my glass to her in response. "No one came looking to kill me, so… thanks. I think?" Then we both laugh and clink our glasses. "Here's to doing one's part. What brings you to Rio?"

She nods her head at Paulo. "I came to see him fight."

"And what did you think?"

"I think… anyone who knows anything in this business can tell that kid is going all the way."

"Yeah. I could've told you that back when he was five. What *really* brings you here?"

"You, of course."

I cock my head at her.

"Come on. You're not going to hide away forever. You're young still, Cort van Breda. Your future is in the professional ring." She nods at Paulo again. "Like him. Like all the others you and Maart have sent into the world. Maart isn't hiding. He's the most sought-after trainer on the planet at the moment."

I put up a hand. "I'm gonna stop you right there." I don't even know this woman's name, and honestly, I don't want to know it. Because that life belongs to some other guy. "You've got me all wrong. I'm perfectly happy to slip into obscurity. And if you doubt that, you have no idea who I am."

She presses her lips together. But everything about her is still smug. Like she knows me better than I know myself. "OK. Then… it was nice to see you. You and all your people look extremely well-adjusted and happy. Congratulations."

"Thanks."

"And… if you ever change your mind…" She slips a business card into my suit coat pocket. "Now you know where to find me." She gives me a finger wave and walks off.

I turn the other direction and get my woman her drink.

Four hours later I'm leading a blindfolded Anya towards a helicopter.

"What the hell is this?" she yells over the thumping sound of the rotors.

She has asked me that four times since this secret journey started.

502

When I put her in a limo after we left Paulo's party.

When I put her on a plane when we got to the airport.

When I helped her into a golf cart that brought us here to the helipad.

And each time I say, "You'll find out."

It's a little less than an hour's ride to our final destination. A two-week getaway in paradise. But we're still about five minutes out when I reach over and pull the silk handkerchief down her face so she can see.

We don't have headphones on. We don't need headphones to talk in a helicopter. She signs, *Where the hell are—*

And that's as far as she gets, because she sees it.

The moon won't be new until tomorrow. But that's OK. That will be day one.

The helicopter lands on the Rock's top platform and even through the dark night, I can see my other family get up from their nests and begin to cry out a 'welcome home.'

When I look at Anya, she's got tears in her eyes. Or maybe that's me?

We get out, the helicopter leaves, and we say nothing. We will probably say nothing this entire trip.

Two weeks?

Two weeks of silence is just a warm-up.

But when we look at each other, and start taking off our fancy clothes—dropping them into piles at our feet—we laugh and giggle like the kids we never were.

Then she takes my hand and we run.

And then we jump.

END OF BOOK SHIT

Welcome to the End of Book Shit. This is the part of the book where I get to say whatever I want about the story (or anything else!). It's never edited and it's always pretty last minute. Though this time, I'm writing the EOBS two weeks before release because I need to get my paperback uploaded for preorder.

So.

I have a lot of feelings about this book. Most of them are good ones. Sick Heart is definitely one of my most favorite stories ever.

Sometimes I finish a book and I'm like… meh. It's a book. I'm not going to tell you which ones I have those feelings about, because for the most part, all my books have about the same rating. Somewhere between 4.0 and 4.8. And to me that means that the people who are generally reading the books like them about equally.

Of course, everyone has their favorites. And like me, their not-so-favorites. But the ratings tell me that it all evens out in the wash. About an equal number of people always seem to like the books and an equal number of people always seem to dislike the books. So I don't want you guys to know which books I don't like. If there was a clear winner in the "I-Hate-This-JA-Huss-Book" category, I probably would tell you because then I would disappoint fewer people when they realized I hated the book THEY loved.

And because I am able to have this perspective on the books, and because I have written so many, and published so many, and gone through the entire book process nearly a hundred times now, I can take a step back and separate myself from the story once it's over.

For instance, people who hated Mr. Romantic – I GET IT. The book was about a guy who was accused of rape in college and had a thing for rape fantasies afterward. That book is definitely what I would call dark.

And Meet Me in the Dark. I mean, the title says it all. You're gonna meet this asshole in the dark. And what you find there is gonna be equally dark. So if people hate Merc, I GET IT.

And in Bully King. Cooper is a jerk. Again, the title explains in very clear language what's going on here. He's a bully. He bullies a girl. And like Nolan in Mr. Romantic and Merc in Meet Me in the Dark, Cooper is looking for redemption. (Though, Nolan didn't *really* need redemption. He did nothing wrong. But regardless, he was still looking for it.)

These are dark books. They have dark heroes. These heroes are broken, they live outside what most of us consider socially acceptable norms, and they do this by CHOICE.

I love all three of those books, by the way. None of them come anywhere near the "meh" feeling I have gotten for some over the years. These three are masterpieces, actually.

But here's my point—Sick Heart isn't about a dark hero. He isn't looking for redemption because he doesn't need redemption. And I do not care what kind of shit people want to write about me for saying that, it's an accurate assessment of Cort the Sick Heart and here's why:

1. He's not into dark shit in bed. He's actually pretty apathetic about sex. Sex to him, and all the adult protagonists in this story, has lost its meaning. Sex is NOT the reason he takes Anya with him to the Rock. He takes Anya to the Rock because he intuitively knows Lazar is a piece of his puzzle and she could be a way to crack that secret. He never clearly articulates this in his thoughts, but it's there. Trust me, I wrote the fucking book, it's there. And despite what one early "reader" said – there is no dubious consent in this book. This person actually complained that Anya didn't agree to the first sex scene because she never said the word YES, even though Anya doesn't FUCKING TALK. There is no dubcon in this book. Anya's view of sex is even more apathetic than Cort's. She gives no fucks at all about sex. But she clearly gives permission in that first sex scene. She is laughing in that sex scene. It is playful. She is drunk, yes. They

all are. But this is not a frat-party-drunk sex scene. This is a we're-still-fucking-ALIVE-celebration sex scene. And even though her permission was given in Cort's point of view, she has no regrets afterwards. She doesn't complain about being taken advantage of. She makes a decision during the fight to help Cort win. She CHOOSES HIM in that moment. She JOINS HIS TEAM. This happens before HE chooses HER. This is part of Anya's permission as well. Furthermore, when they arrive at the Rock and Cort hands her the hose to wash him off, Anya understands this is an act of trust. That he is trusting her not to hurt him. He literally hands her a way for her hurt him and she rejects it. If she were feeling taken advantage of in the first sex scene, she would've missed that subtle act of trust he was showing her. She would not have cared if she hurt him with the water hose. And she did care, because she says, very clearly, at the end of that chapter, "I won't.".

Now. Perhaps Anya SHOULD'VE felt taken advantage of. That's another topic. OK? I get that. Maybe she should've felt that way. But it doesn't matter. The only thing that matters is that she DIDN'T feel that way. And the reason she didn't feel that way was because SHE HAS NO FUCKING FEELINGS ABOUT SEX ANYMORE. It has lost all meaning to her. She does not care how her body is used. Her strength comes from HER SILENCE. She is a MENTAL NINJA. She cares about her WORDS because her speech is what she controls. Her silence is a way to make sure no one ever really KNOWS if they have HURT HER or not.

2. Cort didn't choose his path in life, he was forced. It's either let them win and kill you, or kill them

first. And in my mind—and Cort's mind too—it would be a greater sin to give up without a fight than it would be to rise in the ranks and take your place as winner. He killed people. A lot of people. But he's not a killer. He's a fighter. And not only is he a fighter – HE IS A SURVIVOR. HE OWNS THAT WORD. He has been through hell and he's still here. He's still fighting. He didn't make the rules, he just lived within their boundaries. Could he have escaped before this moment in time? No way in hell. He got out in the end because he was finally in a place where he had no other choice but to put it all on the line. He and his friends finally had some control over things and everyone played their part. At what other point in his life would his camp all have put their lives on the line to break free? There was never a reason to rebel before now. They could always fight back, take out a few people here and there, and then what? Nothing would change. They would not get away, they would all be killed. It is not until Cort has earned his freedom that they finally see a way out and that way out is through Cort.

3. The darkness in this book has nothing to do with Cort. The darkness in this book is all about the evil people who run the world that Cort and Anya live in. They were used up as children. Both of them should be dead by now, but they aren't. They fought. They SURVIVED. Yes, all the vicious scenes in this book that deal with the sick ways in which they were used are a part of MY FICTION. But unfortunately, child sex trafficking isn't a fiction. It's a real thing. And if me writing a love story about two SURVIVORS of that dark world creates the perfect storm of conditions for you to rail and rage against me, then that's all you. Not me. It's got nothing to do with me. All I did was

write a book to highlight the fact that child sex trafficking exists and it's the VICTIMS that get left behind who MATTER.

IN SICK HEART – I MADE THE VICTIMS MATTER.

AND I DID THAT BY TURNING THEM INTO SURVIVORS.

AND IF MY GREATEST SIN IN THIS BOOK IS THAT I GAVE THESE TWO SURVIVORS A **LOVE STORY**, WELL…

This is where I usually say…go fuck yourself. ☺ But I'm gonna show some restraint today and say something else instead. Because I understand how sick the premise of this book is. I get it.

But this is why I put a trigger warning on it, bitches. OK? I did my part. I hate trigger warnings. I almost never use them. But I did this time because I understand how disturbing the backstory of Cort and Anya is. This world my characters live in is sick in the heart. And I wanted to give readers the chance to OPT OUT. If you picked up the story and read it and then got angry because I wrote a love story about two people who survived the most horrific childhoods imaginable, that's ALL YOU.

Don't blame me. I didn't do anything wrong and I will never apologize for the words I wrote in this book.

OK. Now that that's all out of the way, I'd like to say one more thing:

If you HATE this book for reasons other than those listed above—the writing, a plot hole, the pacing, my unusual use of paragraph spacing (my editor tried to change that but I changed it back, so it's fine if you hate it. I knew what I was doing…) the personality of the characters, the unlikelihood of a little boy surviving out on an abandoned oil rig for three months and being fed by a bird, whatever it is — well, then that's totally fine.

I don't care if people hate my stories.

BUT I ABSOLUTELY CARE IF PEOPLE MISCHARACTERIZE **MY** STORY TO USE IT IN **THEIR** POLITICAL AGENDA.

I am not political. I don't even watch the fucking news. And other than the snow storm that just dumped three feet of snow into my driveway overnight, I have absolutely no idea what is happening in the world right now because I live in the literal middle of nothing.

Every day of my life I see more cows than people and I don't own cows, guys. The rancher across the road does. I see more of his cows than I do people in this world on a daily basis.

I unfollow anyone in my social media that posts about politics. It's nothing personal, and I don't unfriend them, I just don't like the way people are divided right now and politics is the number one way people self-segregate themselves into groups.

When I go on Instagram I like to look at pictures of crystals, and flowers, and books, and outer space. I like quotes about giving no fucks and Stoicism.

When I'm on Facebook I hang out in my reader group, Shrike Bikes, where we have a strict no politics rule. I really don't look at anything else.

And I do absolutely nothing on Twitter but post up new release pics or posts about books on sale because Twitter is a cesspool of unavoidable hate.

So if you think this story is part of MY political agenda, you're WRONG.

That's YOUR political agenda speaking, not mine. Because I don't have one.

I write stories that make people question things because if I do have an agenda (and I don't – I refuse to be invested in changing people's minds about their world view), then my agenda would be QUESTION EVERYTHING.

That's it. That's what I stand for.

Question. Everything.

Don't just accept what you are told. Go find the answers for yourself.

And I know that this EOBS won't change anyone's mind, but I've said my piece about it and everyone gets a chance to hear my point of view.

Not one damn thing about what I have written in this book can be misconstrued. It has all been spelled out for you.

Either you are the type of reader who wants to lie about my motivations so they fit your world view, or you're not. I already wrote that EOBS in Bossy Jesse. And trust me, the mean bitches came out of the floorboards like cockroaches to put that EOBS down after it was published. You can see these sad, unhappy people on display anywhere reviews are written. They don't even realize how sad they are. They just keep throwing HATE anywhere they can to make themselves feel special, and better, and "worthy".

But that's got nothing to do with me.
That's all them.
So who gives a fuck.

Thank you for reading, thank you for reviewing, and I'll see you in the next book!

Julie
JA Huss
March 15, 2021

I had written a whole other End of Book Shit about some other points in the story before I got this particular feedback from someone that pissed me off. So I'm gonna paste that below so you can read it. But I'm not gonna put that part in the audiobook version because even though I like what it says, I don't want to say those words out loud anymore. This EOBS I wrote above is the "true" End of Book Shit and what happened to my story between writing that first one and this one is the only thing that matters.

So here's the first EOBS:

Welcome to the End of Book Shit. If you're new here, this is the part of the book where I get to say anything I want and just generally write about the story and process. I don't really edit this, so ignore the typos. And normally I write these very last minute. Usually a day or two before publication, but I'm writing this on February 18, 2021 because the manuscript is going to the audio publisher tomorrow and I actually have no idea when this book will release.

Sick Heart.

I came up with the title of this book over a year ago and it was on my schedule to be written like 6 times and it never got done. I had made the first cover long before I ever started writing it. I had made the second cover long before I started writing it. And this cover it released with is the third design. That's how long this book sat on my "to be written" list. □

I finally started writing it in August of 2020, but I was also trying to finish up the final Bossy Brothers book and the final Harem Station book, so it got set aside for several months before I went back to it in January 2021.

So this book took me a while. And when I started it I had plans to write a MMA fighter book. Probably enemies to lovers. The girl was the daughter of a man who did horrible things to the hero when he was a small child. And the hero was a major dick to this girl because she was his revenge plan. It was going to be very "on trope". Very enemies to lovers/captive romance.

Obviously, that's not how it really turned out. Though most of that is still in this story and there are dark undertones floating around in the background, it's not a dark book at all. I think it's actually one of the most romantic books I've ever written.

There is a lot of violence, for sure. But learning to fight and taking your hits as you do that is a very different type of violence. I definitely didn't set out to write a "learn to fight" book. And that's not what Sick Heart is.

Sick Heart is just a love story about two people who each control only one thing in their lives.

Speech.

And they don't need to learn to fight. They've been fighting for so long, it's now second nature.

Anya was already a warrior. She was just different kind of warrior.

And Cort's heart wasn't really sick, he just turned it off to survive.

This is the point, I think.

Because people often say I write dark books. But you know what? That's not really accurate. I mean, some of them are definitely dark. But I don't actually write books about dark things or people.

I write books about survivors of dark circumstances.

Every single dark book I've ever written was about survivors.

I first started writing books about the global dark underworld in 2013. Tragic started out about an abused girl running away. Manic was a little glimpse into her ordeal. And Panic was her coming to terms with the fact that she willingly took part in something very dark and disturbing. And back in 2013 I was hesitant to put in the stuff about human trafficking.

Not because it was dark and disturbing.

I didn't want to put it in there because I didn't think people would believe it.

Because I didn't believe it. I really didn't think this shit was happening.

Modern-day slavery? A global network of slave traders? WTAF are you talking about?

This was my worldview at the time. So I was pretty uncomfortable putting human trafficking into that series.

But in it went. And... well. The story kept going. And since the human trafficking was already in there, I kinda had to see it through.

I would just like to stop here and say I'm a little bit into the conspiracy stuff. BUT – and this is a HUGE BUT – my interest was always just about aliens.

lol

Like, for real, that's as far as it went for me. I am so in to Ancient Aliens—because I'm actually a science nerd and I want explanations for all the weird shit on this planet we can't explain. I am simply a seeker of truth. Most of you already know this about me. And a lot of you have probably read my Junco Sci-Fi series. So that was the totality of my interest in conspiracy theories. All that other shit about Kennedy, and 911, and what have you – that shit could all go fuck itself.

I just didn't care.

But now I was stuck in this new world of human trafficking and there was no way to back out, so I just went with it. I made up child assassins and a global shadow government called the Company. And listen, of course I knew that there was a conspiracy theory already floating around out there about the global shadow government, right? It's called the New World Order and I didn't invent it. I just didn't believe in it.

But that's why it's called fiction, so whatever.

I kept going.

And it was fun. Good god, who doesn't love James Fenici? Right? I loved writing the Company books. Little Sasha Cherlin. Harper and Nick Tate. A little sprinkle of my man, Ford.

Those were some good times.

But then... then I wrote a book called Meet Me in the Dark and that's where shit got a little too real for me. Because even though it's really hard to find evidence for all these wacky conspiracy theories, there is some hard, damning evidence of a little US government program called MK-Ultra.

They fucked with people's heads.

This was a real thing.

And when I discovered that, I didn't even know what to do with that information. I just finished the book and did my best to forget about it.

But it was there. I've written this sentence in books at least three times – Once you know things, you can't un-know them.

So once I knew that this mind-fuck shit was real, well... my imagination took off and I've been running with it ever since.

And that's all fine. There is a market out there for romantic conspiracy stories. Obviously. I've done pretty well with these books.

But the reason I bring this up is to highlight my journey of acceptance. Right?

In the Rook & Ronin series I came to terms with the fact that human trafficking exists.

In Meet Me in the Dark I accepted that mind-control programs—whether effective or not—were something the US government was in to.

I didn't really believe there was a Company out there, but I was exploring what it might feel like to be caught up in it using fiction.

And in order to keep writing about these characters and this world, I had to keep going. I had to dig a little deeper each time I started a new spin off.

The Misters was about the corrupt media.

The Dirty Ones was about the corrupt elite.

Three, Two, One was about a sex cult.

In To Her was about underground crime syndicates.

Bossy Brothers was about information warfare.

Bully King and Ruling Class were about secret rituals.

Creeping Beautiful is about living on the 'inside'.

And when it finally came time to write Sick Heart I remember sitting down and asking myself... OK. Where can these assholes hide where no one can see what they're up to? Because if I'm gonna write a story about an underground MMA fighting ring where every fight is a death match, not even these smug, uber-elite assholes can do this in the open.

And by this time (summer 2020) we're neck-deep in our very own "dystopian future" filled with corporate data-mining, and facial recognition cameras on every corner in big cities, and social media trying to control the world via access to information.

So where can 'they' hide where I haven't (fictionally) found them yet?

And the answer, of course, is the ocean.

I have set books on many a private island. That's no longer even interesting, I've done it so much. And the idea that the super-elite use private islands for nefarious things such as human trafficking isn't even in question anymore. Epstein and Maxwell are real-life sick fucks who made the news and now we know, right? Now we know this shit is real.

So, I wasn't going to put the fights on an island.

I have always been kind of fascinated with offshore oil rigs. They don't look very big when you see a picture of them, but they are huge and often hold hundreds of people. And the life of an off-shore oil-rig worker is very non-traditional. I'm not going to get into it too much because it's all beside the point. I didn't put the fights on the rigs, I put them on the installation ships because these ships are floating cities and they live under different rules than the rest of us. This is the part of these conspiracy stories that I like to explore.

The ship in the beginning of the book is modeled after a real oil-rig-installation ship called Pioneering Spirit and it is largest ship ever built (as I write this).

This ship is part of the reason this book took so long because in order to write that first fight scene I had to look at videos of the inside, kinda learn how the cranes operate, and how the ballasts work. I needed to know what the inside of the command center looked like and I had to get a general idea of what it was like to be on this ship, so I scoured websites that hire people to get a feel for cabins and watched recruiting videos. I needed to know all kinds of shit about this stupid ship before I could get past that opening fight sequence.

But get this… the things you find when you go looking are fucking weird. I had never heard of Pioneering Spirit when I started this book. I did a basic Google search for "Largest ship in the world" and this thing just popped up. And I didn't give any fucks at all about who owned the ship or how it got its name, I just wanted to see some freaking pics and vid of this thing so I could model my fictional ship after it.

But I wanted to give you guys a little information about the ship for the EOBS so I did a little post-book research just twenty minutes ago and it turns out that this Pioneering Spirit ship is owned by a company, which is owned by a man whose father was a Waffen-SS Nazi and was linked to another company that used slave laborers for the Nazi war effort. And the owner of the company that built the Pioneering Spirit originally named the ship after his father, the Nazi, but naming a ship that had the attention of the entire world after a Nazi caused a "controversy", so it got changed to Pioneering Spirit.

There's that saying, right? You can't make this up. I most definitely *could* make this up, but I don't need to. This is real.

I run into these coincidences when I write these stories all the time (See the End of Book Shit for Mr. Match for proof). I didn't know any of this when I started the book. And I swear to God, the longer I write these crazy books set in the dark underground world of absolute shit-bag people, the more I realize that truth is stranger than fiction.

My big revelation in 2013 was the idea that people are bought and sold like animals.

Right now, somewhere on this planet, there are slave traders buying and selling human beings.

This is a fact.

And my new revelation when it came time to write Sick Heart was so much worse than just "humans" being trafficked.

It was children.

That's the dark side of Sick Heart.

But again, this book isn't about trafficking. It's not about the abuse Anya or Cort dealt with as children. It's not about any of that.

Of course, all that stuff matters.

But then again, none of it matters when you're living it. Because if you're living with it, the only thing that matters is that you survive.

My stories are about surviving.

Sick Heart is about all the ways in which you fight.

It's about all the things you do to cope.

It's about coming to terms with who you are, and what you've done, and then taking a stand for yourself, and hopefully, others like you.

And I know there are readers out there who will leave me a review and say this book is dark. And they're just wrong.

This book is about HOPE.

And if their lives are so damn perfect that they can't relate to the world my characters live in, then good for them.

Not everyone is that lucky.

So that's my story.

And I'm sticking to it.

I hope you enjoyed Sick Heart. I fell in love with these people and I left the ending open for a book two, but we'll see how that goes. Also—fun fact—this is the longest book I've ever written and comes in at just under 130,000 words. An average romance novel is about 70,000 words so… you got your money's worth with this one, unicorns!

Anyway, thank you for reading, thank you for reviewing, and I'll see you in the next book.

P. S. If you'd like to know how all my stories connect, you can find that info on the next few pages.

JA Huss
February 18, 2021

Sick Heart is a standalone book. None of the characters who appear in this story can be found in any other story I've written. (yet). :)

But if you want to know the complete story of this world from start to finish, here are all the related books and characters (with ages).

Rook and Ronin Series

The entire Company beginnings start in this series. But each series is its own entry point. You can jump in and read them out of order as long as you follow the specific series reading order.

Tragic
Manic – Vaughn Family and Sick Boyz appear here.
Panic – Vaughn Family and Sick Boyz appear here.
Ford – Sasha Cherlin (age 12) and Merc first appear here
Spencer – James Fenici first appears here – Five is born, Vaughn Family and Sick Boyz appear here.

The Company - Rook & Ronin Spin-offs

New entry point into the series. This is the true beginning of the shadow government called The Company.

The Company – James and Vincent Fenici age 28, Sasha Cherlin age 13, Nick and Harper Tate age 18. This is the **full story of the "Santa Barbara Incident"** where Adam and Donovan's fathers die (Creeping Beautiful).

Meet Me In The Dark – Merc, Sasha Cherlin age 21, Sydney Channing (Company Girl like Indie and Sasha)

Three, Two, One – STANDALONE BOOK – Jax Barlow first appears

Wasted Lust – Sasha Cherlin, age 24, with Jax Barlow.
Nick Tate, age 29, plays a major role and the rest of the Company characters also show back up. First appearance of Angelica Fenici and "other Adam". **Wasted Lust takes place DURING Creeping Beautiful.** Specifically when Indie is 15 years old and the "Company falls" and when Nick meets Adam in Daphne, Alabama. Vaughn Family and Sick Boyz appear here.

Happily Ever After – last book in the Rook & Ronin series many years later.

The Mister Series – Rook & Ronin/Company Spin-off – new entry point into the series

Mr. Perfect
Mr. Romantic – First appearance of the Silver Society – i.e. The Company
Mr. Corporate – First appearance of "Five"
Mr. Mysterious – Spencer's daughters
Mr. Match – All the Rook & Ronin Kids come back to play.
Mr. Five (or just Five) – Ford's son and Spencer's daughter
Mr. & Mrs. – Ford and Spencer show back up with all the kids. – Vaughn Family appears here.

The Bossy Brothers Series
Rook & Ronin/Company Spin-off – new entry point into the series

In to Her – STANDALONE BOOK – Logan first appears

Bossy Brothers: Jesse – First appearance of The Way – i.e. The Company

Bossy Brothers: Joey

Bossy Brothers: Johnny – Logan shows back up Indie first appears at age 14, Chek's first appearance

Bossy Bride: Jesse and Emma – Chek and Wendy mentioned

Bossy Brothers: Alonzo – Chek and Wendy mentioned, Vaughn Family and Sick Boyz appear here.

Bossy Brothers: Tony – Vaughn Family and Sick Boyz appear here.

Bossy Brothers: Luke – Nick and Lauren Tate show up.

Creeping Beautiful – Rook & Ronin and Company Spin-off – new entry point into the series

The complete story of Nick Tate, James and Vincent Fenici, "Wendy", "Chek", Indie Anna Accorsi, Adam Boucher, Donovan and Carter Couture, Core McKay, and Nathan St. James.

Creeping Beautiful (book 1)
Pretty Nightmare (book 2)
Gorgeous Misery (book 3) – Coming fall 2021
Lovely Darkness (book 4) – Coming fall 2021

Kings of High Court College

Standalone Duet with no crossover characters but is still inside the "Company world".

Bully King
Ruling Class

ABOUT THE AUTHOR

JA Huss is a New York Times Bestselling author and has been on the USA Today Bestseller's list 21 times. She writes characters with heart, plots with twists, and perfect endings.

Her books have sold millions of copies all over the world. Her book, Eighteen, was nominated for a Voice Arts Award and an Audie Award in 2016 and 2017 respectively. Her audiobook, Mr. Perfect, was nominated for a Voice Arts Award in 2017. Her audiobook, Taking Turns, was nominated for an Audie Award in 2018. Her book, Total Exposure, was nominated for a RITA Award in 2019.

FIND HER HERE
www.facebook/authorjahuss
@jahuss
www.jahuss.com